PRAISE FOR *THE EXPEDITER*

"It's fun to watch professionals at the top of their game, which in this case means not only the characters in this great story, but David Hagberg himself as he creates a world-spanning crisis that only Kirk McGarvey can save. The nonstop action races the clock with the fate of millions waiting for the winner."

—Larry Bond, *New York Times* bestselling author

"*The Expediter* involves a standoff between China and North Korea that threatens the world and is terrifying in its very plausibility. Kirk McGarvey faces the darkest and most desperate assignment of his career. *The Expediter* is a brilliantly realized novel."

—Douglas Preston, *New York Times* bestselling author of *Blasphemy*

PRAISE FOR DAVID HAGBERG

"Hagberg is known for being prescient about terrorist events. One can only hope America's real-life enemies haven't thought to study this series."

—*Publishers Weekly*

"David Hagberg writes the most realistic, prophetic thrillers I have ever read. His books should be required reading in Washington."

—Stephen Coonts, *New York Times* bestselling author of *The Assassin*

"David Hagberg runs in the same fast, high-tech track as Clancy and his gung ho colleagues, with lots of war games, fancy weapons, and much male bonding."

—New York *Daily News*

THE
EXPEDITER

DAVID HAGBERG

A TOM DOHERTY ASSOCIATES BOOK
NEW YORK

This is a work of fiction. All of the characters, organizations, and events portrayed in this novel are either products of the author's imagination or are used fictitiously.

THE EXPEDITER

Copyright © 2009 by David Hagberg

All rights reserved.

A Forge Book
Published by Tom Doherty Associates, LLC
175 Fifth Avenue
New York, NY 10010

www.tor-forge.com

Forge® is a registered trademark of Tom Doherty Associates, LLC.

ISBN 978-0-7653-4980-4

First Edition: March 2009
First Mass Market Edition: December 2009

Printed in the United States of America

0 9 8 7 6 5 4 3 2 1

This novel is for Lorrel, as always.

This is a work of fiction, so I've moved some locations, mostly within the city of Pyongyang, to suit my story. My apologies to students of geography and to Kim Jong Il.

PYONGYANG,
DEMOCRATIC
PEOPLE'S REPUBLIC
OF KOREA

ONE

At precisely midnight Huk Kim pulled back the covers, got out of bed, and checked to make certain that the sleep agent she'd given her Japanese roommate hadn't worn off yet. But the girl was totally out of it, and in the morning she would remember very little of what had happened after their dinner in the hotel's dining room two, and absolutely nothing after her head had hit the pillow.

Kim was a thirty-one-year-old, short, slightly built South Korean woman, and her movements were quick, almost birdlike as she tied a folded plastic trash bag around her waist with shaking hands, then dressed in dark slacks, a lightweight dark pullover, and sneakers.

She was frightened to the core, as she had been on the previous kills, but she had no way out, short of leaving her husband, something she couldn't even conceive of doing.

Checking a second time to make certain her roommate was deep asleep, Kim slipped out of her twelfth-floor room and made her way to the end of the deserted corridor, then downstairs to a service area at the rear of the hotel where deliveries were made each morning between four and seven. From there she was able to get outside without being seen, something that would have been impossible from the lobby.

The evening was pleasantly warm, and almost totally dark and silent. Other than the few lights around the hotel, and a few on the bridge across the river, North Korea's capital Pyongyang lay sleeping in darkness, only a pin-prick of light here and there to hint that a city of more than two million people existed less than two hundred meters away.

She shivered. She loved her husband and the fabulous money they were making together, but she hated the work, doing it only for him. Assassinations were usually carried out at night so that the shooters could get away. After five hits in three years, Kim had learned to depend on the dark but she hated it.

Keeping to the deeper shadows, she moved across the driveway that led up to the single road circling the small island of Yanggak, then held up in the bushes and hedges to wait for her husband, and to watch for the policemen who traveled on foot in pairs.

Yanggakdo International Hotel was the city's only ac-commodation for unapproved foreigners, such as South Koreans or Japanese, and for everyone who came into North Korea in a tour group. No one was allowed out of the hotel or off the island after dark, and the road and two bridges leading across the river to the mainland were pa-trolled 24/7 by special police armed with short stock versions of the AK-47 assault rifle.

A dark figure darted up from the service driveway, and Kim eased farther into the hedges until she was certain it was her husband Soon, then she showed herself and he came across to her.

"Any signs of the cops?" he asked, keeping his voice low.

"Not yet," she said.

They pulled on black balaclavas.

Soon was slender, but well-muscled with a square face and dark almond eyes that Kim had always found devastat-ingly attractive. They'd met six years ago when she'd been assigned as a brand-new second lieutenant to his South Ko-rean Special Forces Sniper Unit outside Seoul. She always smiled when she thought about the exact moment she'd first laid eyes on him, handsome in his captain's uniform, self-assured, even cocky. She'd fallen instantly in love with him, and had told him so on the spot.

They began sleeping together that weekend, but regulations would not permit them to be married or to even have an affair. Two years later they resigned their commissions, got married in Chinhae, the small town on the south coast where she was born, and started to look for work, finding it almost immediately as assassins for hire by South Korea's Mafia.

She had been trained for urban warfare assassinations, but killing enemies of South Korea was a completely different thing than killing rival businessmen or gang leaders, or lately, important politicians. She hated every minute of it, but loved her husband more.

Soon pointed two fingers at his eyes and then through the hedges at a pair of figures slowly approaching along the path on the other side of the road, and Kim's stomach did a slow roll.

There had been no possible way for them to bring weapons here, so before Soon had agreed to take the hit he and Kim had spent the better part of a week cooped up in their apartment doing research online, finally coming up with a plan that could work if they ran into no snags. She'd tried to talk him out of it, arguing that if anything went wrong, if they made even one mistake, they would pay with their lives.

"I don't want to lose you," she'd pleaded, but he'd laughed and took her in his arms.

"Not a chance," he'd whispered in her ear.

When the police reached a spot directly across the road, they suddenly stopped. Kim and Soon remained absolutely motionless. One of the cops lit a cigarette, the odor of cheap tobacco wafting on the slight breeze, then they continued down the path.

Kim and Soon crawled through the hedges, careful to make no noise. Keeping low, they raced across the road and onto the path directly behind the cops.

She'd been trained in the Army for this part too, though in practice she'd never had to use her skills for real. This time was different and she thought that she might be sick to her stomach at any moment.

One of the cops, sensing something, started to turn when Soon reached him, jammed a knee in the man's back, and reached for his head.

Kim hit her target a split instant later, jumping up, slamming her knee into his back, and yanking his head back, breaking his spine and his neck. He collapsed without a sound.

Soon was dragging his target into the brush between the path and the river, as Kim rolled off her target and looked at his face. He was just a kid, probably a teenager, and he was still alive, but paralyzed from the neck down, making it impossible for him to breathe. She reared back, turned away, and threw up, a buzzing inside her head, the path and the road spinning out of control.

When she looked back, the kid's eyes were still open but he was dead, and she was able to get a grip on herself.

Soon came back to her. "What are you doing?" he demanded.

"He wasn't dead."

Soon glanced at the boy's face. "He is now." He grabbed the cop's arms and dragged his slight body into the brush where it could not be spotted from the path or the road, or even from one of the windows in the top story of the hotel. No boats were on the river at this time of the night so it was unlikely that the bodies would be spotted from that direction.

Soon started getting undressed, and Kim pulled the balaclava off her head then took off her sneakers, her slacks, and dark pullover. She untied the plastic bag from around her waist, opened it and stuffed her clothing inside. Soon was already stripping the cop he'd killed of everything but the man's underwear. The uniform, belts, cap, shoes, and the AK-47 all went into the bag. He gathered the edges and blew air into the bag, inflating it like a balloon and sealed it with one of his shoelaces.

When he was finished he helped Kim with hers.

It was just past 12:30 A.M. when they slipped into the river and started swimming toward the city, the current weak, but the water cold.

TWO

Cold had seeped into Kim's bones by the time they reached the mainland, and she needed her husband's help to climb the steel ladder and pull the plastic bag out of the water. They were in a narrow park just off Otan Kangan Street, the main thoroughfare along the Taedong River that wound its way through the city. Trees and rosebushes and many statutes of the Dear Leader and his father Kim Il Sung, plus heroes of the war against the Americans, dotted the park.

Nothing moved on the broad avenue nor on the bridges they could see to the north. Even the two fountains in the middle of the river that by day shot geysers nearly five hundred feet into the air had been shut down. Electricity had always been a major issue in the North and it was getting worse, so at night cities went dark and silent.

Bad for the people, but good for assassins, Kim thought.

She and Soon opened the plastic bags and quickly dressed in the cops' uniforms. The Russian-designed, Chinese-made AK-47s were fully loaded with thirty-round magazines, but there was no spare ammunition nor had the cops carried pistols.

They tied the bags out of sight on the top rung of the ladder leading two meters to the river, so that in the unlikely chance someone passed this way in the next hour their clothes wouldn't be discovered.

"Ready?" Soon asked as he slung the rifle over his shoulder.

She nodded, and they headed north along the river, keeping in the park for now.

Their destination, the Chinese Embassy, was nearly three kilometers to the north, near the Floating Restaurant and the Taedong Gate, which nearly five centuries ago was the main entrance into the walled city. China had been allowed to move its embassy out of the diplomatic area of Munsudong, and into the historical section of the city by Kim Jong Il as a show of friendship.

They had studied detailed maps and satellite shots of the city, and when they had arrived here with the Japanese tour group thirteen days ago they'd kept their eyes open. Twice on the conducted tours they had actually driven past the embassy. Both of them knew at least this section almost as well as if they had lived here.

This was just another job, Kim kept telling herself. A Russian living in Tokyo had sought them out through a Mafia connection they'd done business with in Seoul. He was called Alexandar but they'd never actually met him. He was only a voice at a blind number in Tokyo, and an encrypted address on the Web. But for each of the other two jobs they had done for him, he'd paid his fees to their Swiss bank account within minutes of their agreement; half to start with and the other half on completion.

Six months ago they'd assassinated a Japanese senator in Tokyo, Soon hitting him with an MP3 Heckler & Koch Room Broom through the open door of the van with stolen plates that Kim had been driving. The senator had just emerged from a taxi and was entering an apartment building in Ginza to see his mistress. The hit had been made relatively easy because of Alexandar's spot-on intel. Three hours later they were aboard a JAL flight to Seoul, sipping champagne, the weapon they'd used wiped clean and left behind.

Three months ago they'd flown to Paris under false passports, and hit South Korea's ambassador to China while he was attending a conference of Far East ambassadors. That job hadn't been so easy, because the man had been surrounded by fellow diplomats and staff most of the time. And whenever he moved between the venue and where he was staying at the Hotel Continental, he was accompanied by security.

Again, however, Alexandar's intel made all the difference. The ambassador was fond of expensive call girls. Soon was able to tap into the hotel's switchboard, and on the second night when the ambassador asked for a call girl to come to his room, Soon intercepted the girl, claiming he was the man who had called for a prostitute, while Kim in a blond wig and revealing dress had gone to the ambassador's room where she fired one silenced pistol shot into his head.

The only flaw in the assignment was the call girl. Soon said he had sent her away. But later in an e-mail Alexandar congratulated them for disposing of the woman, who would have been a dangerous loose end.

Now making their way through Pyongyang's dark streets on their third assignment for the Russian, she thought about that night in Paris. It was the only time since they'd been together that they'd argued. She'd told her husband that she was disappointed and frightened of what they were becoming.

"The army trained us to be snipers," Soon had told her.

"To kill the enemy," Kim had shot back angrily. "Our ambassador to China was not our enemy."

He'd tried to be patient with her. "We're not politicians. We're shooters. That's what we do." He'd laughed. "Don't think so much."

She'd been infuriated and the argument had lasted the better part of the week, until he'd worn her down, and she'd finally stopped thinking so much.

The payoff for each of the other two hits had been $400,000. But for this one he'd offered twice as much. After a full week of trying to come up with a way for them to make the kill and then get out of the country with their lives intact, Soon had made a counteroffer of $1.5 million. They needed the extra money because the assignment would be next to impossible.

Kim had been proud of her husband for cleverly getting them out of the assignment without upsetting their employer. Alexandar was hiring contract assassins, not suicidal fanatics. But within the hour they got confirmation from their Swiss bank that $750,000 had been deposited to their account, and Soon would not be stopped, although he promised that with their payoff they would have enough to get out of the business.

"We'll be able to retire, maybe buy a small house on the sea, help your parents and your brother. Maybe take vacations to the Riviera—real vacations."

"If we survive," she'd warned.

"You worry too much."

Maybe not enough, she thought as they hurried across the broad avenue and down one of the branching streets just south of the Taedong Gate. The farther they penetrated into the city's downtown, the weirder it got for Kim. Nothing moved. It was as if a plague had wiped out everyone. She was used to Seoul, which like every Western city never slept. But here no sirens sounded in the distance, no dogs barked, no late-night revelers staggered up the street on their way home from a party. At this moment she even wondered if birds sang during the day. She couldn't remember hearing any during the two weeks they'd been here. That was impossible, of course, she just hadn't been listening.

Three blocks from the river they ducked into the doorway of the Democratic Workers Bank, housed in a squat, five-story building, dark at this hour of the night. Kim's heart was in her throat, they were so close to disaster, and she could taste her fear on her lips as if she had been sucking a copper coin.

The Chinese Embassy was across the street in a broad three-story building behind a tall iron fence. The structure had once housed an insurance company, but now its roof bristled with antennae and satellite dishes. No guard was at the entry, but closed-circuit television cameras were mounted atop the fence next to the gate and at the corners of the building.

A few lights were on in the upper-story windows, and they could hear an engine running somewhere behind the building. The Chinese were generating their own electricity.

From their vantage point they were at an angle to the gate, with a shooting distance of less than forty meters. It would be impossible for them to miss at that range.

Kim shrank back into the deeper shadows. She wanted to be anywhere else than here. She had pleaded with Soon to give the money back to Alexandar, but he had refused.

"He accepted our terms, and now we're obligated."

It was a few minutes before two when a Mercedes Maybach was scheduled to arrive and take Chinese Ministry of State Security General Ho Chang Li to a meeting with Kim Jong Il at the president's palace. They were to shoot him to death before he made the meeting.

THREE

At exactly two, lights came on in front of the embassy and a pair of ceremonial guards emerged from the front door and marched to the gate. They wore white gloves, stainless steel helmets, and were armed only with pistols in patent leather holsters at their sides.

Soon cycled a round into the AK's chamber and slipped the safety catch off. Kim did the same. Her heart pounded wildly and her mouth was suddenly dry. If they turned around right now they could make it back to the hotel and dispose of the two bodies. In a few hours they would be on the flight back to Beijing and then home. They could tell the Russian that the general had been too heavily guarded so the assignment had become impossible.

Headlights flashed at the end of the block and a black Mercedes sedan glided up to the embassy and came to a stop in front of the gate. The driver, dressed in a plain olive drab tunic leaped out of the car, and opened the rear door.

For a minute nothing happened, but then the guards opened the gate and a tall man dressed in a plain dark suit came out of the embassy and walked across the narrow courtyard. He stopped under the lights at the gate long enough for Kim to recognize that it was the general from the photographs she and Soon had studied.

"Wait until he comes through the gate," Soon whispered. "You take the guards. I'll do the general and the driver."

Kim's nerves were jumping all over the place, but as soon as she raised the rifle to her shoulder and got a sight pattern on the guards, her training kicked in and she automatically settled down.

General Ho said something to one of the guards then stepped through the gate.

Soon fired first, hitting the general in the chest with at least two rounds, shoving him violently back through the gate.

The guards were slow to react, offering Kim nearly static targets. She squeezed off one round, catching the first guard high in the chest, switched aim and fired two shots, hitting the other man in the torso, driving him off his feet.

She was dimly conscious of Soon firing beside her as she switched aim back to the first guard who was struggling to draw his pistol, and fired one shot, hitting him in the head, taking off the back of his skull.

Suddenly the night was silent.

Across the street General Ho was down, half through the gate, and the driver was crumpled in a heap on the sidewalk a couple of meters away. An impressive amount of blood was pooling around the bodies.

"Let's get out of here," Soon said. He stepped out of the shadows and headed back the way they had come, without looking over his shoulder and without running.

Kim fell in beside him, the city still fantastically quiet. She felt numb, a sense of unreality and disbelief at what she had done. Two more men were dead because of her, and she knew that she would never be able to forget the sight of the blood.

At the corner near the Taedong Gate she looked back, and thought she caught a movement on the street in front of the embassy, but then she and Soon crossed the deserted broad boulevard that paralleled the river.

"Are you okay?" Soon asked her.

Kim looked up at him. His face was animated. She nodded. "I just want to get the hell out of here. The flight can't come too quickly."

"The tough part's over with, sweetheart."

"We still have to get across the river without being seen, and hope nobody discovered the bodies over there."

They reached the park and Soon glanced down the boulevard. "Once they get their act together every cop in the city will be concentrating on the embassy. When they finally get someone who knows what he's doing we'll be long gone, and another three-quarters of a million dollars closer to retirement."

"Let's just get across the river and back to our rooms first, okay?" Kim said. She was shivering thinking about the swim, and because she was starting to come down from the kill.

They heard the first siren somewhere across the city when they reached the ladder where they'd left their clothes. By the time they'd undressed and sealed the uniforms and weapons in the plastic bags other sirens had joined in, but all of them were to the north, converging on the Chinese Embassy as Soon had predicted would happen.

Kim was the first into the water, and she was immediately colder than she'd ever been in her life. Holding the partially inflated bag ahead of her she pushed away from the wall and started for the island. She expected at any moment to hear a patrol boat coming upriver, spotlights searching for them.

Soon swam up beside her. "How are you doing?"

"I'm cold," she told him. She could think of nothing else except being safe in bed in his arms. But it would have to wait until they got home. They'd traveled here under different names, not as husband and wife. Soon had figured they would be more anonymous that way. In addition, everybody on tour groups was required to share a room, which meant that Soon's and Kim's roommates would be able to vouch for them if questions were asked.

"Do you want me to help you?"

"No, I'm okay."

"You sure?"

No, I'm not sure, she wanted to scream. She didn't think that she'd ever be okay after this night. No matter what happened to them from this point on, she would carry this night as a scar inside her head. She didn't think that she'd ever be able to forget the look in the young cop's eyes as he lay dying outside the hotel. He'd had no idea what was happening to him or why. He just knew that he couldn't breathe and a woman was looking at him. Her face was the last thing he'd ever seen.

The river current seemed much stronger, and the distance across to the island much farther than the swim across to the mainland. When they reached the seawall, Kim was unable to help herself up the ladder, and Soon had to haul her over the seawall where she fell to her knees, shivering almost uncontrollably. She was in the middle stages of hypothermia, and she was quickly losing the ability to think rationally. The night was dark and her husband's face right in front of her was out of focus as he pulled her clothes out of the plastic bag and helped her get dressed.

When he was dressed, he held his body against hers for several minutes, her shivering finally subsiding and her awareness of the night sounds coming back into focus.

Lights had come on across the river, and sirens seemed to come from every direction.

"Can you make it back to your room?" Soon asked.

She nodded. "But I might need some help getting across the road. What about the bodies?" She was feeling extremely sleepy.

"I'll take care of them," Soon told her, and Kim sat back on her heels as he quickly dressed the dead policemen, wiped down the AKs, slung them over the cops' shoulders, and rolled the bodies into the river.

The bodies would sink because of the weight of the weapons, and would slowly drift downstream. With any luck they wouldn't be discovered for several days.

Soon stuffed one of the plastic bags into his pocket, and the other into Kim's. They'd brought the bags into the country to use for dirty laundry, and it was possible that some bright customs inspector would notice if they didn't bring them out.

He helped her to her feet, and once she was steady, they crossed the still-deserted road. No lights had come on in the hotel in response to all the commotion across the river. In this country it paid not to be curious. If there were sirens, it meant official police or military business. It was best to turn away.

They got inside and although he was taking a risk, Soon helped his wife to the door to her room, two floors above his. He held her in his arms for a long moment, and then they kissed.

"You did a good job tonight," he told her.

"I'm afraid," she said. Something would go wrong at the last minute. She was convinced of it. Only there was nothing either of them could do except continue with the plan.

"I know," Soon said compassionately. "But just hang on for another few hours and we'll be out of here." He kissed her. "Now try to get some sleep."

Kim slipped inside her room, expecting her Japanese roommate to be awake and demanding an explanation. But the woman was still out of it, and Kim undressed and climbed into bed, yet sleep was a very long time coming even though she was bone weary.

FOUR

North Korea's State Safety and Security Agency was finally coming alive with lights and activity when Counter Insurgency Colonel Pak Hae was passed through the gate. It was a full ninety minutes after the shooting at the Chinese Embassy and Pak had a lot on his mind as he drove around back and parked his Russian-made Lada sedan in his slot. This sort of a violent crime was almost completely unknown, even in a city as large as Pyongyang.

He was a small man, typical of most North Koreans, with dark hair and eyes and an olive complexion. This morning he was dressed in his uniform with decorations, and tall black boots because if what that fool in operations had babbled on the phone was even half true he would need a clear indication of his authority. Unlike the typical North Korean, however, Pak had been educated in the West, after first learning near perfect English in the Cabinet General Intelligence Bureau School One outside of Pyongyang near Kim Jong Il's primary Residence Number 55. By twenty-five, he had degrees in political science and languages at U.C. Berkeley under the cover of a South Korean.

When he'd graduated fifteen years ago he had returned home without hesitation, although at the odd moment he sometimes stopped to consider what his life might have been like had he remained in the West.

The Counter Intelligence Headquarters, located just outside the Munsudong diplomatic quarter, was housed in a massive five-story building, flags flying, satellite dishes and telephone intercept antennae on the roof. Five thousand people worked here including one hundred fifty men and women in Pak's small section, which was tasked with the specific job of finding and arresting spies among foreigners.

He got out of his car and entered the building through one of the rear doors, the guard snapping to attention as he passed. Judging by the activity alone he would have guessed that they were preparing for war, which he thought could very well turn out to be the case.

Taking the elevator up to the third floor he refused to come to any conclusions before he was given all the facts. But if a Chinese diplomat actually had been gunned down on his way to a meeting with Dear Leader the repercussions would be nothing short of stunning, possibly even stunning enough to force the one thing that nearly everyone in North Korea wanted: removing Kim Jong Il from power so that the rebuilding of their country could finally begin.

The common room, which housed some of his research clerks, translators, and preliminary analysts in cubicles, was bustling with activity, everyone listening in on intercepted telephone conversations from every embassy and hotel switchboard in the city. No one bothered to look up as he crossed the large room to his office behind glass windows.

His secretary hadn't arrived yet, but his aide, Sergeant Ri Gyong, was at his desk talking to someone on the phone. He was short, like Pak, but muscularly built, with a broad peasant's face, heavy brows, and eyes that seemed to smile perpetually, as if he found everything and everyone a big joke. But it was a cover. During his military service Ri had served as a hand-to-hand combat instructor in the Reconnaissance Bureau's Special Operations forces that had been modeled after the Russian Spetsnaz troops. And he had been one of the best: tough, aggressive, intelligent. He'd been offered an officer's commission, but had turned it down. As he explained once to Pak, he was a simple man who liked to take orders but never to give them. "Besides, when something goes wrong it's the officers who take the blame, not the grunts."

He crashed down the phone with no smile on his face this morning. "You're not going to believe this."

"It's true then?" Pak asked, his stomach sour.

Ri nodded. "How much did operations tell you?"

"Just that there was a shooting outside the Chinese Embassy and one of their diplomats might have been killed," Pak said. He laid his cap down and started to undo the top button of his tunic.

"Better not do that yet, Colonel, you're wanted at the embassy."

"That bad?"

"Worse. I'll fill you in on the way over. But that was one of Dear Leader's people on the phone just now. He wants an explanation, and he mentioned you by name."

He and Ri went back downstairs where they got into Pak's Lada and headed to the Chinese Embassy. The only cars on the roads were police, though a military truck filled with troops was parked at the Okyru Bridge. Pak put the blue official light on the roof of the car so that they would not be stopped.

"It was no ordinary diplomat who was killed," Ri said. "His name is Ho Chang Li. General Ho, Guoanbu."

Pak was caught by surprise, and he glanced at his sergeant. "What the hell was a Chinese Ministry of State Security General doing wandering around the streets at that hour of the morning?"

"Dear Leader sent a car for him. The killers hit not only the general and two Chinese guards at the gate, but they got the chauffeur."

"Killers?" Pak asked.

"Yes, and you're not going to like the next part. Major Chen claims the shooters were our cops." Chen was chief of security for the Chinese Embassy.

"That's nuts."

"I'll leave it to you to tell him that," Ri said. "But he also mentioned you by name."

"I've become a popular fellow all of a sudden."

"Better you than me," Ri said.

They came around the corner by the Taedong Gate, dozens of police and military troops all over the place. The street in front of the embassy was blocked at both ends by barricades. Four armed soldiers led by an officer manned the nearest barricade, and Pak had to stop.

He held out his identification booklet, and the lieutenant studied it and Pak's face carefully before he handed it back and saluted. "They're waiting for you, Colonel, but you'll have to walk the rest of the way. The investigators want to keep the crime scene uncontaminated for as long as possible."

Two ambulances were parked just up the block from the embassy.

"Have the bodies been moved?" Pak asked.

"No, sir."

Pak backed up and parked behind a military jeep, then he and Ri passed through the barrier and headed down the street to the scene of intense activity in front of the embassy. He had the thought that if this had happened in gun-happy America every television, radio, and newspaper journalist in the world would have gathered like vultures for a feast of carrion. Such things were called media circuses, and rightly so. Something like that was impossible here, and gladly so. Some freedoms were worthless.

Major Shikai Chen, dressed in gray trousers and an open-necked white shirt, stood just outside the gate watching a team of medical examiners and forensic field technicians going over the four bodies. He was a short, slightly built man in his late forties, with round glasses that made him appear scholarly. He glanced up when Pak and Ri came around from behind the Mercedes, his expression unreadable.

"When you've finished looking, the bodies will be moved and this mess cleaned off your street," he said coolly.

"I've finished looking," Pak said. "Can you tell me precisely what has happened here?"

A hint of irritation crossed Chen's eyes, but he nodded. "Very well." He turned to the chief medical examiner standing over General Li's body. "You may proceed. But I want the autopsy report on my desk within twenty-four hours, and the general's body prepared for its return to Beijing."

Pak thought that it was extraordinary that a Chinese officer was giving orders to a North Korean doctor, but he said nothing.

Chen turned back. "Two uniformed police officers waited in ambush, there, across the street in the doorway of the bank, and when the car and driver came for General Ho's appointment with your premier, they opened fired without warning, causing the destruction you see here."

Ambulance attendants were coming down the street with gurneys for all four bodies. Pak turned and looked at the bank where a police photographer was taking pictures of something on the ground. Presumably shell casings where the shooters stood in the shadows of the doorway.

He turned back. "Obviously someone carried out the assassination, but it wasn't our people," Pak said. "We have no reason for it. China is our ally."

"Rebels. Malcontents. Traitors," Chen shot back heatedly.

"Even if that were so, why kill one of your spymasters, Major?" Ri asked. "Unless he was here to spy on us."

Chen bridled and stepped forward. "The ambassador will be calling on your premier as soon as he receives instructions from Beijing. I suggest you find out who did this before the situation gets out of hand."

"Naturally," Pak said. He glanced up at the embassy

windows and the closed-circuit television cameras above the gate and on the building, and suddenly he had a sour feeling in his stomach. "Witnesses?" he asked. He nodded toward the cameras. "Tapes?"

"Yes," Chen said. He took a cassette tape from his pocket and gave it to Pak. "They kept to the shadows for the most part so there aren't many details, except their uniforms and weapons."

For the first time he could remember, Pak was at a loss for words. Such an act was unthinkable here, unless Ri had hit upon something. But even if it were true that the Chinese had mounted a spy operation, he couldn't imagine Kim Jong Il ordering the assassination. At the very least, relationships with their only real friend would be severely strained. At worst it could mean war, and Pak knew that if it came to it, Dear Leader was crazy enough to use the six nuclear weapons that had been hidden from the international inspectors. It was a chilling thought.

"Keep in touch, Colonel," Chen said. "For all of our sakes."

FIVE

Kim woke up a few minutes after eight, bleary-eyed and groggy, and it took her a few moments to get her bearings and remember what she'd done last night. The finality of it came crashing down on her so hard she buried her face in her pillow. The worst part was the look in the young cop's eyes as he lay dying.

Her Japanese roommate Sue Makewa was already up, and probably downstairs having breakfast, which was just as well because Kim didn't think she could face anyone just now. She needed twenty minutes to get her act together.

She took a long, hot shower, and dressed in a fresh pair of jeans, a designer T-shirt, and a pink baseball cap with a Nike logo. Most of her packing was done, but she put her dirty clothes into the plastic bag, and stuffed it into her single suitcase.

Sue Makewa came in, a bright smile on her pretty, round face. "Good morning, sleepyhead," she said in English. It was the tour group's lingua franca. In addition to the eight Japanese and three South Koreans, an Australian couple had joined at the last minute in Beijing.

"Did you sleep well?" Kim asked.

"Like a dragon, until you started talking in your sleep and woke me up."

Kim was horrified and it must have shown on her face.

"Don't worry, I don't speak a word of Korean," Sue told her breezily. "So your little sex secrets are still safe. But it sounded like your boyfriend was being tough on you. Anyway the bus will be here any minute, so we'd better get downstairs."

Kim busied herself finishing her packing. She'd never talked in her sleep, or at least she didn't think she had. Soon had never mentioned it, and he was a light sleeper. Her roommate had no reason to lie about something like that, and it was very likely that she didn't speak Korean, very few Japanese did. Koreans believed that they had migrated across the Sea of Japan and were the first, other than the aboriginal natives, to populate the islands. This view had always infuriated the Japanese, which was one of the reasons they had been so brutal during their occupation of the peninsula in World War II.

Sue zippered up her two bags and set them by the door. "I don't know about you, but I'm ready to go home. I'm tired of someone looking over my shoulder 24/7."

"Me too," Kim said.

"Do you have any relatives here?"

"None that I know of," Kim said. "But even if I did they wouldn't have let me see them on this trip. That kind of stuff takes a different set of paperwork. And a lot of it."

Sue shook her head. "Bastards," she said. "We could have had the same setup if the Russians had invaded like they did in Germany. I would have hated it."

"We do," Kim said. "Have you ever been to Seoul?"

"Once. It's sorta like Tokyo."

"Now you've seen how it is here. Make the comparison. It'll be a long time, if ever, before we'll get together."

"That's crappy."

"Yeah, crappy," Kim said, surprised. It was the first time in the fourteen days they'd been together that her roommate had actually talked to her about something other than the tour. But then, she thought, perhaps she'd been too wound up to listen until now.

"We'd better get downstairs, the bus should be here any minute, and we don't want to give Mr. Tae a heart attack," Sue said. "He's been pretty decent."

Every foreigner visiting North Korea was assigned a guide, more like a watchdog, to make sure no one wandered off the official path or took unapproved photographs. Tae Kwon Hung was the senior guide for their group, and he had been kind, though Kim had been wary of him the entire time. She was sure that he was a cop sent to spy on them, specifically on her and Soon.

Kim zippered her hanging bag, doubled it over, and did up the clasps. This morning in the lobby would be the first real test. The guards they'd killed would have been reported missing by now, and if the hit were traced to someone from this hotel no one would be leaving North Korea any time soon.

Their room was on the eighteenth floor of the forty-five-story hotel that had been built just a few years ago, specifically for tourists and especially tour groups. By

Western standards it was right out of the sixties or seventies, but here in the North it was luxurious by comparison to any of the other hotels in the city.

The elevator was full by the time they reached the ground floor and the general mood among all the tour groups leaving this morning was upbeat. Everyone seemed glad to be going home.

Mr. Tae and the other guides were waiting for them near the doors, as were the guides for three other groups. Four buses were lined up outside to take them out to the airport, but the noise level was low. Everyone was anxious to leave, but just about everyone was nervous about last-minute complications.

Kim caught a glimpse of her husband coming across the lobby. He looked haggard, as if he hadn't got any sleep last night. But she'd seen no sign on his face that anything was wrong, and she breathed a little sigh of relief.

Uniformed guards were standing around, looking bored, but there was no unusual activity that Kim could detect. She turned to their guides as Mr. Tae began his farewell speech, blaming the Americans for all their troubles, and Dear Leader for all the guidance and bounty in the workers' paradise.

The assassination last night of General Ho was going to cause a ripple in paradise, Kim thought. She wondered how Kim Jong Il was going to explain it to the Chinese. It was one conversation she wished that she and Soon could hear.

SIX

It had taken most of the morning before they could find a video playback unit and a small black-and-white television to view the surveillance tape from the Chinese Embassy. Pak was sitting at his desk, watching the assassination in stop action for the fifth time, when Ri came in with their morning tea and noodle soup from the cafeteria downstairs.

"You pick out anything new?" Ri asked, setting the breakfast tray on top of a file cabinet.

"They were waiting in the doorway of the bank when the car came for the general, but there's no way of telling how long they were there beforehand," Pak said.

Ri gave him his tea and soup and chopsticks. "The cameras should have caught them coming up the street."

"Not if they remained in the shadows," Pak said. He rewound the tape to a time two minutes before the hit and stopped it. "It's too bad the cameras didn't pan, but the sidewalk to the east and west of the bank entrance is in shadows. They could have easily reached the doorway without being spotted."

"Right, and made their escape the same way," Ri said.

Pak started the tape, and sipped his tea as he watched.

Two guards in shiny helmets came out of the embassy and walked to the gate. A minute later, headlights flashed from the left, and the Mercedes that had been sent to pick up General Ho slid into view and pulled up. The driver jumped out and opened the rear door. Almost immediately the general emerged from the embassy, crossing the narrow space inside the fence as the guards opened the gate.

Pak sat forward. "Now."

General Ho stepped through the open gate, the view from the camera catching him from behind. At that exact moment two figures emerged from the shadows across the street, and raised their AKs.

Pak stopped the tape. "What do you see?"

"Two cops in uniform," Ri said. "Armed with Kalashnikovs. One of them smaller than the other. Hard to tell, but they're probably Koreans. Definitely not Americans, or even Japanese."

"What else?" Pak prompted.

Ri studied the image, but then shrugged. "I don't know."

"They could have fired their weapons from *inside* the doorway. The cameras were in plain sight, they couldn't have missed them, so why did they step out?"

The answer dawned on Ri all at once. "Because they wanted to be seen."

In the bright muzzle flashes they were able to catch a few more details of the shooters' faces, especially the taller of the two.

"Definitely Korean," Ri said.

Pak rewound the tape and watched the shooting again. "What's wrong with what we're seeing?" he asked half to himself.

Ri shrugged. "They fired eight times, you can count that from the muzzle flashes, which jibes with the number of shell casings found. And they were damned good shooters. They never missed once. Better than I could do."

"Better than any of our cops could do," Pak said.

"Unless they got lucky."

Pak stopped the tape at the clearest image of the two shooters, and it dawned on him what was wrong. "The one on the left. His uniform doesn't fit him."

"Those guys get their lousy uniforms from the same place the Army does."

Pak looked up. "Have you ever seen a Korean so well fed that his uniform was too tight?"

For a second Ri drew a blank, but then all of a sudden his face lit up. "Holy shit, you're right. South Koreans."

"Yes. And who do you suppose sometimes trains South Korean snipers?"

"Who?"

"The CIA."

"They wanted to be picked up by the surveillance cameras to make the Chinese believe that it was our people who did the shooting," Ri said. "But why? What's the point?"

It was ingenious, Pak had to admit. Bold, with a very small chance of success, and yet the bastards somehow got across the border, probably through one of the tunnels down south, made it all the way up here, and found uniforms somewhere.

"To start a war between us and China," Pak said. "I need to know if any of our cops have gone missing in the past twenty-four hours. Not just here in the city, but anywhere in the country."

"If they're from the South maybe they brought everything with them," Ri suggested. "Less risky that way."

"They'd have made sure the uniforms fit like they're supposed to. Baggy."

"I'm on it," Ri said and he went to his desk and started telephoning.

Pak rewound the tape again to the beginning and tried to watch from a fresh perspective, as if this were the first time he was seeing it. The guards came out of the embassy. The car arrived and the driver opened the rear door. The guards opened the gate and the general came out. Moments later the shooters stepped into view and opened fire.

He rewound the tape. The guards came out, the car arrived, the guards opened the gate, the general came out.

And it struck him. The shooters not only knew that a car was coming to pick up the general, they knew the exact time it would be there, and that was impossible. He suspected that only a handful of people could have known such details. A few in the Chinese Embassy, and in the Guoanbu back in Beijing, and a few on Dear Leader's staff.

He would have bet his life that Dear Leader's staff had not been compromised, and it was inconceivable that the South Koreans had the wherewithal to penetrate Chinese security to such an extent they could have come up with intel that good.

But the assassination had taken place.

The tape came to the shooting and Pak studied the images of the two figures. The one on the left was the largest, and his uniform was too tight, but the one on the right was slightly built, more typical of a North Korean. His uniform was a loose fit.

Only a few spy agencies anywhere in the world had even the remotest possibility of penetrating Chinese intelligence: Russia's FSB, Britain's MI6, Israel's Mossad, and America's CIA.

Russia wouldn't be interested in starting trouble between China and North Korea, nor would Israel. England had some commercial interests on the peninsula, but South Korea's chief partner was the United States.

Pak stared at the television screen but the images weren't registering. Dear Leader was insane, there was little doubt about it. But he was a wily politician who had been trained by his father, practically from birth, to run the country. Maybe his constant warning that America was bent on destroying him and North Korea was correct after all, and not just the ravings of a madman trying to turn attention away from his failed policies.

Ri hung up the phone, an odd expression on his face. "You were right," he said. He glanced up at the clock on the wall. "And we've got twenty-five minutes to catch them."

"Catch who?"

"The bodies of two cops were fished out of the river around dawn, their necks broken. They were fully dressed, but their AKs had been fired. Eight times."

"Who were they?"

"Doesn't matter, Colonel. What matters is that they were assigned patrol duty on Yanggak Island."

"Yanggakdo Hotel," Pak said. "Someone from one of the tour groups."

"That's right," Ri said. "And the next flight to Beijing leaves in twenty-five minutes."

SEVEN

At Sunan International Airport, Soon and his roommate, a slightly built South Korean from Inch'on, were first off the bus, and along with Kim and others were herded into the departing passengers' hall.

The airport was busy this morning handling the four tour groups plus a smattering of North Korean and Chinese businessmen who had their own separate line. This close to finally getting out, everyone's spirits had improved markedly since the hotel lobby.

"I thought Beijing was horrible, but this place is in a time warp," Sue said softly. "I'm glad we're getting out." They were in line to get their boarding passes.

"Me too," Kim whispered back. Her heart was pounding, her legs weak, and her palms wet. She felt like a wreck.

Mr. Tae came over. "What was that?" he asked politely. He was a small man with thinning gray hair. He'd taught English in high school before he was given this job.

"I was telling Kim how interesting this visit has been," Sue said. "The time went fast."

Mr. Tae nodded his appreciation even though it was obvious Sue was lying. "Maybe you will come back someday."

Sue nodded. "Maybe."

Kim forced a smile and nodded. She felt stupid, as if everything she was thinking was showing on her face. But Mr. Tae merely smiled at her, and walked back to the head of the line to make sure no one in his group was running into a problem.

"Guys like that have got to wonder why people like us come here," Sue said. "I mean I can understand why you're here but the only reason I came was because of the thesis I'm writing on the two Koreas."

"Did coming here help?" Kim asked, for something to say.

"Not really. I could have gotten almost everything I needed from the Internet, except for the feel of the place."

After their names were checked against the passenger manifest they were issued boarding passes and Mr. Tae led them through a gate where they surrendered their bags and were given claim checks. Before the luggage was loaded aboard the plane every piece would be opened and searched by an army of men, then sealed with customs tape.

Just before immigration, Mr. Tae handed back their passports from which the North Korean visas had been removed. "As you have seen for yourselves, we are a peaceful nation of humble people. My sincere wish is for you to take that message home with you."

"Thank you," someone from the group said, and everyone else nodded their assent. He'd been a pleasant guide, not as strict or demanding as they'd been told some of the others could be.

The airport was going to be the most difficult time, Soon had warned her back in Seoul. "You'll have to keep yourself together, no matter what's happened to that point. They'll know that a Chinese general was gunned down in front of his embassy, but we'll be okay if they haven't found the dead cops."

"What if they do?" Kim had asked. "They'll know that it's someone from the hotel."

"In that case the airport will be locked down, probably all morning while they check us out. But our papers are legitimate, we'll leave no fingerprints or DNA, and if no one spots us swimming across the river there'll be no way for them to single us out."

"What about the cameras at the embassy?"

"Pyongyang is dark at night. Depending on the situation in the street it's doubtful they'll pick out much more than the fact that we're wearing police uniforms." He took her in his arms. "They won't see our faces, I'll make sure of it."

"I'm frightened," she admitted.

"You'd be a fool if you weren't," he said. "One step at a time, babe. One step at a time."

Kim looked up out of her thoughts in time to see her husband heading down the hall right behind his room-mate to the door out to the bus that would take them to the Russian-built Tupolev jetliner, and her heart soared. They were actually going to make it. She forced herself to remain calm.

Sue presented her passport, boarding pass, and baggage claim check to the uniformed immigration official, a pinch-faced little man with round steel-framed glasses and a scowl. He studied the documents and then looked up several times from the passport photo to intently study Sue's face. Finally he checked something against a list, and handed her paperwork back.

"See you on the bus," Sue said over her shoulder and headed down the corridor.

Kim laid her papers on the counter and fought the urge to hold her breath. Armed soldiers were stationed in the airport, so if something went wrong there would be no possibility for her to run. Without Soon she felt alone and vulnerable.

The immigration agent took a long time comparing the information in Kim's passport to a list on a clipboard. She had developed an urge to use the bathroom on the way out to the airport, and now the pressure was almost overwhelming.

"Have you been to Chosun before?" the official asked using the North Korean word for the country.

"No," Kim stammered. "This is our . . . my first trip."

"Do you have relatives here that you tried to meet?"

"I may have relatives here, but I don't think so. I'm from Chinhae, in the south. We have been fishermen for many generations."

"I know where Chinhae is located," the official shot back harshly.

Mr. Tae was at her shoulder. "Is something out of order?" he asked pleasantly.

"This foolish woman is attempting to give me a geography lesson, instead of answering a simple question."

"I'm sorry," Kim said. "I didn't come here to meet anyone."

The official wanted to argue, but he closed her passport and slapped it down on the counter. "Go home."

Kim gathered up her papers. "Thank you," she told the official. She turned to Mr. Tae. "Thank you," she said and hurried down the corridor.

A brisk wind was blowing across the tarmac when Kim emerged from the door and walked across to the big yellow bus. The air stank of burned kerojet and something else she couldn't identify.

The same aging Tupolev jet that had brought them here from Beijing was sitting on the apron one hundred meters away, its forward hatch open and boarding stairs in place. Their luggage was already starting to come out of the terminal. A couple of Air Koryo crewmen were doing a walk-around inspection, while a fuel truck topped off the tanks. The jet looked as if it was unfit to taxi to the runway let alone take off. The paint scheme was peeling, mottled patches showed along the fuselage where sections of the aluminum skin had been replaced, and something that looked like oil had leaked on the ground directly beneath one of the engines.

Kim resisted the urge to turn around and look back at the terminal, but she was certain that she could feel eyes on her back. Someone in the terminal was watching her from one of the windows, waiting for her to make a mistake, waiting for her to incriminate herself, waiting for her to suddenly make a mad dash for the bus.

Soon and his roommate were seated together near the back of the bus seemingly engaged in deep conversation. Kim walked back and sat down next to Sue a few rows forward.

"To tell the truth I'm more frightened of flying out of here in that thing than getting stuck here," Sue said.

"Oh, I don't know," Kim mused, and Sue laughed.

When the bus was full they were held for a couple of minutes, until the refueling was done and the truck lumbered away, before they were taken across to the aircraft.

Kim snuck a quick glance back at the terminal but no one was coming after them, and then she was following Sue up the boarding stairs and into the shabby jet.

They were seated in one of the middle rows, and a few minutes later Soon appeared in the crowded aisle with his roommate Yi Hwang-jap, and she looked up, risking a shy smile as her husband passed. His eyes narrowed slightly, but the gesture spoke a thousand words; they were almost home free, all she had to do was hang on for a little longer and they would be together again in Seoul.

"He's cute," Sue said, and Kim was startled.

"I hadn't noticed."

"Is that why you couldn't keep your eyes off him this entire trip?"

Kim had no answer, and after another few minutes the hatch was closed, and as the jet's engines came to life one of the attendants began explaining the emergency procedures.

EIGHT

Pak's Lada was smoking badly by the time he and Sergeant Ri reached the airport and were stopped at the security checkpoint so that their credentials could be checked. The instant the young guards saw Colonel Pak's red identity booklet they stiffened to attention and saluted. From this point the terminal blocked the taxiway.

"Has the jet to Beijing taken off yet?" Pak demanded.

"I think it is leaving at any minute, sir," one guard said, handing back the ID booklet, as the other raised the barrier.

Pak slammed the car in gear, floored the accelerator, and they shot through the gate and raced toward the road around the terminal that would give them access to the airfield.

"Radio the tower and order them to hold the plane," Pak told his sergeant.

"If we're not in time we can always tell the crew to turn around," Ri suggested.

"If the assassins are actually aboard the plane, they wouldn't hesitate to hijack it."

"Still time to order up a couple of fighters to shoot it down."

"And what happens if we kill more Chinese citizens?"

"I see your point," Ri said. He got on the radio, switching to the tower's frequency, as they reached the south end of the terminal building and turned out onto the apron that led to the taxiways and runways. The big Tupolev was lumbering toward runway 07, its engines trailing thick plumes of black exhaust.

"Sunan tower, this is Colonel Pak Hae, State Safety and Security Agency," Ri said into the telephone handset. "Copy?"

Pak headed directly across to the taxiway behind the jetliner.

"That's right, State Safety and Security Agency," Ri was saying. "I want that jet stopped before it reaches the runway. I want its engines shut down, its hatch opened, and all passengers and crew held on board."

Pak couldn't hear the other side of the conversation, but Ri suddenly shouted.

"I don't give a shit who's aboard. This is a matter of state security, you idiot. Dear Leader has ordered us here." Ri grinned. He loved throwing his colonel's weight around.

The jetliner was fifty meters away from turning onto the active runway when it slowed down and came to a ponderous halt. The engines immediately began to spool down. The truck with the boarding stairs came out from the terminal, as the aircraft's forward hatch swung open.

Pak drove under the starboard wing and swung directly in front of the airplane, blocking any possibility that the pilot could change his mind and try to reach the runway.

He and Ri got out of the car and walked back to the hatch as the truck pulled up and slowly maneuvered the stairs into position. One of the flight attendants was standing at the open hatch, a frightened expression on her pretty round face.

"Take out your pistol," Pak told his sergeant as they started up the stairs. "If anyone makes a move shoot them."

"Anyone?" Ri asked, impressed. He pulled out his Russian-made 9 mm Stechkin autoloader.

"Anyone," Pak said.

At the head of the stairs he showed his identification booklet to the attendant and then to the pilot and copilot.

"How long will we be delayed here?" the pilot asked.

"Until I say so," Pak replied. He turned to the attendant. "I want the passenger manifest."

"Yes, sir," the young woman said.

The aircraft was almost completely full. The passengers were sitting up and watching Pak and especially Ri with his drawn pistol. No one looked happy, and a lot of them were obviously frightened. Only the handful of Chinese businessmen, none of whom had apparently heard about the shooting, seemed to be indifferent.

The attendant handed Pak a clipboard with the names, nationalities, passport numbers, and seat assignments of the one hundred and twenty-five passengers. Twenty-two of them were South Koreans—thirteen men and nine women.

Pak moved into the cabin, stopping at the third row. The two South Koreans seated in A and B were old men, one of them with a long white beard and traditional peasant's hat. They'd most likely come to visit relatives.

Seven rows back he passed two women, one of them Japanese. Her seatmate, a South Korean, looked petrified, as if she expected to be shot at any moment. Pak gave her a reassuring smile and moved aft.

The next three South Korean males were a father and his two teenaged sons from Seoul, seated with a woman.

Pak stared at the father for a hard moment, but he was too slightly built to be one of the shooters from the surveillance tape, and his sons were both too young and too small.

He looked up in time to catch the eye of a man four rows back, who immediately turned away. He was identified on the manifest as Kwan Sang-hung, from Seoul, well built for a Korean, typical for a Southerner. His seatmate was Yi Hwang-jap, also from Seoul, a much smaller man, with narrow shoulders and a round face.

They were the shooters; Pak was almost 100 percent certain of it.

"Keep on your toes," he told Ri, and he walked aft to the pair, who both turned and looked up at him.

The smaller man seemed to be extremely nervous, but the other one was calm. He was a professional.

"Let me see your passports," Pak said.

"Is there a problem?" Yi asked, handing his over. "Everything was in order in the terminal."

Soon handed over his passport, and so far as Pak could tell it was legitimate, or else a damned good forgery. The few visa stamps were for Japan. Yi's passport looked real as well, but it contained no visa stamps.

"What was the purpose of your trip, Mr. Yi?" Pak asked.

"I've always wanted to see the North—Chosun. I'm a history teacher. I can tell my students about my trip."

"What else did you do while you were here?"

"I don't understand."

Pak turned to the other man. "Your story is the same, Mr. Kwan?"

"I'm not a teacher, but I was curious about what it was like up here."

"Were you satisfied?"

Soon shrugged. "I like the South better."

"I imagine you do," Pak said. He stepped back. "On your feet, both of you."

"What?" Yi stammered.

"Your papers are not in order. You're coming with us. On your feet."

No one in the aircraft made a sound, and for a long moment Pak was sure that the schoolteacher was going to cry out for help, but then Soon unfastened his seat belt.

"Better do as they say," he told his seatmate. "We'll catch the next flight home."

Yi wanted to do something, anything but stand up and leave the aircraft. He looked like a cornered animal ready to bolt or fight back, but there was nowhere for him to go, nothing for him to do, and he finally realized it.

He unfastened his seat belt and got awkwardly to his feet. "What about my luggage?"

"Don't worry about your luggage," Pak said. He let the man step out into the aisle, and quickly patted him down. Then he turned him around and secured his wrists with a plastic restraint.

"Am I under arrest?"

"For now," Pak said. He handed the man forward to Ri, and turned back to Soon who'd already spread his arms.

"What are the charges?"

"No charges yet," Pak said. He patted the man down for weapons, but there were none.

Soon turned around and held his wrists behind his back to be secured.

"This has happened to you before," Pak said.

"I was a cop in the Army."

"You should not have come here, Mr. Kwan," Pak said.

"Evidently not."

As soon as the prisoners were settled in the backseat of the Lada, Ri covering them at gunpoint, baggage handlers came out to the jetliner, opened the cargo bay hatch, and began unloading the luggage until they found the suitcases matching the numbers on Kwan's and Yi's claim checks. Pak had them load the bags into the trunk, then got behind the wheel and headed away.

"Nice car," Soon said.

Pak glanced at his image in the rearview mirror.

"Shut your mouth," Ri warned.

"No, let him talk," Pak said. He drove toward the south end of the terminal building. "I'd like to hear his views on how much better things are in the South."

"There's no comparison with this shit hole, but you people are so cut off up here you'd never understand," Soon said. He glanced over his shoulder as a start truck trundled out to the jetliner to power up the engines.

"Why are we under arrest?" Yi asked fearfully. "I've done nothing."

"You were identified across the street from the Chinese Embassy early this morning," Pak said.

Yi was thunderstruck. "That's not possible, sir. I was in my hotel all night." He looked at Soon. "Mr. Kwan will verify it."

"I doubt it, because he was there with you."

"No," Yi protested. "Tell him that we never left the hotel."

"We never left the hotel," Soon said. "Anyway, don't you people have guards posted at the bridges?"

"Actually you two were quite ingenious," Pak said. He pulled up at the security checkpoint and rolled down his window. But the guard glanced at the prisoners in the backseat and Ri's drawn pistol, and immediately motioned for the barrier to be opened.

"I swear on my honor that we didn't leave the hotel," Yi pleaded as Pak drove through the gate and headed back into the city. "We never had access to an automobile."

"Of course not," Pak agreed. "It's why you killed those two cops, stole their uniforms and weapons and swam across the river. What are their mothers to be told? That they died defending the motherland?"

"Murder?" Yi squeaked.

"For those two deaths alone, you'll face a firing squad. But the other, General Ho, why did you assassinate him? What did you hope to gain?"

Yi had lost his voice.

"Of course you're not on your own," Pak said reasonably. "Your planning was too good, and certainly your passports are first-class. Not amateur. But your knowledge of the general's schedule was nothing short of brilliant. Who sent you to do this thing? Was it the NIS?"

Neither man answered. Pak turned onto the main highway and they drove in silence for ten minutes until in the distance behind them they heard the roar of the jetliner taking off. Soon turned and looked out the rear window.

"You almost made it," Pak said. "Except that we found the bodies of those two cops faster than you thought we would. Just chance, I'm told, that they turned up so fast a couple of kilometers downriver from the hotel."

"Now you want our confessions," Soon said.

Something about the man's attitude was slightly bothersome to Pak. He was too calm, too self-assured. Yi was understandable, but not Kwan.

"We'll have them sooner or later, won't we," Ri said. "The easy way or the hard way." He glanced at Pak. "Funny how these sorts usually take the hard way. Do you suppose it's because they're stupid, Colonel? Or brave?"

"Okay, you win," Soon said. "We did it. But we didn't swim, would have got our clothes all wet and messy. We smuggled a hang glider and flew to the other side. You should teach your people to look up every now and then."

"Hang glider?" Yi whispered.

"He's right. It wasn't a hang glider. It was a rowboat. You'll probably find it floating somewhere downriver."

"That's a lie," Yi protested weakly. "I was asleep in my bed the entire night. I didn't even wake up until Mr. Tae telephoned us that it was time to come down for breakfast."

"Okay, we used a mini-sub."

"Those cops you killed were good boys," Ri warned. "Let me shoot this one now, Colonel."

Pak was missing something important here, but he couldn't put his finger on it. "Who hired you to do this?"

Soon looked out the window. The divided highway they were on was almost completely devoid of traffic, but people on foot were walking into the city in the median. In the distance the empty shell of the Ryugyong Hotel rose like a massive black pyramid from the city's center. It had been designed in the eighties to be the world's largest luxury hotel, but bad engineering and lack of money had permanently stalled the project.

Almost no traffic moved downtown, though there were a fair amount of people on foot, and less than a half hour after they'd left the airport, Pak drove through the gate into the agency's compound and around back to his parking space.

The morning was pretty—sunny, mild, only a light breeze. A lot of people would be in the parks today, the lucky ones among them there to eat their lunches. For most North Koreans lack of food was the major issue in their lives. On the surface Pyongyang was a modern, beautiful city. But people here were slowly starving to death, while less than two hundred kilometers to the south people in Seoul were getting fat like Americans.

"I think we'll find the truth once you're inside," Pak told his prisoners.

He and Ri got out of the car and opened the rear doors.

Soon got out and sniffed the fresh air as if he knew he'd never smell it again, but Yi got out, shoved Ri aside, and bolted for the front entry.

"Stop!" Ri shouted, but the little man kept running.

Pak was on the opposite side of the car from his sergeant. "Don't shoot!"

Ri fired once, the bullet hitting Yi high in the middle of his back, and he was flung forward onto the pavement, his head bouncing once and then he lay perfectly still.

"Goddamnit, I said don't shoot!" Pak shouted in frustration.

"But he was getting away," Ri said.

Two armed guards from the front came back in a run, their AK-47s at the ready.

"Everything is okay!" Pak shouted. "Stand down."

The guards pulled up just before Yi's body, not sure what had happened or what they were supposed to do. Almost no one in Pyongyang had any experience with this sort of thing.

"He was trying to escape," Ri said.

"One of you return to your post and call for a doctor and an ambulance," Pak said. "The other one stay with the body."

The guards saluted, and one of them headed back to the front of the building.

"You won't be able to ask that poor bastard any questions," Soon said sardonically.

"Makes you my best bet," Pak told him. He turned to Ri. "See what the man has in his pockets, then meet me upstairs."

"Sorry, I was thinking about those two cops."

"I know," Pak said.

He took Soon by the elbow and led him to the back entrance, and downstairs to the lockup and interrogation center.

The booking clerk looked up as Pak came through the swinging doors with his prisoner, and placed Soon's passport on the counter. "Suspicion of murder."

"From last night, sir?" the clerk asked, pulling a form from a tray. He was a young man with narrow cheeks and a permanent scowl.

"Yes. Once he's processed I want him prepped for interrogation. I'll be back this afternoon."

"What'll it be, drugs or torture?" Soon asked with a smirk.

Again something bothersome, something not quite right, niggled at the back of Pak's head. "Whatever it is you won't like it, but we'll get our answers."

When a pair of guards came out to take charge of the prisoner Pak headed upstairs to his office to see if the Chinese had come up with anything new before he drove out to brief Kim Jong Il. He wasn't looking forward to the meeting. Being anywhere near the man was always dangerous.

TEN

The flight to Beijing was a little under two hours, and Kim managed to hold herself together by burying her nose in a magazine and pretending to read. Everyone aboard was shook up because of what had happened on the taxiway, even the flight attendants were subdued, and no one was doing much talking.

In the terminal at Capital International Airport Sue shook her hand. "I'm sorry about those guys, especially the one you smiled at. Did you know him?"

Kim didn't know if she trusted herself to speak. She wanted to curl up in a ball in some corner and let it all out. She shook her head. "No."

"Well, he's in some big trouble now," Sue said. "Maybe he has family or friends, someone at home who can find out what's going on, and help him out." She shook her head. "Dirty bastards. I'm sorry I came on this trip."

Kim nodded. "So am I."

"I'm off to catch my flight," Sue said. "Good luck to you. And don't be too shook up. Just be glad it wasn't you they grabbed."

They shook hands and Sue scurried down the corridor to catch her JAL flight back to Tokyo, leaving Kim standing flat-footed while people streamed around her as if she were a boulder in the middle of a stream.

What came next? After the initial shock of witnessing Soon and the other man being led off in restraints, she'd asked herself that same question over and over. The problem was she didn't know where to begin, except to get on the Korean Airlines flight back to Seoul.

She turned and headed down the busy corridor to the KA gate, her entire body as numb as her brain.

From the very beginning she and Soon understood that sooner or later either of them could be killed. It was the risk they'd agreed to take when they joined the South Korean Special Forces, and it was the risk they agreed to take when they resigned their commissions so that they could be married and turn freelance.

But that life had been so stupid, she reflected now. She was young and she'd believed in Soon; everything he told her seemed like poetry to her ears. He made perfect sense. They were well trained and they needed money to live. More would be better than less.

In part, she supposed, she had gone along with him not just out of love, but because like him she'd never been able to play by the rules. As a kid she'd always been in trouble with her parents and at school, where she'd been a rebellious tomboy. It was something unusual for a South Korean girl from a pious Buddhist family, and no one knew what to do with her.

In college where she studied social history and geography her grades were lackluster at best, and she had the reputation of sleeping around, though that part was mostly untrue. She had drifted, never really getting in step with the people around her, until an uncle suggested that she join the Army. "Rules are for everybody," he'd preached. "Perhaps in the Army you will learn that means you as well."

After she graduated she got an apartment in downtown Seoul, and found a job working for the automobile giant Kia Motors in the advertising department where she was supposed to write reports on the social conditions in countries where advertising money was being spent. Like any large corporation, Kia depended on maintaining its good name, and was careful not to make some social faux pas because no one was aware of some obscure taboo.

She'd lasted less than three months at a job she considered stupid, working mostly for men who she thought were interested in her only because she was good-looking, and with women who were jealous.

The Army, which was having recruitment problems, welcomed her with open arms; it liked tomboys. She'd breezed through Officers Candidate School with top marks, and in Special Forces school she was the lead woman in her class, and beat all but a few of the men.

She'd found a home, a place where she could be herself, excel at something and be valued for just that, and not her looks. For the first time in her life she was happy.

Then she met Soon, and she realized overnight that she'd never even known the meaning of the word. He became her entire life. The sun rose and set on his existence. Every moment of the night or day that she wasn't at his side was darkness, and every moment she was at his side was sunshine.

The flight to Seoul was already loading passengers when she reached the gate and handed over her boarding pass. Before she entered the jetway, she turned to look back down the corridor in case some miracle had occurred and Soon was racing to catch up with her.

But he wasn't there, and she suspected that she might never see him again.

Unless Alexandar could help.

Walking down the jetway to the aircraft she promised that she would do whatever it took to get her husband back, lies, theft, murder, or sex. If lying and killing and murder were not enough for the Russian she would gladly sleep with him, if only Soon could come back.

ELEVEN

The day was turning out to be sunny and mild as Pak drove out of the city and into the countryside along the Dandong Highway that led northwest to the Chinese border. The well-maintained road was all but deserted, and passing through Changsan Park, he felt a momentary pang for the bustle of the West.

Roads like this in California at this hour of the day would be streaming with cars of every make and vintage. Parks would be filled with mothers pushing baby carriages or dressed in spandex tights with tiny plastic helmets perched on their heads riding ten-speed mountain bikes along the paths.

Everyone would be listening to music, either through headsets or boom boxes or in their cars, which vibrated with the bass notes. America was a musical nation.

Here it was quiet, by contrast. A graveyard compared to a fairground. Pak's car had no radio except for communications, which he'd turned off, so he drove in silence. He turned off the main highway about twenty kilometers outside the city, and followed an unmarked highway up into the heavily wooded hills until he reached a tall fence topped with razor wire. A Special Forces soldier came out of a guardhouse and motioned for him to pull up at the reception gate. A Kalashnikov, muzzle down, was slung over his shoulder and his uniform and boots were as crisp as his movements as he approached the car.

"Your papers," the guard said, and Pak handed them out.

"What are you doing here?" the soldier asked, inspecting Pak's identity booklet. He looked up to compare the photograph.

"To present my report on a situation in the city that developed early this morning. I'm here on orders from Dear Leader," Pak said. He could see another soldier inside the guardhouse talking on a telephone.

"Are you armed?"

"Yes," Pak said. He took his shoulder holster and Russian-made PSM pistol out of the glove compartment and handed them through the window. The semiautomatic fired a small 5.45 mm bullet, but its compact size was an advantage. It could be carried in a shoulder or ankle holster or even in a trousers pocket without detection.

"Your weapon and identification booklet will be returned to you when you leave," the soldier said. "Do you know the way, Colonel, or would you like an escort?"

"Is he in the main house?"

"Yes."

"I know the way."

"Do not stop or turn off the main road," the soldier warned. "You will be expected." He stepped back and the electric gate trundled open allowing Pak to drive through.

Residence 55, which was Kim Jong Il's official home, was actually an elaborate compound in the sprawling hills. The main house was a rambling two-story building nestled on the shore of a man-made lake dotted with islands, all of which were connected by walkways.

Nearby, but partially hidden by the crest of a hill, was the main security building where Dear Leader's guards were quartered and where his personal intelligence directors who made up the real power behind the Cabinet General Intelligence Bureau met and worked.

In front of that particular building, for whatever reason no one knew, a running track and athletic field had been constructed along with a parade ground and grandstand where Kim Jong Il could review his private Praetorian Guard army.

Sprinkled here and there in the woods were several smaller residences for some of Dear Leader's family members and for a few close personal friends, though precious few, even those high in the government, knew who was staying out here at any given time.

A pair of buildings housed a theater for live music and dance performances and a state-of-the-art movie theater with a library of thousands of titles, mostly American. Watching American movies was one of Dear Leader's major preoccupations, that along with his love of fine French cognacs cost the state millions of dollars of scarce foreign exchange every year.

Pak pulled up at the end of a long, tree-lined driveway in front of the big concrete and steel house. The entrance was hidden behind an elaborate screen of flowers and topiary. A dozen Korean flags fluttered in the light breeze, and getting out of the car he could smell the fragrant odors. Somewhere in the distance he could hear water flowing in fountains, and the sun reflected brightly off the expansive windows in the house.

He'd been out here to personally brief Dear Leader on three other occasions, and each time, like now, he'd felt a profound sense of peace and well-being mixed with the sense that an incredible malignant force was just inside.

An old man in a plain gray tunic buttoned to the neck, Dear Leader's pin on his lapel, came out of the house and bowed before Pak. "Your presence is most welcome, Colonel Pak. He's waiting for you inside. Please allow me to present you."

Pak followed him up the walk through the maze of bushes and dwarf trees. He'd not seen this particular servant before, but the man seemed genuinely pleased by the presence of a counterinsurgency colonel.

"Can you tell me his mood this morning?" Pak asked cautiously.

The old man smiled faintly. "Tread with care, Colonel. This business has upset him worse than the Americans and the nuclear inspectors. Shall we say, Dear Leader is volatile at the moment."

"Thank you," Pak said, and he genuinely meant it. The warning might help him get out of here alive.

"Oh, you are most entirely welcome."

Linking verandas, balconies, and wooden patios ran the entire length of the back of the house, which faced the lake with its islands. The place wasn't as elaborate as some of the palaces Saddam Hussein had maintained before his fall, but it could have been the Beverly Hills estate of a wealthy movie producer.

Kim Jong Il, his hands clasped behind his back, stood rocking on his heels looking out across the lake when the old man left Pak off and disappeared back into the house. No one else was around; no advisers, no guards, no one watching to make sure that Pak made no false moves.

"Thank you for coming on such short notice, Colonel," Kim Jong Il said, his voice soft, delicate, almost feminine. He turned to face Pak across a distance of seven or eight meters. He was dressed in a dark blue jacket unbuttoned at the neck, matching wool slacks, and softly polished black shoes. His pushed-up dark hair, sharply receding forehead, jowls, and large, steel-framed glasses made his round face seem chubbier than it was. His tight-lipped smile was more enigmatic than usual.

"My pleasure is to serve, Dear Leader," Pak recited the formulaic response.

"I understand that you have made excellent progress already."

"Yes, sir. We made a preliminary identification of the two assassins and arrested them as they were trying to make their escape by air back to Seoul by way of Beijing."

Kim Jong Il's eyes tightened perceptibly, but he said nothing, nor did he motion for Pak to come any closer.

"One of the assassins was shot trying to make his escape, thus proving his guilt. But the second assassin is at this moment being prepared for vigorous interrogation. I can speak with confidence that our State Safety and Security Agency will solve this crime to your satisfaction in the shortest time possible."

"You say that they are Koreans?"

"Yes, sir. From the South."

With no change in his expression, Kim Jong Il suddenly screamed at the top of his lungs. "South Koreans! Trained by the war-mongering CIA! The Chinese are convinced that I ordered the assassination of General Ho! Their ambassador says they will cut off aid to us! Their ambassador actually threatened me with a military attack!"

Pak stood absolutely still, as neutral an expression on his face as he could possibly maintain.

"They do not believe me," Kim Jong Il said, his voice back to normal, almost sad as if he were having a difficult time accepting that anyone would question something he'd said. He turned again to look at the lake, his hands clasped behind his back.

Pak didn't know if he was expected to continue with his report, leave, or remain where he stood.

"I am convinced that it is the Americans behind this deed," Kim Jong Il said. "I want you to personally find the proof and bring it to me. In this investigation you shall have the power of all Chosun behind you. You may use anyone, go anywhere, and commandeer anything and any amount of money you need to accomplish your task."

"Yes, Dear Leader."

"You must be quick. If our friends launch an attack against us I will unleash the dogs of hell upon their heads. Do you understand?"

"Yes, sir," Pak responded evenly. The man was talking about nuclear weapons.

"Succeed and you live, Colonel Pak. Fail and you die. We all die." Without glancing back, Kim Jong Il walked to the nearest set of stairs and, head bent low, headed down one of the paths that led to a footbridge to one of the islands.

Pak walked back through the house to his car. Two South Koreans had done the shooting, but Dear Leader did have a point; the Americans had the most to gain by meddling in North Korea's strong relationship with China. The only problem was apparently no one over there really understood the depth of Kim Jong Il's insanity. If China actually attacked, Dear Leader would not hesitate for one second to embroil the entire region in a nuclear war that would not only mean the end for Chosun, but mass murder on a scale in the millions.

Time was his chief enemy now.

TWELVE

It was well after lunch by the time Pak got back to his office and took the elevator down to the interrogation center. He lit a Chinese-made cigarette, the only kind available in Pyongyang unless you were a foreigner, and leaned against the wall looking through the one-way glass at what was being done to their prisoner, his stomach doing a slow roll. He never liked these sorts of things.

Mr. Kwan was strapped to a chair in the middle of the small white-tiled interrogation cell, his head lolling forward. Dr. Gi Song had just finished giving him an injection and stepped away, an indifferent look in his deep-set black eyes.

"This is far as I dare take it," he told Sergeant Ri who was perched against the edge of the steel table facing the prisoner. "Any more and the drug could kill him, or at the very least scramble his brains badly enough so that he would probably never recover."

"Not much use to us like that," Ri said.

"No," the doctor agreed, but it was clear that he didn't care. The prisoner was an enemy of the state, and Dr. Gi was a true believer. Pak had never cared for him.

But there were times like these when his skills were a necessary evil.

"When will he be ready?"

"The drug works fast," the doctor said. "A minute or two. What's he done?"

"Pissing in public," Ri replied caustically. He didn't like the doctor either.

"Not so bad."

"On a photograph of Dear Leader."

"The hell you say," Dr. Gi said. "The bastard." He

tossed the hypo in his bag, gave Kwan a last contemptuous glance, and left the room.

When he was gone, Pak stubbed out his cigarette and went in. "One of these days the good doctor is going to realize that you've been playing with him, and he'll report you."

"You'll save me," Ri said. "How did your meeting go?"

"I'm still in one piece."

"That's something," Ri said.

Soon was starting to come around and he looked up, a stupid expression on his face. He'd been drooling and the front of his shirt was spotted.

"Has he been cooperative?" Pak asked.

"Says his name is Kwan Sang-hung, he's an electrical engineer from Seoul, and he came here on a tourist visa because he wanted to see what life was like in the North. He says he never left the hotel."

"What do you think?" Pak asked. The prisoner was looking at them.

"He's lying, of course," Ri said. "But there's something else going on. Like he's waiting for something to happen. Doesn't seem to be afraid for his life though. He's a cool customer."

"A professional."

"Yeah, but a professional what?"

"Mr. Kwan, is that your real name?" Pak asked the prisoner.

"No."

"What is your real name?"

"Huk Soon."

"Well, Mr. Huk, why did you come to Chosun?" Pak asked.

"To assassinate a Chinese intelligence officer," Soon replied.

"That was too easy," Ri said. He was staring at the prisoner and Pak could see that his sergeant was also bothered by something.

"It's too bad we had to shoot your partner," Pak said. "But who hired you to come here and kill General Ho?"

Soon smiled, more saliva sliding down his chin from the corner of his mouth. "No, you didn't," he said, his words slurred and his South Korean accent thick.

"You were right there, and watched the whole thing," Ri said.

Soon's smiled widened and he shook his head. "You waited too long. She's already home."

"What are you talking about, you crazy bastard?" Ri demanded.

Soon just looked up, a silly grin on his face.

"We arrested the wrong man," Pak said. The more slender of the two figures in the shadows outside the Chinese Embassy had been a woman. It had never occurred to him.

"It's a good thing I didn't shoot this one instead," Ri said.

"Find out if any of the passengers on that plane are still in Beijing for whatever reason. Maybe we still have a chance."

"They'll be long gone by now," Ri said.

Pak was impatient. "Just make the call, please. Maybe there was mechanical trouble, or a problem with someone's papers, or a weather delay."

"It was the wrong guy," Ri muttered as he left the interrogation room.

Pak pulled a chair over and sat down close to the prisoner. He took out his handkerchief and wiped the man's chin. "What is her name, Mr. Huk, can you tell me that?" he asked pleasantly.

"Huk Kim," Soon replied, and Pak was startled.

"Your wife?"

Soon nodded. "Yes."

"Were you working for the South Korean government? Did the NIS send you here to assassinate General Ho?"

"No."

"But you're in the military."

"Not anymore," Soon said. "We quit."

"Who hired you? Was it the American CIA?"

"Alexandar," Soon mumbled. He was starting to fade, and was becoming increasingly difficult to understand.

"Alexandar who or what?" Pak prompted.

"Used to be KGB, I think. But he's in Tokyo now. Rich bastard. Mafia."

Soon's head started to loll. Pak slapped him lightly on the cheek to bring him back. "How do you contact him?"

"Internet."

"What's his address?"

"Too complicated. Kim knows."

Pak sat back. The Russians? It made no sense for them to want to destabilize relations between Chosun and China. So far as he knew no problems existed between Putin and Dear Leader.

Soon was on the verge of passing out again, and Pak slapped him harder. "Alexandar is a KGB agent. Is that what you're telling me?"

"He's a businessman now," Soon mumbled.

"Who does he work for?" Pak demanded.

Soon's eyes focused for a moment. "Just like us, I suppose. For the highest bidder."

Pak nodded, trying to work out the possibilities. The prisoner was not lying, that was impossible under the influence of the cocktail of drugs that had been injected into his system. But he'd talked too easily. Answered every question without evasion. It was as if he was proud of himself.

The light faded from the prisoner's eyes and he slumped

forward, the straps holding his wrists to the arms of the chair keeping him from falling to the floor.

Ri was just coming down the stairs, a sour look on his face, when Pak emerged from the interrogation room. "No luck," he said. "The flight to Seoul landed two hours ago."

"Have someone get our prisoner cleaned up and back in his cell, I'm through with him for now. But I want him treated well. Give him all the food he wants, showers, clean uniforms, and exercise every day,"

"I don't have it that good," Ri complained.

"No. But we're not going to trade you to China."

"What's next?"

"You and I have to do some homework, and then I have to arrange for a flight out."

"Where're you going?"

"New York."

NEW YORK/SARASOTA

THIRTEEN

The only decent jetliner in North Korea's small fleet was an aging Tupolev Tu-134 twin turbofan, on which their Russian-trained mechanics lavished loving care. If the need ever arose for Kim Jong Il to get out of the country in a hurry this was his personal aircraft.

It was five in the morning and still dark when Pak's car was cleared through the gate and Sergeant Ri dropped him off at the rear of the terminal where the plane was being refueled and inspected. The entire area was bathed in harsh white spotlights, armed soldiers everywhere.

"Make sure that nothing happens to our prisoner," Pak said getting out of the car. He retrieved his single nylon sports bag from the backseat. "Especially no more drugs. When the time comes I want him perfectly sane."

"Dr. Gi might have something to say about it."

"If you get into any trouble while I'm gone call Dear Leader's people. Tell them that you work for me and you'll be protected."

Ri looked at him like he was crazy. "The last thing I want is to be noticed by his people."

"If you need help you can get it."

Pak started to turn away, but Ri called after him, "Who're you going to see in the States?"

"Someone I think can help us," Pak said.

His credentials were checked before he was allowed to get anywhere near the airplane, and then when he went aboard the flight attendant, a pretty girl in an Army sergeant's uniform glared at him. "Welcome aboard, sir."

"Am I late?"

"Yes, sir. May I take your bag?"

Pak shrugged. "No." He glanced at the pilot, copilot, and flight engineer who had finished their preflight inspection and were on the flight deck preparing the jet for takeoff, then went down the aisle to a window seat a few rows back next to an emergency exit hatch.

The only person aboard the plane other than himself, the cockpit crew, and their replacements seated forward, was Lin Hun-Haw, deputy ambassador to the U.N. who was on his way to New York to try to convince the Security Council that North Korea was not responsible for the assassination, a task nearly everyone thought would fall on deaf ears. Lin was in his early sixties, slightly built and somewhat stoop-shouldered, with a scowl that seemed to be permanently etched on his face.

"You're late, Colonel," he said sharply, as Pak was stowing his bag in an overhead bin. "Explain yourself, before I allow you to continue with me."

Pak and Ri had spent the afternoon, all of the evening, and most of the morning trying without success to come up with something on an ex-KGB agent named Alexandar who apparently lived in Tokyo and had ties to the Mafia, but Internet service in North Korea, even for high-ranking intelligence officers, was practically nonexistent. They'd also secured a second set of papers, including credit cards, identifying Pak by name, but as a South Korean-born American businessman, as well as the flights and rental car he would need once he got to the States. Right now he was tired and impatient. What he was going to the States to do was nothing short of dramatic and had about a zero chance of success, but so far he'd been unable to think of anything else.

"Telephone Dear Leader, I'm sure that he will be happy to answer your questions," Pak said. He took down a pillow and a blanket. The flight from Pyongyang straight through to San Francisco, then on to Chicago, and finally New York, including fuel stops, would take nearly twenty-four hours. Once on the ground Pak figured he wouldn't be getting much sleep for a few days, so he wanted to get as much as possible in the air.

Mr. Lin was glaring at him.

"Both of us are on important missions, Mr. Deputy Ambassador," Pak said. "Either telephone Dear Leader, or give the order for us to take off now." He turned to the attendant. "In the morning I'll want breakfast, and I'll require that the crew patch BBC London back to me on my headset."

The girl opened her mouth to say something, but Pak sat down, buckled himself in, reclined his seat, and closed his eyes. By the time the engines were started and began to spool up, he was asleep dreaming of the faces aboard the tourist flight to Beijing. One of the women had been the second assassin. For some reason the thought astounded him.

FOURTEEN

The interminable flight east over the vast Pacific Ocean was made bearable for Pak because he slept most of the way. In the late morning when he awoke, he took a sponge bath in the head, then ordered an American breakfast of bacon and eggs, which, according to the attendant, was quite impossible. He settled for a Tsing Tao Chinese beer and a cigarette, and sat by himself staring out the window at the continuous deck of clouds far below, wondering how it would be to return to California.

His four years at U.C. Berkeley seemed like a dream to him now. He'd enrolled undercover as a South Korean adult student so he'd been allowed to live in an apartment off campus. Blend in, he'd been told by his handler back in Pyongyang. "But take care that you do not assimilate. The culture is seductive."

But he had assimilated, at least to a degree. It would have been impossible to operate undercover as a student otherwise. He'd developed a taste for Coca-Cola, but not for American beer and definitely not for McDonald's hamburgers, though he liked the fries. Television had been too frantic for his tastes, traffic on the highways too intense, and most of the music too loud, too discordant.

But there'd been a girl, a graduate student in international studies, who'd come to live with him his last year. She'd be forty now, in a good career, possibly at the U.N., married with children. She'd said that she was in love with him, but that nothing could stand in the way of her career. Maybe later, she had told him.

He'd never married, never had the time or found any of the North Korean girls very interesting, and he thought about his U.C. Berkeley lover from time to time, wondering how it would have been had he defected, gone to work for the U.S. government, maybe even the CIA, and looked her up.

Deputy U.N. Ambassador Mr. Lin slipped into the seat beside him. "I just looked at the passenger manifest. You're not on it."

Pak turned from the window. "No."

"How will I explain your presence when we land in New York?"

"It won't be necessary, because I'm getting off in San Francisco," Pak said. "So far as you and the crew are concerned I was never aboard."

"You can't just walk off an airplane. There will be customs and immigration officers, security police, officials watching our every move."

"That's not your concern, Mr. Ambassador. I simply ask that no matter what happens you have no reaction."

"Impossible," Lin fumed.

The attendant came back. "Captain Lee informs me that if you wish to listen to a commercial radio broadcast you will have to join him on the flight deck. We do not have the provisions to feed it here to the main cabin."

Pak unbuckled his seat belt. "If you'll excuse me, sir."

Lin got up and stepped back in the aisle. "I don't think you're going to like what you'll hear."

"I don't think so either," Pak said, and he went forward to the open flight deck door.

The flight engineer was in the galley drinking a glass of tea, and the pilot invited Pak to have a seat at the officer's position.

"We can pick up BBC London on shortwave, Colonel," the pilot said. "But if you're interested in what's happening down there, I can give you the CNN feed from Hawaii, we just passed over the islands."

"CNN is fine," Pak said, and he donned a set of headphones as directed and a moment later an announcer was speaking in English about the developing serious situation between the Chinese and North Korean governments.

In Pyongyang, the Korean Central News Agency had made no mention of the assassination or of the escalating tensions with China, but CNN featured the incident as its lead story. The facts were from the Chinese point of view. They were identifying General Ho as a high-ranking diplomat who'd been sent to Pyongyang to discuss ongoing terms of the nuclear disarmament agreement that North Korea had made, and the increased Chinese aid that was being offered in exchange for a new stability on the peninsula.

It was speculated that Kim Jong Il had refused to give

up the six to eight nuclear weapons already built, and had threatened to unleash a nuclear war unless Beijing backed him up. And some analysts were predicting that China would invade its ally and take Kim Jong Il down, which would in all likelihood mean an exchange of nuclear weapons that would probably spread to Seoul, Taipei, and even Tokyo.

So far there had been no response from North Korea, though Deputy U.N. Ambassador Lin Hun-Haw was currently en route from Pyongyang and was expected to make a statement tomorrow to the Security Council.

Pak lowered the headset and glanced back at Mr. Lin, who was seated on the armrest of one of the seats, staring at him.

"Are you finished, Colonel?" the pilot asked.

"Yes, thank you, I've heard enough. How soon before we land in San Francisco?"

"Depending on ATC, we'll be there around 2000 hours."

"Do you understand what is required?"

The pilot was uncomfortable, but he nodded. "Yes, we understand what you mean to do. We'll cooperate with State Security."

"Good man," Pak told him. "If something goes wrong you've never heard of me. Perhaps I was a stowaway."

FIFTEEN

Pak, dressed in gray slacks and a dark blue windbreaker with SFO SECURITY in gold letters on the back that had been hastily prepared for him by Special Branch, dropped down into the electronics bay beneath the cockpit floor when the aircraft came to rest to be refueled. It was twenty minutes after eight, local, which made the timing tight, but not impossible.

He glanced up at the captain and copilot and nodded, but said nothing. Their nonpassenger was leaving by the basement door, and once he was on the tarmac he was no longer their concern. Captain Lee reached over his armrest to close and lock the access hatch, plunging Pak into nearly complete darkness, except for the jewel lights on the equipment panels.

A star fastener tool had been taped to the wheel well hydraulics maintenance hatch, and Pak set to work removing the twelve fasteners that held it in place. Five minutes later he set the tool aside, and carefully prized the hatch up from its seal and set it down.

The pavement was two and a half meters below, and Pak immediately smelled a combination of odors; kerojet, hydraulic fluid, diesel fumes from the refueling tanker, and another, perhaps that of the sea. He climbed down into the well, replaced the hatch overhead, then threaded his way through the landing gear struts down to the nose wheels where he held up for a moment in the relative darkness.

Strong lights bathed the aircraft and the fuel truck that had rumbled out one hundred meters from the main terminal building. No one was being allowed off the aircraft, and no one would be subject to a customs check until they landed in New York City early tomorrow morning, so security was minimal.

Pak climbed down off the wheels, and nonchalantly walked around to the other side of the truck so that it was between him and the airplane, and headed across the tarmac to the open door of the baggage bay beneath an empty Delta jetway.

A few people were at the terminal windows above, watching the airplane and the security officer walking away, but he didn't expect anyone would be sounding an alarm. A North Korean diplomatic aircraft had been isolated and was being refueled, and a San Francisco Airport security officer was walking back to the terminal. Nothing was out of the ordinary, yet Pak was relieved when he reached the empty baggage bay and discarded the blue windbreaker that had covered his sport coat, laying it nonchalantly in plain sight on one of the rails.

He took out the thick manila envelope stuffed in his belt at the small of his back and his small nylon bag, which he had strapped to his waist, and looked around.

A small pile of luggage was stacked ready to be transported out to a connecting flight due in sometime tonight. Pak selected a small, dark blue overnight bag, and stuffed his things inside with what appeared to be a man's dirty laundry. He crossed to a security door into the access hallway that connected all the airlines' baggage handling areas in the international and domestic terminals, as well as the Bay Area Rapid Transit station beneath garage G.

Passengers arriving on international flights had to pass through customs and immigration before they could reach the BART trains. But there was no security in the access tunnels, because entry from the terminal side could only be made through code-locked doors.

Just before the corridor passed through to the domestic G terminal, Pak opened a door that led down a short corridor and out to the BART terminal. No one was in sight, and hefting his piece of stolen luggage he stepped out and walked down to the terminal. Only a half-dozen passengers were waiting for the next train into the city, and no one paid Pak the slightest attention as he bought a ticket from one of the kiosks using a credit card under his work name of Joseph Yee, a businessman from San Francisco.

The train arrived a few minutes later and Pak got on

with the others for the twenty-minute ride into the city. Looking out the window as they left the terminal, he was struck by the notion that he could simply get off the train downtown, and lose himself in the city. Or, perhaps he could telephone the FBI or CIA and ask for political asylum in exchange for what he knew about the assassination of General Ho. He would certainly get their attention because he would be considered a high-value intelligence asset.

But no one would believe him. Kim Jong Il was insane and Pak Hae was part of the scheme. He was here in the States to spread disinformation. It's what Washington wanted to believe. The West had blinders on when it came to North Korea. Dear Leader was certifiably insane, but he was not stupid as most everyone over here believed, even though he had played the U.S. and her allies as fools for years. He was a master of the game. From time to time he would back off the nuclear issue, allowing inspectors into the country to see what he wanted them to see, but only long enough to get some much-needed fuel oil, medical supplies, and grain, before he would kick them out again until it was time to reopen the negotiations.

This had been going on for a very long time, and yet no one over here got it. Nor did he think anyone here would get it this time. Except for the man he had come to see.

He had reached the conclusion that the only help North Korea was going to get—help that would be believed by Beijing—would have to come from her chief enemy, the United States. Even as the thought had first come to mind, he'd wanted to dismiss it as utterly foolish, with absolutely no chance of success.

Pak got off at San Bruno, the first stop, and went directly over to a kiosk where he got a ticket for the train back to the airport, due to leave in five minutes.

The American would have to be influential, someone of the stature of a Jimmy Carter, with the on-the-ground experience of a Colin Powell, the legendary intelligence skills of an Allen Dulles, and the ruthlessness and brains to see both sides of an issue. He would have to be a risk-taker. Someone who'd always thought out of the box.

When Pak had returned home from college in the U.S., he'd earned his masters and Ph.D. at Kim Il Sung University in the history, philosophy, structure, and notable personages of the Western intelligence apparatuses. Especially in the United States.

Four men, beginning with Allen Dulles, America's first true spymaster, had the most influence on how the U.S. looked at and dealt with the world from the standpoint of intelligence-gathering activities. In Pak's estimation, besides Dulles, the others included William Colby and Donald Suthland Powers. All three of those men were dead.

He had come to the United States to ask the fourth man to help avert a nuclear war.

It was a few minutes past nine thirty by the time he was back at terminal G, and made his way to the U.S. Airways counter. He was booked on flight 784, which left at 10:45, and would arrive in Tampa, Florida, first thing in the morning where he had reserved a rental car for the short drive down to Sarasota.

Now that he had come this far, he wasn't at all sure what sort of a reception he would get, except that he could very well be shot on sight.

SIXTEEN

Kirk McGarvey and his wife Kathleen were finishing a late breakfast, early lunch by the pool behind their house on Casey Key a few miles south of Sarasota when the telephone rang. It was nine in the morning of what promised to be a lovely early fall Florida day, after a long, hot, humid summer.

They had decided to sail their forty-two-foot Island Packet south to Key West, and then up the East Coast and off to the Bahamas once the hurricane season was officially over next month. It seemed like years since they'd been anywhere together. Between McGarvey's "projects" as Katy called them and his work at USF's New College teaching Voltaire, plus Katy's fund-raising efforts for three major charities plus the Ringling Museum of Art, there never seemed to be much time.

Katy answered the phone. It was their daughter Elizabeth, who was calling from the CIA's field operations training base, known as the Farm, near Williamsburg that she and her husband Todd Van Buren directed. She wanted to talk to her father, and she sounded a little breathless.

"Have you been watching the news the last couple of days?" she asked. She was in her late twenties and the spitting image of her mother at that age; slender with a good build, an oval face, beautiful large eyes, short blond hair, and just a hint of an attitude that to invade her space might be risky.

"You mean the North Korean thing?" McGarvey asked. He'd retired as director of the CIA a couple years ago, at the age of fifty, after a career as a black operations specialist in which he had killed people. Often he wasn't proud of what he had done for his government, but his targets had all been truly bad people.

He was a tall man with a solid build, a pleasant face, and gray-green eyes. Not so long ago he'd come out of retirement to take on a freelance assignment for the Agency in which he'd killed Osama bin Laden, and he still kept himself in top condition with a daily regimen of hard exercise.

"What's your take on it?" Liz asked. Whenever anything came up on the international scene, she always called her father to get his read, which would in turn be passed along to the officer candidates at the Farm.

"Kim Jong Il is crazy enough to do something like that, if he had a reason. But it'd have to be big. As it is he's practically cut his own throat."

"If China crosses his border will he go nuclear?"

"I expect he would, and I expect the Chinese know it. If I were giving advice I'd go for a surgical strike. Find out where he's hunkered down and take just him out. I don't think anyone else over there would have the stomach to launch."

Elizabeth was silent for a moment or two. "How's Mom?" she asked.

"Just fine. Do you want to talk to her again?"

"No, I've got to get back to work," she said. "Has anyone from the Building called you?" The Building was what employees called CIA headquarters.

McGarvey glanced at his wife, who was staring down at their dock on the Intracoastal Waterway, a pensive expression on her face.

"No, should Dick have called?" McGarvey asked. Dick Adkins was the current DCI.

"There're some rumors floating around," Liz said tentatively.

"Like?"

"Could have been a South Korean hit."

"NIS has the people for it, but unless they know something that we don't, I wouldn't think that they'd be that stupid. If Kim Jong Il goes nuclear he's bound to do it up right. He'd take out Seoul and probably Tokyo."

Again Elizabeth hesitated. "That's about what Todd and I came up with," she said. "But that's not all. If it comes to that China wouldn't hesitate to level Pyongyang, and while the region is going up in flames we think they'd probably hit Taipei, and we'd be sucked into it."

McGarvey had come to the same conclusion when he'd seen the first bulletin on CNN that a high-ranking Chinese diplomat had been assassinated in Pyongyang. "I assume that the president is trying to calm down the Chinese," he said, though nothing had been mentioned on the news.

"He's called in the ambassador, but Daddy, I don't think anyone up there really knows what's going on or what to do," Liz said. "Totally off the record, I don't think Dick can handle the intel. And without that the White House and State are blind."

"Dick's a good man."

"No question about it. But he's never been in the field. He's never—" She paused.

"Killed a man, like I have," McGarvey finished it for her.

"Daddy, we're frightened up here."

"You have every right to be," McGarvey said. "Have you heard anything from Otto?" Otto Rencke was the CIA's resident genius. He and McGarvey were close friends and had a lot of mutual respect for each other. Their history together went back for more than ten years, and in that time Otto had practically become family. A few years ago he had even saved the lives of Mac's wife and daughter in an operation that had begun to unravel. It was a debt of friendship impossible to repay and even harder to forget.

"No," Liz said. "I was just about to ask you the same thing."

"I'll call him right now, and see if he's turning up anything. In the meantime the Chinese haven't mobilized on the border, so there's still time."

"I don't think it'll be a land war," Liz said.

"You're probably right," McGarvey told his daughter. "Let me call Otto and then Dick and I'll get back to you."

"Okay," she said in a small voice. She was a tough, well-experienced CIA field officer, but sometimes she was still a little girl who needed a father to assure her that everything would turn out all right.

"That didn't sound promising," Katy said after McGarvey hung up.

"She's nervous," McGarvey admitted.

"Should I be?"

"I don't know yet, but we could be headed for trouble."

She was studying his face, her gaze penetrating. "Personal trouble, or U.S. of A trouble?"

McGarvey was about to answer her when the motion alarm for the front of the house tripped and a light on the eaves behind them flashed. He entered a code on his cell phone, bringing up the closed circuit television image of the driveway.

A dark blue Ford Focus had pulled up in the driveway and a slightly built Oriental man, dressed in gray slacks, blue blazer, and a white shirt got out. He was carrying a thick manila envelope.

"Company," McGarvey said, getting up.

"Anyone we know?" Katy asked.

"Nope," McGarvey said. "Stay here."

"Get rid of them, Kirk," she said, but he had started up to the house and didn't hear her.

SEVENTEEN

He got to the entry vestibule and took his pistol from a drawer in the hall table as the doorbell rang. Putting the gun in his pocket, he opened the door.

"Mr. McGarvey," the man said, his English very good. "I'm very glad to catch you at home. I've just come from Pyongyang. My name is Pak Hae and I'm a North Korean Intelligence officer here to ask for your help."

McGarvey stared at him for just a beat, then glanced out at the car. "Are you alone?"

"Yes, sir."

"Officially?"

"With Dear Leader's sanction," Pak said. "May I come in and explain why I'm here? I think time is not on our side."

McGarvey stepped aside to let the North Korean in, and when the door was closed, he forced the man up against the wall, and took the manila envelope and set it aside. "Spread your arms and legs."

Pak did as he was told, and McGarvey quickly frisked him, coming up with his California driver's license in another name, several credit cards, and photographs of a family he probably didn't have.

"I'm not armed."

"It's good for you that you're not," McGarvey said. He glanced inside the thick envelope, which contained some files, in English, and a series of crime scene photographs, as well as two shots of a man in prison garb.

"Those are for you."

"How did you know who I was and where to find me?"

"My doctoral thesis was about important U.S. intelligence officers past and present. And I do my homework well."

Over the years Mac had thought he'd lost his capacity for surprise. But this now was something else. "If this is about the Chinese general who was hit in Pyongyang, you've come to the wrong place for help. Give me one good reason why I shouldn't get the FBI out here."

"We didn't do it, and of course no one believes us, so I'm here to ask you to help prevent a nuclear war."

"Why me?"

"Because you're a man of honor, whose word the Chinese respect, especially after the incident in Mexico City last year. If you were to prove that we didn't carry out the assassination, you would be believed."

"Your premier is crazy enough to have ordered it, especially if General Ho was there to try to talk him out of his nuclear program."

"Yes, he is just that crazy, but it wasn't us."

"The South Koreans wouldn't have done it either," McGarvey said. "They know damn well that if the situation ever got out of hand the first nuke would hit downtown Seoul before they could do anything about it."

Pak hesitated for a moment. "You've heard something."

"Just a rumor that it could have involved a South Korean shooter."

"A pair of them, freelancing for an ex-KGB agent with deep pockets living in Tokyo."

"No reason for the Russians to get involved," McGarvey said.

"Not officially, we agree with that much," Pak said. "But they were South Koreans, ex-NIS, husband and wife. We managed to arrest the husband intact, but the wife is back in Seoul."

"Ask for the South's help."

Pak managed a slight smile. "Dear Leader believes that South Korea is behind the hit, at the direction of the CIA. He's ordered me to find the proof."

"So you came here," McGarvey said, intrigued despite

his natural skepticism. "You've got balls, Colonel, I'll give you that much."

"Will you help?"

"I'll hear you out," McGarvey said. He picked up the files then led the North Korean back to his study, which looked out across the backyard. Katy was still seated at the table waiting for him.

He drew the blinds and motioned for Pak to have a seat across from him as he spread the files and photographs out on the desk.

"That's outside the Chinese Embassy," Pak said. "A car came to take General Ho to a meeting with Dear Leader, and the assassins knew the precise time it would be arriving."

"Someone in your government must have leaked the schedule."

"That's possible," Pak conceded, "but not likely."

"They got the intel from somewhere."

"That's only part of our problem. We've had the South Korean in our custody long enough for the Chinese to distrust anything he might tell them if we handed him over."

"This him?" McGarvey asked, studying the photos of the man in prison garb.

"His name is Huk Soon, his wife Kim. But that's all we know about them. They don't show up on any of our databases. And neither does the Russian Soon says hired them. All he knows is the name Alexandar and an old e-mail address, which when we checked didn't exist."

"How'd they get past your security?"

"They flew in as tourists, and on the last night they snuck out of the hotel, killed two policemen, dressed in their uniforms, and used their weapons to kill not only General Ho, but the chauffeur and two Chinese Embassy employees."

McGarvey put the last photo down. "There's no reason

for the kill except to destabilize your relationship with China. And the only countries who might benefit are South Korea and us."

"Exactly," Pak said. "Mr. McGarvey, I went to U.C. Berkeley, and I think I know the U.S. well enough to believe that no one in your government is stupid enough to engineer something like this. Nobody would win."

"Obviously someone thinks so."

"Only a madman."

"Kim Jong Il," McGarvey said.

"We've tried to assassinate him, but he's surrounded himself with impregnable security. Sooner or later he'll die, like his father, only there will be no replacement. When he's gone we can begin rebuilding our country, and someday reunite with the South."

"You'll have to survive until then."

"We need your help."

McGarvey turned away. The North Koreans had every reason to lie, and it was not unlikely that Kim Jong Il was crazy enough to pull off a stunt like killing a Chinese intelligence officer and blaming it on the South Koreans and the CIA. The only motive that made any sense was if the Chinese had tried to pressure North Korea to drop its nuclear program once and for all. It was possible that General Ho had threatened Kim Jong Il and the madman had ordered the assassination.

The one loose straw that didn't fit was an ex-KGB officer by the name of Alexandar living in Toyko who had hired the killers. It was so fringe that it had the ring of truth.

He turned back. "Go home, Colonel."

Pak got up, took a pen from his pocket, and wrote a New York telephone number on the back of the manila envelope. "You can contact me in Pyongyang through this number. It connects us with our U.N. delegation's secured communication section."

"I don't know if I'm going to do anything about this," McGarvey said, and yet he didn't know how he could possibly stay out of it. If China attacked North Korea the U.S. would almost certainly be sucked into the mess, and a great many people, maybe millions, would be incinerated.

"We can pay you—"

"This isn't about money," McGarvey shot back. "But if it were you wouldn't be able to afford me."

"I understand," Pak said.

"I would have to come to Pyongyang."

"That could be arranged."

"And I would need the freedom of access to any place or any person, including Kim Jong Il."

Pak hesitated. "You can't know how dangerous that would be."

"More dangerous than a nuclear war?"

Pak shrugged. "Please hurry," he said, and he went back to the vestibule and let himself out.

McGarvey watched the security camera image in his cell phone as the North Korean got in his car and left, never once looking back.

EIGHTEEN

McGarvey telephoned Otto Rencke at his office in the OHB, the Old Headquarters Building at Langley. His official title was Director of Special Projects, the only one anyone could think to give the computer and mathematics genius, who most of the time was in a cyberworld of his own.

His slight frame topped with an overlarge head and

long, out-of-control, frizzy red hair marked him as an odd duck, and his generally sloppy appearance—unlaced sneakers, torn jeans, and dirty T-shirts—convinced most people who met him for the first time that he was probably a street person rather than one of the most powerful and feared men inside the Company.

Fact was that the entire national intelligence computer system, from the CIA and NSA to the Defense Intelligence Agency and FBI's mainframe, was by and large Rencke's creation. He was the only man on the planet who completely understood how the vastly complicated networks actually functioned, and how with a few strokes on his keyboard he could bring the entire system to a screeching halt.

"Oh wow, Mac, did Liz call you this morning?" Rencke gushed.

"About a half hour ago," McGarvey said. "She wanted to know if we'd talked about what's going on. Sounds like panic on the seventh floor."

The DCI's office was on the top floor of the OHB just down the hall from the Watch, where five analysts plus a watch commander kept tabs on everything happening in the world in real time, 24/7. All the doors were kept open up there because Dick Adkins and most of the directors before him wanted to know what was happening at all times. Adkins was in the habit of wandering up and down the hall, peering into the various offices and centers, especially the Watch.

If there were any hint of trouble up there, everyone would feel it.

"No one knows what's going on. Bob Snow says he's working the problem, but so far his people are coming up empty-handed and the prez is making noises." Snow was the Deputy Director of Intelligence, the directorate that was supposed to figure things out.

"I'm coming up to Washington this afternoon, I want you to set up a meeting with Dick, and with Carleton Patterson and Howard McCann." Patterson was the CIA's general counsel and McCann was the Deputy Director of Operations.

"You know something, kemo sabe?"

"I'm not sure," McGarvey said. He glanced up as Katy came to the door, but she didn't say anything. "I want you to track down a Russian, ex-KGB supposedly working out of Tokyo. All I have is the name Alexandar and a dead e-mail address. He may have hired a husband-wife team of shooters—former NIS—who did the hit. Apparently he's got money, which means he's probably a player."

"Holy shit," Rencke said quietly. "You got their names?"

"Huk. Soon and Kim."

"A little bird's been whispering secrets in your ear?"

Katy turned and disappeared around the corner.

"I'll explain when I get up there," McGarvey said. "I don't think that you'd believe me if I told you over the phone. In the meantime see what you can come up with."

"Most of my programs have been pretty quiet lately," Rencke said. "Which direction do you want me to go?"

"The shooters are freelance, so maybe they've taken other jobs," McGarvey said. He was thinking on the run, but the moment Pak had denied North Korea's involvement, he'd had the odd thought that somebody might be taking a run at Kim Jong Il's regime from the outside, though he couldn't think why.

"I'm on it."

"Look for a pattern."

Rencke was silent for just a moment. "Son of a bitch," he said. "I can think of a couple of possibilities right from the get-go if the idea is to completely isolate the bastards, if that's what you had in mind."

"Exactly," McGarvey said.

"Bad stuff, Mac," Rencke said. "They might actually bring the Dear Leader down, but it'd be the biggest mess since the Nazis invaded Poland. All of us would be in it."

"Yeah," McGarvey said. "I'll see you this afternoon."

"Can you get up to Sarasota within the hour?"

"Yes."

"I'll book you on the flight leaving at quarter after eleven. You'll have your e-ticket on your cell phone by the time you get there."

Upstairs in the bedroom Katy had pulled out his hanging bag and was packing. She was brittle. "How long will you be gone this time? I need to know so I can pack for you."

"A day or two," McGarvey said.

There'd been plenty of other moments just like this one. In fact early in their marriage she'd given him an ultimatum—her or the CIA. He'd chosen neither and instead had run to Switzerland where he'd hid from everyone, including himself, while their daughter had grown up without a father because he'd been too stupid to know when to shut his mouth, when to bend with the wind, and when not to overreact.

"Right," Katy said. "Warm or cold climes?"

"For now, just Washington."

She looked up, her lips compressed, a flinty expression in her normally soft eyes. "Is it the thing between China and North Korea?"

McGarvey nodded.

She glanced toward the door to the stair hall. "He didn't stay long. Was he one of ours asking for your help?"

The other thing he'd learned the hard way with Katy was not to try to protect her by lying. Her life had been in jeopardy more than once because of what and who he was. She deserved to know what might be coming her way.

"He was a North Korean intelligence officer. They want me to prove they didn't order the assassination."

Her mouth dropped open. "You're joking," she said. But then she shook her head. "But you never joke about things like that."

She wanted to laugh and cry at the same time, he could read it in her tone of voice and her body language.

"I wish I was."

"Kirk, you can't seriously believe those people. Kim Jong Il is nuts and his finger is on the actual nuclear trigger."

"I don't know what to believe yet, sweetheart, that's why I'm going up to Washington to talk it over with Dick." He went across the room and took her in his arms. She was shivering. "And that's all I'm going to do."

"For now," she said, parting. "But whatever happens take care of yourself and come back to me. I don't look good in black and I'm too young to be a widow and anyway there's only ever been you."

WASHINGTON

McGarvey's flight was late getting into Dulles, and it was a few minutes after six by the time he got out to CIA headquarters, after-work traffic terrible on the Beltway. Rencke had left word for him at the visitor's gate, and although he didn't recognize any of the uniformed officers, they were expecting him and he was given an unrestricted pass.

"Welcome back, Mr. Director," one of them said.

"Just for a visit," McGarvey said. He put his visitor's pass on the rental car's dash and drove the rest of the way up, parking in front of the OHB.

Rencke was waiting inside the main arrivals hall, his red frizzy hair flying all over the place. When he was excited he tended to hop from one foot to the other, which he was doing now. But none of the security officers or the departing employees streaming past paid him the slightest attention. They were used to him.

He gave McGarvey a big hug. "They're waiting for you upstairs," he gushed. "We can talk on the way."

"You came up with something?" McGarvey asked, falling in beside Rencke.

"Yeah, but it makes no sense unless you're going to tell me that someone from North Korea paid you a little visit."

McGarvey was startled. This was over the top even for Rencke. "How the hell did you come up with that?"

Rencke grinned. "You called me with some stuff you

couldn't have known any other way." He laughed. "Who was it?"

"Colonel Pak Hae, State Security."

"He's claiming Pyongyang is being framed and they want you to prove it because last year you saved Beijing a big embarrassment, and you've got pull," Rencke said. "Is that right?"

McGarvey nodded. Traffic in the first-floor corridor, which also served as the CIA's museum, was beginning to thin out.

Rencke was delighted. "Am I good, or what?"

"What do you have for me?"

"First of all your Russian is probably Alexandar Turov, once upon a time a general in the KGB. His specialty was arranging wet work, *mokrie dela.* He was one of the heavy hitters, you know. Never actually played the violin, but he was a damned good conductor."

The name was vaguely familiar to McGarvey. "I don't think our paths ever crossed, even indirectly."

"They wouldn't have. So far as I can tell he's just about always been a behind-the-scenes guy. But he's a deal-maker. Made a ton of money during and just after pere-stroika, but for some reason he disappeared from Moscow about eight years ago and maybe set himself up in Tokyo. There're few hints that the FSB sent people after him, to try to get back some of the money he stole, but they disappeared."

"Is he on any of our lists?"

"Nope. He's just another Russian security officer who turned entrepreneur," Rencke said. "They're a dime a dozen. And that's the good news. The bad is that there's actually nothing solid that puts him in Tokyo or anywhere else for that matter. He's apparently gone deep, and he's damn good. But I'll keep on it, and I'll bag him sooner or later."

"What else?"

"The two ex-NIS shooters aren't on anyone's list. As far as South Korean LE knows they're clean."

"Did you get an address?"

"Yeah, but there's no telling if it's legitimate. No phone or computer records in their names, but I'm still working on it."

"Could mean they're hiding something," McGarvey said. "What else?"

"There might be a connection that I've got my darlings chewing on, but there's no color yet," Rencke said. His darlings were his computers and from time to time their monitors changed color, sometimes going to lavender, which meant that one of the programs that was digesting data came up with a threat to U.S interests. The deeper the color, the more serious the threat.

"With the shooters?"

"Six months ago Japanese Senator Hirobumi Tokugawa was gunned down on the way to his mistress's apartment in Tokyo. Possibly a pair of shooters, but no arrests have been made. Then three months ago South Korea's deputy ambassador to China, Roh Tae-Hung, was shot to death along with a call girl in Paris. Possibly two shooters, one of whom might have impersonated the call girl to get into the man's room. No suspects, no arrests."

"Where's the connection?"

"Besides the possible husband and wife team, both men were soft on North Korea's nuclear program," Rencke said. "Lots of anti-American sentiment out there. Some folks would like to see the country put back together. Pyongyang's nuclear weapons and rockets combined with South Korea's money and manufacturing capabilities would make it a powerful force in the region."

"Someone doesn't want to see that happen," McGarvey said. "But what about General Ho?"

"He may not have gone to Pyongyang to talk the North Koreans out of their nuclear program," Rencke said. "The

Chinese aren't saying. He could have been there to offer Kim Jong Il China's support."

They stopped at the elevators. "What's the Russian's motive?" McGarvey asked. "Can't be money if he's as rich as you say he is. And if he manages to start a war, Tokyo will be on the hit list."

Rencke shrugged. "Maybe it's his ego. Maybe he's in the game because it amuses him. And if he still has some solid connections with the FSB he'd have plenty of warning to get out of Dodge before Dear Leader sent a nuke across the pond."

"There's more to it than that."

"There always is," Rencke said, a momentary look of weariness crossing his features. "I'll see what else I can come up with."

They took the elevator up to the third floor, where Rencke got off. "When are you going over there?"

"I don't know," McGarvey said. He handed the manila envelope to Rencke. "This is what Colonel Pak brought out for me."

Rencke's eyes widened. "He actually came to Casey Key, to your house?"

"Yup," McGarvey said. "I'll come down to see you when I'm finished upstairs."

TWENTY

The DCI's secretary, Dhalia Swanfeld, a pleasant-looking but formal older woman, looked up with a little smile as Kirk McGarvey entered Adkins's outer office. She'd been McGarvey's secretary when he was the director of operations, and had advanced with him during his short tenure as director of the CIA.

"Good evening, Mr. Director," she said. "It's good to see you again."

"How are you?" McGarvey asked.

"Just fine, sir. They're waiting for you inside."

McGarvey glanced at the door. "What's their mood?"

"Curious why you're here now of all times," she said. "But a little relieved, I think." She picked up the phone and announced him.

Dick Adkins, reading glasses perched on the end of his narrow nose, was seated at his desk, facing the DDO Howard McCann and Carleton Patterson, the former New York corporate attorney who'd been the CIA's general counsel on a temporary basis for ten years.

They all looked up when McGarvey walked in.

"Good to see you, Kirk," Adkins said, rising. He was a slightly built man a few years older than McGarvey with a pale complexion and light blue eyes that showed he was under a lot of tension.

McGarvey waved him back. "I'm not so sure you're going to be so glad after I tell you why I'm here." He sat down. "Carleton."

Patterson nodded. "How're you enjoying retirement? Bored yet?"

"Sometimes," McGarvey admitted.

"You picked a hell of a time to show up," McCann said, glaring. He counted himself a modern spymaster, and he'd never liked McGarvey or any man of action. Finesse was the new motto of the directorate, which had even been renamed the National Clandestine Service.

"Why's that, Howard?" McGarvey asked. "Because of the North Korean thing, or have you gotten yourself worked up about something else?" He didn't much care for McCann either.

"Christ," McCann swore. "You're out. Go home."

Adkins held up a hand. "Wait a minute, Howard," he said. "Okay, Kirk, what did you bring for us?"

"I assume that the president is talking to the Chinese in greater depth than we're hearing on the news."

Adkins nodded. "He's buying some time for us to figure out what the hell Kim Jong Il is playing at. We know the guy's stark raving mad, but this makes no sense."

"It doesn't to them either," McGarvey said. "North Korean intelligence contacted me this morning. Said they didn't order the assassination. It was done by a pair of South Korean ex-NIS shooters working for us."

McCann was furious. "Goddamnit, Dick, I told you the shit would start raining down around our heads unless you convinced the president that we need to take the son of a bitch down before the region goes nuclear."

"It wasn't us," Adkins told McGarvey. "But if Kim Jong Il's people believe it, why'd they come to you?"

"They want me to come over to Pyongyang and prove they didn't do it."

McCann was struck speechless for the moment.

"Moderates?" Patterson asked.

McGarvey nodded. "They don't like Kim Jong Il either. And they're desperate to somehow convince Beijing that someone else was behind the kill. They think I'm the one for the job."

"That's quite impossible, of course," Patterson said. "You do understand that if you tried to help them it would be construed as an act of treason against our government. Even if they're telling the truth, and Kim Jong Il wasn't behind it, you couldn't get yourself involved."

"He's already involved," McCann said sharply. "He's listened to the bastards, and he's come here to convince us . . . of what?"

"The shooters were hired by an ex-KGB general, Alexandar Turov, who's living in Tokyo."

"The Russians?" Adkins asked. He too was incredulous.

"No," McGarvey said. "Apparently he's just an expediter working for somebody else."

"Who?" Adkins asked

"I don't know."

"But you believed your bosom buddy, is that it?" McCann demanded. "Is that why you didn't report this to the Bureau's counterespionage people—you've got pals over there too—and let them take it from here?"

"Because I believed him," McGarvey said.

"No," Adkins said. "I agree with Carleton 100 percent. I'll get you together with Bob Everhardt and someone from the Korean desk to debrief you and afterward we'll see where we're at." Everhardt was chief of the DO's counterintelligence staff, and one of the people McGarvey had hired as DDO.

"In the meantime we're faced with a situation that could go could nuclear at anytime."

"That's for the politicians to work out," Adkins countered.

"Which is only possible if they have good intel," McGarvey shot back. This was about the reaction he thought he'd get. But he had to make the try.

McCann took out his cell phone. "I'll get security up here to arrest him until we can straighten this shit out."

"I don't think you want to do that," McGarvey said mildly, getting up.

McCann glared up at him. "You won't get out of the building."

"For Christ's sake, Howard, leave it," Adkins said. He turned back to McGarvey. "Ball's in your court, Kirk. You know what's at stake, professionally as well as personally."

"I've always known," McGarvey said, and he walked out.

TWENTY-ONE

Rencke's office was on the third floor, and although he was authorized to have a secretary, and there was a desk and funding for that position, he'd always declined the offer. He worked at his own pace and he didn't want someone looking over his shoulder, or arranging his itineraries, or, God forbid, trying to clean him up. He owned one suit, one white shirt, and one tie, which he only ever used for funerals.

McGarvey's key card authorized his entry, and he knew the four-digit code for the door lock. The desk in the outer office was piled with files, maps, and satellite images, as were the couch, two easy chairs, and coffee table. It looked as if it had not been cleaned since Rencke had moved in.

Rencke was seated at a bank of computer monitors in the shape of a U, his fingers flying over one of the keyboards. Three eighty-two-inch flat-panel monitors on which were displayed the real time outputs of various spy satellites around the world were lined up above the computers. McGarvey recognized the images on one of them as downtown Pyongyang.

"Where will it be first," Rencke asked without turning around. "Seoul, Pyongyang, or Tokyo?"

"Before I try to find Turov and whoever hired him, I'm going to need more answers," McGarvey said. "Huk Soon is still in Pyongyang, but his wife Kim made it out."

"Seoul it is," Rencke said. He looked over his shoulder. "Ten minutes ago the Chinese brought their missile and air forces up to a stage one alert. DEFCON four."

"Any response from Pyongyang?"

"Not yet. But I think we're running out of time. And if

the shit does go down, you're going to be in a seriously unhealthy place."

"How soon can you get me over there?"

"Are you packed?"

"Bag's in the rental car out front."

"An Aurora is rolling out at Andrews. I'll drive you over there now, and take care of your car first thing in the morning. By the time you're airborne I'll have an NIS guide-interpreter standing by. They want this thing to go away as much as everybody does, so they're going to co-operate."

"What did you tell them?" McGarvey asked.

Rencke grinned. "You're looking for an old friend, but they want more," he said. He finished with his keyboard and got up. "Whatever I get I'll download to your sat phone, so you better keep it with you at all times, kemo sabe."

On the way out of the office, McGarvey remembered one last thing. "Send someone down to Casey Key to keep an eye on Katy. If Colonel Pak could get to me that easily, he certainly could get to her."

"The babysitters are already in place," Rencke said. "Nobody who doesn't belong will get within five klicks of her even when she goes out shopping."

"Thanks."

"How'd they take it upstairs?"

"Not good."

"Gee, what a surprise, and I'll bet Howard was leading the charge."

McGarvey had to smile despite the situation. "Do you suppose he doesn't like me?"

SEOUL

TWENTY-TWO

After descending to refuel over the Pacific, the SR-91 Aurora had climbed back up to its cruising altitude of 130,000 feet where the stars were visible and the curvature of the earth was apparent. Three and a half hours after taking off from Andrews, the pilot, Air Force Major John White, radioed back to McGarvey that they were starting their descent and were less than thirty minutes from touchdown at Oasan Air Force Base outside Seoul.

McGarvey had managed to get a little sleep, though the flight suit and bladder bag were uncomfortable. "Any reason I can't use my sat phone?"

"Now you can," White replied. "Just don't mention where you are, sir."

The aircraft's exotic shape and fuselage covering made it even more stealthy than the F-117A, and Aurora pilots were ordered to stay as high up as possible for as long as possible, and spend the minimum of time taking off and landing, limiting the visual sightings.

Rencke answered on the first ring even though it was midnight in Washington. He'd been waiting for the call. "You should be just about there," he said

"Half hour," McGarvey said. "Who'd you set me up with on the ground?"

"Captain Ok-Lee Lin. She's NIS which started out to be a problem because they refused to deal with you unless you were coming in on Company business."

"If word gets back to Adkins through official channels, I'll be all but dead in the water."

"You're there on a black project involving the North Korean thing, I had to give them that much," Rencke said. "But I told them there might be a leak here at a very high level, so any communication with us has to be through you. No mention of your being in the country will be made to anyone, including our embassy."

"I'll bet they loved that," McGarvey said.

The South Korean National Intelligence Service had been distrustful of the CIA since two years ago, after one of its agents operating in the North had been burned. It had been strongly rumored that some of the intel that the NIS had shared with the CIA had somehow leaked.

"It was the only way I could get them to cooperate," Rencke said. "When this is all over we can kiss and make up. In the meantime I figured this was top priority."

Something was missing. "Has anyone from upstairs been down to see you yet?"

"Not a word," Rencke said. "Kinda odd, don't you think? Howard especially would have to figure that you and I had talked."

"Has anyone tried to hack your systems?"

Rencke chuckled. "Not possible, Mac, I shit you not. Leastways not by anyone here on campus. They warned you to stay the hell out of it. Maybe Howard is giving you enough rope to hang yourself."

But there was more to it than that, McGarvey was convinced of it. He'd seen things like this before. As soon as a national crisis hit us, like 9/11, everyone got superbusy trying to cover their own asses.

"What assets have we got trying to figure out what really happened in Pyongyang?" McGarvey asked.

"Until you showed up everyone was convinced that Kim Jong Il ordered it."

"Just to show the Chinese that he can't be dictated to?"

"Something like that," Rencke said. "It's what the president wants to hear. He doesn't want another war, so he's siding with the Chinese, telling them what a shit Kim Jong Il is, and that he oughta be taken out with as little damage to the country as possible. It's gonna happen, the president just wants the Chinese to finesse the situation, because if they push too hard Dear Leader will launch."

The Korean peninsula had come into view out the canopy, and Major White was practically diving the Aurora straight in.

"Anything new on Turov?"

"Nothing yet," Rencke admitted. "But I'm going on the assumption that he's our man, and that he *wants* to be reached by the right sort."

"Someone who needs his talents."

"That's right, but for now he's probably lying low until this blows over. He might already have left Tokyo, but a man like him will always have his ear open for something new. Which means he can be contacted."

"When you get to him, what are you going to offer?" McGarvey asked.

"President Haynes, and I'm going to ask that he hire you as the shooter."

TWENTY-THREE

Huk Kim got out of bed at last, and padded into the bathroom where she looked at her face in the mirror. Her eyes were red-rimmed and puffy, her complexion sallow. She'd managed to hold back the tears on the flight to Beijing and then here to Seoul and even in the taxi to the apartment.

But the moment she'd walked in the door without Soon, she'd broken down.

From the day she'd laid eyes on him, he had been the center of her universe. She never did anything without him, or at least without his face, his feel, and his strong masculine smell in her mind. She made no decisions without him. Every thought she had was about him. Her entire future was intertwined with his.

Now he was gone.

She splashed some cool water on her face, dried off, and went into the living room, but stopped. She'd completely forgotten why she was there.

For several long seconds she stood in the middle of the room trying to remember something. Maybe she was losing her mind, she thought, and she turned to tell Soon what a little fool she had become. But of course he wasn't there. He hadn't come back from Pyongyang with her.

She'd almost forgotten about how he'd been marched off the airplane by two men, one of them brandishing a pistol. They were cops, or maybe state security, they had the look. Now he was either in an interrogation cell or he was dead.

In Pyongyang. In North Korea.

Suddenly she knew why she'd finally woken up and why she was here, what she had to do.

She got her cell phone from her purse where she'd dumped it and her hanging bag by the door last night when she'd returned. She flipped it open, got a dial tone, and with fumbling fingers entered a local number.

Alexandar could normally be contacted on the Internet, using a sophisticated encryption program that he'd sent as a download to Kim and Soon's laptop. If the entry procedures and passwords were wrong, the program would erase itself as well as the laptop's entire hard drive.

In an emergency he could be reached at a redialer number that was unique to the operator. Her number was different from Soon's. It was the only secret she'd ever kept from him, and it had been at his insistence. "Our lives could depend on it," he told her.

It seemed to take forever before the call went through, and when it rang she let go of the breath she'd been holding.

After two rings the connection was made, though no one answered.

"We have a problem," Kim said, trying to keep her voice as even as she could.

For several long seconds she pressed the phone to her ear, hoping that he would be there, that he would answer her, but the connection was broken and she had a dial tone again.

TWENTY-FOUR

The Aurora landed at Oasan Air Force Base shortly before ten in the morning local and was immediately directed to an empty maintenance hangar at the opposite side of the field from the operations terminal. Flying in, McGarvey got very little chance to see anything of Seoul from the air because of their speed and the extreme angle of descent, and once they were inside the hangar the main doors trundled closed before the aircraft engines had fully spooled down.

A boarding ladder was brought over as the canopy came open. Major White was already standing up when McGarvey undid his harness and unplugged his helmet and took it off.

"Good flight?" the pilot asked.

"A short flight," McGarvey replied. "Thanks for the lift."

A tech sergeant in flight-line coveralls helped McGar
vey out of the aircraft and down the ladder where a briga-
dier general was waiting at the bottom. He didn't look
happy, nor did the young, slightly built Korean woman
dressed casually in blue jeans, white blouse, and Nikes,
standing next to him.

"Tom Handleman—division commander," the general
said. He didn't bother to shake hands. "I hope you're here
to help straighten out the situation, I'd just as soon not go
to war."

"Let's hope not," McGarvey said. He turned to the
woman. "Captain Ok-Lee?"

"Yes," she said, shaking hands. "Your reputation pre-
cedes you, Mr. Director." Her English was only slightly
accented.

"Former director," McGarvey said. "I'm here as a civilian."

"Right."

The tech sergeant got McGarvey's bag from a compartment in the belly of the fuselage and brought it over, then
helped him remove the flight suit, boots, and bladder bag.

"Will you be needing anything else on base?" Handleman asked.

"I don't think so," McGarvey said.

Ok-Lee drove a C-class Mercedes very fast and expertly
in heavy traffic into the big city. The morning was bright
and warm, but a haze of smoke hung over the industrial
complexes, and curled along the Hangang River busy
with commercial traffic. Every second vehicle on the
highway seemed to be a van or truck of some sort. Seoul
was a prosperous place, everything happening at a breakneck pace.

"I've booked you at the Westin Chosun downtown in
Gwangh-wamun," the NIS agent told him.

"I'm not going to do much sightseeing," McGarvey said.

Ok-Lee gave him an odd look. "Why exactly have you come here, Mr. McGarvey?"

"To help stop World War III, if it's not already too late."

"CIA hasn't given us anything worth a damn," Ok-Lee said. "And I'm not afraid to share with you that we're at a complete loss what to do next, although the suggestion has been made to try to get someone up there and eliminate Kim Jong Il."

"The NIS has tried that before."

"More than once," Ok-Lee said bitterly. "Maybe we'll get lucky this time."

They drove for a while in silence, the industrial parks in the outskirts giving way to apartment buildings and occasionally American-style shopping centers.

"What's the mood here?" McGarvey asked. "Anybody running for the hills?"

"Just a trickle. But we've been resigned to the fact that the crazy bastards have nuclear weapons and rockets, and there's not a lot we can do about it." She glanced over at McGarvey. "I hope you brought something we can use."

"A name."

Ok-Lee's eyes narrowed. "Are you telling me it's true that one of our own people made the hit?"

"Probably two of them, a man and a woman," McGarvey said. "The guy is still in Pyongyang, but the woman presumably made it out."

"Give me her name and we'll have her in custody by lunch," Ok-Lee said, but then she frowned. "Unless you're telling me that they were actually working for your people."

"No, but there's more to it than that," McGarvey said. "I want to find her with as little fuss as possible."

"And then what?"

"Then we'll have a little chat about who they were really working for."

The Westin, built in 1914, was Seoul's first Western hotel, and had been kept up-to-date through the years. McGarvey had been debriefed there a few years ago after an assignment in Japan, and then had spent a couple of days lounging around until it was time to go home.

Ok-Lee flashed her credentials to the bellman and ordered him to hold her car. She directed McGarvey across the broad, old-fashioned lobby to the bank of elevators. "You're already checked in," she told him.

"Under my own name?"

"Any reason why not?"

"Not yet," McGarvey said.

His top-floor suite looked to the west toward city hall and the broad, traffic-choked boulevards that cut through the modern skyscrapers. It could have been just about any large city anywhere in the world, a place in which to lead an anonymous life below anyone's radar.

McGarvey checked out the rooms including the palatial bathroom, as well as the phones and table lamps, but so far as he could tell the suite had not been bugged.

Ok-Lee watched him until he was done. "No one knows you're here."

McGarvey smiled. "You do, and so does your boss."

"We want you to succeed," she said.

"Their names are Huk Soon and Huk Kim, former NIS snipers, or at least they went through the training and had commissions before they resigned," McGarvey said.

He opened his bag on the bed and took out a small leather satchel about the size of a dopp kit as Ok-Lee made a call on her cell phone and said something in rapid-fire Korean, only the Huks' names understandable to him.

Her eyes widened slightly when McGarvey pulled his

9 mm Tactical SG Compact Wilson pistol and Slimline quick-draw holster from the satchel and attached it to his belt at the small of his back, but she went to the desk where she quickly wrote something on a piece of hotel stationery, then hung up, and pocketed the phone.

"If you fire your weapon anywhere in South Korea you will be in some serious shit, Mr. McGarvey, no matter why you came here."

"I'll keep it in mind," McGarvey promised. "Did you find out where she lives?"

Ok-Lee wanted to pursue the issue, but she nodded tightly. "Where did you get these names?"

"I can't tell you that now, you wouldn't believe me anyway, Captain," McGarvey said. "Shall we go find her?"

She said something in Korean half under her breath.

"That didn't sound nice," McGarvey said.

"It wasn't," she replied.

TWENTY-FIVE

Kim had never used the emergency number to contact Alexandar so she had no idea how long it would take for him to get back to her. But it seemed like hours since she had made the call, and the confines of the third-floor apartment were getting to her. She felt as if she were just as much a prisoner here as Soon was up north.

For the tenth time in the last hour she went to the window and looked down at the street. Nothing seemed out of the ordinary to her. This was a small, old-fashioned neighborhood straight north of downtown, and just a few blocks from the Sungsin Women's University where she'd gotten her degree in political science. She almost wished she were back there now, her life had been simpler then.

The streets here were narrow and lined with ground-floor shops on both sides, and apartments in the second and third stories above.

It was hard to imagine that Alexandar wouldn't contact her. She'd gone online and checked their Swiss account. The final payment of $750,000 had already been deposited, which meant that he wasn't dissatisfied.

But there was no telling how he was going to react when she told him that Soon had been taken off the plane in Pyongyang.

Once on a Saturday morning in bed, after they had made love, she'd asked Soon what would happen if one of them were ever to be arrested.

"All depends who arrested us and for what," he'd told her. "Maybe it would be a good-looking meter maid in Paris, because I forgot to pay a parking fine. We'd go back to her place so I could bargain for my freedom."

He was laughing at her, and she slapped his chest. "I'm serious."

"Let's deal with that if and when it ever comes up," he'd said. "Now I'm hungry."

Soon joked about almost everything, but now it had come up, and she didn't know what to do.

She'd refused to turn on the radio or television, and everything outside seemed normal. But she and Soon had been certain that the assassination of a Chinese general in Pyongyang, apparently by a pair of local cops, would create an international stir.

She got dressed in a pair of jeans, a light sweatshirt, and flip-flops and let herself out of the apartment. The old woman who managed the building was sweeping the vestibule and she looked up and grinned when Kim came down the stairs.

"Mr. Huk not back with you?" she asked. "I not see him."

"No, he had some more business in Nagasaki," Kim said, her heart in her throat. She wanted to cry.

"Maybe best we all get out of here," the old woman said, but she shook her head and went back to her sweeping.

Kim wanted to ask the old woman what she meant, but she was afraid she already knew.

Outside she started down the street toward the market a half block away to buy a packet of cigarettes, maybe a bottle of wine, and something to eat for supper. And a newspaper. The tiny store run by an old man with a long mustache and a tiny black hat was on the corner, newspapers and magazines displayed on racks in front.

From across the street she could read the blaring headlines: WAR IMMINENT in Seoul's largest newspaper, the *Hankyoreh Shimbun*. ALERT! the *Gook-Min Ilbo* warned, CHINA RATTLES HER SABERS! The headlines were also plastered across the front page of the English-language *Seoul Times*.

A small three-wheeled mini-truck, belching smoke, rattled past and Kim crossed to the market, where she stopped in front of the newspaper rack, unable to help herself from staring.

"Very bad news, Mrs.," the old man said from the doorway. "You want newspaper?"

Kim looked up, startled. She hastily picked one of the papers randomly then went inside the shop where she bought a pack of Marlboros, a bottle of Australian Merlot, and one of the rice bowls with noodle soup and fish that the old man's wife made fresh each morning.

"Where's Mister, haven't seen him for more than two weeks?"

"He's still away on business," Kim said absently, paying for the things.

"Too bad."

Outside she recrossed the street and headed back to her apartment. She wanted to get home so that she could read the newspaper stories to find out if anyone suspected the shooters had been anyone other than North Korean cops.

It was perfectly clear to her now what Alexandar wanted to accomplish by the assassination of General Ho. But why? It made no sense that the Russians would want to foment trouble between China and North Korea. Only the U.S. could possibly benefit by the hit.

She was momentarily stopped in her tracks. Soon believed that Alexandar was only a middleman, an expediter, who did nothing more than hire shooters. A freelancer. And the CIA was notorious for hiring foreign talent to do some of its dirty work.

A C-class Mercedes passed and Kim wouldn't have paid much attention except that it pulled up and parked in front of her apartment building.

Her heart skipped a beat and her knees went weak. She crossed to the other side of the street where she sat down at the one small table in front of the neighborhood kimchi shop, as a slightly built Korean woman in jeans got out from the driver's side. A moment later a tall, somewhat husky man wearing a sport coat and khaki slacks got out from the other side. It was obvious to her, even at this distance, that he was an American.

They went inside as the owner's daughter came out of the shop. "May I help you?"

"I'd like some tea, please," Kim said.

The girl went back into the shop, leaving Kim to stare at the car's license plate. She couldn't quite make out the numbers and letters, but the plate was slate-gray, federal government.

The woman was NIS and the man was CIA. She was convinced of it.

And now she had no idea what she was going to do.

TWENTY-SIX

On the strength of Ok-Lee's NIS credentials, the old woman who managed the building let them into the Huks' apartment, although she didn't like it and she wasn't shy about letting them know how she felt with a steady stream of Korean.

"What was she saying?" McGarvey asked when they got inside. He'd drawn his pistol and stood in the entryway.

"That they're her favorite tenants," Ok-Lee said. "That they've been away, and if the government was paying attention to business as it should be, we wouldn't find ourselves in the mess we're in."

"Somebody came home," McGarvey said pointing to the hanging bag lying on the floor.

"You're right," Ok-Lee agreed. She knelt down and opened the bag as McGarvey cautiously crossed the living room and checked out the kitchen and single bedroom.

"No one's home," he said, holstering his pistol, and coming back to where Ok-Lee had spread the contents of the bag in the middle of the living-room floor.

"A woman's clothing, and it looks as if she's been gone for more than just a day or two, most of it's dirty. She stuffed all of it in this big plastic bag."

"She's tidy."

Ok-Lee was troubled. She shook her head. "Koreans don't do things that way. We would handwash our things, especially our underwear, every night and hang them to dry."

"Maybe the Huks are modern Koreans."

"Maybe," Ok-Lee said, but something about the plastic bag bothered her.

"Anything else interesting?"

"No," Ok-Lee said, getting up and looking around. "Nice," she said.

The apartment was very well decorated with Danish furniture, expensive rugs, a large plasma television, and Bose sound system. Library shelves held several hundred DVDs plus a lot of large format art books, as well as a collection of world atlases and country guides. Most of the books were in Korean so Ok-Lee had to translate.

"They like to travel," McGarvey said.

"Let's see what else they like to do," Ok-Lee said and she and McGarvey searched the apartment, starting with the living room, moving the furniture around, checking behind wall plates, light fixtures, and inside every book and CD.

An hour later Ok-Lee came across a laptop computer beneath some sweaters on a closet shelf in the bedroom. "Here we go," she said, laying it on the bed, but McGarvey stopped her before she could open the lid.

"If they're who I think they are, this could be important," he said. "I don't want to screw it up by doing something wrong."

"Booby-trapped?"

McGarvey shrugged. "Maybe not to explode, but at least to erase the hard drive. I have somebody who can take care of it for us."

Ok-Lee bridled. "These are Korean citizens we're investigating, not Americans."

"And I'm here to help," McGarvey said. "For now let's do it my way, okay?"

"I'm sticking my neck way out here, just on your reputation, Mr. Director."

"So am I," McGarvey said.

After a moment she nodded. "I was told to cooperate, so I will. But don't bullshit me, McGarvey, or I'll cut you off at the knees."

"That's fair," McGarvey said. "In the meantime did you notice what we *didn't* find?"

Ok-Lee looked around. "No."

"Money, passports, letters, bills, credit card statements, checkbooks," McGarvey said. "This place is too clean."

"Safety deposit box?"

McGarvey handed her a key attached to a plastic tag with Korean figures. "This was in a drawer under some socks. Spare apartment key?"

"This says nine, the apartment is three," Ok-Lee said. "This is a key to a storage locker or unit somewhere. See the number inscribed on the key?"

"Can you trace it?"

She smiled. "Do you suppose the key is booby-trapped?"

"No, but the storage locker might be."

TWENTY-SEVEN

It seemed forever to Kim before the man and woman emerged from the building and climbed into the government Mercedes. The only reason they had taken so long was if they had searched the apartment, and Kim was sick at heart by what they had found.

The man was carrying the laptop that held Alexandar's encrypted program and the records of all their transactions, including the Swiss bank account and password.

She forced herself to wait a full five minutes in case they might double back, but finally she paid her bill, gathered her groceries, and crossed the street.

The old woman came out of her ground-floor apartment, an angry scowl on her deeply lined face. "The government people were here, Mrs. What do they want?"

Kim's stomach was churning. She shook her head. "What government people?"

"They wanted to see inside your apartment. But I told them to mind their own business and take care of the country."

"But they went upstairs, and you let them in," Kim said, her voice stern to hide her fear. With Soon under arrest in Pyongyang everything was falling apart.

"No choice," the old woman shot back. "Why did they come here? Are you in some kind of trouble?"

"No, nothing like that," Kim said. "But I honestly don't know why they were here. Maybe it was a mistake."

"Yes, a mistake all right," the woman said, and she watched as Kim went up the stairs. "You better fix it, Mrs."

But without Alexandar's help Kim didn't know how.

She ignored the mess in the apartment, and went back to the bedroom to find the key. But the contents of the chest of drawers had been rifled and it wasn't there. She stood flat-footed in the bedroom staring at the open drawers in despair. The two most important and incriminating things were gone. The NIS had come here with an American and had taken the computer and the key.

First Soon and now this. But how had they known to come here?

At that moment her cell phone vibrated against her hip, startling her so badly she jumped. She opened it with fumbling fingers. *"Ye?"* Yes? she said in Korean.

"Why have you called?" a man asked in English. It was Alexandar, she had no doubt of it.

"We have a problem," Kim said, switching to English.

"What problem?"

"Soon was arrested. They took him off the airplane before we could take off."

The phone was silent.

"They have my husband, and now we have to rescue

him," Kim blurted. "I'll return the money, all of it, but you have to help me."

"You made a mistake," Alexandar said. "You and your stupid husband."

Kim's fear instantly turned to anger. "Listen, you bastard, we've kept records. I know enough to see you hang."

Alexandar laughed. "Don't threaten me. If anyone hangs it will be you. But listen to me, I'll help because you and you husband have done very good work for me, and there'll be more of it. For now I want you to stay inside your apartment and I'll come to you tonight."

The relief was sweet but it lasted only a moment. "There's something else. I went to the store and when I got back a man and woman were here. The woman was NIS, it was a government plate on her car, but I think the man was CIA."

"How do you know this? Did they see you?"

"They didn't see me, but he had the look," Kim said. "How could they possibly know about me and Soon?"

"What foolish little secrets did they find in your apartment? Tell me that you and your husband have been careful."

"They got the laptop."

"That's okay, they'll fry the hard drive if they try to open it."

"And the key is missing," Kim said.

"What key?" Alexandar demanded.

"To our storage locker where we keep our equipment and other things."

Again the phone was silent for several seconds, but when Alexandar came back he didn't sound angry, or even overly concerned. "You'll have to clear out of your place right now, and you'll never be able to come back."

"Where should I go?"

"Check into the Westin Chosun downtown under a

work name, and I'll find you there tonight," Alexandar promised.

"Why that hotel?"

"No American would stay there, it's too old and inconvenient. We'll get this straightened out first, and then find a way to get Soon out. I have a few friends up there who'll arrange something for us. But in the meantime you'll have to do one thing for me. It's important."

"Anything," Kim promised.

"They'll be back, the NIS officer and the American, if that's who he is. I want you to hang out somewhere near your apartment, and get a photograph of the man. But you mustn't be seen. Can you do that?"

"Yes, but how do you know they'll be back."

"Once they find your locker, they'll be back," Alexandar said.

TWENTY-EIGHT

At the stoplight three blocks from the apartment, Ok-Lee used her cell phone to pull up an NIS program that accessed a broad range of civilian databases, such as phone books, Web sites, utilities, and business addresses. She entered the seven-digit number from the key and within seconds an address for a storage center came up.

"That's impressive," McGarvey said.

Ok-Lee smiled faintly for the first time since picking him up at Oasan. "The CIA doesn't have this capability?"

"Our privacy laws are a bit stricter than yours."

"Yeah, right," Ok-Lee said. The light changed and she headed down the street, turning left at the corner. "This place is across the river. What do you think we'll find?"

"Family heirlooms if I'm wrong," McGarvey said.

"And if you're right and the locker is booby-trapped?"

"We'll see when we get there," McGarvey said. "But the apartment wasn't rigged, because they're good South Koreans and they wouldn't want to hurt innocent bystanders. So, if the locker is in a crowded area where people are likely to be nearby, it should be safe."

"You're guessing," Ok-Lee said. She was getting angry again. "I think we should call a bomb unit out here."

"Is your shop clean?"

"Cleaner than yours," Ok-Lee shot back.

"Look, if anything gets out the whole deal could fall apart. Trust me."

"Sorry, Mr. Director, you're CIA and right now that's not such a good thing around here." She reached for her cell phone, but McGarvey put a hand over hers.

"You asked how I knew that her husband never made it out of Pyongyang," he said. "A North Korean intelligence officer came to my home in Florida with photographs, and asked that I help prove that Kim Jong Il didn't order the assassination."

Ok-Lee's mouth dropped open, but she recovered quickly. "He's blaming it on the CIA?"

"That's right, but no one else believes it," McGarvey said. "Especially the Chinese who're convinced that the guy's totally insane and could push the button at any moment."

Ok-Lee concentrated on her driving for a minute. "He would. Beijing would get it, but so would we, and probably Tokyo. He's made the threats before."

"Which is why I agreed to see what I could do," McGarvey said. "But I need your help, I can't do it alone."

Forty-five minutes later they came onto a narrow street bustling with vehicular and pedestrian traffic. Small shops selling mostly household items such as pots and pans, rugs, bath towels, and soji screens were busy.

Ok-Lee found a parking spot half up on the sidewalk across from the storage business, the front of which was covered by a steel accordion fence, closed now. The sign above the fence was in Korean. "This is it," she said.

"What's the sign say?" McGarvey asked.

"Roughly, it says Mr. Pim's Handy Storage, with a number to call if you want to rent a locker."

Inside the accordion gates a narrow corridor ran to the back of the building, a half-dozen padlocked doors on either side. The key fit the lock in the gate, and McGarvey swung it aside.

"We're taking a big chance here, goddamnit," Ok-Lee said. People streamed past on the sidewalk. "If this place blows, a lot of people will get hurt."

"I know," McGarvey said. It was the mantra of the terrorist who believed that there were no innocent people, but Kim and Soon were not terrorists, they were hired guns, and he understood the difference.

He headed down the corridor, Ok-Lee right behind him.

"This one," she said five doors down on the left. "*Ahop.*" Nine.

McGarvey ran his fingers around the door frame, searching for anything that might indicate the presence of fail-safes, something normally unnoticeable that would indicate someone had tampered with the door or had opened it. But whatever tradecraft the Huks used, fail-safeing their storage space wasn't included.

"Anyone taking any notice of us?" McGarvey asked as he bent close to examine the heavy-duty brass padlock.

"Not so far," Ok-Lee told him. "Is it clean?"

"Looks like it," McGarvey said. The lock opened with a well-oiled snap, and when he took it off the hasp and eased the door open, Ok-Lee stepped back a pace.

The storage room was about five feet wide and twice that deep, six aluminum suitcases along one wall and a couple of cardboard file boxes along the other. A bare lightbulb dangled from the ceiling.

"Make sure no one comes back here," McGarvey said and he went inside and switched on the light.

Starting with the cardboard boxes he found several thick files in Korean, along with what looked like surveillance photographs of men coming out of or going into what might have been office buildings, or in a couple of cases government buildings, getting in or out of automobiles—mostly Mercedeses—or sitting at sidewalk cafés.

One of the boxes contained an assortment of South Korean passports in a number of different names, all with photographs of Huk Soon or Huk Kim, in various light disguises, along with several envelopes that contained as much as $10,000 in cash in various currencies.

"What have you found?" Ok-Lee asked from the doorway.

"Passports, money, and files on what were probably their targets," McGarvey said. "We've got the right people."

He moved next to the aluminum suitcases, none of which was locked, which he found astounding, considering what they held. In addition to various styles of men's and women's clothing, along with wigs and makeup, three of the suitcases were filled with weapons; one of them with the Russian 7.62 mm Dragunov sniper rifle with a high-power scope; one with the very hard to find American-made .50 caliber Barrett rifle that had an effective kill range of one thousand meters. Shaped cutouts in the thick foam lining held a Steiner night vision scope, the ten power Leupold & Stevens day scope, two box magazines, a tripod, and a silencer. The third aluminum case held a variety of pistols, among them a small Beretta and a couple of German-made 9 mm SIG-Sauer P226s, along with ammunition, spare magazines, silencers, and cleaning and repair kits.

Ok-Lee stepped inside and looked over McGarvey's shoulder. "Shit, those are sniper rifles," she said. "I've got to get my people down here to go through this stuff."

"No," McGarvey said, looking up at here. "That's exactly what we're *not* going to do."

Ok-Lee tried to argue but McGarvey held her off.

"We know who she is, we know where she lives, and we know she's probably desperate to get her husband out of Pyongyang. She's probably already turned to the one person in the world she thinks can help her."

"Alexandar Turov."

"That's right," McGarvey agreed. "But this guy's a pro. If we take this place apart, or put it under surveillance he'll spot what's going on and back off."

"If we get the woman, and Pyongyang has her husband, we can convince the Chinese—"

"Convince them of what?" McGarvey demanded. "Beijing's not going to believe Kim Jong Il, and they're certainly not going to believe your people. At this point they're convinced that the North Koreans made the hit."

Ok-Lee nodded to the file boxes. "We have this stuff."

"Doesn't prove a thing."

"What then?" Ok-Lee asked. She was desperate now, and McGarvey almost felt sorry for her.

"We need the Russian, and if we back off the woman will lead us to him."

"If we lose her, we're faced with a nuclear war here."

"Don't I know it," McGarvey agreed.

TWENTY-NINE

Kim had stuffed what clean clothes she had left into the hanging bag by the front door, and replaced her makeup and a few other toiletries. The fear that had been eating at her gut since Pyongyang was still with her, but now it was tempered by Alexandar's promise to help rescue Soon.

She took the four potted plants off the stepladder by the living-room window and carried it out into the corridor where she stopped a moment to listen at the rail for any sign that the old woman was snooping around on the landing below. Everyone else in the building was still at work, and the stair hall was quiet.

Taking the stairs silently, in her bare feet, Kim raced to the top floor where she placed the ladder beneath the opening to the attic crawl space, climbed up, pushed the cover aside, and hauled herself through.

Careful not to slip off the joists, she scrambled to the far corner, where she retrieved a small plastic bundle, about the size of a loaf of bread, returned to the opening, and lowered herself to the top rung of the ladder where she pulled the cover back in place.

Her heart was hammering now. She had no idea how long it might take for them to find the storage locker and discover what it contained, but she didn't think she had much time left here.

She hurried downstairs to the apartment, where she placed the pots back on the ladder, and went into the kitchen where she cut open the bundle from the attic. Inside was their emergency kit in case something went drastically wrong. Passports in work names they'd never used, driver's licenses, credit cards, family photographs, even an overdue parking ticket for a car they didn't own, along with a few thousand dollars in cash, and two Walther PPK pistols, with silencers and one magazine of 7.65 ammunition each.

The kit was never meant to support them for much longer than a few days, but if they ever had to get out of the country in a hurry, and this was all they could take, it would be enough.

She stuffed the empty bag into the trash can then put everything except for her passport and papers into the hanging bag. Her things went into her purse, along with a camera cell phone, and she changed into a dress and decent shoes, her heart hammering even harder by the time she was finished.

For a few seconds she hesitated at the door, gazing at the apartment where for the past few years she and Soon had been deliriously in love and happy. They had planned on finding a small villa or house somewhere along the Mediterranean coast either in France or perhaps northern Italy once they had enough money in their Swiss account. Soon had figured ten million euros would do for a modest retirement. With the money from their latest hit they were more than a third of the way there.

But all of that was finished, or at least it was on hold until they could get Soon out of Pyongyang, and even with Alexandar's help she didn't know how it was possible.

Downstairs the old landlady came out of her apartment. "Are you running away?"

"Soon wants me to come back to Nagasaki," Kim said, trying to keep her voice neutral.

"Government people come one minute and next minute Mrs. clears out. Something is plenty fishy here."

"Nothing's fishy," Kim said. She patted the old woman's arm. "I'll be gone for just a few days. Be a dear and water my plants, would you?"

The landlady's eyes narrowed. "Maybe Seoul is not such a good place to be right now. But maybe Nagasaki isn't so good either." She nodded toward the door. "What do I tell them if they come back?"

"The truth," Kim said. "That I've gone to Nagasaki to be with my husband."

"Come back if you can. You and Mr. are good people."

Kim managed a smile, and went out and walked to the end of the block where she hailed a taxi.

"The Westin Chosun," she told the driver.

THIRTY

McGarvey and Ok-Lee sat in the car across from the storage building, the engine idling. No one on the bustling street had paid them much attention, though McGarvey figured he had to stand out as a foreigner, so somebody was watching.

"Let's go," he said.

"If she's on the run she'll have to come back here for her papers and money and a weapon," Ok-Lee said. "This is the one place in Seoul where she's bound to show up sooner or later."

"Unless Turov gets here first and kills her," McGarvey replied. The woman was a loose cannon that the Russian couldn't afford to ignore. If she had made contact with him, which he was sure she had, he would have to show up here.

"All the more reason to put a watch on the place," Ok-Lee argued. "We've got some pretty good people who know how to blend in."

"One person, and they're not to make a move without

contacting you first. She won't do us any good if she gets in a shoot-out. With her husband under arrest in Pyongyang she's desperate enough to try something like that rather then let herself be taken."

"Done," Ok-Lee said. She pulled away from the curb and around the corner at the end of the block she made a call on her cell phone and talked in rapid-fire Korean for several minutes.

McGarvey figured that no matter how hard the president was trying to convince Beijing that hitting North Korea was not the answer, the situation here was spiraling out of control. He figured they only had a few days, maybe one week at the most, before Chinese missiles launched from mobile platforms near the border rained down on Pyongyang. Kim Jong Il would only have minutes to respond, which meant that he would be preparing his missiles right now, which in turn would convince the Chinese that their only option was to make a first strike.

But the part that puzzled him the most was who had hired Turov to find shooters willing to get inside North Korea and make the hit. Again and again he came back to the same question: Who had the most to gain by destabilizing the relationship between North Korea and China? And each time he came back to the same troubling answer: The U.S. had the most to gain.

"Do you want to go back to the hotel now?" Ok-Lee asked.

McGarvey looked up out of his thoughts. "How soon will somebody be in place down here?"

"Within the hour."

"Good," McGarvey said. "What did you tell them?"

Ok-Lee was troubled. "I lied, Mr. Director," she said. "And I didn't like it very much, because I've put my career on the line for you, possibly even my freedom."

"In that case you'd better start calling me Mac. Mr. Director is too formal."

Ok-Lee turned away to concentrate on her driving. She shook her head and said something half under her breath in Korean. "My name is Lin," she said. "Where do you want to go?"

"Back to the woman's apartment," McGarvey said. "I want to take another look and have a word with the landlady."

"I don't think she'll tell us much."

"I'll ask the questions this time, and you can translate."

The old woman came out of her apartment the moment McGarvey and Ok-Lee walked through the front door. She was still dressed in old faded baggy gray slacks and a flowered top mostly covered by a worn cotton jacket. She held a broom in both hands as if she was ready to defend herself and she looked angry.

She said something in Korean.

"She wants to know why we've come back to bother an innocent old woman," Ok-Lee translated for McGarvey.

"Because we know that she lied the first time, and liars go to prison," McGarvey said harshly.

Ok-Lee wasn't happy. "She's just an old woman protecting her tenants."

"Tell her."

Ok-Lee translated, and the landlady backed up a half step.

McGarvey took out his pistol and transferred it to his jacket pocket. "The truth now, where are the Huks?"

The old woman's eyes widened in fear, and she mumbled something.

"They're both gone. To Nagaski," Ok-Lee said.

"But the wife came back," McGarvey pressed. "Her suitcase is upstairs on the floor."

"Yes, but she left again, to go back to Nagasaki. She asked me to take care of her plants for just a few days."

"When did she leave?" McGarvey demanded. "No lies now," he said menacingly.

Ok-Lee translated, and the woman replied. "Maybe less than two hours ago. She came in just after you left, and went out fifteen minutes later."

"Shit," McGarvey swore. He turned and headed up the stairs in a dead run.

"She knew someone was coming," Ok-Lee said right behind him. "She was watching the apartment."

"Call your surveillance people and tell them to get someone over to the storage locker right now."

At the top McGarvey slammed his shoulder into the apartment door, popping the lock and half tearing the wooden frame away. The hanging bag was gone, the dirty clothes still lying in a heap where Ok-Lee had dumped them.

He stopped for just a moment to see if anything else seemed out of the ordinary, something that was different from a couple of hours ago.

A small wooden stepladder that held the potted plants the old lady was supposed to water while Huk Kim was away caught his attention. Something wasn't quite right. He walked across the room and stared at it, but nothing caught his eye.

In the bedroom the chest of drawers was still open, but now most of the clothes were gone, and in the bathroom the makeup and other things that had been laid out next to the sink were also missing.

The woman had waited outside until he and Ok-Lee were gone, then had come up here, repacked her bag, and took off. But not to Nagasaki. Somewhere else.

McGarvey left the bedroom and went into the kitchen as Ok-Lee was finishing her telephone call.

"Someone will be in place within fifteen minutes," she said. "Have you found anything?"

"She packed in a hurry," McGarvey said.

Nothing seemed out of place in the tiny kitchen, and McGarvey was about to turn away when he spotted a bundle of plastic with some duct tape and something else stuck to it stuffed in the trash can between the tiny fridge and the two-burner gas cooktop. He walked over and pulled it out. The package smelled faintly of gun oil, and a small clump of what looked like spun fiberglass.

Back in the living room he stared at the stepladder for just a moment, until he had it. "Go upstairs, Lin, and see if there's a way to get into the attic. A covered opening in the ceiling. Something like that."

Ok-Lee turned and went out leaving McGarvey to stare at the stepladder. She was back in under a minute.

"It's there just down the hall from the head of the stairs," she said.

McGarvey nodded to the stepladder. "She took the pots off the ladder, took it up the stairs and got into the attic. When she brought it back she didn't put the pots in exactly the same places. You can see it in the dust rings." He held up the plastic package. "This is what she was after up there. Her escape kit."

Ok-Lee understood immediately. "She's armed now."

McGarvey nodded. He'd always maintained the same sort of easily accessible escape kit for the day he had to go on the run. "Not only that, she has a new set of IDs and money."

"Shit," Ok-Lee said.

"Let's go back to the hotel and see if a friend of mine can find out what's on the woman's laptop," McGarvey told her.

THIRTY-ONE

As soon as Kim had checked into the Westin and brought her bag up to her eighth-floor room, she went downstairs, crossed the lobby, and one of the doormen hailed her a cab. She'd directed the driver to take her to a shopping arcade a block and a half from her apartment, and walked the rest of the way where she got a sidewalk table at the kimchi shop.

The same Mercedes C-class with government plates was parked at the curb, and her heart skipped a beat as the same man and woman came out the front door. She'd almost missed them.

The waiter came out and she ordered tea. He left as the American came around to the passenger side of the car, giving Kim just seconds to take out her cell phone and get off a few shots, one of them a three-quarters profile.

She hastily lowered the phone to her lap and turned away as the man looked directly at her. She held her breath, hoping that they had no recent photographs of her, and girded herself for the necessity of killing them both if she had to.

Nothing was going to stop her from trying to rescue Soon, not the NIS and certainly not some suit from the CIA.

The waiter came back with her tea and she reached for the pistol in her purse as she glanced across the street, but the American had gotten into the car and was closing the door.

Kim took some money out instead and paid for her tea. The waiter politely thanked her and went back inside as the government car pulled away and turned the corner at the end of the block.

She closed her eyes for several long seconds, the tightness in her gut slowly easing.

Obviously the NIS knew enough about her and Soon to come here, though they'd had no contact with anyone at the agency since they'd resigned their commissions several years ago. More troubling than that was the presence of the American. The NIS might be routinely checking all of its retired snipers, which was something they would not ask for help with from the CIA. So what was the man doing here?

She called Alexandar's contact number, and when the connection was made downloaded the four photographs she'd managed to take of the American.

"I've checked into the Westin Chosun, like you asked, and I'm heading back over there now until you show up." She looked across the street as her landlady opened the front door and began to sweep the sidewalk as if she wanted to get rid of any trace the woman and the American might have left behind.

"Please hurry," Kim said. "There's no telling what the bastards are doing to Soon. We have it get him out of there right now."

She waited several long seconds in the hope that Alexandar would pick up, but the connection remained silent and she finally closed the phone and put it in her purse.

It was turning out to be a lovely fall afternoon, but Kim felt a chill thinking about her husband, and she shivered.

THIRTY—TWO

McGarvey ordered a couple of beers from room service then used his sat phone to reach Rencke at Langley. It was 3:00 A.M. in Washington but his friend answered on the first ring.

"Oh wow, what've you got, Mac?"

"A laptop from the Huks' apartment, and it's probably bugged," McGarvey said.

"If they're the right ones."

"She took a runner right after we showed up the first time. Told her landlady that she was going back to Nagasaki to be with her husband."

"Do you think she's going to somehow get back to Pyongyang and try to rescue her husband?" Otto asked. He was excited.

"That's what she probably wants to do, and I think she's probably called Turov to ask for his help."

The connection was silent for a moment and McGarvey could see Rencke in the chaos of his office, staring up at the monitors hanging from the ceiling.

"He'll kill her," Rencke said.

"I think he probably meant to kill them both when they got back from Pyongyang," McGarvey said. "Mission accomplished, whatever the hell the mission was, and now it's time to eliminate the loose ends."

"Have you opened the laptop's lid?" Rencke asked.

"No, should I?"

"Definitely not. I gave you a serial port cable with your sat phone. Do you still have it?"

"Right here," McGarvey said. He'd taken it out of a pocket in his hanging bag.

"Connect the laptop to your phone and I'll take it from there."

"Don't I have to turn the laptop on first?" McGarvey asked.

"I'll do that from here."

"How?"

Rencke chuckled. "Kemo sabe, do I tell you how to shoot a gun?"

McGarvey set the laptop computer on the desk and plugged it into the sat phone.

"Got it," Rencke said. "Give me an hour."

"One more thing," McGarvey said. "Can you find out if the North Koreans are getting their missiles ready to launch?"

"Dick asked me that this afternoon, and I'm on it," Rencke said.

"It'll be too late by then. How about the Chinese?"

"They went to DEFCON three about two hours ago," Rencke said.

"We're running out of time."

"Yeah," Rencke said. A green light on the front of the laptop came on. "One hour, Mac."

THIRTY-THREE

Driving across the river to NIS headquarters in the Naegok-dong district after dropping McGarvey off at the Westin Chosun, Ok-Lee had time to examine where her loyalties lay most strongly.

She was a field officer in her country's intelligence service and she held a strong belief and pride in the republic.

But she was also a realist, as many intelligence officers became before they turned into cynics. Reuniting the nation, North and South, which was a dream of nearly every man and woman on the peninsula, would never happen so long as Kim Jong Il was alive. But she also realized that confronting the maniac head on was nearly the same as suicide.

It was what they were faced with now, and the trouble was that no one on the fifth floor had any real idea of what to do next. Everyone seemed to be waiting for the Americans to talk some sense into Beijing, because no one believed that Kim Jong Il could be reasoned with, or trusted to keep his word if he did promise something.

And then there was Kirk McGarvey, arguably one of the most effective intelligence officers since World War II, come here to Seoul with a wild story of Russian intermediaries and South Korean assassins.

The thing was that in Ok-Lee's estimation he was the only man on the planet who seemed to have any real idea what to do and how to go about it. The apparent leak back at Langley bothered her deeply, but the NIS wasn't free of its spies, and anyway the instant he had introduced himself at Oasan she had begun to feel that it would be okay to turn over the entire problem to him. He could handle anything, you could see it in his eyes, in the way he held himself, and in the tone of his voice as much as what he said.

McGarvey was a man who exuded competence and self-confidence and at first she had resented his effect on her, though if half the stories about him were true he was a man among men, something rare.

At thirty-four, Ok-Lee's love life was all but nonexistent. The few men she dated were either misogynists, as many Asians were, or they were simply stupid, conceited, or worse, weak.

Her sister said that Ok-Lee would never get married and have children because she was too hard. "If some man actually tries to get close to you the first thing you try to do is have a mental arm wrestling contest with him. Who wants that?"

She couldn't respect a man who would lose to her, but if it ever came to it she had a feeling that McGarvey wouldn't lose.

NIS headquarters was housed in a sweepingly modern building somewhat taken after the CIA's Old Headquarters Building. She was passed through security at the outer gate, then drove up to her parking spot, and took the elevator to her cubicle on the third floor in National Security Law Operations.

Bak in-Suk, chief of the Foreign Section, came out of his office, a skeptical look on his small, round face. He had married last year, but before that he and Ok-Lee had dated a few times, and he was one of the few men she'd ever found even slightly interesting. He was bright, and his major fault was that he knew it, but they were still friends.

"Did he bring anything we can use?"

Ok-Lee dropped her purse on her desk, and shook her head. "He's chasing a dead end, or at least I think he is."

"They must be damned scared to send a guy of his background out here," Bak said. "Is that why you sent a surveillance team to watch some storage locker?"

"I did it to humor him, there's nothing there."

"It's a waste of resources, with all the shit coming down around our heads."

"You asked me to babysit the man, and that's what I'm doing," Ok-Lee said. "Look, does anyone upstairs have any idea what's going on?"

Operations was running full tilt because of the crisis and yet the only sounds were a few muffled telephone conversations and the plastic clatter of dozens of computer keyboards. Bak looked down the corridor between the cubicles to see if anyone who could overhear them was coming.

"Doesn't matter who took the bastard down, Beijing is blaming it on Dear Leader, and nobody knows what the fuck to do," Bak said, keeping his voice low. "They're hoping that sooner or later the crazy son of a bitch will come to his senses and apologize. The Chinese will make some more threats for a few weeks, but everything will start to calm down and this time next year it'll be business as usual."

"Is that what you think?"

Bak shrugged his narrow shoulders.

"Anybody heading for the hills yet?"

"We've had a couple of sick calls, not many," Bak said, and he smiled. "Thanks for sticking with me on this one. You got a crappy assignment, but at least it looks like we're doing something constructive."

Ok-Lee felt rotten about lying to him, but if the agency's director and his staff had no idea what was going on, or what to do about the situation, she had to at least give McGarvey a fighting chance. "He wants some phone records on a couple people who used to work for us."

"Anyone important?"

"No."

"Well, get him his phone records, and whatever else he wants," Bak said. "Who knows, maybe you're wrong and the CIA does have something we can use."

He turned and went back to his office leaving Ok-Lee to sit down at her desk and power up her computer.

Coming up with the Huks' service records was easy, but beyond that she ran into an almost total blank, except for the address of their apartment. They had apparently met shortly after graduation from Sniper School and according to a Military Investigation Unit report they'd begun sleeping together almost immediately, which was strictly forbidden by Sniper Service regulations.

They'd been reprimanded twice, the first time verbally by their commanding officer, and the second in the form of a letter placed in their files, warning them to either quit the affair or face disciplinary action.

Two days after the written warning, they'd both resigned their commissions and disappeared into civilian life.

The record stopped there. Beyond that it was as if they had dropped off the planet. No records existed for them in the Driver's License Bureau, they'd not applied for passports or federal identification cards, they apparently had no jobs because they never filed income tax forms, nor had they ever been injured, because their names did not show up on the registries of any hospital in the country, and neither had they violated any law, not even something so minor as a parking ticket because their names were not in any police or court databases she searched.

If either of them had a telephone, land line or cell, no records existed so it was impossible to learn if they'd ever made calls to Tokyo.

Ok-Lee printed out their service records, and sat back for a minute or so staring at their photographs. They were a handsome couple, the woman, Huk Kim, much smaller than her husband Soon. But the biggest difference between them, apparent even in the military ID photographs, was the look in their eyes. Soon was a hard charger, while Kim seemed to be much less driven. His was the typically determined attitude of a Sniper Service officer, but hers was much softer, maybe even a little uncertain of what she had gotten herself into.

An act on the woman's part, Ok-Lee wondered? According to McGarvey they had been the shooters in Pyongyang, and the papers, money, and weapons in the storage locker seemed to confirm it. Now the husband was either dead or in a military prison in the North, and the woman was on the run.

Ok-Lee telephoned McGarvey at the hotel. "I hope you've had better luck with the laptop than I've had here."

"I've got somebody working on it," McGarvey said. "Did you come up with anything?"

"They were officers in the Sniper Service, and they were having an affair, but rather than give that up they resigned their commissions. Beyond that, except for the address of the apartment where they slept together, I'm drawing a blank. No voter records, no driver's license, no phone records, nothing."

"I should have something later this afternoon," McGarvey said. "Why don't you keep digging, and then come over here around eight, I'll buy you dinner."

Ok-Lee smiled. "How do you know I don't have a husband and a dozen kids waiting at home for me?"

"No ring," McGarvey said simply.

"Eight," Ok-Lee said, but she thought it was something more than a bare ring finger.

THIRTY—FOUR

Kim was standing at the window of her fifth-floor hotel room, looking down at the building rush-hour traffic when her cell phone lying on the nightstand chimed. She caught it on the second ring.

"*Ye.*" Yes, she said.

"Where were those photographs taken?" a man demanded in English. It was Alexandar; she recognized his voice, but he sounded angry.

"In front of the apartment," she said. "I think he's an American, probably CIA."

"You're damned right he is, or was. Name is Kirk McGarvey, and he was a shooter for the Agency until they brought him back to the Building and made him the director. He's supposed to be retired now, so only something very big would bring him here to your apartment."

"I didn't know," Kim said.

"What the hell did you and your husband do to attract his attention?"

"Just the job."

"I mean where did you two fuck up? How did your names get into a CIA database?" Alexandar shouted.

Kim sat down on the bed, her heart pounding. Soon had never seemed so far away as he did now. She desperately needed him here with her. "I don't know what you're talking about," she said. "We went there, did the job you hired us to do, and Soon and another man were arrested and taken off the plane. Obviously they've found out who Soon is, and under drugs he might have told them about me and where we live, but they wouldn't have shared that information with the CIA. If anything they might have turned him over to the Chinese."

"He hasn't left Pyongyang."

"Soon is still alive?" Kim asked excitedly. It was if a terribly heavy burden had been pulled away. "You know this for a fact?"

"He's alive," Alexandar said. "Did you recognize the woman?"

It was hard to keep on track now that she knew Soon hadn't been executed. "NIS, probably. She was driving a car with government plates."

"She's Ok-Lee Lin, a minor field officer in the Security Law Operations Center. She was probably sent to show McGarvey around. What else does the NIS know about you?"

"They can't know anything about us. Soon made sure of it after we left the service."

The circuit was silent for several seconds, but then Alexandar was back. "It still doesn't explain why he came to Seoul."

Kim looked over toward the door. Soon was alive and she was going to make sure he got out. "Will you help me?"

"Yes, of course I'm going to help you," Alexandar told her, the anger suddenly gone from his voice. "But first we have a bigger problem to take care of and you're going to help me deal with it."

"What problem?"

"Kirk McGarvey," Alexandar said. "We're going to kill him, you and I."

Kim's heart leapt to her throat. "I can't," she sputtered. "I wouldn't know how to begin to find him."

"No problem," Alexandar said. "He's right there at your hotel in a suite on the top floor."

Kim almost dropped the phone. Her first instinct was to run, right now. Grab her things and get out, but Alexandar's insistent voice was in her ear.

"Unless we kill McGarvey I won't be able to help you get your husband out. Do you understand?"

"I can't do this thing," Kim said, trying to keep herself together. She was on the verge of tears again. "Not alone. Not without Soon."

"I'll help you."

"How? Not from Tokyo."

"I'm here in the city, very close to you," Alexandar said, his voice soft now, reassuring. "And what you have to do will be dangerous, but you won't be on your own, I promise you."

Kim didn't know what to say. She was consumed by visions of her husband. She was lying next to him in their bed in the apartment, where they'd been so happy between assignments.

"Do you trust me?" Alexandar asked.

It was never supposed to be this way. Soon had promised her in the beginning that they would get out as quickly as possible.

"Do you believe that I won't let you down?"

She nodded. *"Ye,"* she said. *"Ye."*

"Very good," Alexandar said soothingly. "Now this is exactly what will happen."

THIRTY-FIVE

It was seven in the evening when Otto's call came from Langley, and McGarvey sat up and put his feet over the edge of the bed. He'd managed only a couple hours of badly needed sleep, but he was supposed to meet Ok-Lee downstairs at the hotel's O'Kim's bar, so it was time to get up and take a shower anyway.

Rencke was excited, and his enthusiasm was like a shot of adrenaline. "We hit the jackpot, kemo sabe."

"You got into the computer?" McGarvey asked.

"Of course I did, the encryption program was just a couple of steps above Stone Age. They're the shooters, all right, and they've done five hits in the last twenty-four months, all for a Russian who they only know as Alexandar. Everything's there, times, dates, places, methods, and payments to their account in Switzerland."

"General Ho is on the list?"

"Yup, and they got paid a mil and a half, U.S. Seven-fifty before the hit, and seven-fifty within a couple of hours after the job was done," Rencke said. "They flew up to Pyongyang via Beijing as part of a tour group. The last night they snuck out of the hotel, killed two cops on patrol, stole their uniforms and AKs, sealed everything up in plastic garbage bags, swam across the river, hiked over to the Chinese Embassy, and assassinated the general, his driver, and a pair of Chinese guards at the gate. They made certain that they were spotted by the embassy's security cameras—to make sure the Chinese knew that it was a pair of North Korean cops who did the kill—then went back and swam across the river."

They'd found the plastic bag that held the woman's dirty clothes. It had bothered Ok-Lee because of its un-Koreaness.

"Pretty slick, actually," Rencke was saying.

"They had to be either arrogant or stupid to keep something like that in a laptop that could go missing," McGarvey said.

"Maybe they thought of it as insurance," Rencke suggested. "If they went down so would Alexandar."

"Did they know who the Russian really was and where he lived?"

"Just that he was somewhere in Tokyo and they guessed he was ex-KGB. But beyond that all they had was an e-mail address, which I checked. It's a dead end."

"They probably had a phone number in case of an emergency and they needed a lifeline," McGarvey said.

"Wasn't in the machine."

McGarvey got up and walked over to the window and looked down at the street still clogged with traffic. It was getting dark and he was beginning to feel that he was missing something important, that they were all missing something important—even the shooters were.

"What else did you find? You said they'd made five hits in the last two years."

"Yeah. Three months ago South Korea's deputy ambassador to China—he was shot to death in Paris—and six months ago the Japanese senator gunned down in Tokyo. They were soft on North Korea, wanted to have an appeasement with Kim Jong Il to avoid a war."

"Who had the most to gain?' McGarvey asked again. It was the part that bothered him most.

"Us," Rencke said. "But it gets even more complicated than that, Mac. Remember Senator Thomas Moore, who got himself shot to death in Tel Aviv last year?"

"It was an accident, stray bullet from one of the refugee camps in Gaza. He was at the wrong place at the wrong time."

"That's what Mossad figured, but according to the laptop, Kim was the spotter and her husband Soon fired the shot."

"The guy was from South Dakota, where's the connection between him and the others?" McGarvey asked.

"I couldn't find anything," Rencke admitted. "So I went to the fifth assassination to see if there was maybe a second pattern."

"And?"

"A little more than two years ago, a German deputy minister of nuclear affairs was in New York giving testimony to the U.N. on his country's sales of nuclear power stations to Iran. The night before he was scheduled to speak, he left his hotel late, and the next morning his body showed up in Chinatown. He'd been shot to death."

"Koestler, or something like that," McGarvey said. He vaguely remembered the incident, because for a couple of months the German press had a field day taking America's "lawless gun club culture" to task.

"Willi Koestler," Rencke said. "And he also threw me for a loop at first, until I finally got it. Moore was positioning himself to be the new architect of a Middle East peace between Israel, Iran, Syria, and Iraq, and Koestler wanted to trade nuclear energy across the region for stability to guarantee the steady flow of oil."

McGarvey turned away from the window. He was still missing something, this just wasn't adding up. "I'm not sure that I follow you, Otto."

"I didn't see it at first either. You gotta step back so you can see the whole thing. With China and North Korea at odds, who has more to gain than us?"

"No one," McGarvey said.

"Correcto mundo, ergo no connection among all five assassinations," Rencke said. "But flip it over, and ask who has the most to lose if China tries to take out North Korea and Kim Jong Il actually launches his six nukes?"

Now McGarvey saw what Rencke was driving at, but it made even less sense. "I don't know if we would have the most to lose, but we'd probably be sucked into the mess, especially if Beijing took the opportunity to hit Taipei."

"Not only that, but if one of the missiles got through and a nuclear weapon was detonated somewhere over downtown Beijing, you could kiss off our trade deals with China until the country stabilized. We'd be back to paying the actual value for everything from T-shirts and ironing boards to cell phones and dog food. Our market economy would get slammed big time."

"With Moore assassinated, we took a step backward from any sort of peace accord in the Middle East."

"Means we keep funding the arms race," Rencke said.

"Plus it continues to be a breeding ground for Islamic fundamentalists," McGarvey said. "And if Koestler would have succeeded, or at least made a dent in the problem, and solved some of the energy needs over there, it would help reduce the poverty levels and take away at least one of the reasons for al-Quaeda to continue the fight. Or at least it would put a crimp on their funding."

"Bingo," Rencke said. "It's not us who have the most to gain, it's us who have the most to lose."

So far as McGarvey could see, they were still at the starting gate. "The Huks worked for Turov. Who does the Russian work for?"

"Whoever it is," Rencke said. "They don't like us very much."

"Keep digging," McGarvey said.

"Will do."

THIRTY-SIX

Kim paced up and down in her room as the hour approached eight when Alexandar had told her to go upstairs, knock on McGarvey's door, and invite herself in for a drink. "He'll arrest me on the spot," she'd responded. "How will that help Soon?"

"But you've got it wrong, my dear. He's not here to arrest you, though he'll probably turn you over to the NIS when he's finished. He came here for information."

"On what?"

"On me, of course," Alexandar had said. "But the thing is, if you show up in the same provocative dress you wore for the hit in Paris, he'll have to let you in. From what I've read he's always been something of a ladies' man. Even left his wife some years ago, and took up with a Swiss cop in Lausanne."

"So he lets me in, then what?" Kim had asked, even though she'd known what would happen next.

"Why, you kill him, of course."

"Not much place to hide a pistol in that outfit."

"Tape it to your thigh," Alexandar had told her. "When the time is right, pull it out and shoot him. He'll check your purse, but I think that he's too much of a gentleman to pat you down."

"What about afterwards?"

"You and I will arrange for Soon's release."

"Where will I meet you?" Kim had asked.

Alexandar had laughed. "Oh, I won't be far. And when you've finished this little job, I'll make contact."

His call had come nearly two hours ago during which time she had given serious thought to what she would have to do in order to have a chance at saving her husband's life, and she had come to the conclusion that assassinating the former director of the CIA wouldn't help. In fact his death would make things worse. The NIS knew about her and Soon, it's why they had shown up at the apartment. With McGarvey shot to death in his hotel room, South Korea's normally tight security would intensify tenfold. Cops with her photograph would be posted on practically every street corner. If she moved she would be taken in, and Soon would never get out of Pyongyang alive.

But Alexandar was still the key. If she could talk to him face-to-face she would make him understand that once she had Soon back the two of them would take Kirk McGarvey as their next assignment for free.

Instead of the sexy cocktail dress she'd worn for the hit in Paris, she put on a pair of jeans, a nice white blouse, and Nikes. She debated going out unarmed, but in the end she stuffed the Walther in her shoulder bag. No matter what happened tonight she was not going to be taken without a fight.

And, she thought at the door, Soon had never trusted Alexandar. The Russian was nothing more than a means to their retirement. He was a man with his own agenda, Soon had argued, and that was staying alive.

She would force a meeting with Alexandar, by going to a highly public place, and he would come to her where she could talk to him in relative safety.

THIRTY-SEVEN

O'Kim's, the hotel's cocktail lounge, was busy mostly with Western businessmen who either didn't care about the impending trouble between North Korea and China or like many others before them were intrigued by hanging out in a possible war zone. It was tempting fate, and it got the adrenaline pumping in a certain type.

McGarvey managed to find a pair of seats near the end of the bar and had just ordered a Rémy neat in a snifter, when Ok-Lee showed up, in a short skirt, tank top, and sandals. She carried a small purse and a manila envelope, and spotting McGarvey at the bar she worked her way across to him.

"A punctual man, I like that," she said, swinging up onto the bar stool.

"A pretty woman, I like that," McGarvey said.

She smiled. "That's quite a sexist remark for a married man with a grown daughter who helps run the Farm, but thanks anyway."

McGarvey laughed. "Happily married," he said. "If you're going to do your homework you might as well do it right." He smiled. "I thought we'd have a drink first before dinner."

"Sounds good," she said.

The bartender came over and she ordered a glass of champagne, then handed McGarvey the envelope. "This is an English translation of our file on the Huks including their ID photographs. A little thin. They weren't in the service long, and when they got out they all but disappeared. And there's nothing on them in any of the databases I searched. Not switching apartments was their only real mistake."

McGarvey glanced at the photos and quickly scanned the Huks' service record as the bartender came with their drinks. "Nothing much here except for the reprimands."

"Take a look at their training evals."

McGarvey flipped to the personnel records that listed the results of their training. Both had gotten the highest grades for not only their marksmanship, but for their stealth skills. They were good snipers, the best according to their supervisor. Their only problem was a tendency to ignore orders.

He looked up. "They know what they're doing," he said. "Have you ever had anyone else in the service go freelance?"

Ok-Lee shook her head. "Not that I know of, but that doesn't mean it's never happened. We just don't make a big deal out of it, leastways not in public."

McGarvey took a drink. "Now we wait," he said.

"For what?" Ok-Lee asked. "We don't have a lot of time here."

"For Turov to come here and for the woman to make a mistake."

"What are you talking about?"

"She knows that we're looking for her, and almost certainly why, otherwise she wouldn't have grabbed her emergency kit and taken off. I think she's probably contacted Turov about the situation with Soon, and the fact that somebody's on her trail, and he's going to come here to kill her."

"That would have to mean he's told her where to go to ground," Ok-Lee said. "Which leaves us nothing."

"Not quite," McGarvey said. "He has to know that I'm here."

Ok-Lee was startled. "How? Unless there's a leak in my section."

"He knows because he's been told that someone wants

to hire him to arrange a hit on President Haynes, and they want me as the shooter."

Ok-Lee was amazed. "He'll never believe something like that in a million years."

"You're right, but I'm betting that he'll be intrigued enough to find out what's really going on, and he'll come to me," McGarvey said.

"Ego."

McGarvey smiled. "Yup. And who knows, maybe he'll try to kill two birds with one stone."

Ok-Lee was troubled. She sipped her wine and stared pensively at her reflection in the mirror behind the bar. "I think it's too big an assumption to think he'd risk everything to come here," she said.

"What's the NIS doing?" McGarvey prompted after a moment.

She turned to him. "Waiting for your government to bail us out," she said bitterly. "In the meantime we know Huk Kim was involved and if I gave the word she would be in custody before morning."

"She's very good at what she does" McGarvey reminded her. "You could wind up with some dead cops, and a dead assassin who wouldn't be of any help."

"Goddamnit, you're playing it too loose and easy," Ok-Lee shot back. "This is my country's life we're discussing."

"Believe me, if I didn't think I could help I wouldn't have come all this way to put my head on the chopping block with yours and Tokyo's and Taipei's." McGarvey leaned closer. "Huk Kim and her husband were the shooters, but Turov was the expediter. He's the only one who can lead us back to the source. Who ordered the assassination and why. Without that we'll never be able to convince Beijing it wasn't Kim Jong Il."

"And without that China *will* go to war."

McGarvey nodded. "I think whomever Turov is working for wants just that very thing to happen."

Ok-Lee sat forward. "But why, for God's sake? What maniac would want something like that? Think of the millions of innocent people who would be incinerated in even a limited nuclear exchange. Think of the millions who would die from their burns and infections in the next few weeks, and more in the coming months and years of leukemia and every other radiation-caused cancer." She looked away, momentarily overcome by what she was saying. "Why?"

"I don't know. But it's one of the reasons I'm going to have a chat with Turov."

"Asap," Ok-Lee said when she suddenly turned around. "My God, it's her!"

McGarvey turned in time to see a slightly built Korean woman darting past the barroom door and disappearing into the lobby.

"Police! Stop that woman," Ok-Lee shouted, jumping off the bar stool. She pulled a pistol out of her purse and took off in a dead run.

Everyone looked up at the commotion but no one made a move to help, or even get out of the way. The situation was happening too fast.

McGarvey was right behind her. "Be careful," he cautioned her. "He's probably here."

Ok-Lee pulled up at the doorway. She held the pistol in both hands, the muzzle pointed up. "A setup?" she demanded.

"I think so," McGarvey said. "Go right, I'll go left."

THIRTY—EIGHT

Kim raced across the lobby, turning several heads, but she didn't have time for stealth. The woman at the bar, who had shouted at her, was the same woman from the apartment earlier today, and the man seated with her was the Amercian.

It was just rotten luck that she had run into them like this, but at least she was sure that they had no idea she was staying here. If they had, they wouldn't have sat down at the bar for a drink. They would have found her room and arrested her.

Halfway to the outside doors, it suddenly came to her that she had been set up. Alexandar had known that one way or another they would come face-to-face, even if she didn't go through with the assassination, at which time he would kill them both.

He'd never meant to help get Soon out of Pyongyang. In fact it was likely that he had planned on killing both of them if they'd made it back.

She looked over her shoulder just before she reached the doors, in time to see McGarvey and the woman emerging from the barroom and splitting up.

A bellman pushing a cart loaded with baggage was just coming from the driveway and she had to sidestep to the left to miss him, and she ran headlong into a tall, stocky man with thick white hair and a flowing mustache wearing old-fashioned steel-framed glasses.

She had only a split second to look up into his eyes, which were startlingly blue but lifeless.

He grabbed her arm.

"Hold that woman!" Ok-Lee shouted. "Police!"

The old man looked up, startled, and he stepped back, releasing his hold on Kim's arm.

It was the opening she needed. No way in hell was she going to be taken here. Not now, not like this, not until she had a chance to figure out how to rescue Soon. She darted outside, the night warm and humid and noisy with car horns and a distant siren, and hurried down the driveway, dodging cars and a couple of taxis.

Traffic on the main avenue was extremely heavy and she didn't have time to wait for the light, so she turned left and almost immediately lost herself in the crowds of pedestrians clogging the broad sidewalk. No one seemed to be in a hurry, and she slowed down with the flow so she wouldn't stand out. She resisted the urge to turn and look over her shoulder.

Alexandar had told her on the phone that he was close, and she thought that it was a real possibility that he'd seen her leave the hotel with McGarvey and the NIS officer on her tail. It meant that not only was she being chased by the American and the woman, but Alexandar could be right behind her, sighting his pistol on the back of her head.

She'd never felt so alone and vulnerable in her life. If Soon were here he would know what to do, how to get away. He'd certainly tell her not to look back, or try to run, either move would make her stand out in the crowd. Blend in, he would say.

She came to the intersection and as luck would have it the walk light was on and she crossed to the other side of the street with the surging crowd.

Soon would also tell her not to rely on anyone else. They'd both worked out the tradecraft that they would need to go to ground if something ever happened. Her only mistake this afternoon and evening was relying on Alexandar to help. Now he too was coming after her.

She headed back in the direction of the hotel, ducking into the broad entry of a busy electronics store that sold everything from cell phones and iPods to televisions and computers.

She positioned herself so that she could see the hotel entrance up the block.

Know your opposition, Soon would say. Find out who they are and how they operate.

Then make your plan.

THIRTY-NINE

At the end of the hotel driveway Ok-Lee pulled up short, McGarvey right beside her. A number of people had come out of the lobby to see what the commotion was all about, but no one made a move to get close to a woman brandishing a pistol.

"We'll never find her by ourselves in this crowd," Ok-Lee said bitterly. "I'm calling for backup before this gets out of hand."

McGarvey was scanning the pedestrians on this side of the street as well as the other. But it was like looking for a needle in a stack of needles. And he forced himself not to look back.

"She knows that we're after her," he said. "And now she'll go to ground. The more cops you put on the street the deeper she'll hide."

"Goddamnit," Ok-Lee said in frustration. She put the pistol back in her purse. "What the hell was she doing here at this hotel? Stalking us? Because it certainly wasn't a coincidence."

"Turov knows I'm here, and I think he probably sent her to try to kill me," McGarvey said. "Or at least force me out into the open."

Ok-Lee was startled and it showed on her face. "Like right now?"

McGarvey nodded. "We're still looking for the woman. Head left, and I'll get across the street."

"We'll never find her—"

"If Turov is watching I want him to think that we're still trying," McGarvey said. "Now move it, but watch yourself."

Ok-Lee offered him a faint smile. "This is *my* city, McGarvey, you'd better watch your own back."

She turned and headed left, almost immediately lost in the crowd. As soon as she was gone, McGarvey started across the busy street, dodging traffic like a bullfighter dancing just out of harm's reach. An S-class Mercedes was suddenly there, the driver laying on the brakes and the horn. McGarvey jumped up on the hood, slid across to the other side, just missed a small three-wheeled van, and slipped behind a bus to the sidewalk. Almost immediately traffic got back to normal.

The bus temporarily blocked anyone standing in front of the hotel from seeing him, and before it moved off he ducked into the corner of a bank's entryway, and flattened against the wall in relative darkness.

Otto's message to Turov had evidently worked, otherwise he would not have sent Huk Kim to the hotel. It would be one man, alone, someone hanging back to watch what was going on. Someone who wouldn't seem overly curious. A Westerner, nevertheless, who would stand out among the much shorter, smaller Koreans. He would be at the hotel, or nearby so that he could monitor the woman's movements as she tried to flush McGarvey out into the open where he could be easily taken. Turov wasn't a martyr. He might want McGarvey dead, but he wouldn't be willing to give up his own life or freedom for it.

Now that the excitement was over most of the people who'd gathered in front of the hotel entrance went back inside. One man, however, headed down the driveway, and McGarvey recognized him as the one who'd been at the doorway, the one who had grabbed the woman's arm for just a moment, before he'd stepped back and let her go.

He appeared to be solidly built, with longish white hair, a large mustache, and when his face was momentarily illuminated by the headlights of a limo coming up the driveway, McGarvey could see that he wore glasses.

Turov?

McGarvey stepped out of the shadows so that he was in plain sight. At the bottom of the driveway the man glanced across the street directly at McGarvey, hesitated for only a split second, then headed to the left, in the direction Ok-Lee had gone.

In seconds he was lost in the crowd on the busy sidewalk.

McGarvey speed dialed Rencke's number, and his friend answered on the first ring.

"Did you get the message to Turov?"

"It took about ten tries until I found a remailer that accepted my query," Rencke said. "And if he's our man he's damned good. Or whoever set up his system is. Are you telling me that he's there?"

"I think so," McGarvey said. He made his way past the fountain in front of the bank and headed in the same direction as Lin had gone, trying to pick out the taller man in the midst of the much shorter Koreans. "Has he replied yet?"

"No, and I don't think he will. That address was closed down within a few minutes after I got through."

"That's okay, because if we're right I think it flushed him out into the open."

"He's there to kill you."

"That's what I figured," McGarvey said, and he caught a brief glimpse of the man. "Got to go, Otto," he said, and he broke the connection, pocketed the phone, and looked for a break in traffic.

FORTY

From just inside the doorway of the electronics store Kim watched McGarvey pocket his cell phone and head down the block in a big hurry in the direction the NIS woman had gone. But he'd waited until the man she'd bumped into in the lobby had come out of the hotel and disappeared in the crowd.

For a moment when McGarvey had crossed the street, Kim had been horrified that he'd somehow spotted her, and she had reached in her purse for her gun. But he'd disappeared behind a fountain two buildings away.

When the bus had moved out of the way she'd spotted the man with the white hair look across the street and then start after Ok-Lee, and because of McGarvey's reaction it had dawned on her that the old man was Alexandar.

McGarvey was looking for a break in the heavy traffic so that he could cross the street, but everything was moving at breakneck speed, practically bumper-to-bumper as was the norm in downtown Seoul, especially at this hour. Just about everyone in this city went full tilt all the time, as if they were trying to catch up with something or someone.

"The Americans," Soon would have suggested. She could hear his voice, and clearly see his face. They were torturing him up there, giving him mind-altering drugs that could fry his brain. If they didn't stand him in front of a firing squad, he would probably come out of the ordeal as little more than a vegetable.

What surprised her was the lack of sirens. According to Alexandar the woman's name was Ok-Lee Lin and she worked as a field officer for the NIS. She should have called for backup. By now sirens should have been converging from all over the city. An ex-military shooter was on the loose, possibly the shooter at Pyongyang. She would be top priority. Important enough to bring the former director of the CIA all the way from the States to find her.

Unless McGarvey knew about Alexandar and the real reason he'd come to Seoul was to find the Russian, possibly using Kim as bait. It would explain what had just happened. McGarvey and Ok-Lee had separated, and as soon as Alexandar had headed after the woman, McGarvey had moved out. Suddenly the NIS officer had become the bait.

Kim hesitated a little longer in the electronics store until McGarvey made it across the street and she was certain that he wouldn't be able to spot her if he looked back.

Her first plan had been to lure Turov to some place public, like the hotel lobby where she could have her face-to-face talk in relative safety. But the presence of McGarvey and Ok-Lee had made that impossible. Then standing here, watching McGarvey, she'd thought about going to Tokyo and somehow finding out where he lived. But something like that would take too much precious time, and if she did make it that far it would be a dead end. Even if she had Alexandar at gunpoint, there was no guarantee that he would cooperate in getting Soon out of North Korea.

She'd also thought that if she could find Alexandar and

put her pistol to his head she could make him tell her who had ordered the hit. She could use the information not only to stop the insanity between China and North Korea, but to gain Soon's release.

She was naïve and she knew it. But something else occurred to her. Something Soon had always insisted on, that they never were to rely on anyone else. They had to do everything for themselves; make their own preparations, get their own weapons and papers, arrange their own travel plans, and do their own research.

It had worked flawlessly for them until this last time. And now it was up to her.

Making sure that McGarvey was finally lost in the crowd across the street, Kim slipped out of the electronics store and headed to the corner in the opposite direction where she found a cab, and ordered the driver to take her to the Yeongdeung-po gu district.

She would not be able to return to the hotel or to her apartment to get her things, so for now all she had were the clothes on her back and the pistol, some money, and most of the escape kit from the attic in her purse. It was enough to get her out of the country, possibly to Switzerland where she could access their money and from there, go anywhere on the planet.

She and Soon had discussed the Caribbean, or perhaps South America. Venezuela's relationship with the U.S. right now was not good. If she disappeared in Caracas, it was unlikely that McGarvey or someone like him would be allowed to look for her. And Chavez certainly wouldn't cooperate.

But that left Soon in the hands of the North Koreans.

Standing in the doorway across from the hotel watching the situation unfold, the glimmerings of another plan had begun to crystallize in her head. One that had almost no chance of success, except that their storage locker in Yeongdeung-po gu held all the papers, uniforms, and weapons she would need, and she would not be going north without a powerful bargaining chip.

Her only hope at this point was that the locker hadn't been cleaned out, and that it wasn't staked out. Beyond that she didn't want to dwell on the details of her crazy plan.

FORTY-ONE

Across the street McGarvey bullied his way through the crowds, trying to catch up with the white-haired man from the lobby, cursing himself for his stupidity. He'd counted on Turov coming after him, not Ok-Lee and Huk Kim.

He called Ok-Lee's cell phone and it rang three times before she answered. She was out of breath.

"*Mu-eot?*" What?

"The guy with the white hair and glasses at the hotel. It's Turov and he's on your back."

"Shit, are you sure?" Ok-Lee demanded. "I can't find the woman."

"Forget her. I'm right behind you."

McGarvey could hear the same sounds of the crowds and traffic in the phone as he was hearing on the street. "Lin?"

"I don't see him yet, but I'm coming around a corner into the courtyard of an apartment tower. It's just across the entrance to the underground arcade, about a block from the hotel. Do you know where this is?"

"No, but I'll find you," McGarvey said, redoubling his efforts. "Stay loose."

"Watch yourself, Kirk. He might suspect that this was a setup and you're on *his* back."

"I hope so," McGarvey said. "I sincerely hope so."

At the corner he was against the light. He pulled out his pistol and held it up as he pushed his way through the knot of people backed up at the curb and raced across the street, cars, taxis, three-wheelers, and mopeds screeching brakes and swerving trying to avoid hitting him.

On the other side he was in time to see a tall, bald-headed man cross the street with the light, and duck down some broad stairs into the underground arcade, and he was suddenly very concerned.

A modernistic glass-and-stainless-steel skyscraper at least thirty stories tall rose from the corner, the main entryway opening at an angle into a broad courtyard planted with greenswards and small trees that led across to an expanse of glass and automatic doors.

The edges along the rise of the building were mostly in shadow and at first McGarvey didn't see Ok-Lee lying on the pavement. He raced past her, pulling up short, and turning back only when he heard her call his name.

She was crumpled in an awkward heap, her pistol lying next to her head, her hands clutching her stomach, blood welling out from between her fingers, soaking her blouse, and already pooling up on the pavement.

McGarvey dropped down beside her.

"One-one-nine," she whispered to him. "Ambulance."

"Hang on," McGarvey told her. He entered the number into his cell phone.

"We're across from the Lotte Arcade," she whispered. "In English, they'll understand."

The emergency operator came on in Korean. "You have a police officer down across from the Lotte Arcade," McGarvey said calmly, scanning the darker shadows for any sign that Turov was still here waiting to take another shot. "Do you understand?"

"Yes, of course," the operator said.

"She's been shot, and she's losing blood," McGarvey explained. "Hurry!" He broke the connection.

"No white hair," Ok-Lee said, her voice weak. "Bald."

Christ, he'd been the guy crossing the street and going down into the arcade. "Take it easy, Lin, the ambulance is on its way. You'll be all right."

"I wasn't expecting it. I was looking for white hair."

"I'm sorry. It was my fault."

"No," Ok-Lee said, trying to rise, but McGarvey gently held her back.

He took off his jacket, bundled it up and eased it under her head as a pillow, and she managed a smile.

"We need to get our stories straight," she said. "They'll want to hold you until they can figure out what happened. In-Suk is going to be all over this." She groaned. "He's still in love with me, I think."

"Don't worry about it."

In the distance they could hear sirens.

"It was a random shooting," she said breathlessly. "We were supposed to meet at the arcade, but you were late. I came over here because I thought I saw something, and a couple of kids shot me. Stupid."

"No," McGarvey started to tell her.

"They'll hold you until it's too late," she said. "Listen to me, I know what I'm talking about. You need to get the bastard before everything goes to hell. You're the only one who can do it."

"I won't leave you like this."

"Don't be a hero."

The sirens were much closer now.

"Don't be a martyr," McGarvey said. "We won't be able to stop him from leaving Korea, not without making such a big fuss he'd be able to sidestep everyone. He'll go back to Tokyo, and I'll find him there."

Ok-Lee suddenly grabbed his arm with a bloody hand.

"Find him, Kirk. Stop this before it blows up. A lot of people are depending on you. Including me."

"Count on it," McGarvey said, his jaw tightening. He was thinking about some other women who had gotten too close to him and had paid the price. He wasn't going to let this one down.

He eased her grip from his arm and placed her hand back on her stomach wound, then reholstered his pistol, took out his handkerchief, and wiped a trickle of blood from the corner of her mouth.

She was passing out, her eyelids fluttering, when a pair of uniformed cops, their pistols drawn, came into the courtyard, and McGarvey raised his hands above his head.

"Ambulance," he said. "Hurry."

FORTY-TWO

Turov made his leisurely way across the Lotte Underground Arcade to the Metro station at Euljiro and took a busy number two train back one stop where he got off at city hall. Up on the street he stopped a moment to listen to all the sirens a few blocks to the south.

It amused him to think that the woman NIS officer would probably bleed to death before she got to the hospital. He had gut shot her so as not to kill her immediately. In that way McGarvey, who'd taken up the chase, would stay with the woman, probably all the way to the hospital. The Americans he'd worked with were all romantics, though most of them would fiercely deny it. And McGarvey was no different.

He waited for the light and crossed with a knot of people to the Radisson Seoul Plaza where he'd been staying since he'd gotten word that the assassination in Pyong-yang had been a success.

He was a man who liked his minor luxuries, and each of the last five times he'd come to Seoul to monitor the Huks' homecomings, he'd stayed at this hotel under a different name and disguise. He tipped very well so that his treatment would be first-class, even though no one on the hotel's staff recognized him from the previous visits.

And that amused him, as did the fact that the Radisson was less than two hundred and fifty meters as the crow flies from the Westin.

He made his way around the large fountain gushing a brightly lit plume of water from a pair of concentric pools and across the driveway past the bellmen into the vast, bustling lobby.

A Japanese woman in a man's tuxedo was playing a baby grand piano at the lobby bar, and a bunch of Western businessman, most of them drunk already, had filled her tip jar to overflowing. The mood of the crowd was the same as it had been at the Westin, fear and excitement mixed with a sense that something momentous, some big historical event, was about to happen and they were the lucky ones to be here to witness it firsthand.

As he waited for an elevator he glanced at the reflection of the lobby entrance in the gilt-edged mirror above the hall table on the remote chance that he was wrong and McGarvey had followed him here.

Ok-Lee would describe the man who'd shot her as a Westerner, but bald. Maybe McGarvey had spotted him crossing the street, and instead of waiting for the ambulance had taken up the chase.

It was not likely, but Turov had built a life on considering every possibility, even the most unlikely, especially when it involved a professional. Men of McGarvey's experience very often did the unexpected.

But the elevator came and Turov rode up to his suite on

the eighteenth floor, careful not to enter until the corridor was empty of staff, none of whom knew him as a bald man in his forties and would wonder what he was doing with a key to another man's room.

He took off his jacket and tossed it on the arm of an easy chair, then crossed to the wet bar where he opened a bottle of Krug, poured a glass, and drank it down. He took the champagne and the glass back to the bedroom where he kicked off his shoes, propped himself up on the bed, poured another glass, and then telephoned the concierge desk.

"I'll be going to Tokyo first thing in the morning, be a dear and book me a seat, would you?" It wasn't necessary for him to specify first-class.

"Sometime after breakfast, Mr. Levin?" she asked.

"Naturally," Turov said. This time he was traveling on an Israeli passport as Dov Levin, a sixty-five-year-old importer of Oriental art, who had an eye for young pretty women, and who, in the few days he'd been here, had established himself as a nice man who was free with his money.

"Will you be returning soon?"

Turov chuckled. "You can never tell when somebody like me will show up."

"Yes, sir. Your e-ticket will be delivered to your room within a few minutes."

"That's not necessary, my dear," Turov said. "I'll collect it at the desk when I check out in the morning."

"No trouble."

"I insist," Turov said. He could see himself snapping her neck. She was a young woman with the flat face that Koreans found attractive, but that he as a Russian Jew found repulsive. "In the morning."

"Yes, sir."

Turov broke the connection, finished his second glass of champagne, then got up and went into the bathroom where he peeled off the flesh-toned latex skullcap that covered his short-cropped dark hair and flushed it down the toilet.

The police would eventually find the wig and mustache where he had discarded them in the storm drain in front of the apartment tower where Ok-Lee had been lurking, but it would tell them nothing more than the man they were looking for had worn a wig.

At forty-three, Turov was in excellent condition. At the KGB's School One he had been an outstanding soccer player, because he had no fear of hurting anyone from the opposing team or any of his own teammates for that matter. He had absolutely no loyalty to anyone but himself, not to his team, not to the school or the KGB, and certainly not to the Soviet Union, which by then was already disintegrating.

At slightly under two meters and ninety kilograms he was within a centimeter and a kilo or two of his college height and weight, and a daily regimen of hard exercise under Minoru Hirobumi, his chief of staff back at the compound in Tokyo, kept him in top form. The exercises, both mental and physical, were not a hobby, they were basic survival, and both men treated them that way.

Turov had no fear of any man, and his major fault was that he also had no respect for anyone. It was the only point of contention between him and his training master, who was a samurai and followed the ancient practice of Bushido that prided honor above all else.

He took the blue contacts out, revealing his dark eyes, then began with the makeup that put age lines in his forehead and neck, age spots around his ears and at the base of his nose and his eyelids, and on the backs of his hands. A pale overlay lotion gave his skin tone a gray cast that made him look tired.

The effect, when he was finished, was subtle, natural. He did not look like a man in his forties pretending to be older, instead he looked like a man in his sixties who was in very good shape for his age.

He brushed a little gray in his sideburns to complete the effect, then dressed in dark slacks, a white shirt, a dark sport coat, and an embroidered yarmulke on the back of his head.

"Mazel tov," he told his reflection in the mirror by the door, before he went back downstairs to have more champagne and dinner, and to spread some money and good cheer so that the staff would not forget him.

McGarvey's crude attempt to engage him with an assassination proposal had been amusing. The pot between China and North Korea had been given its final stir and soon it would be time to decamp to Sidney or Melbourne.

But he had to consider the possibility that McGarvey would come to him in Tokyo and he would have to kill the former CIA director. He decided that it would be one of the most pleasurable things he'd ever done.

FORTY-THREE

Kim got out of the cab a couple of blocks from the storage locker and blending in with the shoppers made it the rest of the way on foot to where she ducked into a shop selling incense sticks and soapstone holders across from the locker on the narrow street. Brightly colored banners and signs were strung from the second-story overhangs, lending a carnival air to the scene.

Kim, who was from the small fishing town of Chinhae in the far south, had been dazzled by the big city the first time she'd come to Seoul. The tall buildings, traffic, and noise had made her homesick. But this district and especially this street reminded her of home, and she'd pestered Soon to find an apartment down here, at least until they had to leave Korea for good. He'd agreed with her, but they'd never seemed to find the time to make the move, and now it was too late.

She bought a small bundle of sandalwood sticks from the polite shop owner, and then lingered over a collection of holders on a table just outside the doorway.

The NIS plainclothes surveillance officer stood out like a sore thumb, leaning against his unmarked car at the end of the block. A cop had come over and they were talking and smoking cigarettes, neither of them doing their job.

Kim watched them for a full minute, trying to make some sense of what was happening. Someone had been sent to watch the storage locker, as she had feared might happen, but the babysitter had his back to the building. It was as if he'd been sent here to keep an eye out for her, but had been told that it wasn't very important. He was putting in his time, nothing more.

Keeping an eye on the NIS officer and cop, Kim made her way across the street, ducking into Mr. Pim's doorway as she pulled out her pistol and screwed the silencer on the finely machined threads on the end of the barrel. Making sure the babysitter hadn't turned around, she hesitated until no pedestrian was nearby and then fired one shot into the lock securing the accordion gate.

The noise from the single suppressed shot seemed loud to her ears, but no one passing on the street seemed to pay her the slightest attention. She eased the gate open, slipped inside, closed it behind her, and scurried back to their locker.

She held up in the darkness for several seconds watching the passersby, half expecting to see the babysitter and maybe the cop at the gate, but still no one was coming to investigate.

The brass padlock could not be opened with anything

as light as the 7.65 mm bullet her pistol fired, but the soft metal hasp and the matching staple that was screwed into the wooden door frame were a different story. She fired two silenced shots, one above and the other just below the staple, waited a few moments to see if anyone was coming, then put the pistol back in her shoulder bag and tugged at the door, pulling the lock and the entire staple plate out of the door frame with a dull clunk.

She stepped inside the room, closed the door behind her, and working by feel in the complete darkness took a couple of shirts from one of the cases, rolled them up, and stuffed them along the bottom of the door. Only then did she switch on the light.

Her heart lurched. They hadn't merely sent a babysitter to keep watch, they'd used the key to get in here and search the place. Most of the boxes and cases had been opened. They knew about the weapons and the false papers and everything else. They knew! And yet they were more interested in Alexandar than in her.

She quickly went through everything, and when she was finished she was reasonably certain that nothing had been taken. Their things had been rifled, but nothing was missing, and that made even less sense to her than the babysitter outside who didn't seem to be paying any attention to his job.

For a long moment or two she stood flat-footed in the middle of the tiny storage compartment, conscious of her rapidly beating heart.

None of what was happening here in Seoul really mattered. Only getting Soon out of North Korea meant anything to her. And she had hatched a wildly impossible scheme to do just that. Soon would tell her that she was crazy. Completely out of her pretty little head.

His voice was clear inside her head, and it brought tears to her eyes.

But she would have to hurry if she was going to save him before his brain was fried from drugs or before the nuclear weapons started to fly.

She had to rummage through a couple of boxes before she found a blue nylon Nike duffle bag, into which she stuffed a set of black camos, including a black balaclava, boots, and night vision goggles. She added another set of identity papers to the ones she'd taken from the attic, some money in North Korean denominations, and a few pieces of civilian clothes to replace what she had to leave at the hotel. Anything else she needed she would have to buy on the run.

When she had the bag zippered up, she hesitated a little longer trying to decide if she should take another weapon, something heavier than the Walther PPK in her purse. But she decided against it. She would try to reach Pyongyang to trade for Soon's life, not try to shoot her way to him.

She reached up to turn off the light when the door was suddenly jerked open, and she turned around to face the NIS surveillance officer from the street corner, what looked like a boxy 9 mm SIG-Sauer in his hand. There was no safety on the SIG, and the hammer was at full cock, so it was ready to fire.

She picked that up in an instant, her NIS training automatically kicking in, and she managed a highly indignant look. The cop wasn't with him, which meant she had a chance here, but only one.

"Who the hell are you?" she demanded. "Is this a stickup?"

"You know damn well who I am, Lieutenant," he said. "You had me spotted on the corner."

"Yeah, well where's the cop who was with you?"

"This has nothing to do with the cops."

Kim shook her head and dropped the nylon bag. "I don't

know who you think I am, but I've got ID," she said. She fumbled for her purse, and the NIS officer stepped through the doorway.

"No, you don't," he warned. "Keep your hands in plain sight."

It was a mistake on his part. As he came into the narrow storage room, Kim raised her hands in front of her and moved toward him.

He reached for her arm, but she stepped aside and batted his gun hand away as she sidekicked him in his leading knee, the bone and cartilage breaking and tearing with an audible pop. He went down with a grunt, and she grabbed his gun hand, and snapped the wrist using his own weight as a lever.

This time he cried out in pain, but Kim dropped down, one knee on his chest, and clamped her fingers around his throat, depressing his carotid arteries, cutting off blood to his brain.

It was mostly over before he had a chance to defend himself, and she watched as consciousness faded from his eyes, and his body went limp.

She held the pressure for a few seconds longer, but then let go and reared back, a sob catching in the back of her throat.

Another few seconds and he would have been brain-damaged. A little longer and he would have died. For simply doing his job. She was a suspected assassin and he had been ordered to watch for her, and take her into custody if possible.

And it had been so easy for her. Easier than this poor bastard would ever realize.

"We're not murderers," Soon had told her after their first hit.

"What then?" she'd demanded. She'd been frightened and sick at her stomach.

"What we always were, Kim. We're soldiers."

He had been holding her in his arms, and she had tried to pull away, but he wouldn't let her.

"We've never killed an innocent person, and I promise you that we never will."

"How can you be so goddamned sure?" she'd cried.

"I just am, and so will you be in time," he'd said. "If it comes to it, and you don't believe that our target deserves to die, then don't pull the trigger. Walk away, and I'll understand." He'd kissed her. "I promise you, just walk away."

She looked down at the surveillance officer, whose breathing was starting to return to normal, picked up the nylon bag, turned off the light, closed the door and gate behind her, and walked away.

FORTY-FOUR

At the Asan Hospital McGarvey was shunted off to a waiting area next to the emergency room while Ok-Lee was evaluated by a team of doctors and nurses. In less than five minutes she was wheeled down the corridor and loaded aboard an elevator. A stern-faced nurse came back to where McGarvey was standing at the doorway.

"You are the American who came with Ms. Ok-Lee?"

"Will she be okay?" McGarvey asked. Turov had gut shot her so that he could make his escape, knowing that McGarvey wouldn't leave her if she had still been alive. A cold fire had always burned in his belly for bastards like that. And there would be payback.

"Her condition is very serious," the nurse said. "She's on her way upstairs to an operating theater now. We'll know better in the next hour."

"Please let me know."

The nurse turned away but then came back. Her expression had softened. "She regained consciousness briefly and told us that you saved her life."

"I'll wait here," McGarvey said.

"It may be hours."

"I'll wait."

The nurse left at the same time two men, both of them obviously cops or intelligence officers, charged into the emergency room, flashing their identification. The admitting clerk pointed them in the direction of the waiting room, and when they spotted McGarvey they came straight back. They weren't smiling.

"McGarvey?" the shorter of them demanded. He had a small face that was screwed up into a mask of anger.

"That's right. You must be Mr. Bak, Lin's boss."

Bak's eyes narrowed. "That doesn't matter. Where is she?"

"Upstairs, they're going to operate. She was shot in the stomach and she's lost a lot of blood."

"And where were you?"

"She wanted to show me the shopping arcade. We were supposed to meet there, but I was late. I'm sorry."

Bak was obviously holding himself in check. He nodded. "You're lying, of course," he said through clenched teeth. "I know your record, or at least some of it. Wherever you show up disaster follows you. I wanted you kept out, but I was overruled." He glanced toward the corridor. "If she dies I'll see that you hang, you son of a bitch, if I have to do it myself."

The agent with him touched his sleeve and said something softly in Korean, but Bak pulled his arm away.

"You requested that a storage locker in Yeongdeung-po gu be placed under surveillance this afternoon. Why?"

"I'm trying to find someone who might want to get something there."

"Who is this someone?" Bak pressed. "It must have something to do with the Pyongyang situation."

"I'm not sure," McGarvey said. He couldn't afford to be hung up here in South Korea answering questions. By now Turov was on his way back to Tokyo, and that was where the answers would be.

Bak stepped closer, an even more menacing expression on his round face. "Well now you can be sure, Mr. Director. The man on surveillance was found by a neighborhood cop semiconscious inside the locker. Can you guess what was found, besides my man, that is?"

McGarvey shrugged.

"False papers, money, clothing, and weapons. Sniper's weapons. The tools of assassins." His eyes never left McGarvey's. "If you expect to get out of Seoul before the bombs fly, you'll have to tell me the truth."

"If I don't get out of Seoul by morning, the bombs just may fly," McGarvey said.

Bak wanted to pull a pistol and open fire, McGarvey could see it in his eyes, and he suddenly realized that the man was probably in love with Ok-Lee, which just now made him doubly dangerous.

"Who shot her? One of the assassins?"

"No."

"You're telling me that whoever shot her has nothing to do with what we found in the storage locker, or what happened in Pyongyang?" Bak asked harshly. "Because if that's what you're trying to do here I'll arrest you right now. Believe me, you won't like our interrogation center."

"I'm sure I won't, but in the meantime you'll still have the same problem on your hands."

"One that you've come here to help solve for us."

"That's right."

"But you won't share information with us."

"There's no time."

Bak turned away, and the other agent said, "Witnesses

said they saw a tall man, a Westerner without hair leaving the courtyard, and that you came afterward. Would you know this man?"

"No," McGarvey said.

"Leave Korea while you can, Mr. McGarvey, before we have to arrest you and forcibly put you on a plane out of here."

"I'd like to stay until morning, at least long enough to find out how Lin is doing," McGarvey said. "Can you give me that much?"

Bak turned back. "What's your interest in her?"

"I'm partially to blame for putting her in harm's way. I want to make sure she comes out of it."

Bak said something in Korean to the other agent, who gave McGarvey a bleak look.

"I'm going to collect your things from your hotel room, and bring them here. As soon as we learn that Captain Ok-Lee is in the clear I'll personally drive you back up to Oasan."

"Thank you," McGarvey said.

The agent hesitated. "Is there anything I need to be made aware of? Anything in your things that might hurt me?"

McGarvey shook his head. "Just dirty laundry."

Around midnight the surgeon came downstairs, his gown and paper booties blood-splattered. He looked tired. By now NIS personnel were all over the hospital, inside and out. One of their own had been shot in the line of duty, and it had probably happened because of an American ex-CIA director. No one was happy.

Bak said something to the doctor, who ignored him, and instead came over and sat down in the chair beside McGarvey.

"Mr. McGarvey, Captain Ok-Lee has lost a lot of blood, but the bullet missed her spleen and her liver so that the damage was confined mostly to the walls of her stomach. She'll recover with no problems, but it will take a great deal of time before she is without pain. Do you understand this?"

"Yes. May I see her?"

"No, not for twenty-four hours at least."

"I can't stay that long."

"She said that you would say something like that."

"She's conscious?" McGarvey asked.

"Long enough to ask me to thank you for saving her life," the doctor said. He leaned closer and lowered his voice. "And for you to find your Russian."

"Thanks, Doctor," McGarvey said. "When she recovers tell her that I will."

TOKYO

Turov took the early morning JAL flight direct to Tokyo, after a big breakfast and a round of hefty tips and good wishes at the hotel. He'd clumped across the lobby, leaning heavily on his cane, and humming an old Israeli kibbutz song loudly enough that everyone he passed had glanced up and smiled. He had played his role to the hilt as he usually did, so that the staff and guests would be sure to remember him as a rich, generous eccentric, not a Russian expediter of murder.

The time before he had been a nervous scholar who had kind words for everyone, and before that he'd taken on the roles of playboy, medical doctor, movie director, and journalist, but always with one common thread, that of generosity and good cheer.

Minoru Hirobumi was waiting for him with one of the Land Rovers at Narita's international arrivals gate. As usual the airport was a madhouse, and as usual his chief of staff was completely unruffled, serene. He was a small man, compact. "Another success, and now we may leave," he said. "Have you decided when and where?"

"Melbourne, but we have some time yet," Turov replied. "The U.S. is putting enough pressure on China to hold off the attack for at least a week. Maybe longer."

"Do you think there will be a war, Colonel?"

"Almost certainly, but don't you think so? It was a slap in the face to Beijing, an international embarrassment.

It's bound to have an effect. It's why Haynes is working so hard."

"The longer the delay the less likely China is to attack, I think."

"You may be correct," Turov said absently. "Maybe they'll need another little nudge."

The airport was fifty miles to the northeast of the city and the Ueno Park District where his expansive home was located behind bamboo walls. Traffic was nearly impossible as usual, but the morning was bright and lovely and Minoru was an excellent driver. Turov stared out the window and let his thoughts drift to the coming confrontation.

In the early days with the KGB he had carried out the occasional assassination, and although he was a ruthless, efficient officer in the field he was even better planning hits. His specialty had been, and still was, finding the right people for the job at hand and then motivating them to do it.

Afterward he killed his assassins, which was ridiculously easy, because none of them ever saw it coming. Fresh off a kill they were usually so hyped-up, adrenaline pumping, that they kept an eye out for the authorities, not their paymaster.

In each case Turov got a particular pleasure not only because a dead assassin would provide a lousy witness, and that he got his money back, but because each kill had given him a sexual rush.

As a fifteen-year-old on the soccer field in Leningrad he'd felt his first surge like that when he'd seriously hurt a forward, breaking the kid's leg, a couple of ribs, and the second and third vertebrae. The forward never walked again, which was a matter of total indifference to Turov, and although he had been kicked out of the game for unnecessary roughness he never forgot his feelings as he walked off the field. It had been better than an orgasm.

He'd never told anyone that, of course, but he was sure that he'd seen the look of comprehension in the eyes of more than one of his victims just before they had died, which made his feelings even more intense.

Minoru had been with Turov since the mid-eighties, and besides his monumental patience he understood his boss sometimes better than Turov understood himself. Among other things he knew when to back off. There were times for questions, times for action, and other times, like now for silence.

Turov knew and appreciated this in Minoru, who had become as near to being a friend as anyone ever had or could, and he settled back in the rear seat with his thoughts about the upcoming battle with McGarvey.

Somehow the CIA had found out about the Huks, and McGarvey had been sent to find Kim, but only to interview her, not make an arrest. Otherwise the NIS would have staked out the apartment, and kept a watch there until she finally showed up. The fact that they hadn't was significant, though it hadn't made sense to him until the clumsy attempt had been made to contact him with a job offer. Then he had understood.

Against all odds the CIA had found out who had hired the Huks to go to Pyongyang and make the hit. Of course what they didn't know was who had hired Turov to expedite the assassination. Had they known that, McGarvey would never have come to Seoul. He would have had another more interesting, and certainly a more devastating target to keep him occupied.

Soon was safe in Pyongyang, because all the drugs in the world could not extract more information than the man had in his head. All he knew was that his paymaster was a man by the name of Alexandar, and that after each hit money was deposited in a Swiss account.

The North Koreans did not have the laptop computer that Kim admitted had been taken from their apartment.

McGarvey had it, and Turov was enough of a realist to believe that, however unlikely, it was at least possible that the computer's memory could be read despite the encryption programs and fail-safes.

It was on that basis that he suspected McGarvey would be coming here. And he'd found that he was looking forward to their meeting. It was time for him to kill someone interesting. Someone worthy. Someone capable enough to offer resistance.

Someone, given the right circumstances, who could provide the nudge necessary to inadvertently make the U.S. push China into attack.

McGarvey had come out here to unravel the mystery of who had killed General Ho in Pyongyang and why. When he was gunned down, apparently by an agent of the North Korean government, the hue and cry from Washington would be immediate.

China would attack, Kim Jong Il would send his missiles flying, and the entire region would go up in flames in a war from which Japan and the Koreas might take a half-century or more to recover, and because of which the U.S. might sink to a second-class power, bankrupt and ineffectual.

Ueno, Tokyo's museum district, was located in the hills northeast of downtown with a lovely view of the city and the bay. Turov's compound was on a broad street of similar compounds above the Tokyo Metropolitan Art Museum. Wealthy Japanese businessmen maintained second homes up here, usually for their mistresses. This was an area of secret, secondary lives, a place where everyone minded their own business to an even higher degree than was common in polite Japanese society.

Minoru had telephoned ahead so by the time they'd pulled up at the rear gate, discreetly hidden behind a screen of foliage, one of the house staff let the Rover pass, first checking to make sure who was in the car.

Security here was tight 24/7. In addition to Minoru, the six people on his staff included two cooks and two maids, plus Sokichi Tanaka and Kotaro Hatoyama who'd come from the ranks of Japanese Self Defense Forces Special Action units. They were not particularly bright, but they knew how to handle themselves. They'd been court-martialed and drummed out of the service for excessive violence after the two of them had taken on seven fellow servicemen after a poker game that had gone bad. All seven had ended up in the base hospital, two of them in critical condition. Only the fact that no one had died, and that the seven had started the fight kept Tanaka and Hatoyama out of the stockade.

All of them, except for the maids, had been recruited eight years ago by Minoru who had the uncanny ability to find the disgruntled, disaffected man, angry with a system that valued discipline and proper reports over action, because he himself had been just such a man.

His father had been a Japanese Ground Self-Defense Force colonel working as liaison to the embassy in Taiwan after the war. He'd married a Chinese woman, and Minoru had been born in the late sixties. When they'd returned to Japan their lives became a living hell. The colonel was kicked out of the army because his wife presented a security risk, and Minoru had been so severely ostracized at school that he was pulled out of classes and home-schooled by his mother, who was a mathematician, and by his father, who had been a military combat officer.

Life had been difficult for the family, and even more difficult for Minoru after his parents died in a house fire. After living on the streets of Tokyo for two years he was accepted at the Waseda University on the basis of his high test scores and his athletic abilities on the non-sumo wrestling mat. In four years he graduated nearly at the top of his class in foreign studies, but no jobs were open to him with the government or industry because of his mixed heritage, except for the military, where despite his degree he was not given a commission.

He did learn ground combat operations, including infiltration-exfiltration techniques, weapons, explosives, and hand-to-hand fighting. After a couple of years he transferred to the Public Security Investigation Agency, called Koancho, that had been loosely modeled after the American FBI. But his situation was no better there because of his parentage, and he eventually landed at the Russian Embassy as a translator and adviser to the KGB officer in charge of special projects—Alexandar Turov— who understood and appreciated him for his abilities and not his Chinese mother.

Since that time there was nothing on this earth that Minoru would hesitate to do for his boss—espionage, treason, murder, even suicide if it was asked of him.

Turov went directly through the sprawling, beautifully but sparsely decorated, traditional Japanese dwelling of interconnected rooms and spaces that could be defined and redefined at a moment's notice by translucent rice paper shoji screens, to the bathhouse open on three sides to the peaceful rock and water garden.

The maids, naked, had prepared his steaming bath. Without a word Turov spread his arms and the women undressed him. He sat on a low wooden stool next to a bucket of water to be washed vigorously with a harsh soap and stiff bath brush. When they were finished they poured the bucket of extremely hot water over him, and then helped him into the neck-deep bath.

Minoru was there with a glass of crackling cold Krug for his boss. "What remains to be accomplished before we leave?"

Turov looked up at him with pleasure and smiled as the girls got into the bath with him.

"An American ex-CIA officer may be coming here,"

he said. He sipped the champagne, the coldness in contrast to the hot bathwater. The yin and the yang. The Chinese had gotten at least that much right.

"Why?"

"To assassinate me. His name is Kirk McGarvey. Do you know it?"

"He was briefly the director of the agency," Minoru said. "His death can be easily arranged, though there may be some consequences."

Turov held his glass out for more wine. "If he does come here, we'll kill him. Otherwise we'll leave well enough alone. He has no proof yet."

"Is that such a good idea, Colonel?"

"We may have no choice," Turov said. "Nero fiddled while Rome burned. And afterward we shall go to Australia to wait for the end of the war."

"The entire house staff will be leaving?"

"Why no," Turov replied indifferently. "Did you think so?"

FORTY-SIX

Japan's Air Self-Defense Force refused to allow the Aurora to enter its airspace so instead McGarvey was shuttled across to Tokyo aboard a U.S. Navy Gulfstream IV VIP jet sent out from Yokosuka to fetch him. No questions were asked because of the current situation and because McGarvey was a former director of the CIA. He could be out here for only one reason.

They landed around noon at Tokyo's much smaller and less busy Haneda Airport ten miles southwest of the city center, and taxied across to the police hangar and out of sight. Customs had been alerted that an American traveling under a diplomatic passport would be arriving, but the two stern-faced men in plain suits who boarded the Navy jet identified themselves as agents with the Public Security Intelligence Agency, PSIA.

"We've been sent to ask what your specific business is in Japan, Mr. Director," one of them said.

McGarvey had glanced at their IDs but hadn't bothered with the names. "I'm here at the request of our ambassador."

"No, sir, you are not," the agent said. "We have the right to search your luggage—"

"Not under diplomatic cover."

"Or refuse you entry."

"That's your choice, but it would be a mistake," McGarvey said. "I'm here to help, if I can, but of course you're aware that we have very little time."

The door to the cockpit remained closed and the young Navy attendant had disappeared somewhere forward.

"Help us with what, specifically?" the other agent asked, his English good.

"I'm looking for a man who may have been involved."

"Not a Japanese citizen."

"No, not a Japanese."

"But this man is expecting you?" the first agent asked.

"Yes."

"Give us his name and we'll find him."

"It wouldn't do you any good, because if I'm right he's nothing more than an intermediary and I'm hoping he'll answer some questions."

"Just like that?" the first agent demanded. He and his partner were more uncomfortable than angry, and McGarvey figured they'd been ordered to try to find out why the former director of the CIA had suddenly shown up in

Japan aboard a U.S. Navy jet direct from South Korea's Oasan Air Force Base, but not to deny him entry.

"Maybe not so easy," McGarvey conceded.

"We won't stamp your passport."

"There's no need, I won't be long."

The two men gave him a bleak look. "If there's any trouble we'll leave it for the police to handle," the first agent said. "Do you understand that you're on your own?"

"I'm here to help prevent a war."

The agent nodded. "Yes, sir. And the last time you were here to help, several of our citizens ended up dead. You're not welcome here."

"Are you denying me entry?" McGarvey asked.

"No," the agent said

"It won't do to have me followed. I'll either disappear or leave the country and you can deal with the situation yourself."

"All you Americans are arrogant," the agent said. He and his partner gave McGarvey one last hard look, then left the aircraft.

The pilot opened the cockpit door and came aft. His name tag read: Halvorson. "Is someone picking you up, Mr. Director?"

"Not this time," McGarvey said gathering his bag. "Thanks for the lift."

"No bodyguard, sir?" Halvorson asked. "The entire country's pretty tense right now. A lot of them are blaming us. They're seeing it as a standoff between us and the Chinese and no matter how it turns out Japan will be on the losing end."

McGarvey shook his head. "First it was Bush and now it's Haynes. Amazing what people think one president can take the blame for. What's happening with the Seventh Fleet?"

"Already out to sea, or will be within twenty-four hours,"

Halvorson said. "We're heading down to Okinawa as soon as we refuel."

"Good idea."

"We can't stick around for you."

"I don't imagine," McGarvey said at the open hatch.

"Well, good luck, sir," Halvorson said.

McGarvey was given a lift by a taciturn man in a utility uniform and white cap with a strap around his chin driving a Follow Me pickup truck from the police hangar across to the busy main terminal.

The monorail into the city was cheaper and much faster but it was crammed and McGarvey wasn't in the mood to stand all the way. After he exchanged some money at one of the kiosks he walked directly across the main arrivals hall to the taxi stand outside where he asked the director with his little white flag for a cab to the Asakusa View, one of the finer hotels in the city.

He wanted his arrival to be noted, and staying at a luxury hotel in the heart of the city would not esacape Turov's notice. I'm here, McGarvey was saying. Do you want to play?

Tokyo was more intense than Seoul had been, in part because the South Koreans had been living with the threat from the North for more than six decades, and in part because the Japanese had been attacked twice with nuclear weapons, and they knew the horror of it.

The cabbie became angry as soon as he realized that his fare was an American, and when they reached the hotel in the city's old section he refused to help with McGarvey's bag, an insult that in other times would have meant his dismissal. Nor did any of the bellmen on duty offer to help. No one shot him angry looks, but the attitude was there.

A harpist played in the tea lounge section of the small

marble lobby, and as had been the case with the bellmen, McGarvey's reception at the front desk was cool, even though he'd stayed at this hotel before, and even though he'd booked a suite for an open-ended stay.

After he'd signed in he carried his own bag upstairs to his rooms on the twenty-fifth floor, where he unpacked his pistol, silencer, and two magazines of ammunition, placing them under his jacket on the bed.

He opened a Kirin beer from the mini-fridge and went to the tall windows overlooking the city and the Sumida River that wound its way through the downtown, and telephoned Rencke in Washington.

It was midnight, but Otto was still in his office. "The entire campus is on emergency footing, ya know," he said "And Dick doesn't even want to know where you are. No one's asking. Not even Howard."

"Anything from the White House that's not been on the news?"

"Nobody's saying anything, but the pressure's on for us to figure out what General Ho was doing in North Korea that would make Kim Jong Il want to take him out. Beijing sure as hell isn't offering any explanations."

"What about the mood in the Building, has anything changed since I left town?"

"It's been less than forty-eight and it's gotten really weird. Frosty. No one's saying or doing anything except to cover their own asses. We're practically drowning in a tidal wave of memos and e-mails. What about you?"

"Turov's our man, and he knows that I'm coming after him," McGarvey said. Shooting Ok-Lee had been nothing more than a setup. Turov wanted a confrontation here in Tokyo, and he wanted it before the missiles started to fly. McGarvey's jaw tightened thinking of Ok-Lee lying in a puddle of her own blood.

"What happened, Mac?"

McGarvey told him everything that had happened

from the moment he'd met the South Korean NIS officer at Oasan until this morning in the hospital when the surgeon had finished saving her life.

"Are you counting on him coming to you?" Rencke asked. "Because if you are I don't think that's such a hot idea. I've managed to dig up some stuff on him, and if this is the right guy he's a bad dog."

"I'm hoping that's exactly what he means to do," McGarvey said. "Send whatever you've got, and I'll take a look at it. In the meantime I want you to find out where he lives. He's a Westerner here in Tokyo, so no matter how low a profile he's maintained he's on someone's radar. Probably not the cops, but most likely the tax authorities, maybe one of the exclusive downtown golf clubs, possibly even one of the *yakuza* families. He'd need security and some sort of arm's-length source of intelligence."

"You're talking about local intel," Rencke said. "He's probably getting the big stuff from his contacts at the FSB's First Chief Directorate. They're still pretty good."

"I don't care about that part of it for the moment. I just want to find out where he hangs his hat and maybe pay him a little visit when he least suspects it. But the clock is ticking."

"I'm on it," Rencke said, and the connection was broken.

FORTY-SEVEN

McGarvey figured that Turov wouldn't wait long to make contact, because he would want to get out of Tokyo as soon as possible. If it was going to happen it would probably be tonight, or certainly no later than tomorrow.

For the moment he couldn't do much but wait.

After he finished his beer, he took a shower, changed into some fresh clothes, and propped himself up in the large bed with the information on Turov that Rencke had downloaded to his sat phone.

The Russian's real name was Nikolai Boyko, born of Jewish parents in Leningrad, both of them dead now. His mother had been a housewife and his father an engineer at one of the electrical generating plants. When it came time for the teenaged Nikolai to get his internal passport he listed his ethnic origin as a Great Russian and not a Jew. That was in the late seventies when a series of pogroms had raged across the Soviet Union. Had he identified himself openly as a Jew his future would have been at an end before he'd even started.

It was a period of we don't ask you don't tell, when competent people were needed to help fight the Cold War. It was the same year he'd been kicked off the soccer team for unnecessary roughness. In every subject he was at the top of his class, but little else showed up in Rencke's research until Boyko was accepted at the prestigious Frunze Military Academy to study ballistic missile engineering, which could have eventually led to a career in the navy and eventually command of a nuclear submarine.

His grades at the academy were nothing short of stellar, easily at the top of his class in every subject, though his name did not appear on the rosters of any of the academy's sports teams, including soccer.

Here Rencke's report became somewhat speculative, based, he wrote, on fragments of testimony given at a closed hearing about the deaths of four seniors. This was in Boyko's senior year.

It was in the late winter of 1987, Boyko was twenty-four, and ready to graduate in the spring. He had evidently nurtured a grudge against the four who had apparently harassed him the entire five years. Jew baiting, it was called, but it was a rare sport at the academy because so few Jews had ever been accepted.

Boyko sat in the upper bleachers of the gymnasium watching the gymnastics team working out. A number of the athletes were of Olympic potential so their practices usually drew a fairly large crowd.

One of them, a cadet named Anatoli Shuskin, on the weight-lifting team, had been the instigator among the four who had given Boyko such a hard time. After each of his successful lifts that night the audience roared its approval. He was sure to win the gold medal next year.

Afterward, when practice was over and the gymnasium began to empty, Boyko waited outside in the bitter cold, until the athletes started to emerge from the locker room, most of them heading back to the dormitories, while others headed toward the restaurants and bars just outside the main gate.

Only seniors were allowed off the grounds without special permission and Boyko had counted on Shuskin and the other three, pumped up by their practice, to want something to eat and drink before heading to bed. There would be the girls from the gym crowd there, of course, and the four of them were almost sure to get laid. Good practice, good food, good drink, and good sex. Anything for the Olympic-bound men, who would graduate in a few months and after the games head out into the fleet.

It was a few minutes after ten when the four of them came out the door and headed beyond the track field, most of the lights on campus off or dimmed for the night. Boyko fell in behind them, keeping to the shadows as much as possible, though it probably wouldn't have mattered because not once did any of them look back.

At the gate, the four men showed their IDs and were waved through, and headed left down the street, traffic light at this hour.

Boyko hung back until they were lost in the darkness

then hurried to the gate, showed his ID and the under-classman doing duty as the gate guard waved him through.

"Lucky bastards," the guard mumbled under his breath as Boyko headed after Shuskin and the others.

The four passed the trolley station in the next block and crossed the street, obviously heading for the Four Bells, which was a favorite hangout for athletes from the academy.

Boyko caught up with them in the next block. "Hey, *pizdas*," pussies. He spoke just loudly enough for them to hear. A half-dozen students were gathered outside the restaurant a block away, and he didn't want his voice to carry that far.

Shuskin, who stood less than one meter seventy, but weighed more than one hundred kilos stopped and turned back. He was built like a god, narrow waist, broad chest and shoulders, and massive arms. The other three, on the weight-lifting team with him, were built nearly the same. No one in the academy had ever messed with them.

For a moment Shuskin didn't recognize who it was standing in the darkness, but when he did a smile spread across his broad peasant's face. "It's the Jew boy," he said. "What do you think, gentlemen, did the kike say something to us?"

"I called you *pizdas*," Boyko said. "Are you too stupid to understand the word? Or didn't your mothers explain the facts of life to you?"

"You little fucker, it's time you learned your manners," Shuskin said.

Boyko turned on his heel and disappeared around the corner down the narrow side street of tailor shops and laundries, dark at this hour.

Shuskin was the first around the corner, and when he spotted Boyko he let out a roar and charged, the other three just a couple of meters behind him.

At the last possible moment Boyko stepped aside,

pulled out the twenty-five-centimeter chef's knife he'd stolen from the mess hall kitchen and had honed to razor sharpness, and sliced the weight lifter's throat to the back of his neck. He moved back just in time to avoid the sudden gush of blood as Shuskin's forward motion propelled him another few meters down the avenue before he collapsed with a horrible gurgling sound.

Boyko turned on the other three, calmly slashing their throats, the same as he had done to Shuskin and none of them stood a chance, they were weight lifters, solid on their feet, not as agile as a former soccer player who still worked out every day.

After they had bled out, he walked back to the academy, first stopping under a streetlight to make sure that he'd gotten no blood on his clothes.

He'd wiped the knife clean, and before he went to his room he put it back in the mess hall exactly where he'd found it, amused that in the morning it might be used to slice the kielbasa for breakfast.

From the school's files Rencke had been able to hack, it was apparent that everyone on campus knew who had committed the murders and why, but there was no hard evidence. Even so the Frunze commandant had been put in a position where he had to do something because of Shuskin's popularity, and at that moment the KGB came to his rescue.

The remainder of Boyko's records were sparse and Rencke admitted that he had to do a lot of reading between the lines to put the pieces together, among his sources the debriefing of two KGB officers who'd defected to the West, one to the U.S., the other to England, who talked about the young Jew who'd been kicked out of Frunze, had become a standout at the agency's School One, and had gone out into the field as a killer for Department Viktor.

He'd had assignments in Washington and London, working out of the Soviet embassies, as well as Mexico City, Bonn, Tokyo, Beijing, and even briefly in Tel Aviv. In each posting he'd apparently learned the language of the country, and everyone who'd ever had any contact with him said the same thing: the man was nothing short of brilliant but ruthless.

"A genius, but a bloody cold fish," one of the defectors had told his SIS handlers outside London. "Just as soon cut your throat as look at you."

Boyko had been recalled to Moscow after the collapse of the regime to help reorganize the KGB into the FSB, but within a year he had dropped off the map, completely disappearing from view.

About this time an entrepreneur who called himself Alexandar Turov burst onto the scene out of nowhere, amassing a fortune within an incredibly short time, apparently by assassinating, or arranging the assassinations of rising star businessmen whose rivals—including the FSB—were willing to pay big money in Western currencies to eliminate them.

Turov, the businessman, invested heavily in Japanese real estate, getting out just before the bust, and then in American tech stocks, getting out of those just before 9/11 when the market went into a tailspin.

After that Turov had apparently retired into obscurity in Tokyo, leaving only the vaguest of rumors connecting him with the man known only as Alexandar, who for a price could expedite a murder of anyone at any time at any place on the planet.

McGarvey phoned Rencke. "How sure are you that Boyko and Turov are the same man?"

"About eighty-five percent," Rencke answered. "Louise thinks maybe seventy-five, but no more than eighty. But she's always been tough, ya know."

"How about Turov as Alexandar the expediter?"

"Less," Rencke admitted. "Maybe just fifty-fifty, or a little better. But I got a feeling about this guy."

"Have you found out where he lives?"

"I'm working on it, kemo sabe."

FORTY-EIGHT

Turov had finished with his bath and a rubdown by the two girls and he was in his sleeping quarters dressing for a simple dinner at home, hopefully with McGarvey, when someone knocked discreetly.

"Come," Turov called softly. He studied his reflection in the mirror on the armoire door, his hair back to its natural dark, and then looked beyond to the shoji screen. As it slid aside he reached for his pistol on the shelf, but it was Minoru and he relaxed.

"The gentleman is lodging at the Asaka View. A suite on the twenty-fifth floor."

"Your information is accurate?" Turov asked. It was an insult but he wasn't in the mood for mistakes, though his slight anxiousness did not show.

"My police informant has been reliable in the past."

Turov finished buttoning the broad sleeves of his white silk shirt before he turned to face his chief of staff. "I only ask because Mr. McGarvey is a dangerous man, and it will not do for us to make an error now."

"A most remarkable man if only half of what I have learned is true," Minoru said softly. He never raised his voice, for him to do so would be impolite, opposite of his Bushido learning. Nor did he ever find the need to repeat himself.

"Your source?" Turov asked, moving across the room to the low table for his glass of champagne. He drank some and refilled the glass from the bottle sitting in the ice bucket. He despised sweet Russian champagne. Only the French knew how to produce a decent vintage.

"In Washington, one of the senator's aides. Do you wish to know this name?"

Turov waved it off. "I can guess who, but it doesn't matter, the record speaks for itself."

"He has had the ear of the past three presidents, he has friends in the FBI as well as all the other intelligence and police agencies in Washington, and of course he still has many friends and contacts inside the CIA."

"How about Homeland Security?"

"I don't know. Do you wish me to find out?"

"No," Turov said. He looked out the open wall to his garden, the placement of the rocks and of the reeds comforting in their orderliness, the sounds of the flowing water soothing in the gentleness.

"He has killed men."

"Many men?"

"Yes."

"As many as I have?" Turov asked, turning to face his chief of staff who had not entered the room, but stood at the open screen.

"Possibly more by his own hand," Minoru said. "He has more years experience than you do."

For some reason this bit of news irritated Turov, but he didn't let that show either. Instead, he smiled.

"He is a formidable man."

"So it would seem," Turov said, controlling his temper with a supreme effort of will. "All the more interesting when I kill him."

"I would not advise it, Colonel."

Turov's left eyebrow rose. "That's why you work for me, and not the other way around."

Minoru nodded. "Yes, sir."

"Now this is what I want you to do tonight after you finish supervising the preparations here."

After Minoru had left, Turov went out to the broad veranda where he drank another glass of champagne, his last, he decided, until this business with McGarvey was finished, and then he would indulge himself while China, the Koreas, and Japan burned.

It would be better than a Dostoyevsky novel, a great and tragic entertainment.

He set his glass aside, and walked back to his small study at the core of the house. The room, furnished only with a small desk and one chair, was completely surrounded by a Faraday cage that blocked any type of electronic surveillance measures, and double rice paper walls that sandwiched backer boards, which made them soundproof.

The WiFi telephone and computer were connected via series of band pass filters to an automatic remailer service in Taipei that had so far proven to be completely reliable. All calls or e-mails in or out of this room were impervious to eavesdropping, even by the American National Security Agency with its sophisticated satellite equipment.

Although it was late on the American eastern seaboard, he telephoned the man who had hired him to have General Ho and the two men before him assassinated. Service for value, his profits had been immense so far. But the job wasn't finished.

"Do you know who this is," he said when the phone was answered after the fourth ring.

"Yes," his contact, code-named Daniel, said, and in that one word it was obvious he was concerned.

"We have a potential problem that will require an additional payment."

"What problem?"

"Kirk McGarvey has become involved. He was in Seoul looking for one of my shooters, and he's followed me here to Tokyo."

"Impossible."

"Nevertheless, he's here. Which means he's getting information from somewhere. A leak from your end?"

The phone was silent for several beats.

"I will take care of this problem," Turov promised. "But it will cost you another five million euros."

"He's a dangcrous man," Daniel warned. "Not so easily . . . eliminated. Others have tried and failed."

"Leave that up to me. If I fail, you will not have to make a payment."

"There'll be serious repercussions. The blowback could be immense, even against the backdrop of what's about to happen out there."

"That part is your problem."

"Maybe there's a better way."

"Better than killing him?" Turov asked.

"Yes. But give me a few hours."

"Very well," Turov said. "If I don't hear from you in that time, I'll expect the first payment in my account. Are we clear?"

"Oh, yes," the voice at the other end said. "Very clear."

FORTY-NINE

It was quarter to seven and McGarvey was about to go downstairs for dinner when his sat phone chirped. By now Turov would know that he was here and would probably be making a move this evening and McGarvey wanted to make it easy for the man by being someplace public.

The caller was Rencke, and he sounded out of breath as he usually did when he had the bit in his teeth. "If Turov is our man, he's got a place on millionaires' row in Ueno, not too far from your hotel."

"Has he got any muscle up there?"

"I don't know. Getting anything on him was really tough. In fact I thought it was impossible, because he's not on any tax rolls, he's not registered with any utilities department, he doesn't hold a Japanese driver's license, and apparently he doesn't even have a relationship with any bank in the country."

"But you found him," McGarvey prompted.

"Yeah. Transfers of foreign funds into and from Japan. I started with Switzerland, an obvious choice, and ran into a blizzard. Seems like half of all Japanese millionaires do at least a part of their banking with the Swiss, mostly to hide some of their money from the tax man. But not so many of them use that route for ordinary living expenses. Turov is hiding behind an Australian corporation, registered under the name Boyko Investments, Ltd. Which makes him one cheeky bastard."

"Hiding out in the open."

"Yeah, but listen, Mac, none of this shit is one hundred percent, ya know. I'm doing a lot of guessing here, tons of extrapolations."

"Boyko Investments has to be too big a coincidence."

"Not so big," Rencke said. "Worldwide there are two dozen companies under that name, and just as many under Turov or some variation of either."

"How many linked back here to Tokyo?"

"Only the one," Rencke conceded.

"Okay, I'm going in to take a look tonight, maybe pressure him into making a mistake," McGarvey said. "How do I find his place?"

"It's near the Tokyo Metropolitan Art Museum. I'll download the directions to your phone. But you could be running into a buzz saw. If he knows you're in Tokyo, he'll expect you to come to him."

"It's exactly what I'm hoping for," McGarvey said. "I think he'll make contact with me tonight here at the hotel, and if he does I'll throw him a little misdirection."

"Well you have another problem you'll have to deal with," Rencke said. "Adkins knows you were in Seoul and he knows that you're in Tokyo. He wants to talk to you asap."

"How'd he find out?"

"I don't know, but I'm trying to run it down. Probably someone from the NIS."

It was possible that Ok-Lee's boss contacted someone at Langley because of the shooting, but McGarvey had another, much darker thought. It was something that had been playing around the edge of his consciousness almost from the moment Colonel Pak had laid out the situation. Who had the most to gain and who had the most to lose if the region went nuclear? The conclusions he was coming up with were taking him down a path he wasn't sure he wanted to go.

Just a few months ago he'd been involved with an operation in Mexico City involving a Chinese intelligence service general that ultimately ended up in an attack against the U.S. that was still under investigation by the CIA.

Now this, involving another Chinese intelligence service general at the center of an operation that could ultimately end up being an even stronger blow against the U.S.

Coincidence? He couldn't make himself believe it.

"I'll call him in the morning."

"He's camped out upstairs until this shit blows over," Rencke said. "Everyone on this side of the pond is going nuts. But I can hold him off a little longer."

"I'll call him now," McGarvey said.

"The directions to Turov's place in Uneo are in your phone. Watch yourself, this guy's good."

McGarvey broke the connection and speed dialed Adkins's private number at his seventh-floor office. The DCI answered on the second ring, and he sounded irascible.

"What?"

"How'd you know that I was in Seoul?" McGarvey asked.

Adkins hesitated only a beat. "Christ, make me a happy man and tell me that you're on the way home."

"Who told you?" McGarvey pressed.

"Howard told me this morning. Said someone from the NIS called him. Evidently you got one of their officers shot up, and she damned near died."

"The guy's name is Alexandar Turov. He hired a pair of South Korean shooters to go up to Pyongyang and take out the general."

"You're not listening, Mac. If it gets out that an American, especially a former DCI, is meddling in this business there'll be no end to the international complications. The general's assassination might even be laid on our doorstep."

McGarvey had always liked Adkins. The man was honest, well-meaning, and a damned fine administrator. But he was no spy. He didn't know when to take a chance, or even how to evaluate a risk to see if the possible outcome was worth it.

"I'll come home as soon as I can."

"Not good enough!" Adkins shouted. "For Christ's sake, Mac, we're looking down the barrel of a nuclear war out there that could spread not only to Japan, but to Taiwan as well, and we'd be right in the middle of it. You sat in this office, you know what's at stake. If need be we'll turn this over to the Japanese authorities to have you arrested and forcibly sent home. But Howard's afraid that you just might resist and there'd be another shooting."

"Turov is nothing more than the middleman, an expediter, and I'm going to ask him for a name."

Adkins hesitated for a moment. "I'll give you a few hours, Mac. It's all I can do, and then I'll have to turn this over to the COS there in Tokyo and ask him to bring you in, even if it means going to the Japanese authorities for help."

"I'll be out of here first thing in the morning, no matter what happens," McGarvey said. "Twelve hours from now. But it's too important and I'm too close to back off now."

"My hands are tied," Adkins said.

"So are mine," McGarvey said, and he broke the connection and stared out the window at the lights of the city.

FIFTY

Of the four restaurants in the hotel, McGarvey had enjoyed the French best from his last time here. The chef was from Paris, and had studied at the Cordon Bleu, earning the Asakusa's kitchen three stars. By seven when McGarvey arrived, the elegant dining room with its Louis XIV furnishings was only half-filled with Western businessmen meeting their Japanese counterparts. No one seemed to be in a hurry, and the noise level in the tall-ceilinged room was muted.

The maître d' brought McGarvey a tie then took him to a small table at a window. "Will someone be joining you for dinner this evening, sir?" He unfolded the linen napkin and draped it across McGarvey's lap.

"Somebody might drop by and ask for me."

"Would you care to leave your name, or would you rather not be disturbed?"

"McGarvey."

"Very good, sir," the man said with a half bow and he returned to his station.

Two waiters came, one to pour Evian in a stemmed glass, the other with bread and butter. When they left a third brought the menu.

"Good evening, sir. May I get you something to drink?

"A cognac, something nice," McGarvey said. "I'm celebrating."

"Yes, sir," the waiter said and he left. Like the other staff he was French, and unlike the Japanese at the desk this afternoon, their attitude was no different toward Americans than toward anyone else.

McGarvey guessed that at least one-third of the Westerners here this evening were probably Americans. It made him wonder if they knew something about the impending war that that no one else was aware of, or did they have faith in Washington brokering a peace between North Korea and China? The Americans who'd been caught in Baghdad during the first and second Gulf wars might have felt the same way. Either that or they were men seeking to make a profit from the war. Only in this case, if Kim Jong Il did launch one of his nukes, Tokyo would probably become an unhealthy place in which to do business.

The waiter returned with the cognac and withdrew to allow McGarvey time to look at the menu, making him also wonder about the French and other foreigners working and doing business here in Japan. The situation was serious, but no one he'd met, other than the Japanese, seemed to be concerned.

He felt an odd sense of unreality, as if he were caught up in some sort of a time warp, someplace outside the current world order.

McGarvey looked up as a short Japanese man in a Western business suit came across the room from the maître d's station. He moved like an athlete, his step light, poised to move very fast if the need suddenly arose.

"McGarvey-san," he said with a slight bow. "May I have a seat?

"That depends on who you are."

"My name is of no importance. But my employer's name may be of some significance to you. Alexandar Turov."

McGarvey took a sip of his drink. It was a Napoleon brandy and good. "Do you mean Nikolai Boyko? I think our paths may have crossed recently in Seoul."

The Japanese man showed no reaction. "May I sit down?"

McGarvey motioned for him to take a seat, and as he did the waiter came over, but McGarvey waved him off.

"The gentleman won't be joining me for dinner."

"Very well, sir."

When he was gone, McGarvey turned his attention back to Turov's messenger. "Well?" he asked coolly.

"Mr. Turov wishes to invite you to dinner this evening, if you haven't already dined, or for drinks if you have."

"Why?"

"He would like to discuss with you a recent offer made on your behalf."

"Do you mean President Haynes?"

"I wouldn't know, McGarvey-san. I'm simply a messenger this evening."

McGarvey studied the man who looked like anything but a simple messenger. Close up it was obvious he was in superb physical condition, and able to keep his emotions in check. Bushido, probably. But something else was in the messenger's eyes and facial structure, maybe a hint of Chinese. If he were of mixed heritage his life here in Japan could never have been easy.

"Tomorrow evening. I'm tired now, jet lag."

"Mr. Turov was most anxious to meet with you tonight."

"What's the hurry?"

The Japanese man didn't bother to answer. He was being toyed with and he knew it.

"Have him come here, if he wants to see me tonight," McGarvey said. "I'll meet him downstairs in the lobby bar."

"That's not possible, sir," the Japanese man said. He produced a business card, English on one side, Japanese on the other, and held it out. "Hand this to your cab driver, it gives directions."

McGarvey ignored it. "I know my way," he said. "Let's say eight tomorrow evening?"

"I'll pass your message along."

"If there is a problem, he can leave word for me with the desk," McGarvey said. "Now if you don't mind, whatever your name is, I'd like to order my dinner in peace."

If the insult bothered the man, he didn't show it. He pocketed the business card, got to his feet, bowed slightly, and left.

Two hours later McGarvey was back in his room, where he telephoned Rencke, and told him about the conversation he'd had with Turov's messenger. He pulled out his dark slacks and dark pullover from his bag, plus the extra magazine of 9mm ammunition and the silencer.

"Dick was down here raising hell. Wanted me to call Mrs. M and have her put some pressure on you."

McGarvey had to smile. "What did you tell him?"

"That if he wanted to try to involve her I'd crash every computer in the building, and it'd probably take a couple of months before we got back to normal."

"How'd he take it?"

"I don't know," Rencke said. "But I've never seen a DCI do a one-eighty so fast in my life."

"I'm going up there sometime after midnight. Do we

have a satellite in position to give me some real-time shots of his house and the immediate surroundings? I'd like to see if he's making any preparations."

"Give me five minutes and I'll have something for you," Rencke said. "But be careful, Mac, he's no good to us dead."

"That's the tough part," McGarvey agreed. "And there's something else I want you to start looking for. Something in Turov's background, maybe even as far back as his KGB days."

"You looking for connections? A bridge from then to now?"

"American connections."

"Shit," Rencke said softly.

"Yeah," McGarvey said. "Shit is right."

FIFTY-ONE

Turov rarely smoked, which was unusual for a Russian, even a modern Russian, but just now he felt the need, and he got an American Marlboro from a cigarette box at his bedside, lit it, and walked out onto the broad platform looking onto the garden.

His American contractor had not called back, which wasn't surprising. And even if he had, Turov had decided that he would take care of Kirk McGarvey in his own fashion. As Minoru had warned, if only half of the stories about the former CIA director were true, he was a dangerous man. And Turov valued his personal freedom too highly to allow a dangerous man to stalk him.

Minoru came out of the main house at the far end of

the veranda and stopped for a moment in the shadows, as if he were a bearer of bad news and hesitated to bring it forward.

The night was still. Only the muted hum of traffic down the hill near the Ueno Station and Metropolitan Festival Hall slightly marred the peaceful silence. The prime house rules were for silence, discretion, and invisibility. All the staff members, except for Minoru, were to carry out their duties as discreetly as possible while at all other times remain in their own wing of the compound. No radios or television were allowed, no voices raised, no musical instruments or games be played. If and when someone needed to celebrate, they would leave the compound. No one complained because the money Turov paid was very good.

Turov remembered his childhood as one of nearly monastic silence. "The man who babbles ceaselessly is the man who is unsure of himself or who does not know what he is doing, and wants to convince you otherwise," his stern father had told him.

Later, at the beginning of his KGB career, he'd learned interrogation techniques from Sergey Kuzin, a master, who taught that the fewer questions asked, the more likely the prisoner will believe he has to say something merely to fill the silence.

"All of them want to cleanse the sins from their souls," Kuzin advised. "In the end they want absolution. Become a sympathetic listener, a Catholic priest who will hear their confessions."

Turov had used the same techniques during his assassinations, sometimes learning the most amazing things. Men and women on their deathbeds had no loyalties to anything other than their own lives. It was one of the other lessons that he'd learned early on, that knowledge is power. More often than not he would return from a kill knowing more about his masters than they wanted.

It would be the same tonight with McGarvey who would confess who had sent him here and why. The information would undoubtedly be valuable.

"Come," Turov called softly.

Minoru came down the veranda to where Turov was standing.

"He refused your invitation for this evening, but said he will come tomorrow at eight."

It was about what Turov expected would happen. "Where did you speak with him?"

"In one of the dining rooms."

"Let me guess, French?"

Minoru nodded. "He also refused your card. Said that he know the way."

That, however, was unexpected, but Turov held back a frown. "Was he very rude?"

Minoru shrugged. "When he is dead his past inelegancies will not matter. But he will come here tonight, possibly very early in the morning when he believes we are asleep."

"I expect that you are correct," Turov said. "But since he didn't accept the card, we shall have to reset the trap. I would like that taken care of within the hour."

Minoru nodded. "Naturally."

"I do not want him damaged too badly. Bring him to me and I'll kill him myself, but first I would like to ask him a few questions."

"As you wish. I have several people in or near the hotel who will call when he makes his move. It will give us plenty of warning."

"Very good, Hirobumi-san," Turov said, using the honorific, and a brief flash of pleasure crossed Minoru's face. "Everything is happening according to my plan. I allowed him to see me in Seoul and he came here as I expected he would. I sent you to speak to him and he will come here."

"One other thing, Colonel," Minoru said. "He referred to you by the name of Nikolai Boyko."

Turov was physically rocked for an instant before he recovered his poise.

"Is this of some significance that we should be aware of?" Minoru asked. "Perhaps I can help."

"It's a name I used a very long time ago. But it has no meaning now."

"Except that Mr. McGarvey's sources of intelligence must be very good. Best that he be eliminated as soon as possible."

"Yes," Turov mumbled, but he was lost in thought about exactly how he would conduct his interrogation of McGarvey.

FIFTY-TWO

McGarvey rose from a sound sleep a few minutes after three in the morning, and went into the bathroom where he splashed some cold water on his face and rinsed out his mouth.

Back in the bedroom he dressed in dark slacks and a dark pullover and placed the Wilson in its holster at the small of his back. He pocketed the silencer, two spare magazines of ammunition, and sat phone, then pulled on his dark sports coat and opened the door a crack so that he could make sure the corridor was empty before he slipped out and headed to the elevators.

Before he'd gone to sleep he'd spent a half hour watching the real-time downloads of satellite images of Turov's compound from a KeyHole bird. But if they had been making any preparations for his arrival, which he was certain they had, they'd been discreet.

He got off on the mezzanine, took the stairs down to the main floor where he made his way past the gift shops to the lobby, and held up just short of the corner. No one was behind the front desk, nor did there seem to be any cleaning or maintenance people doing their work. Only one figure in a bellman's uniform was stationed near the front doors. Outside a lone cab was waiting.

McGarvey stepped back. It was a setup, of course. The bellman was there to report to Turov the moment McGarvey showed up and got into the cab. His people would be waiting, which was what McGarvey had expected.

He went back to the stairs and took them one floor down to the service area in the basement. At this level the hotel was already alive for the coming day, in fact areas such as the laundry never shut down. Everyone was busy here, so he had no difficulty reaching the loading dock area without trouble. It was the same everywhere, the man who moved smartly as if he had a purpose and he belonged usually never attracted more than a passing glance.

Three small delivery trucks were pulled up and deliverymen in white gloves, white coveralls, and bright yellow caps were busy unloading cartons of what were probably canned goods, along with fresh-cut flowers in long boxes, and three large aluminum cases covered in frost that were removed from the truck by a small forklift.

As inside, no one paid the slightest attention as McGarvey jumped down from the dock, made his way between the trucks, and up the ramp to the street level where he turned away and headed down the all but deserted street.

Under ordinary circumstances if he were stopped by a cop who wondered what a *gaijin* was doing wandering around the streets at this hour of the morning he might be questioned. But if that happened and the cop called in the incident, he would probably be told to forget it. No one in Tokyo wanted trouble from the former CIA director. If he wanted to go for an early-morning walk he was breaking no laws. In any event PSIA had taken an interest and that would be enough for any beat cop unless there was some serious trouble involving a Japanese citizen and/or a firearm.

The only vehicles on the streets at this hour were delivery vans, street cleaners, and garbage trucks, plus the occasional car or SUV. The nearest subway station was at Tawaramachi on the Ginza Line where McGarvey figured he would find cabs waiting for the early wave of workers coming into the city. Although he would stick out he didn't think he would be refused a ride.

He reached the station without trouble, where again he held up in the shadows across the street. A half-dozen tiny vans with green lights were parked at the cab stand in front, the drivers gathered outside for a smoke before the rush began. Nothing seemed out of the ordinary to him. If he had been spotted leaving the hotel he hadn't picked up any indication of a tail, nor did it appear as if Turov had sent someone here to wait for him.

The Russian had been in the business for a long time, and that he had survived for so many years meant that he was a careful man. He would have to know that McGarvey was coming sometime this morning, and he would have made preparations.

McGarvey stepped out into the light and crossed the street as a red double-decker bus rumbled past. One of the cabbies said something and they all looked up as McGarvey approached.

"Does anyone speak English?"

"No trains yet," one of the drivers replied.

"I need a cab," McGarvey said.

The cabbie said something to the other drivers, and

they all started to turn away, until McGarvey pulled out a hundred dollar bill.

"I want to go to Uneo."

"*Hai,* you have directions?"

"The Ueno station."

The driver shrugged and nodded toward the entry to the subway station behind him "Take the train."

"I want to go now."

The driver said something to the others, who laughed. But then he took McGarvey's money. "We go now," he said.

FIFTY-THREE

Turov was lying in his bed, fully awake, listening to the gentle sounds of water flowing over the rocks in his garden and thinking about his later days in the KGB after the breakup when he'd been recalled to Moscow to help reorganize the service, especially Department Viktor.

Nobody knew what was going to happen next. Germany had collapsed and like a row of dominoes the first piece tipped by Gorbachev's hand started the chain reaction. All of Eastern Europe collapsed, and no Soviet soldiers were sent. The Balkans became independent, and nothing happened. Finally the entire Soviet Union disintegrated, and except for Chechnya there was no fighting.

By then Bokyo, as he was known in those days, was a colonel, and was considered too dangerous a man to have around, especially if that fool Yeltsin actually instituted the rule of law, as he promised to do. The colonel had assassinated people by his own hand, and had arranged the murders of others. But worst of all he'd collected information from the deathbed confessions of his victims who had tried to bargain for their lives. Troubling information about high-ranking men in the Kremlin. Information that could not be allowed to reside in the possession of one man.

Two Department Viktor men, Nikolai Tsumayev and Yevgenni Lakomsky, both of whom Boyko had trained, were sent to his apartment under the guise of a friendly visit, but with orders to kill him. They brought vodka, good dark bread, and pickles, but Boyko wasn't home, so they went downstairs to wait for him. Tsumayev went to the back of the apartment building, while Lakomsky stayed out front.

By three in the morning when Boyko still hadn't shown up, Lakomsky went around back to have a smoke with his friend, but Tsumayev's throat had been cut. His body had been propped up in a sitting position against the wall, his severed penis stuffed into his mouth.

Boyko's message couldn't have been clearer.

Lakomsky brought the department Lada around back, stuffed his partner's body in the trunk, and drove away to report to his boss, General Igor Mokretskov, who had ordered the hit but with the warning that it had to look like Boyko had been killed by a burglar. The general had been stealing money from KGB funds for years. It was something that Boyko had learned nearly a year earlier.

Later that day when an aide came out to the dacha, three badly charred bodies were discovered. The Moscow city prosecutor's office quickly determined that Lakomsky and Tsumayev had tried to rob the general, who killed them both by slashing their throats, and then stuffed their penises into their mouths. When for some unknown reason the general tried to burn their bodies, the gas can he'd used to douse the corpses had caught fire, burning him to death.

But it had been a senseless crime, because the general had little or nothing except for his dacha in the country and an apartment in the city and the furnishings. He had almost nothing in his bank accounts and very little cash in either residence. He'd not been a rich man.

Boyko resigned his commission a month later and went into business for himself, using as his start-up money the five million U.S. he had convinced the general to transfer before he burned the man alive.

A dark figure came to the open shoji screen, and knocked lightly on the frame.

"Yes?" Turov asked, raising his modified Steyr GB 9mm pistol, the tiny laser sighting dot centered on the figure's chest.

"McGarvey has left the hotel," Minoru said. "He walked to Tawasamachi Station where he got a cab."

"Was there time to put someone in place to follow him?" Turov asked, lowering the pistol.

"No. But he must be on his way here."

Turov sat up. "I agree. Have Tanaka and Hatoyama assume their positions. If the opportunity arises to capture him alive and relatively undamaged, do it, otherwise allow him to come here and we shall deal with him inside the walls."

"Is that wise, Colonel?"

"You asked that once before," Turov said sharply, but without raising his voice. "Do not repeat yourself to me. Do you understand?"

"*Hai*," Minoru replied. "Where will you be?"

"Around," Turov replied.

Minoru nodded, and turned to leave, but Turov called after him.

"Hirobumi-san. You may inform the men that I will remain inside the perimeter."

"Yes, sir."

"You and I will leave for Australia when we have finished here."

"What about the staff?"

"Tell them nothing," Turov said.

When Minoru was gone, Turov went out onto the veranda where he smoked another cigarette. He would miss this place, its serenity, but he'd known for the past year that the time was coming when he would have to leave. It would not be for Australia, as he had told Minoru but somewhere with amenities, somewhere he could put his fortune to best advantage, somewhere he could continue to put his talents to good use.

Back inside he got dressed all in black. He fitted the pistol with a suppressor. Noise outside of the compound needed to be kept at a minimum, and he was willing to trade the slight loss of accuracy because of the silencer for it.

Before he went out he placed a phone call to Captain Hirashi Sekigawa, who was in charge of the Tokyo Metropolitan Police, Keishicho, Division of Uneo. He was a longtime friend of the special residents here, who saw to it that his meager salary was regularly supplemented.

"Sorry to telephone so early in the morning, Hirashi-san."

"It's of no concern," the cop replied. "How may I be of assistance?"

"I think that I may be the target of a burglar sometime this morning," Turov said. "It's tedious I know, because crimes of this nature hardly ever occur in Japan, and especially not here."

"I will immediately send a detail out to you."

"No, please don't disturb your men. Now that we've been alerted we'll handle it here ourselves. I merely wanted to inform you that there might be a slight disturbance here, but it will be nothing you need concern yourself with."

"I understand," the cop said. "Thank you for the call."

"A messenger will arrive at your home within twenty-four hours."

"You're most kind."

"Not at all," Turov said. He broke the connection, then left his bedroom, slipped out the rear entrance of the compound, and disappeared into the night.

FIFTY—FOUR

The Ueno train station, its front façade brilliantly lit, was quiet at this hour, but by six this would be a madhouse of workers streaming in from the country. Across the street the soaring Tokyo Metropolitan Festival Hall was also lit up, and above, rising into the hills, were the Keneiji Temple Pagoda, the Toshogu Shrine, and Turov's compound.

"No trains for two hours now," the cabbie said, pulling up.

"Thanks for the lift," McGarvey said, getting out. "Maybe you want to stay here, I might need a ride back."

The driver said something in Japanese that didn't sound complimentary, powered the rear door shut, and took off.

When the cab had disappeared around the corner, McGarvey walked across the street, his hands in his pockets. He went around the west side of the Festival Hall and headed along narrow tree-shaded streets in the general direction of the pagoda and shrine, coming a few minutes later to one end of the Koenguchi Park with its long esplanade and reflecting pool.

This entire area was a district of museums and parks that could have come directly out of central casting for a Japanese travelogue; footpaths that meandered through stands of cherry trees, arched wooden bridges crossing ponds and narrow streams, traditional old buildings mixed with the modern built after the war, and broad avenues surrounding warrens of narrow streets that hadn't changed much in a century.

Otto's directions placed Turov's compound on a long street that ran roughly parallel to the slope of the hill just below the zoo but above the pagoda and shrine and connected with the main road back down to the train station. If they were expecting him tonight, they would be waiting somewhere below the compound in the trees that ran along the street, thinking that it would be natural for him to come up the hill from the station.

Instead he headed across the connecting street toward the Metropolitan Art Museum until he came to a spot where a path went into the zoo well away from the main entrance and just above the upper end of Turov's street. He would be coming at them from an unexpected direction courtesy of the real-time satellite images Otto had sent over.

It took nearly ten minutes for him to make his way beneath the monorail, to the front entrance where he headed down the street moving from one shadow to the next. The lower side of the street was tree-lined park and museum land, while the large houses on the length of the upper side were all hidden behind a tall, ugly unpainted concrete block wall, broken here and there only by thick wooden gates.

McGarvey pulled up at a spot about thirty meters from the gate to Turov's compound when he spotted a movement in the trees farther down the road. A man stepped out of the woods for just a moment then stepped back. It was a setup.

He reached for his pistol at the small of his back when someone stepped up from the trees behind him.

"If you pull out your gun we will be forced to kill you, Mr. McGarvey," a man said. His English was heavily accented but good.

McGarvey withdrew his hand and turned around. Two men had come out of the woods where they had been waiting for him to come down from the zoo. One of them held a silenced pistol, the other an aluminum baseball bat. Both of them were Japanese and looked streetwise and hard.

He'd probably been spotted leaving the hotel, and it was possible that someone had watched him come up from the train station.

They hadn't shot first and asked questions later, which told him that Turov wanted to talk. The Russian had to be nervous that someone was coming at him. It was something McGarvey had counted on. But this was their territory and Turov had years to perfect his defenses. All Mac wanted was this sort of a response. Only he was going to play the next part by his rules, not by the Russian's.

"I'm not surprised he sent a couple of street hoods like you to do his dirty work," McGarvey said easily. "I suppose he's hiding inside like the coward he is until you soften me up."

"The colonel said not to kill you if possible, just to wait for you to show up and then bring you in," the one with the bat said. "He didn't care if we had to carry you."

McGarvey shrugged. "That's if you can actually hit me with your little toy. But if you try, I just might stick it up your ass."

The man said something in Japanese and he suddenly brought the bat up. He started to swing as he stepped forward, but McGarvey moved out of the way at the last instant. He grabbed the man's arm just above the elbow and propelled him sprawling on his face.

The second man had raised his pistol but McGarvey was too close, and he easily batted the muzzle away with one hand, while pulling his own weapon with the other and firing one silenced round into the man's knee.

As the guard grunted in pain and collapsed to the ground McGarvey reached down, yanked the pistol from his hand and turned as the first guard was scrambling to his feet, the aluminum bat still in his hand.

"Let's not try that again," McGarvey said. "If I have to kill you, who'll help your partner back to the house? I just came here to talk to your boss, nothing more."

The guard dropped the bat. "I don't think you're going to like what the colonel has to say to you. He's waiting across the street."

"Right," McGarvey said. He holstered his own gun, ejected the magazine from the guard's weapon, which was a lightweight Austrian-made 9 mm Glock 17 pistol, thumbed the seventeen rounds onto the ground, dropped the magazine, and quickly fieldstripped the gun, letting the parts lay where they fell.

Both men watched him warily, neither making a move against him.

"I'm going to walk back down to the train station now, where I'm sure there'll be a snack bar or café, someplace to get a cup of coffee or tea," McGarvey said. "Ask the colonel to join me. Just him, no one else. We'll talk."

"You'll never get away from here alive," the man with the shattered kneecap said.

McGarvey suddenly pulled out his pistol, and jammed the muzzle into the man's forehead. "Maybe I'll just kill you both and let your boss man figure it out on his own."

"Go."

McGarvey nodded down the block. "If you try to follow me make sure you kill me, because if you don't I'll make it my mission to put a bullet in your brain. *Wakari-masuka?*" Do you understand?

"*Hai,*" the man on the ground said.

He looked at the other man, who nodded tightly after a moment.

"Sensible," McGarvey said, and he walked back up the

hill toward the entrance to the zoo, ready for Turov's man to take up the chase. But it never happened, and ten minutes later he was heading down to the station.

FIFTY-FIVE

McGarvey picked an all-night tearoom on the train station's upper level from where he had a good bird's-eye view of the nearly deserted main arrivals hall and the front doors. He'd bought the early edition of *The Japan Times*, Tokyo's main English-language newspaper, and brought it and a pot of green tea to a table near the railing.

Except for an old man standing at a tall table, and the counterman, he was the only person in the shop. When neither of them was looking, McGarvey laid his pistol on the table and covered it with the newspaper

Turov, wearing jeans and an open-collar white shirt, came into the station, glanced up to where McGarvey was seated and then headed directly across to the escalators, which hadn't been switched on yet. He made his way up to the second level, moving easily as if he were a man without a care in the world.

He hesitated for just a moment at the broad entrance to the tearoom, taking in the old man and the employee behind the counter, then came directly across to McGarvey and sat down.

"Glad you could join me," McGarvey said. This close he could see the irritation in Turov's eyes. "Though my reception earlier wasn't friendly."

The Russian shrugged. "You pushed and I pushed back. No harm."

"Your man with the shattered kneecap might not agree."

"He's expendable."

"We all are," McGarvey said.

Turov nodded. "What are you doing here, Mr. McGarvey? What am I to you?"

"I had your shooter cornered in Seoul, until you interfered," McGarvey said. "But the NIS officer you shot will recover and I'll find your shooter and a direct link back to you."

"I suppose it would do no good to say that I haven't been to Seoul, or anywhere in Korea for that matter, in years. But here you are, looking for something. What answers do you think I have for you?"

"We know your Department Viktor background, and we have some pretty good evidence that you've become an expediter, a middleman for assassinations. What we don't understand are the last three hits you arranged, including General Ho up in Pyongyang, unless you thought that you could start a war out here."

"It would seem that the situation is heading in that direction," Turov said. "I too read the newspapers, but it doesn't mean I had anything to do with the general's assassination. As for the other two I'm not sure who you mean, though I can guess."

"It's not you who wants a war, of course," McGarvey said. "I suspect that you're indifferent to what's about to happen, so long as you can get yourself far enough away until the shooting stops. What we're interested in is who hired you and why?"

"Even if I had been involved you'd be correct in believing that I wouldn't care. The motives of my paymasters would mean nothing to me."

Turov started to reach in his pocket, but McGarvey moved the paper aside for a moment, revealing the pistol.

Turov smiled. "Are you going to shoot me simply because I attempted to take a handkerchief out of my pocket?"

"Russians don't use handkerchiefs. Keep your hands on the table."

Again a look of irritation crossed Turov's eyes. "As you wish," he said. He glanced down at the arrivals hall. "It will get quite busy here in a couple of hours. Do you mean to hold me until then? Is someone else coming?"

"Only until I find out who hired you."

"If you do shoot here in public you'll never leave Japan alive, you do understand that, don't you, Mr. McGarvey? Doesn't matter that you once ran the CIA, I'm sure that the PSIA isn't overjoyed you came here. And even if you told them that you believed I was a killer, they wouldn't do anything without proof. I have friends here, and at this moment Japan blames the current trouble on your government."

McGarvey held his silence.

"It's all about money," Turov said to fill the silence. "Without proof you can't fight its power."

"Witnesses?"

Turov shrugged. "What will she tell you?" he asked. "Assuming you find her. I'm told that the NIS has stopped looking. Curious, don't you think? In any event the South Koreans certainly would not wish to take the blame for General Ho's assassination."

"I know where her husband is," McGarvey said, letting his voice drop as if he were sharing a secret with a conspirator. "He probably knows more than his wife."

"No one believes him. Certainly the North Koreans don't, even if he's still alive."

"We'll see," McGarvey said. "In the meantime you've given me all the proof I need that you set up the assassinations."

"Won't do you any good," Turov replied indifferently.

"Nor you if I put a bullet in your head."

"I know what you've done and what you're capable of, and even if everything I'd heard is true it doesn't matter,"

Turov said. He got to his feet. "Now that I've met you I realize that you're simply not worth the effort to kill unless you persist."

"I'll find the proof and I'll be back," McGarvey said.

"Go home or die here in Japan," Turov warned. He turned and left the tearoom.

McGarvey watched the Russian go down the escalator, cross the arrivals hall, and walk out the front doors, never looking back. He'd found one of the answers he'd come looking for. Turov was their man, there was no doubt about it. But that left the who and especially the why. The business of starting wars usually fell to governments. The issues usually were too sweeping to interest an individual. Power, territory, national self-defense, uprisings, the overthrow of a dictator or rotten regime.

In this instance North Korea had no reason to pick a fight with China, no matter how insane Kim Jong Il was. It was a war that they couldn't possibly win. Even if they successfully launched all of their nuclear weapons into China, it would not be a decisive blow.

South Korea had no reason to start such a war, which without a doubt would spread to Seoul. In any event Kim Jong Il had intimated that he was willing to open another round of peace talks, which would include the nuclear issue.

Nor was Japan interested, because Kim Jong Il had made it plain in public statements that one of his targets would be Tokyo. No one believed it was anything but rhetoric. But the Japanese weren't about to test it.

Which left the why. What country stood to gain the most?

He pulled out his sat phone and speed dialed Colonel Pak's number in North Korea.

PYONGYANG

FIFTY-SIX

A few minutes before midnight McGarvey was waiting on the commercial pier at Nagato, a small town on the north coast of the west end of the main island of Honshu. The night was pitch-black under an overcast sky, with a light fog creating halos around the few lights. Nothing moved along the water's edge.

Somewhere out in the bay that connected with the Korea Strait what sounded like a highly muffled outboard motor was incoming. It was impossible to tell how close it was or the exact direction from which it was coming, but Colonel Pak had instructed McGarvey to be on this dock at this hour.

"We don't have much time," McGarvey had argued. "Can't you arrange to fly me over?"

"Under ordinary circumstances it would take weeks or even months to arrange," Pak had told him. "Right now it would be impossible."

A twenty-foot center console runabout appeared out of the mist, one man at the helm and another figure standing up in the back. As they reached the end of the pier the second figure waved, and McGarvey saw that it was Pak.

The helmsman nudged the engine in reverse for just a second or two and the boat came to a nice stop against the dock. McGarvey tossed his bag down to Pak and then jumped aboard.

"Were you followed?" the North Korean asked.

"If you mean by the PSIA, no," McGarvey said.

Pak pushed them away from the dock and the slightly built helmsman in the uniform of a North Korean merchant seaman gunned the engine as he swung the wheel and they headed smartly back out into the bay.

"We're crossing to Wonsan on one of our hydrofoils that makes a twice-a-week run to Nagasaki mostly for medicines and other supplies," Pak said. "We got lucky with the timing."

"I wasn't aware that Japan was still doing this for you."

Pak nodded tightly. "Even now. In exchange our navy has stopped its incursions into Japanese waters." He looked McGarvey in the eye. "We would have stopped anyway. We can't afford the fuel."

"Kill your Dear Leader."

"It's been tried," Pak said. "Is that why you want to come to Pyongyang? You still don't believe me? Or have you learned something?"

"I want to talk to Huk Soon, if you haven't fried his brains yet."

"He's alive and in one piece, and you will be allowed to interview him, but he won't tell you anything that wasn't in the material I gave to you. And afterward you will have to leave."

"Then we're wasting our time," McGarvey said. "You might as well take me back to the dock. I can reach Tokyo by this afternoon and Washington in the morning."

"You're not going to walk away from this, Mr. McGarvey. I know at least that much about you. Considering what's at stake you're in for the duration."

"Not if you restrict my movements."

"Yes, we know how you operate," Pak said. "If we allow you to run around Pyongyang shooting at people it will only make things worse."

"That's already happened, Colonel," McGarvey replied sharply. "It's why you came to me in the first place."

Pak was clearly uncomfortable. "My hands are tied."

"Bullshit. You not only made it to the States, but you managed to reach my house without trouble. Your hands are anything but tied."

A large double-decked ferryboat appeared out of the fog, sitting low in the water, its foils submerged now that it was at a standstill. Pak said something to their helmsman who immediately slowed down and circled around to the port side of the ship.

"China gave us two of these last year," Pak told McGarvey. "They'd been used in Hong Kong and Macau. Eighty-five kilometers per hour. They were made in your country by Boeing. We'll reach Wonsan a little after noon."

"And then?"

"And then what?"

"We know who assassinated General Ho, but if you want to know how they did it, who hired them, and why, so that you can prove to Beijing that you're not lying, I'll need a free hand."

"I'm afraid to ask exactly what you mean."

"I'll need to keep my pistol and my sat phone and I'll need free access for Huk Soon and myself anywhere in the city."

Pak said something under his breath that McGarvey didn't catch.

"I think you've been given a carte blanche to do whatever it takes to prove your people didn't assassinate the general and to do it fast," McGarvey said.

They'd reached the ladder that had been lowered for them. The gate in the rail above had been opened but no one was there. Davits to lift the runabout back aboard dangled from the stern and their helmsman waited patiently for his two passengers to get off.

"I think you don't believe me," Pak said. "You think we may have done it, and now this is an elaborate setup to convince you of our innocence. If we can do that you could go to Beijing and make a case that they'd accept."

"The thought had occurred to me," McGarvey said. "You want to go to Pyongyang to prove that I'm telling the truth."

"Or lying."

Pak nodded. "Okay, Mr. McGarvey, we'll do it your way. Only understand that you'll never leave Pyongyang alive if I am lying to you and you manage to prove it."

"Fair enough," McGarvey said.

He followed Pak up the boarding ladder to the lower deck and inside through a hatch. What had once been filled with passenger seats was now an open cargo area that was filled mostly deck to overhead with cardboard cartons. Some were marked with the symbol of the International Red Cross while others bore the markings of the French organization MSF Médecins Sans Frontières—Doctors Without Borders.

"You see, at least this part is the truth," Pak said. "There is a place forward where we can have something to eat and get some rest. It'll take eight hours to get to our dock."

FIFTY-SEVEN

The night was anything but silent, even here at a remote section of the DMZ well east of the hustle and bustle of Kaesong and Panmunjon. Huk Kim, dressed in black camos, had lain in the tall grass one hundred meters out from the barren no-man's-zone that marked the north-south border since just after nightfall, watching for the change of guard at midnight, and the patrol routine on both sides of the tall razor-wire-topped fence.

Even this far out the squawk of the communications radios in the guard towers, the hardy growl of the Humvees on this side and the Gaziks on the other, and the occasional voice could have guided a blind man. The harsh lights atop the towers lit the one-hundred-meter barren strip of land between the fences that stretched from coast to coast across the peninsula.

It was less than one hundred kilometers as the crow flies from downtown Seoul to the town of Chorwon on the DMZ, and it had taken Kim less than two hours to get here, but it seemed as if she had stepped into another time and place, another world so barren and yet so filled with danger all she wanted to do was turn around right now and go home.

Soon would be waiting for her at the apartment, demanding to know where she'd gone and why. "What could you have been thinking, you little fool," he would ask, a puzzled smile on his face. "The tunnel was for getting out, not in. We were going to use it if we got into trouble that night."

But they *were* in trouble, and the only way she knew to reach him was through this tunnel, one of more than a hundred that crossed under the DMZ, and one of only a sparse handful that were supposedly unknown by the North, and all but forgotten and abandoned by the South because the risk of cave-ins and flooding was considered to be too great.

"Try to put a hundred men with their equipment through there, or worse yet a couple of mechanized vehicles and the roof will come down, no doubt about it," Soon had told her two days before they'd flown to Pyongyang via Beijing. "But just two people, moving carefully, making no sounds, could get through okay if they had to. But only if they had to," he'd warned.

An armored personnel carrier rumbled up the dirt road from the direction of the American–South Korean compound and stopped at the observation post. Two soldiers got out and climbed to the top of the tower, while four others entered the fortified bunker on a small rise just before the no-man's-zone.

Moments later two men climbed down from the tower and the four who had been replaced came out of the bunker. All of them got into the APC, which headed to the next observation post three hundred meters to the east.

It would take the new team several minutes to get settled down for the midnight to 0400 shift, during which time they would be focused outward, toward the North and not checking their rear, which was SOP in case North Korean infiltrators made it through the DMZ.

Keeping low, Kim grabbed her nylon kit bag and backed slowly to a narrow cut in the hill that during heavy rains and the spring snow melt was a raging stream that flowed down to a wider creek with high mud banks. At the bottom she was hidden from view by anyone watching from one of the observation towers on the DMZ, and from the main road that led back to Chorwon a few kilometers to the southwest.

Shouldering the bag, she hurried along the creek to a stunted tree growing almost straight out of the bank that here was about three meters above the surface of the slowly flowing water.

She scrambled down to the creek, and making absolutely certain that she was alone, shoved the tree up and to the right, taking half the riverbank with it, and revealing a pitch-black hole large enough to accommodate a jeep. Soldiers and vehicles could gain access by coming up the shallow creek, except during the floods.

Kim did not consider herself overly claustrophobic, but she didn't like the dark, and she especially didn't like the sounds of running water coming out of the hole.

She took a red flashlight out of a pocket, and shined it through the opening. A sloping gravel-lined ramp led straight back into the hill at a fairly steep angle, but she couldn't make out a thing beyond a few meters.

A dog barked somewhere in the distance, and girding herself, Kim stepped into the tunnel, pulling the tree that had been fitted with some sort of a swivel base back into place. Suddenly the only noises were those of the running water and of her ragged breath. There was a very strong possibility that she would die down here before she made it under the DMZ and the two kilometers to the exit.

She took a deep breath, let it out slowly, and started down the slope. There was even more than a strong possibility that Soon would be executed for his part in the assassination. This was a risk she had to take if she had any chance of saving him.

Ten meters in she came to the slowly moving water that looked like swirling black oil in the red beam of her flashlight. Evidently the creek had found a fault line and had eroded the bank to partially flood the tunnel. But there was no way of knowing how deep the water was, or even if the passage was clear all the way to the other side.

She shined the light on the rock ceiling two and a half meters overhead. She wasn't an engineer but it looked sound to her, although some water was dripping down in places. Every couple of meters it was shored up by heavy wooden beams that also looked solid.

Soon said the tunnel had been abandoned and all but forgotten by both sides because it was far too dangerous.

"Soon," she said softly, and simply speaking his name out loud gave her strength. "Please help me."

She stepped into the water and slowly headed farther down the tunnel. The gravel underfoot was slippery and twice she nearly fell, but after fifteen or twenty meters the flow never got any deeper than her waist, and shortly after that the level began to recede until it was only up to her ankles.

The tunnel had been built wide enough to accommodate a jeep and a column of soldiers, that along with
the other tunnels crossing under the DMZ could in the
time of war allow a sizeable number of men to the other
side. But it was a two-way street, and had been from the
start. In time of war the North could just as easily invade
the South. And either side could set up explosives that
would bring tons of rocks crashing down on the heads of
the invading forces.

With that thought in mind, Kim slowed her pace, re-
signing herself to not reach the open air possibly until
morning. But it was a thing that had to be done for her
husband.

"Soon," she whispered his name aloud.

FIFTY-EIGHT

It was first light of a hazy morning when the supply boat
reached Wonsan, threading its way through a series of
islands inside the broad bay. This was North Korea's
major seaport and standing out on deck with Pak, Mc-
Garvey counted a half-dozen cargo ships in a harbor that
could have easily accommodated five times as many.

"Is it usually this busy?" McGarvey asked.

Pak gave him a sharp glance. "No use taking shots at
me because I can't defend what has become of my country."

"How do your people feel about what's happening in
the South?"

"Most of them don't know, or believe whatever they've
heard is propaganda. Anyway it doesn't pay to openly
criticize."

"Relatives from the South were allowed to visit at one time. They must have brought stories with them."

"Yeah," Pak said, a bitter note in his voice. "Why do you think the border was closed?"

McGarvey leaned against the rail as they came up the harbor past the cargo ships to the military docks, where several small patrol craft were berthed. Farther up the inlet several low-slung concrete buildings, steel doors covering the seaside openings, were heavily guarded. McGarvey picked out at least four gun emplacements.

"Submarines?" he asked.

Pak smiled. "We don't have strategic submarines. Anyway I suggest that you don't mention what you've seen here until you get home."

"Our satellites have enough pictures."

Four navy ratings helped with the dock lines, but neither they nor the crewmen who shoved out the boarding ramp said a thing as Pak and McGarvey got off the boat. Officially no passengers had been aboard, especially not an American.

"One of our Special Operations Brigades is based here, but I'm sure you know all about that too," Pak said. "They're tough boys and they don't take very well to activities in their backyard that they know nothing about. So we're getting out of here immediately."

An old Lada sedan trundled through a security gate at the end of the dock and headed their way.

"Our ride?" McGarvey said.

Pak nodded. "My sergeant, Ri Gyong. He's a fine man, but he's like a lot of cops, he looks only straight ahead."

"Will he be a problem?"

"Not unless you pull out your pistol and discharge it. In that case you wouldn't want to be anywhere near him. He's a good man."

"He's bought the party line, but you haven't. Interesting mix."

Pak gave McGarvey another sharp look. "He's a realist. And as far as he and the rest of my staff are concerned you were never here, and the sooner we can take you back to Japan the happier everyone will be."

"Fair enough, as long as you understand that my whereabouts are known to a few key people."

Pak shrugged. "Your disappearance inside Chosun would present us with no greater a problem than we're already facing. But you're here to help us."

"I'm here to find out who killed General Ho and why," McGarvey corrected. "Don't forget it."

The car pulled up and Ri got out. He looked McGarvey up and down but didn't offer to shake hands. "So this is him." His English was heavily accented but understandable.

"He's here at great risk to help us," Pak said.

"How's your prisoner? Still alive and in one piece?" McGarvey asked.

"I don't like arrogant American bastards coming here to tell us our business," Ri shot back angrily.

"I don't blame you, I wouldn't like it either. But I'm here because I was asked to help. And the sooner I find out what I came to find out, I'll be out of your hair."

After a moment or two Ri nodded. "We're treating him better than he deserves."

"Then let's get it over with," McGarvey said. He tossed his bag in the backseat and got in as Ri got behind the wheel and Pak rode shotgun.

They were waved through the open security gate, which closed behind them, and headed through the city of 300,000 that despite the apparent lack of activity on the docks was bustling. Although there wasn't much traffic on the roads the broad sidewalks were busy as were the many parks they passed. Banners seemed to be hung from every available light post and government building, and no public park was without a statue of Kim Jong Il or his father Kim Il Sung. Unlike cities in the West, there was no litter along the roadways, nor did there seem to be any grafitti, such things were not allowed in North Korea.

On the way out of the city toward the mountains in the distance they passed a collection of buildings and quads that looked like the campus of a university, young people uniformly dressed in gray trousers and white shirts hurrying between classes.

"Do they teach anything about the West?" McGarvey asked.

"Oh, yes, history is a major subject," Pak said, and he managed a slight smile. "But it would be nothing you would understand."

"Is that why you went to school in the U.S.?"

"To know our enemies is to understand how to defeat them."

"Spare me," McGarvey said.

"How well do your countrymen know us, Mr. McGarvey?" Pak asked. "When I was in California everyone took me for a Japanese. They didn't know the difference. And that included the professors."

"Were you treated badly?"

Pak looked away momentarily, and he shook his head. "No. In fact parts of it were good, even though it was always noisy. I never got used to that." He turned back. "Obviously America is not going to shrivel up and blow away with the wind, as Dear Leader wishes, but if we are pushed he will use our nuclear weapons."

Ri said something in Korean, but Pak waved him off.

"It's a war that we could not possibly hope to win. But no one in the region would win. Not China, not South Korea, not Japan. Perhaps not even Formosa."

"Millions of people would die," McGarvey said. "It's the only reason I agreed to come here."

"What madman would benefit from such a thing?" Pak asked inwardly, but then he focused on McGarvey again. "It's not Dear Leader."

"Are you sure?"

"Yes," Pak said. "I've bet my life on it."

"And mine," McGarvey replied.

FIFTY-NINE

The sun had just topped the eastern horizon when Kim got off the narrow blacktopped road, scrambled into the drainage ditch that ran beside it, and flopped down in the tall grass. She was filthy dirty from the nightmarish trip through the tunnel beneath the DMZ, hungry, and now that she was back in the North frightened nearly out of her wits.

For a time back there, when she knew that she could not take another step in the absolute darkness, she'd reached out and touched the sleeve of Soon's night fighter camos. And they had started their conversation.

"If you must do this, darling, I'll guide you," he'd told her. "But you have to know how foolish you are. You made it back to Seoul without being caught, and you even managed to elude Alexandar and Kirk McGarvey, the CIA officer he warned you about. Why take this chance now?"

"It's the only way I can save you," she'd replied, not able to see a thing but comforted by his feel and his scent. At one point she'd almost switched on her flashlight so that she could see him, but had decided against it in case they were closer to the tunnel's end than she figured, and someone outside might catch the flash.

She'd slipped and fallen to her knees in the ice-cold water and slime covering the tunnel floor, and for a moment she'd known she didn't have the strength to get up and continue. But Soon's hand was in hers and he'd drawn her to her feet.

"If you're going to do this foolish thing, you need to be careful," he'd warned her. "Once we're outside I won't be with you."

"I don't know if I can do it," she'd cried, her head in a muddle.

"Go back home, then, sweetheart. You can't do a thing for me in Pyongyang."

She'd tried to see his face through the pitch-black, but it had been impossible. "But I can do it. I have a plan."

"What are you talking about?"

"I'm going to offer them a trade."

Soon was angry, she'd heard it in his voice. "What, trade you for me? Never."

"No, not that, darling. I'll trade both of us for someone else. For the man responsible for the hit."

"Alexandar?" Soon had demanded. "They'll never believe you. Besides, we have no proof."

"Someone else," she'd said. "And they'll believe me even without written proof." And she'd patiently explained to her husband how she'd come up with the idea and the facts she would present to shore up her claim. In the end he was impressed, as she'd known he would be.

"It just might work," he'd said. "But first you have to get out of this tunnel and away from the DMZ before daylight. At that point this is what you'll have to do next."

Lying in the grass beside the road, looking back the way she'd come, Kim felt an overwhelming sense of weariness. Yet she was grateful that Soon had been there for her, because she was certain that she would never have made it this far without him.

Nor would she have thought to do what he had told her, but then he'd always been smarter than her, with more experience and a practical head on his shoulders. It was one of the many reasons she loved him.

From here the DMZ's fences and towers were lost in the hills in the distance, at least five kilometers away. Nothing moved in either direction on the highway, nor did she see any farmers in the small rocky fields that had been hacked out of the scrub brush and forests. But the morning was pleasantly warm, especially after the long night in the cave.

She took the K-bar knife out of her pack, peeled away a grass plug one meter wide in the side of the ditch then dug a hole that deep. She dropped the knife into the hole along with her Walther PPK and spare magazine. She took off her boots, dropped them into the hole, and then peeled off her sodden camos and used them to clean herself as best as she could. She dressed in slate-gray cotton pants, a tunic blouse, white socks, and flip-flops. Everything else she'd brought across, except for her South Korean ID, a credit card, and some money, went into the hole along with the nylon bag. She shoveled the dirt over the top of the things, tossing the rest of it that wouldn't fit into the tall grass, and finally replaced the plug.

She wiped her hands with tufts of grass then stepped up onto the highway to make sure she'd done it the way Soon had suggested. If a North Korean army patrol caught her armed and dressed in the dark camos they would probably shoot first and ask questions later. Dressed the way she was now she might make it far enough away from the border to be picked up by the cops to whom she'd tell her story.

No one riding in a car or on a bicycle, or even passing this spot on foot would notice that anything had been disturbed here.

With a last glance over her shoulder to make sure nothing was coming from the direction of the DMZ, Kim headed north toward the town of Ich'on twenty-five kilometers away. As tough as the tunnel had been, it was the easy part. But now that she had come this far she couldn't turn around.

"Soon." Her husband's name formed on her lips.

SIXTY

The divided highway to Pyongyang was in good repair, neatly trimmed hedges along the median, but no road signs and very little traffic—mostly military vehicles or farm trucks and only the occasional car, plus a few bicycles. It was well before noon by the time they reached the city center and dropped Ri off at the Security Agency's headquarters.

"Is this where you're keeping Huk Soon?" McGarvey asked Pak.

"Yes. And you will be allowed to interview him as soon as he's made ready."

"I want to talk to him now."

"You will within the hour," Pak said, taking the wheel and heading away. "He's one of the assassins, we know that for a fact, because he confessed to us, which makes him enemy number one. We took certain measures when we questioned him, not unlike those your people use at Guantanamo Bay, and for just about the same reasons. Ri will get him cleaned up for you and give him something to clear his mind."

It was an argument that McGarvey couldn't counter. He'd been to Guantanamo and had even helped with the interrogations of several al-Quaeda combatants. "We don't have much time," he said.

"I know," Pak said. "I'm taking you to your hotel and afterward I'll bring you to see the assassin."

Pyongyang, a city of nearly three million people, was like just about every major capital city in the world with broad avenues, granite government buildings, parks, statues, and monuments. But it was too clean, no litter, no graffiti, no trash anywhere, and there were no traffic jams, nor were the sidewalks jammed, the entire place seemed weirdly quiet.

"I may not be staying overnight," McGarvey said. "It depends on what Soon tells me."

"You don't have a choice. The earliest you could leave is tomorrow. There's simply no other way out."

The Pyongyang Koryo Hotel was a twin tower modern edifice in the heart of downtown where the international nuclear inspectors had stayed, and where foreign businessmen were put up. A revolving restaurant was on top of each tower, and by North Korea's Spartan standards this place was the ultimate in luxury.

The usually busy parking lot out front was nearly empty, as was the orange bronze and glass soaring lobby. None of the bellmen or front desk staff were smiling, and when Pak walked directly to the bank of elevators with his foreign guest everyone suddenly got very busy.

"Normally you would have been assigned two escorts," Pak said on the way up. "But all you'll get is me."

"I'm not surprised the hotel is practically empty. Pyongyang is not a safe place to be right now."

"No."

"What about Mrs. Pak? Did you send her into the country?"

Pak gave McGarvey a bleak look. "There is no Mrs. Pak—neither my mother nor my wife. I might have a

couple of cousins in the South, but no one else. I'm surprised you didn't do your homework."

"I didn't think that part was important," McGarvey
said. "Have you ever thought about going south?"

Pak glanced up at the ceiling and then at McGarvey.
The elevator was bugged. "No," the North Korean intelligence officer said. "My time in California cured me of
any dreams like that. I enjoy stability, orderliness."

"I'm sure you do," McGarvey said.

His room on the fourteenth floor was pleasant enough
with a queen-sized bed and a small television set atop a
dresser. One chair sat behind a desk, which held a telephone that only connected with the front desk through
which any outside calls had to be placed. Internet service
was banned to all but a few high government officials, so
there was no computer connection. Tall windows looked
out across the city toward the Taedong River.

McGarvey tossed his bag on the bed, and started to
check the table lamps for bugs, but Pak stopped him.

"That's not necessary in this room for the moment. Ri
had it cleaned this morning."

"A good man to have at your side."

"Yes, he is," Pak agreed.

McGarvey took his pistol out of his bag, checked the
magazine and the action, and holstered it beneath his
jacket at the small of his back.

"Nice pistol," Pak said. "But when did you switch from
a Walther PPK to a Wilson?"

McGarvey had to smile. "A while back. Evidently
you've done your homework."

"Some."

McGarvey took out his sat phone and when he had a
signal speed dialed Rencke's number in Washington. The
Special Projects Director answered on the first ring.

"You're in."

"Yeah," McGarvey said. "What's the situation on the ground?"

"It's getting bad, kemo sabe. Everybody's screaming bloody murder for us to do something. And everyone on the hill is blaming the White House, but Haynes is dragging his feet for some reason. It's almost as if he wants China to take out Pyongyang. Preemptively. And that's just nuts, ya know."

"What's Adkins doing?"

"He says he's collating," Rencke said, and McGarvey could hear the strain in his friend's voice. "Spends most of the day and night in the Watch. But listen, Mac, something else is going on. I don't know what it is, but one of my secondary search engines is going ballistic on me."

"What are you coming up with?"

"You know that polonium 210 op you worked on in Mexico? Well, the Bureau's still searching for the shit because we know damned well that thirty or forty kilos of it got across our border, but nobody's having any luck."

"What's that got to do with this situation?" McGarvey demanded.

"I don't know, Mac. Honest injun, I don't. But one of my programs says there may be a connection. And it's the deepest lavender I've ever seen."

McGarvey had been facing Pak, but he turned away and walked to the window, his thoughts racing over the facts of an incident he'd handled just a few months ago involving a Chinese intelligence general carrying out a rogue operation from his embassy in Mexico City. The general had been desperate for money to maintain a lavish lifestyle he'd become accustomed to, and he'd worked a deal, possibly with Iranian intelligence, to smuggle polonium 210 into Mexico and then get it across the border into the U.S.

Some traces of radiation had been discovered in a motel in El Paso and a truck stop outside of Tucson, but the trail had gone cold. In any event after Mexico City the problem had been turned over to Homeland Security and the FBI, and McGarvey had gone home.

The underlying problem that had not been solved was the source of the money, though almost certainly it had come from the Middle East, probably Iran and possibly even Saudi Arabia.

"Is it the money trail?" McGarvey asked.

"That's what I'm thinking, but so far everything I'm coming up with points toward Prague. But I'm still working the problem."

"Let me know as soon as you can," McGarvey said. "I'm getting the same feeling that all along we've been missing something."

SIXTY-ONE

It was nearly noon by the time the police car came down the highway from Ich'on, and made a U-turn directly in front of Kim and stopped. Both cops got out and walked back to her.

"Where are you going?" one of them asked. Both men were short and slightly built, their uniforms hanging on their frames.

"To Pyongyang."

"On foot?"

"No," Kim said, taking her identification card out of her pocket and handing it over. "Whoever you telephone after you arrest and question me will come out to fetch me." Her heart was beating rapidly and her mouth was dry. For this to work these country cops had to be willing to stick their necks out a little, something that wasn't often done up here in the North.

The cop who'd taken her card glanced down at it and his eyes suddenly went wide and he fumbled for his pistol on his hip. "You're a spy!" he shouted.

"No," Kim said, trying to keep her voice calm. She raised her hands over her head. She'd didn't want to get shot to death by some fool cop after coming this far.

"You're from the South," the other cop accused her. Both of them had their pistols out now and pointed at her.

"I've come across with some information that your Safety and Security Agency in Pyongyang is going to be real interested in. But they'll be needing it right away."

"How did you get across the border?" the first cop asked.

"I found a tunnel," Kim said. "Listen to me, this is about General Ho's assassination last week and the trouble with China."

The cops were looking at her like she was from Mars. "Search her for weapons," the one who's been driving ordered.

The second cop holstered his weapon, but did not secure the flap before he came over and frisked her, his hands lingering on her breasts, and on her crotch. He was a moron, and Kim thought how simple it would be to grab his pistol and using his body as a shield kill the other cop and then him. But she endured the search without saying or doing a thing.

"Nothing," the cop said.

Kim took the small amount of money she'd brought over out of her pocket. "You forgot this," she said, holding it out.

The cop who'd frisked her snatched it out of her hand.

"Now, I've come a long way and I'm tired and hungry."

The cop still holding the pistol on her glanced again at the ID card. "How do I know this isn't a forgery?"

Kim couldn't believe what was happening. "Why the hell would I fake a South Korean national identity card and give it to the first North Korean cop I saw?"

"So that we'd take you to jail and feed you."

"Listen to my accent, you idiots. Do I sound like I'm from here?"

"We'll keep her money," the second cop suggested.

"And this fake identity card," the other one said.

It was like being in a comedy and if she hadn't been so frightened she would have laughed at them. Suddenly she spat on the pavement in front of them. "Fuck Dear Leader," she said.

The cop raised his pistol and pointed it directly at her head, and she raised her hands higher.

"My name is Huk Kim, I know who ordered General Ho assassinated, and at this moment my husband Soon is being held in Pyongyang as a suspect in the shooting. If you don't want to feed me some of your fine grass soup, at least take me to jail and inform your superior officer who I am before it's too late."

"I think it's already too late for you," the cop with the pistol said. "Whoever you are and wherever you've come from you'll soon learn that your humor is not appreciated. But you'll get your wish to get to jail, and so will all your family when we round them up."

"No wonder you're starving to death up here," Kim said.

The second cop pulled her arms behind her back, roughly cuffed her, and shoved her in the backseat of the blue-and-white cruiser. She had survived the DMZ and now these cops without being shot, but the ball was in their court. It was possible that they would put her in a cell and leave her there until they figured she would finally tell them who she really was.

But there was no time. Everyone in the world was talking about the assassination and the possibility of war, but here no one knew a thing. It was pitiful. And frightening. All she needed was for one more piece of luck, a cop downtown who would dare to make a call to Pyongyang about her. It was her only hope.

SIXTY—TWO

Pak drove back to his office down the middle lane reserved for official traffic, keeping his silence all the way. They were passed through the gate by the sentries and went immediately around to the rear of the massive granite building and parked. Pak shut off the car and turned to McGarvey.

"Who were you talking to on your satellite phone?" he asked. "Somebody at the CIA?"

McGarvey figured there was no use lying. He nodded. "A friend."

"What money trail? And what's this about missing something all along? Would you care to explain?"

"Assassinations cost a lot of money. We think that wherever it's coming from might be funneled through a bank or banks in Prague."

"That's nothing new," Pak said. "What have you been missing all along?"

"The obvious, Colonel, who's supplying the cash and more important, why."

Pak stared at him for a moment or two. "Then you believe me."

"I think that you've told me the truth, so far as you know it."

"But there's more," Pak said.

"There always is," McGarvey replied and he started to open the door, but Pak stopped him.

"I meant that General Ho's assassination was just part of something much bigger. Is that what you're thinking?"

"I want to see Huk Soon now."

"Goddammit, we're fighting for our lives here," Pak said, and McGarvey could hear genuine fear in the man's voice. "It doesn't matter what you think of my country, you understand what's at stake here. We asked for your help and you came."

"That's right, but before I go back to Washington with this I'm going to make damned sure of what really happened here. And to do that I'll need to talk to Huk Soon."

Pak hesitated. "You'll need to leave your pistol at the security desk. No weapons are allowed in the cell area."

"Then get him dressed and bring him up here," McGarvey said. "We can go for a walk away from the tape recorders."

"You must be crazy."

"No, but I'm getting sick of arguing with you. Either bring him up here so that I can talk to him with no one listening—so that he believes no one is listening—or take me back to Wonsan so I can catch the ferry. The sooner I'm out of this workers' paradise of yours the happier I'll be."

Pak hesitated again.

"Do it, Colonel. And you and your sergeant can follow us."

"Where do you think you're going to take him?"

"Out the gate and across the street to the park, for now."

"Don't get out of the car until I return, or you'll probably be shot," Pak said. He got out and went into the building.

Sitting back, McGarvey contemplated phoning Rencke again to get more details about the search for the source of the money that was directed to the general in Mexico City for the polonium operation and to Turov in Tokyo for the three assassinations. If the source could be pinned down, they might be able to get a heads up for whatever was coming next. He did not think fomenting a confrontation between China and North Korea was the endgame, nor was smuggling the radioactive material into the States the entire story.

If the situation here did escalate into an exchange of nuclear weapons, and if the polonium was used for mass murder in some major city, maybe New York or Washington again, what else could be coming toward the U.S.?

Islamic fundamentalists were at war with the entire world, against the Hindus, the Jews, and the Christians, and the most worrisome part was that the level of sophistication had risen dramatically since 9/11. Bin Laden dead no longer mattered. A new leadership, willing and able to keep out of the public's view, even out of sight of their own soldiers, was directing the battles now, and they were good.

Afghanistan and Iraq had been misdirections, as were al-Quaeda's mountain hideouts on the Pakistan border. The hot spots were constantly shifting—Mexico City, Paris, Tokyo, here—and would continue to do so, leaving the U.S. to fight an enemy that had no headquarters and no clear battle plan that could be met by a counterattack.

But Otto and his machines were working the problem, and McGarvey was certain that if anyone could crack the code it would be Rencke.

Pak and Sergeant Ri emerged from the building, leading a man dressed in a gray jacket buttoned up to the neck, gray slacks, and slippers, and came over to the car as McGarvey got out.

"Huk Soon," Pak said.

The man's eyes were slightly glazed, but it didn't appear as if he had been beaten too badly. He was taller and heavier than either Pak or the sergeant, and probably in much better physical shape even now.

"Are you up for a walk?" McGarvey asked.

Soon's eyes widened. "You're an American," he said, and he started to say something else, but McGarvey held him off.

"We'll be alone, no microphones, no jailers, no one to listen to what you have to tell me. Do you understand?"

Soon nodded after a moment.

Ri wanted to argue, but he went ahead and cleared the way with the guards in front, so that McGarvey and Soon were able to walk out and cross the street into a pretty park where people were strolling, some sitting on park benches, others practicing tai chi. McGarvey's size and Western clothing attracted attention but for the most part people were too polite to stare or come close.

"I've seen your wife Kim in Seoul," McGarvey said.

"She made it okay, that's good," Soon replied. He glanced over his shoulder at Pak and Ri who were out of earshot. "You're American, CIA? What the hell are you doing here?"

"Trying to stop World War III."

"Did the NIS ask for your help? Have they arrested Kim?"

"We tried but she got away from us, which is too bad for her, because Alexandar Turov, the Russian who hired you, came to Seoul to kill her."

"I don't know what you're talking about."

"We tossed your apartment and found the key to the storage locker. We also found your laptop computer and my people cracked it. We know about all your hits, including the ones in Paris and Tokyo."

"Now you want to make a deal," Soon said. "That's slick. What do I get in return? A ticket out of here?" He shook his head. "That won't happen, and I'm surprised they let you in, but they probably won't let you leave."

"They asked for my help, and I came, not because I give a shit about some two-bit hit man who cares more about money than what might happen because of him. And when I do get out of here, I hope they stick it to you."

"Point taken. But the question stands, what's in it for me?"

"Your wife's life. Or don't you give a shit about her either?"

Soon looked away and they walked in silence for a little while. "What do you want?"

"Tell me what you know about Turov."

"I didn't even know his last name until you told me," Soon said. "He's just been a name on an e-mail, and the guy who deposits money in our account."

"How did you find him?"

"I didn't. He found us after we did a contract kill for a Korean mafia family."

"Turov's just an expediter," McGarvey said. "Did you ever get a hint who he was working for?"

"I had the idea that whoever hired him had something to gain, otherwise they wouldn't have spent that kind of money."

"Who did you figure that would be?"

Soon stopped and looked at him. "The United States, of course," he said. "That's why you're here, isn't it?"

"I want you to show me how you and your wife did it."

Soon nodded over his shoulder. "Think they're going to allow that?"

"Count on it."

SIXTY—THREE

The operations center at the State Safety and Security Agency had been quiet all morning despite the turmoil outside over the Chinese thing, and despite the unprecedented arrival of the American under Colonel Pak's supervision. And Lieutenant Hang-gook Ma, today's duty officer, was damned glad of it, because the last few days had been a nightmare. Dear Leader had turned his gaze toward them, and that never was a good thing. The slightest mistake could mean a man's life.

Most of the ten clerks on the main floor were doing busywork, typing reports from information that came in from not only around the capital city but from all the outlying districts across the country. Nothing important.

Hang-gook stepped out of his glass-enclosed office and stopped for a moment to survey his domain. On most days he was proud of his position, nothing much ever happened. But just now he would have given a year's pay to be somewhere else. Cleaning streets, anything. He was a slightly built man, with a narrow face, intensely dark eyes, and a thin mustache that he thought made him look like an Indian movie star.

A cup of tea from the cafeteria downstairs would go good now, he decided, and he started across the room when one of his corporals who was speaking on the telephone looked up and waved him over.

"Can't you handle whatever it is?" Hang-gook asked.

"This is the police in In'chon. They've arrested a woman who was impersonating a South Korean spy."

"Ridiculous," Hang-gook said. "Why would anyone want to do something like that?"

"Shall we pass this along to Colonel Pak? We might catch him before he leaves the building."

"What, are you stupid? We won't be bothering the colonel over something like this, especially not now."

"Yes, sir. They want to know what to do with their prisoner."

"Let her go or shoot her, I don't care which," Hang-gook said. "I'm going for tea."

"Yes, sir," the corporal said and he turned back to the phone. "Do whatever you want with her, but don't waste a cell and don't feed her no matter what sort of wild stories she's telling you. But first find out who she really is."

Hang-gook turned and walked away when the corporal suddenly swore. The lieutenant stopped and turned back. All of his clerks had looked up at the outburst.

"Wait, you idiot, I want you to tell this to my lieutenant."

Hang-gook had a tickle at the back of his head, and an unsettled feeling in his stomach that something was about to happen that he'd fervently prayed never would; he was going to be put in a position where he would have to make a decision.

The clerk was holding out the phone for him, a neutral expression on his narrow face. He was passing the buck and glad of it.

The connection was lousy as was most telephone service from outside Pyongyang and at first Hang-gook had trouble understanding what the man was saying, except that he was Sergeant Hwang Jong-li the chief detective in Ich'on about one hundred and fifty kilometers to the southeast.

"Who is this woman you're talking about? Have you identified her?"

"She was carrying only an identity card from the South. Says her name is Huk Kim, and that you're holding her husband Huk Soon. She's telling some wild story about an assassination. Frankly I was about to turn her over to the hospital."

This was even worse than anything Hang-gook could ever have imagined. It put him directly in the middle of the most important investigation in the history of Chosun. Dear Leader himself had taken an interest, and whatever happened, whatever decisions were made—good or bad—he would know.

"How do you know the woman's telling the truth?"

"I don't know anything of the sort, Lieutenant. Her story is too fantastic to believe, but I don't know what she's up to. She talks like a Southerner, although her clothes are definitely from here."

Hang-gook glanced at his clerks, but all of them had gotten back to work. Even the corporal had turned away and was furiously typing something.

"What do you want us to do with her?" the cop from Ich'on asked.

Hang-gook tried to reason out his responsibilities. If the colonel were here the decision would be his. But Pak had left strict instructions that he was not to be bothered this morning, for any reason.

"Lieutenant?" the irritating cop's voice was like an insect in Hang-gook's ear.

"How much persuasion did you need to make her talk?"

"None," the detective replied. "She kept repeating the same story, and insisted that I contact State Security because she knew who was behind the assassination."

Suddenly enlightenment was Hang-gook's. In his mind this was the finest zen moment of his life, and he smiled for the first time since the killings in front of the Chinese Embassy. This meant the right sort of recognition, even promotion to senior lieutenant.

"Bring her here," he told the detective, his voice in his own ear calm, but crisp.

"What? We don't have the fuel allocation."

"Never mind about that. Listen very carefully now. This woman is of supreme importance to state security. I want her brought to my office, and I am giving you just ninety minutes in which to do it."

"I'll need authorization—"

"You have it from Dear Leader who is personally interested in this investigation," Hang-gook said. "Do I make myself clear?"

The line was silent for a long moment "Of course, Lieutenant. I'll personally escort her."

"And make sure that she talks to no one else. No one!"

"Is it true then, what she's told us? The assassination?"

"I suggest for your sake, Detective Sergeant Hwang, that you completely forget everything that you have heard. Bring the woman here and your name will be mentioned favorably in my report."

SIXTY-FOUR

Ri went back across the street to get the Lada after Mc-Garvey had explained to him and Pak what he had in mind. And now riding across the river to the Yangakdo Hotel on the island, the sergeant was in a black mood, and kept up a steady stream of objections in Korean.

"I don't think he believes you," Soon said to McGarvey. They were seated together in the backseat.

"Doesn't matter," McGarvey said.

Pak, who was riding shotgun in the front, looked over his shoulder. "Then what does matter, Mr. McGarvey?"

"I want him to show us how he did it."

"I told you—" Soon said.

"Without the help of the Pyongyang police, or maybe some of Colonel Pak's people."

Ri said something under his breath, but Pak calmed him down. "He's perfectly right to doubt us."

They took a left on the paved road that ran round the shoreline, past the International Cinema and finally the forty-five-story modern hotel that was used almost exclusively by tour groups. The hotel's employees, mostly Chinese, were treated the same as the tourists, never getting off the island without an escort.

The normally busy parking lot was practically empty as was the expansive lobby when they showed up. Every tour group scheduled since the assassination had been canceled. No one on the hotel staff had been told why, and no one, according to Pak, was asking any questions.

Ri pulled up in front, but no bellman came out, nor did either of the clerks at the front desk or the manager standing nearby approach as Soon led McGarvey and the two State Security agents across the lobby to the elevator.

"How close do you want me to play this?" Soon asked.

"I want everything," McGarvey said.

"My room was on the tenth floor, Kim's was on the twelfth," Soon said on the way up. "At midnight we got out of bed, got dressed in dark slacks and dark pullovers, and met downstairs."

"Were your roommates involved?" Pak asked.

"We drugged them so they'd sleep through the night."

They got off on the tenth floor and Soon led them first to his room halfway down the corridor from the elevators, and then to the emergency stairs at the end. "It was our last night here so we'd had two weeks to figure out the hotel's routines. Between midnight and three in the morning were the quietest hours. All the cleaning people were done, and the breakfast staff didn't start until around four."

The four of them followed Soon down to the service level one floor below the lobby. The laundry, heating plant, electrical distribution room, and maintenance areas were down a broad corridor to the left, and the room service kitchen, pantries, walk-in coolers and freezers, and the loading dock were to the right. The few staff on duty momentarily stopped what they were doing to look up at the strangers, one of whom was obviously a foreigner, but immediately turned away.

"The kitchen was deserted at that hour so it was no problem getting out of the hotel from the delivery entrance," Soon told them.

"Did you steal a truck?" Ri asked. "None were reported missing. Anyway how did you get past the checkpoint on the bridge?"

"We didn't steal a truck."

"Then how did you get across the river?"

"They swam," McGarvey said. "They killed the cops for their uniforms and weapons, and stuffed everything, including their own clothes into plastic bags."

"We found one in the bastard's suitcase," Ri said. "We never thought they really swam accross."

They had walked up the driveway and crossed the road to the bushes along the river where Soon waited for his wife to join them. They had seen the police patrols from their hotel windows, and knew the cops traveled in pairs on foot.

"You waited in the bushes and killed them," Ri said. "Bastard."

"We needed their uniforms and their weapons," Soon replied matter-of-factly.

"You're taking this well," Pak observed.

"From the moment you pulled me off the Beijing flight I knew that I was a dead man walking. But my wife escaped and she knows how to take care of herself."

"You don't care about those two cops you killed?" Ri demanded. He couldn't get over it.

"No. They were North Koreans, the enemy." Soon turned away and looked across the river. "We swam over from here and it was damned cold. Kim had a lot of trouble, even more on the way back."

"Then what?" McGarvey asked, expecting the sort of explanation Soon gave him, because he knew that with a little bit of luck it would have worked. But one big question remained.

"We're not taking a swim this morning," Pak said. "We'll drive over."

Back on the mainland Ri pulled into the park where Soon and Kim had gotten out of the river and changed into the police uniforms. The day was bright and warm, and a lot of people were out and about, but as before in the park across from State Security headquarters, no one paid them any attention.

"Where'd you leave your clothes?" Pak asked.

"We put them in the plastic bags and hung them on the seawall. There's a ladder."

"From that point you strolled up the street over to the Chinese Embassy, in the open, knowing that no one was about to stop a couple of police officers making their rounds," Pak said.

"Weren't you worried about a passing patrol car?" Ri asked. "If a supervisor had come along you could have been in trouble."

"We stayed in the shadows mostly," Soon replied. "Anyway we didn't see anyone until we got to the embassy."

"They stayed out of sight until the car pulled up and General Ho walked out of the embassy," Pak told McGarvey. "Then they stepped out into the open so that the security camera taped them shooting the general, the driver, and the Chinese guards. We were given a copy of it."

"Taped two North Korean cops pulling the triggers," Ri said.

"Afterward we came back here, got out of the uniforms, and swam back across the river and got back into the hotel the same way we got out."

"They both would have gotten away if the bodies of the police officers they'd dumped in the river hadn't turned up so quickly," Pak said. He shook his head. "How much were you paid?" he asked Soon.

"A lot of money."

Ri wanted to take him apart on the spot. "The Colonel asked you a question."

"It doesn't matter how much," McGarvey said. "I want to know how he knew the precise time the general would be leaving the embassy."

"Alexandar told us."

"How did he know?"

Soon shrugged. "His intel has always been the best, and this time was no different. I didn't question it."

The implication suddenly struck Pak. "That's impossible. Even if this Russian ex-KGB officer of his was still connected with Moscow there's no way that the general's schedule could have been known."

"I expect that the Russians have penetrated Chinese intelligence," McGarvey said. "Either that or the leak's here, someone on Kim Jong Il's staff."

"Not here," Pak said. "Even so why would the Russians want to start a war between us and China? It doesn't make any sense."

"Why don't you ask your friend," Soon said. "The CIA sent him here to make a deal with me. The Americans are the only ones who want this war."

SIXTY-FIVE

Handcuffed in the backseat of the diesel-powered Toyota police cruiser racing down the nearly empty highway into Pyongyang, Kim had plenty of time to rehearse her lines. She would only get one shot and she'd have to be convincing. It was worth her life to save Soon's, but it would have to be played just right. Not every North Korean was as stupid as the two cops who'd arrested her.

"Who are you taking me to see?" she asked the detective who had interviewed her.

"Shut your mouth," he said, glancing at her reflection in the rearview mirror. "We're almost there and I'll be well rid of you."

"Maybe if you help me you'll get a promotion."

The detective said something she couldn't quite catch, but she was certain that he was frightened. Whoever he had called must have been important because the man drove like someone possessed by an evil ancestor.

They crossed the river on the Okyru Bridge and suddenly they were in the city, on the broad Mansudae Street, the government buildings huge and imposing, and the reality of the situation hit her for the first time since Soon had convinced her to take the job.

They were murderers who had brought the region to the brink of nuclear war, and no matter what happened neither of them would walk away from this alive. It was almost funny in her mind, and she stifled a laugh, but she'd never really thought of herself as a killer until this instant—except for the two cops outside the hotel that night.

He would call her a perfect little fool when she showed up, but she knew that he would be secretly glad that she had come to be with him. Life without him was impossible. She'd felt that the instant he'd been taken off the airplane. By rights she should have jumped up then and there and turned herself in.

The detective stopped at the gate in front of the State Security Headquarters Building and handed out his identification booklet to the uniformed guard, a Kalashnikov slung over the man's narrow shoulder.

"You're expected. Drive around to the back, but stay in your vehicle until someone comes for you," the guard said, handing the booklet back. He glanced at Kim in the backseat then stepped away and waved them through.

A young man in a corporal's uniform was waiting for them. He had the detective let Kim out of the car and unlock her handcuffs. "Go back to Ich'on, and say nothing to anyone about this. Do you understand?"

The detective nodded dumbly and handed over Kim's

ID. She felt a brief pang of sorrow for him. He'd only been trying to do his job until she'd shown up. And now she had brought him trouble.

"Is this all she had with her?" the corporal demanded.

"Yes."

Kim held her silence. If she'd wanted to make trouble she could have mentioned the money, but it wasn't worth it. She would gain nothing.

The detective gave her a bleak look, then got in his car and drove away, belching black smoke, as the corporal took Kim upstairs to operations on the third floor.

Lieutenant Hang-gook came to his office door as the corporal appeared with the woman prisoner from Ich'on, and it was all he could do not to rub his hands together like a greedy moneylender, something his wife pointed out he did whenever he was nervous or overwrought. Like now.

Everything on the floor went dead silent as the corporal brought Kim across.

"This is the prisoner's wife," he said unnecessarily. He handed over the South Korean identity card. "It doesn't look like a forgery to me, sir."

"I'll be the judge of that," the lieutenant said. The woman was small, but with a full round face and a hint of muscles. Best of all she seemed frightened and unsure of herself, as well she should be if she was telling the truth.

"I would like to see my husband," Kim said, and Hang-gook could hear the South in her accent.

"Go back to your duties," he told the corporal, and he motioned Kim into his office where he closed the door. For just a moment he wondered if he was doing the right thing by conducting the initial interview himself and not immediately taking her downstairs to the lockup and then calling the colonel. But he couldn't pass up such a golden opportunity.

"Is my husband okay?"

"Why did you come here, if you're who you say you are?" Hang-gook asked, rubbing his thumb and forefinger over the sleek plastic of her ID card. He couldn't feel any irregularities that might indicate it had been tampered with.

"To trade for his freedom."

For just a second Hang-gook wasn't sure he'd heard right. "What are you talking about? He admitted that he's an assassin, and if you really are his wife, that makes you a killer as well."

"That's right, I helped assassinate General Ho, the driver that Dear Leader sent to the Chinese Embassy, and the Chinese guards at the gate. I also killed one of the police officers outside our hotel on Yanggak Island."

"Neither of you will ever leave Chosun alive," the lieutenant blurted before he could stop himself.

"My husband will, because of what I came to tell you."

"Whatever you have stored in your head, we can find out," Hang-gook warned.

"But you won't have the proof until I'm sure Soon is across the border."

"Proof of what?"

"Who hired us," Kim said. "It was the American CIA. They want China to destroy your Dear Leader and his cronies."

"We know this already—"

"Our paymaster was Kirk McGarvey. He came to Seoul to kill me so I wouldn't talk."

Hang-gook stared at the woman. Nothing would ever be the same in his life from this moment on. She was the golden Buddha here to bring him salvation from someday retiring as a fifty-year-old junior lieutenant with a pension so small he and his wife would have to beg from their relatives just to survive.

"If I find out that you've lied, I may shoot you myself," he said, careful to keep the excitement from his voice.

"We worked for a Russian doing business in Tokyo, but he was hired by McGarvey. And I can prove it."

"Yes, what is this proof?"

"When Soon is free."

Hang-gook suppressed a smile. "Stay here. Don't move. Don't do anything foolish, and I'll bring you to see your husband." He jumped up and rushed out of the office.

No one had gotten back to work but that didn't matter right now. He motioned for the corporal who came over.

"Sir?"

"The American who Colonel Pak brought here. He has a room at the Koryo. I want you to go over there right now and search it."

"For what?"

"Anything incriminating."

A cunning look came into the corporal's eyes. He too sensed opportunity. "Shouldn't we call the colonel?"

"Not yet," Hang-gook said, not able to keep the excitement from his voice. "That stupid woman told me that Dear Leader was correct, it was the Americans. And Kirk McGarvey was the one who gave the orders. If we can prove this for the colonel . . . anything is possible."

"Give me ten minutes," the corporal said and he left.

Hang-gook stood for several moments lost in thought, and when he turned back all of his clerks were staring at him. "Have you nothing better to do?" he demanded, and everyone scurried back to their desks like frightened mice.

He went to the door of his office but then hesitated, and turned back again. "Someone call downstairs and have the prisoner Huk Soon brought up. I'll sign for him." He wanted to see the look on his face when he saw that his wife was here.

One of his clerks got on the telephone and after a brief conversation hung up. "The prisoner is gone, Lieutenant.

Colonel Pak and Sergeant Ri signed for him an hour ago."

It made no sense to Hang-gook. The colonel fetches the very American who engineered the assassination and then releases the prisoner. He couldn't get his mind around any set of circumstances that would fit such bizarre facts. Unless Colonel Pak was so brilliant he had lured the American here, or was a traitor.

He opened his office door and looked in at the woman who had hunched her feet up under her and sat crouched on the chair as if she were a cat ready to spring. She turned to him.

"May I see my husband now?"

"Just a few more minutes," he said unnecessarily, and he closed the door and perched on the corporal's desk, the other clerks studiously avoiding looking his way.

Ten minutes stretched to twenty before the corporal called from the hotel. One of the clerks answered and handed the phone to Hang-gook who was beside himself with nervous energy. If he were wrong, if the woman was telling some crazy lie, he would be in a great deal of trouble.

"It's here," the corporal shouted. "She's telling the truth."

"What did you find? Tell me!"

"Two CIA files with photographs of Huk Soon and Huk Kim. I don't read English but it's them, and I've seen pictures of the CIA's seal."

The relief was more than sweet. "Good. Bring them here."

"I'm on my way."

Hang-gook broke the connection then called the agency's radio communications section and had them reach Colonel Pak on his car radio.

The call went through almost immediately. "This is

Lieutenant Hang-gook, I'm so sorry to interrupt you, sir, but I have some information that's for your ears only."

"Standby," Pak said, and he was back a minute later. "Yes, what is it?"

"The other assassin showed up this morning in Ich'on, and I had her brought here, on my authority."

"You have the wife?" Pak demanded.

"Yes, sir, but that's not all. She claims that Kirk Mc-Garvey, working for the CIA, was the one who ordered the assassinations."

"That's impossible."

"Sir, I sent one of my men to the Koryo to search Mc-Garvey's room. He found CIA dossiers on Huk Soon and his wife." Hang-gook closed his eyes. He felt like a man teetering on the edge of the cliff. "She said he came to Seoul to try to kill her. And, as incredible as it seems, I think that's why he came here. He means to finish the job, and maybe kill the husband."

"Fantastic," Pak said. "We'll come back immediately."

SIXTY-SIX

At State Security headquarters they were passed through the gate and Ri drove around back and parked. After the radiophone call ten minutes ago Pak's mood had subtly changed, and McGarvey figured that the colonel had gotten some bad news.

"Anything I should know about before we go up?" McGarvey asked. "Your phone call back in the park?"

"It concerns you," Pak said coolly. "Someone who wants to see you showed up."

Ri took charge of the prisoner and just inside the door Pak held out his hand.

"I'd like your pistol now."

Rats' feet were pattering at the back of McGarvey's head. The situation was wrong. "No."

Ri stopped and glared at him. "The colonel asked for your weapon."

McGarvey stepped back. They were in a small entry room. A security door with a keypad led to the downstairs corridor. The only way out was back to the car, and McGarvey knew that he wouldn't make it to or through the front gate without being shot down.

"I won't go anywhere unarmed," McGarvey said to Pak. "It's the deal we made when you came to ask for my help, remember?"

"Who do you think you are, you bastard," Ri said, and he started to reach for his weapon, but Pak held him off.

"Our guest is correct, and I don't think he means to shoot anybody today. He's here to help us prove that we did not assassinate General Ho. And I think we'll learn something instructive upstairs. Keep your pistol, Mr. McGarvey, if it makes you feel more comfortable."

Ri wanted to argue, but he entered the code on the keypad and the door buzzed open. The corridor was busy but no one paid them any attention, and they took the elevator up to the third floor and down the hall to the operations center.

The clerks stopped what they were doing and Hang-gook jumped up from where he was perched on a desk, talking with the corporal, relief on his round face.

"Where is she?" Pak demanded.

Hang-gook nodded across the room. "I put her in my office."

"And the files?"

Hang-gook handed him a large green envelope, tied

shut with a red ribbon, of the kind used by couriers carrying classified documents between departments.

"Good work, Lieutenant," Pak said. "I'll take it from here if you don't mind us using your office until we get this sorted out."

"Of course not."

This was the heart of badland, and McGarvey had been tense from the moment he'd gone aboard the ferry to Wonsan, but at this moment he wondered if he had made a serious mistake coming here. He'd been in over his head any number of times, but this was about as bad as it had ever been, and the moment they walked into the lieutenant's office and Huk Kim jumped up from the chair into her husband's arms, he realized it was even worse than that.

"You little fool, what are you doing here?" Soon demanded. "How did you get up here? Are you out of your mind?"

"I had to come back for you," she cried. "And I told them everything, how we got here and how we killed the general and the others, and about Alexandar and about—" She spotted McGarvey in the doorway and she stopped in midsentence. "It's him," she said breathlessly, her eyes wide.

The office was very small, and the five of them were crowded practically on top of one another. McGarvey reached back and shut the door. The woman was desperate enough to try to get up here, and inventive enough to accomplish it. But she'd not come empty-handed. She'd come to trade something for at least her husband's release.

"Do you know this man?" Pak asked.

"Yes, his name is Kirk McGarvey. Alexandar told me that it was the CIA who hired him, and that McGarvey fed him the intel and the money."

Soon looked as surprised as the others.

"Is that how it was?" McGarvey asked him.

The man nodded after a brief hesitation. "According to Alexandar."

"Quite a coincidence you coming to the States to ask for my help," McGarvey said to Pak.

Pak opened the green envelope and extracted the two dossiers that had been lifted from McGarvey's hotel room. "Can you explain these?"

"I did my homework after you came to see me. We figured these two might have been the shooters, so my first stop was Seoul, where we would have had the woman, except she had help from Alexandar Turov, their Russian contact."

"You know this Russian?"

"We came up with his name as a probable expediter, and I spotted him in Seoul where he was trying to kill Kim to keep her quiet."

"He's lying," Kim said.

"Then why did you run?" McGarvey asked.

"To get away from you," she replied. She turned to Pak, desperation in her voice. "I can prove it's him. Let my husband go home, and I'll cooperate. Dear Leader will have what he needs to stop the war."

"No," Soon said. "I won't leave without her."

"I've had enough of this," Ri said, reaching for his pistol beneath his jacket.

McGarvey stepped to the left, batted the sergeant's hand aside just long enough to pull his own pistol and jam the muzzle against the man's temple.

Pak was pulling out his own gun when the much larger Soon shoved him roughly to one side and grabbed the Russian-made 5.45 mm PSM out of his hand.

Ri reached up and grabbed the barrel of McGarvey's gun. "Fire in here and you'll never get out of the building alive."

"You're probably right," McGarvey said. "Why don't you give it a try?"

Pak said something in Korean, and after a brief hesitation Ri let go and dropped his hand to his side.

"What next?" the colonel asked.

"You came to me in the States, why?" McGarvey asked.

"Because I thought that you were an honorable man, who the Chinese trust, and you would be able to help find out what really happened."

"If I had been the one behind the hit, I wouldn't have come here," McGarvey said.

"If it wasn't you paying Alexander then it was someone else from the CIA," Soon said. "You bastards are the only ones who stand to gain anything from this."

"You can't get out of this building alive, you know that, of course," Pak told McGarvey. "Put down the weapons, let us take you into custody, and we'll deal with your government through the U.N. in New York."

"You and I are leaving with the woman, while Soon stays behind to keep your sergeant quiet."

"No—" Kim protested, but her husband cut her off.

"What do you have in mind?" Soon asked.

"Turov wants to shut her up, so I'm going to use her for bait," McGarvey said. "But first I'm going to take her to Washington to convince my government that North Korea wasn't behind the shootings."

"I'll never see you again," Kim cried.

Soon ignored her. "Getting out is impossible."

"Not impossible," McGarvey said. "I can't guarantee what will happen to your wife in the end, but at least she'll be away from here. Will you help?"

"Yes," Soon said without hesitation.

"No, please," Kim cried.

"It's the only way, darling," Soon said.

McGarvey took Ri's pistol from its holster and pocketed it. "Your colonel's life depends on your cooperation, do you understand?"

Ri looked at him, his eyes narrowed. "I know that I'll piss on your still warm body and enjoy every second of it."

"Right," McGarvey said, and he turned to Pak. "You and I and the woman are going to walk out of here, get in your car, and drive out the front gate. If you give me your word that you won't try to cause any trouble, I'll give you my word that I won't draw my weapon and open fire, killing a lot of innocent people."

Pak said nothing.

"I don't think North Korea had anything to do with the assassination, and I'll do what I promised you, I'll find out who did order it."

"Even if it's someone in your own government?"

"Even that," McGarvey said.

Pak nodded. "Very well, though I don't know how the hell you think you can get out of the city let alone the country."

McGarvey turned to Kim. "Cooperate and we just might make it in one piece. If not, you and your husband will certainly die."

"Go with him," Soon said. "Please."

She was distraught, but she reached up and gave her husband a kiss on the cheek and then nodded.

Soon switched aim to Ri.

"We need a half hour," McGarvey said. "If he moves or tries to call for help, shoot him."

"He won't," Pak said.

SIXTY-SEVEN

In the operations center Hang-gook jumped up, but Pak waved him back. "Keep everyone out of your office for the next half hour. We have one more thing to do with this prisoner and then I'll be returning."

"Yes, sir," the lieutenant said. He gave McGarvey a suspicious look. "But what if I need to reach you? Will you be monitoring your radio?"

"Of course."

"Will Sergeant Ri need any help with the other prisoner?"

"No, and they're not to be disturbed," Pak said. "We just need a half hour."

"I understand, sir," the lieutenant said.

On the way down in the elevator, Kim was shivering and she seemed to be unsteady on her feet.

"When's the last time you had something to eat?" McGarvey asked. In some way she reminded him of his daughter Elizabeth who would almost certainly have tried to pull off the same stunt to save her husband, Todd.

"What do you care?" she demanded angrily. "You're going to get Soon and me killed. That's why you came here after me."

"She's lying and you know it," McGarvey told Pak.

"I have to go with what I learn. My hands are tied. If you're not involved, we'll find out."

"In the meantime everyone in Pyongyang just might get incinerated," McGarvey said. "Thanks to this woman and her husband. For money."

"You ought to know," Kim said. "Colonel, you have to believe me. If you can stop this bastard from taking me out of here, and if you can arrange to get my husband back to Seoul I can prove he was the one who arranged everything."

"He's not going to get out of Pyongyang alive and neither are you," Pak told her.

"I don't want to die," she blurted.

"You should have thought of that before you and your husband became assassins," McGarvey said harshly. Yet that's exactly what he had made a career of doing. There was a distinction between what he and they did, though it was a narrow one and depended on which side of the fence the observer was on. He'd always worked under that slim margin, and he'd spent more nights than he could count wondering if what he had done was the right thing.

No one stopped them down the first-floor corridor, nor did the armed guards at the front gate ask any questions, just waving the Lada through.

"You have a half hour," Pak said. "Where do you want to go?"

"The Chinese Embassy," McGarvey said.

Pak was startled. "You're crazy if you think they'll talk to you let alone take you in. And even if they did you wouldn't be allowed back out."

McGarvey took out his sat phone. "Just drive."

Pak turned right and headed down the broad Okryo Street along the river toward the Taedong Gate.

McGarvey and Kim were seated in the back, and suddenly she made a lunge for the door, getting it half open before McGarvey managed to grab her by the arm.

She screeched something in Korean, and for a few seconds it was all McGarvey could do to keep her from tumbling out of the moving car.

"If you tell the Chinese she was one of the shooters they'll kill her," Pak said.

Kim moaned something unintelligible, but she calmed down.

"I won't tell them a thing, except that she's important to the investigation," McGarvey said. "You could have taken advantage of the situation just then, why didn't you?"

Pak glanced at McGarvey's reflection in the rearview mirror. "You had your gun pointed at my head the entire time."

"Plausible deniability."

"I think you Americans call it covering your ass."

McGarvey got a signal on the phone and speed dialed Rencke's number. Wherever Otto was, in his office, in his car, or at home, the call would be rolled over to him. He answered on the second ring.

"Oh wow, what's going on, Mac?"

"There's no time to explain now, but I need your help. I've got one of the shooters with me and I'm making a run for the Chinese Embassy. The colonel who came to see me in Sarasota is driving us over there, at gunpoint. Find out who their chief of security is, explain what I'm working on, and convince him that I need a ride out of Dodge."

"Major Shikai Chen," Pak said.

"Hang on one," Rencke said.

"His name is Major Shikai Chen."

"Are you sure, Mac?" Rencke asked.

"Yeah," McGarvey told him. "We're on our way over now, but this situation won't stay stable much longer."

"I'm on it," Rencke promised.

"We're less than ten minutes away from the embassy," Pak said. "But no matter if Major Shikai allows you inside, you will never be allowed to leave Chosun without Dear Leader's permission."

"I know," McGarvey said. "That's why I'm going to explain everything to him too, and ask for just that."

SIXTY-EIGHT

By the time they reached the Chinese Embassy, Rencke had not come back on the line. The street was blocked at each corner by four troop trucks and what looked like at least fifty North Korean soldiers in camouflage combat uniforms and armed with Kalashnikov assault rifles.

A lieutenant colonel got out of a Russian-made Gazik parked directly across from the embassy and walked up the street toward them.

"This is trouble," Pak said. "These guys are Reconnaissance Bureau—special forces—and they don't screw around. Let me do the talking."

"You're supposed to be at gunpoint," McGarvey said.

"I'll figure out my explanations later," Pak said. "But both of you, keep your mouths shut if you want to survive the next five minutes." He got out of the car, his movements deliberate, his hands in plain sight.

"What is State Security doing here," the lieutenant colonel demanded. "Haven't your people caused enough trouble already?" City police were under the control of the agency.

Kim quickly translated for McGarvey.

"I'm delivering two people to the Chinese—"

"The hell you say," the lieutenant colonel said, and he started to step around Pak who put out a hand to stop him.

The troopers at the nearest barrier, realizing that something not right was going on, snapped to, their weapons at the ready.

"I suggest that you take your hand off my person if you want to live much longer," the Reconnaissance Bureau officer warned.

"I'm going to reach inside my jacket for a letter—not a

weapon," Pak said. He moved his right hand to his pocket and stopped.

A half–dozen troops raised their weapons higher, ready to shoot, but the lieutenant colonel motioned for them to hold off.

Pak carefully took out Kim Jong Il's letter and handed it over. "This will explain my position."

The lieutenant colonel quickly read the letter, glanced up at Pak, and reread the letter. He handed it back, his expression neutral. "I'll check this out, Colonel, if you'll give me a few minutes."

"Check it out if you will, but I'm making my delivery."

Rencke was back. "They're looking at the car outside their embassy and they've agreed to let you and the woman inside, but they don't want to start an incident with the Recon Bureau."

"What'd you tell them?"

"Just your name. But it was enough. The major should be coming out of the front gate now."

A slight man in dark trousers and an open-collar white shirt stepped past the Chinese security guards at the gate and stopped.

"I've got him," McGarvey said. "Let's go," he told Kim. He got out of the car, and reached back to help her, but she batted his hand away and jumped out.

Together they walked past Pak and the Reconnaissance Bureau lieutenant colonel, McGarvey acutely conscious of how delicate the situation was.

Major Chen stepped aside as they reached him and motioned them through the gate, which the security guards closed after them. McGarvey didn't look over his shoulder to see if Pak had driven off as they crossed the narrow courtyard and entered the front stair hall of the four-story building.

"We agreed to bring you this far, Mr. McGarvey, on the strength of your reputation," Major Chen said, stopping in the middle of the hall. "Now, considering the importance of the current situation, we will require an explanation."

"The North Koreans did not kill General Ho, and I've been asked to prove it," McGarvey said. "This woman may hold the key, but only if I can get her back to Washington immediately."

Major Chen's left eyebrow rose. "We have never met, but I was told that you are an unusual man." He looked at Kim. "We have the ambassador's aircraft standing by at the airport, but I'm not sure we would be allowed to get to it, or if it would be allowed to take off. What proof?"

"I can't say right now—"

"You of all men must appreciate the urgency of our position. If we initiate an attack that stupid bastard will probably launch, and we couldn't do a thing about it until afterward."

"It's why I came here."

"Without your government's sanction," Major Chen said bitterly.

"I need your help."

The Chinese intelligence officer was clearly frustrated. "I can't do a damned thing for you. They won't let you out of here."

"Yes, they will, if you're willing to fly us to Washington."

"You have to get to the airport first."

McGarvey raised the sat phone. "Otto?"

"Here."

"Can you contact Kim Jong Il's people, explain the situation, and allow me to talk to him with a translator?"

"Holy shit, Mac. I'm on it."

Major Chen was impressed and it showed. "I was not told that you were a surprising man."

No one else was in the stair hall and the building was all but silent, though somewhere in the distance McGarvey thought he could hear a muffled conversation, two people arguing about something.

Kim was getting shaky on her feet and McGarvey sat her down on a wooden bench with carved dragons. But it took nearly ten minutes before Rencke was back.

"You owe me one, kemo sabe," Rencke said. "He's on the line. No names, not his, not yours."

"Right," McGarvey said, and the call was switched. "You understand that I have agreed to help."

He could hear the translator in the background, but there was no response.

"I may have the proof that we need. But I must get to Washington as soon as possible."

Again he could hear the translator, but no answer.

"It will require that I have safe conduct to the airport, along with my prisoner, and clearance for the Chinese ambassador's aircraft to leave North Korean territory."

Still there was no reply, and a moment later the connection was broken.

"They're gone," Rencke said.

Major Chen walked to the long narrow windows flanking the door. "They're leaving," he said. He turned back and looked at McGarvey. "You Americans say, son of a bitch. That's a good expression. What now?"

"We need a ride to the airport and the use of your ambassador's airplane."

Major Chen allowed a slight smile. "I think that is possible."

McGarvey raised the sat phone. "We're on our way out."

"I'll arrange something from Beijing," Rencke said. "That was some spooky shit."

"Yeah," McGarvey said. "But there's more to come."

WASHINGTON

SIXTY-NINE

Rencke had rounded up a C-20G Gulfstream IV VIP jet at Yokosuka Navy Base in Japan, and had it at a quiet corner of Beijing's Capital International Airport by the time McGarvey and Kim arrived from Pyongyang. The transfer went smoothly, and once they were aboard and outbound for Hawaii, Kim was fed rice and sushi by an attractive petty officer, and afterward she had put her seat back and had fallen asleep.

"May I get something for you, sir?" the girl had asked McGarvey.

"A Martell straight up, if you have it."

"Of course."

"And let me know when the pilot thinks it's okay for me to use my sat phone."

"Right now, I think, but I'll check."

She came back with his drink and gave him a smile. "I was right. It's only cell phones that give our electronic gear trouble."

"Thanks," McGarvey told her. "Do we have an ETA for Andrews?"

"At this point it looks as if we'll be landing around 0600, and that includes refuels at Midway and Long Beach. If that changes I'll let you know." She glanced at Kim. "You look as if you could use a few hours sleep yourself, sir."

"You're right," McGarvey said and when she went

forward he took out his sat phone, got a signal, and phoned Rencke.

"You're out."

· "We took off from Beijing about an hour ago," McGarvey said. "Should be arriving at Andrews around six in the morning. Does anyone know where I've been?"

"If anyone does they're not mentioning it. Howard's spending most of his time covering his ass up on the Hill, and Dick has been over to the White House four times in the past thirty-six hours."

"What about Rodgers?" Richard Rodgers, III, was the new Director of U.S. Intelligence, supposedly with oversight over the CIA and the other thirteen intelligence agencies.

"For the moment this belongs to us, and no one else, so when the actual shit hits the fan we'll be the only agency to take the hit," Rencke said almost bitterly. He'd always known how the game was played, and for the most part he'd always been above it. "Everyone else will come out fairly clean and they'll be the first ones up to speed, and not hamstrung by a bunch of bullshit congressional committees."

"Time to retire?" McGarvey asked.

"I'm thinking about it, Mac, honest injun. But retirement hasn't seemed to have done you much good."

"Have you found out anything new on Turov?"

"No, and that's damned odd. Given the time and a push in the right direction my search engines can scan just about any system, but the shit I'm coming up with now is superficial. Driver's licenses, property deeds, a Citation jet. He's a wealthy Russian ex-pat living in Japan, but I can't get a lock on what he does for a living, or how he's come up with his money after he left Moscow."

"From what I saw he's not living *that* large in Tokyo, in fact he's practically invisible," McGarvey said. "What about his contacts, any luck there? According to the shooters, it was Turov who gave them the general's precise schedule. It's my guess the Russians may have penetrated Chinese intel and Turov got his information from Moscow, because it doesn't look as if anyone on Kim Jong Il's staff was the source."

"There's been a few rumblings over the past six or eight months that the FSS was trying to score big, but that's all I've heard. I'll check on it though."

"How about us?" McGarvey asked. It was a thought that had been niggling at the back of his head since he'd learned of the existence of the Russian expediter in Tokyo. For years the CIA had been trying to penetrate the Chinese intelligence apparatus, Guoanbu, first in Washington, then in New York at the U.N., and over the past few years in Beijing itself, but the Company had only a limited success.

"I'm not sure," Rencke said softly as if he were worried that someone might be eavesdropping. "I don't generally stick my nose in McCann's business unless I have to, but I caught the whiff of a rumor that we might have finally gotten someone inside last year, right after that deal you were involved with in Mexico City. Your burning General Liu and his operation threw the Guoanbu a curveball and while Beijing was trying to get its shit together we might have gotten someone inside. But so what?"

"Find out for me, please," McGarvey said. "And if we do have someone in place, find out who's handling the product."

Rencke was silent for a long second or two, and when he came back on the line he sounded even more guarded than before. "You're thinking that maybe Turov's source is here, inside the Building?"

"I don't know what I'm thinking, Otto. But the way things stand we've got the most to gain by China flattening Kim Jong Il's regime."

"You're right, but it doesn't necessarily mean that we're

behind it," Rencke said. "Dick wouldn't have anything to do with something like that, he doesn't have the guts or the imagination. He's bland not insane. And anyway, we're probably talking big money here and there's been no sudden drain on our finances for any sort of a black project. I know that for a fact, because I went looking for the funding for the Mexico City operation and came up empty-handed. So far as I know the Bureau thinks the big bucks came from Mexican drug money laundering. That stream alone tops eight billion, so a few hundred million here and there wouldn't have made much of a dent."

"It still comes down to a problem of motivation," McGarvey said. "The Mexican drug cartels have no reason at all to engineer anything like this."

"No," Rencke admitted. "But Turov's intel might have nothing to do with money."

"I think it has," McGarvey said.

"Okay," Rencke said after a moment. "I'm on it. What about when you get here?"

"Is the Cabin John safe house free?" The house was actually a small estate along the Potomac River that the CIA had confiscated in a sting a few years ago. McGarvey had used it a couple of times, but not recently.

"Hang on," Rencke said. He was back in twenty seconds. "It's been empty for six months. A caretaker goes out there a couple of times a month to check on it. He's not due for another ten days, but that might not be such a great place to hide the woman. It won't take housekeeping long to find out you're there."

"I'm counting on it," McGarvey said.

"Shit," Rencke said softly. "I don't like this, kemo sabe, I shit you not."

"Trust me, I don't either."

"I'll pick you up at Andrews."

* * *

McGarvey telephoned his daughter who along with her husband directed the CIA's training base outside Williamsburg. "Van Buren," she answered tersely. She always seemed to be in a hurry.

"Hi, sweetheart, it's me."

"Daddy, where the hell are you? Mom's been going nuts."

"I'll be landing at Andrews first thing in the morning, and hopefully this business will be resolved in a few days, but it's not going to be pretty."

"Well, the shit's been hitting the fan around here in the last twenty-four hours. We're at DEFCON three, and the word on the street is that might be bumped up to two unless something happens to defuse the situation out there right now."

"What about the Russians?"

"They're in it too. Putin is calling for restraint, but his Rocket Forces are on alert, and just about every naval vessel in Vladivostok has lit off their power plants and headed out to sea."

"I need a favor from you and Todd," McGarvey said. "I'm bringing somebody in with me, and we're going to the Cabin John house. I'm going to use her as bait, and I'm going to need some muscle. But it'll have to be completely off the books."

"For how long?"

"Twenty-four hours at the most."

"Do you need a detail to meet you at Andrews?"

"I don't want to attract that much attention. Otto's meeting us and driving us out."

"I'll send someone."

"Thanks."

"Shall I call Mother?"

"No," McGarvey said, and when he looked up, Kim was awake and staring at him, an enigmatic expression in her Oriental eyes.

SEVENTY

Turov was finishing his simple rice and fish dinner on the teak deck at the edge of the garden when his Nokia 110 encrypted cell phone burred softly. Only four people had the ability to communicate with him over the state-of-the-art phone that used an advanced 10.2 kilobit RAS key encryption with a 2.6 kilobit random key, and then only if the message was of extreme importance.

Clearing his mind of all his preconceived notions about what would likely happen next so that he could never be surprised, he answered the call. "Yes."

"This is Daniel. He arrived two hours ago with the woman."

"Were you able to find out where they went?"

"It's a CIA safe house on some acreage a few miles outside the city, near Cabin John just above the river. Are you thinking about going after them?"

"We don't have much choice," Turov said. "She has to be eliminated for obvious reasons, and he knows who I am. The bastard actually showed up outside my door and demanded to have a meeting."

"Did you—meet him?" Daniel asked.

"At a railroad café."

"And he didn't kill you?"

Turov cut off a sharp reply, but he was getting tired of hearing how good McGarvey supposedly was. If for no other reason than that, plus the man's supreme arrogance, the ex-CIA director was going to die. "We were in a public place. It would have been impossible for either of us to make a move."

"What did he want, for heaven's sake?"

"He thinks that he has what he needs to prove I was

behind the assassination. All he's looking for is the source of my money, and we know where that leads."

"You don't know this man," Daniel said softly.

"You needn't worry, he will be taken care of. You can leave that part up to me."

"Are you coming here yourself?"

"Of course not," Turov replied impatiently. "But I've sent someone who is quite capable."

"He'd better have help," Daniel warned.

"Tell me about this Cabin John house. Are there security measures in place, and does he have anyone with him other than the woman?"

"I don't know the details offhand, but I expect he and the woman are alone. He certainly doesn't have anyone from here. Will you need me?"

"That's not necessary," Turov said. "We'll manage. There's no need for you to expose yourself." It was exactly what he wanted Daniel to do.

"I can help."

"How?"

"I've got to check out a couple of things first, and then I'll call you. Just have your people hold up until you get word from me. But no matter what happens the woman has to be eliminated."

"She could make trouble, but she couldn't prove anything," Turov said. "McGarvey is using her as bait, as I knew he would. He wants me to come to him, and I will, but not quite in the way he expects."

"This could go south in a New York minute," Daniel said.

"Not if your fail-safes are intact."

Daniel was suddenly guarded. "What do you know about my tradecraft?"

"Nothing, nor am I interested," Turov said. "We're both protected that way." It had been Daniel who'd approached him eighteen months ago, and although he knew the man's real background, he wasn't sure about the source of the money, though he had a few guesses. "McGarvey and the woman will be eliminated very soon, and what comes afterward will be up to you, and your . . . interests."

"There will be some serious fallout over McGarvey's death."

"Against the backdrop of a nuclear war, no one will notice."

"Don't count on it," Daniel said. "Don't count on anything."

"I don't," Turov replied, but the conversation had gone as he had expected it would. "Now tell me exactly where this Cabin John house is located."

Minoru was in his room at the Hay-Adams Hotel when Turov's call came through.

"He's brought the woman to Washington, as I thought he would."

"But there was no sign of her in Seoul."

"That's the surprising part," Turov said. "Apparently Mr. McGarvey isn't the only one who's inventive. A U.S. Navy aircraft met them in Beijing after they'd flown in from Pyongyang aboard the Chinese ambassador's plane. Evidently the woman crossed the border and was picked up by the police."

"She was trying to rescue her husband?" Minoru asked in wonder. "But that makes no sense, Colonel. What could she have hoped to accomplish? Break him out of jail or something?"

"I think she went up there with a bargaining chip."

"What could she have offered them?"

"Maybe she was trying to put the blame on McGarvey. It's the Americans who want this war."

Minoru started to reply but he caught his breath. "You knew that he would be coming back here to lure you in. He's using the woman for bait, but that means he somehow convinced the North Koreans to let him take one of the assassins with him. What did he have to offer them?"

"Me, of course," Turov said. But at the back of his head he knew that he was missing something, something very important, and it was maddeningly close, but just outside his ken.

"What do you want me to do?"

"Kill them both as quickly as possible," Turov said. He gave Minoru directions to the CIA's Cabin John safe house, and the name and contact information of an ex-KGB enforcer living in Alexandria and working openly as a Russian affairs adviser mostly to entrepreneurs wanting to do business in Moscow.

"It might be easier if I went in alone," Minoru said. "Bound to be a surveillance and security setup out there. One man on foot makes less of a fuss than two."

"There'll be more than two of you. McGarvey will be expecting someone to come after him. He's an assassin and so is the woman, so neither of them will hesitate to pull the trigger, and both of them are experts."

"How many shall I take with me?"

"At least two."

"How about afterward?" Minoru asked.

"My jet is standing by for you at Dulles. Get back here as quickly as possible."

"What about your KGB friend and his people?"

"Those that survive will be expendable," Turov said. "I'll expect you will see to it."

"It could get messy."

"I expect it might, but you'll probably have some help from inside."

"Could you explain that?" Minoru asked.

"Later, when I find out for sure. But when it's over that person would have to be eliminated as well."

The McLean office of Valeri Lavrov was housed in a two-story brick-and-wood building set back in a heavily wooded business complex one block off Dominion Drive. Minoru, driving a rental car, found the place and parked on the street in plain sight. It was after the morning rush hour and traffic was light, the day very pleasant. Some children were in a playground, and he watched them for a minute or two thinking ruefully about his unhappy childhood, but then he telephoned the office, and a receptionist answered on the first ring.

"All Russian Consulting, how may we be of service?"

"I'm an old friend of Mr. Lavrov's, from Tokyo," Minoru said. "I would like to have a word with him."

"I'm sorry, sir, but he has someone in his office at the moment. Would you care to leave a name and number where he could reach you?"

"Tell him that Alexandar is interested in doing business. He'll want to know that straightaway."

"The moment he's free I'll give him your message."

"He'll want to know now, please," Minoru insisted politely. "I'll hold."

The woman hesitated.

"This involves a great deal of money."

"Please hold," the receptionist said, and she was gone.

Lavrov came on the line within seconds. "Where are you?"

"I'm parked on the street in front of your office in a dark blue Dodge Charger," Minoru said.

"Who the hell is this?"

"I work for Alexandar, and he's sent me here to hire

you and a few friends for a bit of contract work. Shouldn't take long, and the money's good."

"How good?"

"You know how generous our friend can be. Probably at least one million for you personally, and expense money for the others."

"How soon would the contract have to be settled?"

"Very soon," Minoru said. "Certainly no longer than twenty-four hours."

"Okay, if you came off the Beltway you passed a strip mall a few blocks back just after the 123 overpass. A McDonald's is on the corner across the street. I'll meet you there in ten minutes."

"You'll be out for the rest of today and probably tomorrow," Minoru said, and he broke the connection and drove off.

The only customers in the McDonald's were two women at a corner table having coffee when Turov's friend walked in, ordered a cup of coffee, and came over to where Minoru was waiting.

He was a short, heavyset man who looked more like an amateur boxer than a former spy. He had been the number two KGB officer in Chechnya working as an operational planner directly with Turov. The story Minoru had been told was that Lavrov had gotten cornered by a force of eight or ten rebels in a war-torn section of the city, and would have been captured and tortured except for Turov's intervention.

The man owed his life to Turov.

"Must be a big deal if he's offering that much," Lavrov said, sitting down. "Last I heard he was bunkering in Tokyo. Not such a healthy place right now."

"This contract has something to do with the issue," Minoru said.

Lavrov grinned. "That has his signature written all over it. So who'd he send you over to knock off?"

"Two people and possibly one other. One of them is a South Korean, a woman."

"One of the shooters from Pyongyang?" Lavrov asked, his smile fading away. Whatever he looked like, he was not some mostly brain-dead punch-drunk.

"Yes," Minoru said.

"Does the CIA have her?"

"Not officially, but she's been taken to one of their safe houses."

"Who's her babysitter?"

"Kirk McGarvey."

Lavrov was shaken. "*Eb tvoiu mat.*" It was the universal Russian expression for something very bad, literally translated as fuck your mother.

"You know of this man?" Minoru asked.

"Yes, and it's going to take more than the two of us."

"We might have some help from inside."

"I don't care. I still want to take more muscle."

"How many operators can you come up with?"

"Four. And I'm going to need more than a million dollars, because if we actually take McGarvey down the fallout will be intense. Every intelligence officer and federal cop will be on our case."

"Only if there are any witnesses."

Lavrov started to object, but then he realized that Minoru meant to eliminate everyone.

"And if it actually comes to a shooting war between China and North Korea, which at this point seems likely, the U.S. intelligence apparatus will have its hands full. You can return to your office and you'll never be a suspect. This war will not be about Russians."

Lavrov shook his head in amazement. "The four guys I want are up in New York. I can get them down here by this afternoon, or early evening."

"Are they reliable?"

"To the highest bidder, which at the moment is me. Two of them were in Chechnya with me and the colonel, and we got out together. The other two were tough guy Moscow mafia. Militia was on their asses when the colonel asked if I could use them for the occasional op over here. I said sure, and he pulled a couple of strings and they showed up in New York."

"Get them here as soon as possible," Minoru said. "In the meantime I want to drive up to the safe house and take a look at the situation."

"We'll fly first to take a look at the setup. I have a friend who runs a small charter aviation service down at Manassas, about twenty miles from here."

"Does he know how to keep his mouth shut?" Minoru asked.

"That's the only kind of friends I have."

At the airport, Sergei Sulitsky, another of Lavrov's friends from the old days, agreed without hesitation to take them on a quick sight-seeing flight, no introductions necessary. He walked off to ready the single engine Cessna Skyhawk TD tied down on the ramp and Lavrov explained the situation to Minoru. Solitsky had been a young KGB pilot when the Soviet Union disintegrated. But he was a Jew and he and his wife and son were stuck in Moscow, penniless and friendless without any prospects. Lavrov pulled a few strings and got the man and his family out and set him up with this business, because from time to time it was handy to have a pilot willing to fly somewhere no questions asked.

They flew at three thousand feet almost due west until they were well outside the terminal control area around Dulles International before they could turn north, reaching the Potomac River just below Whites Ferry a few minutes before four.

Lavrov, seated up front, directed Sulitsky to follow the river toward Washington.

"We're only fifteen miles from the city, and that's restricted airspace," the pilot told him. "I could lose my license if I cross the line."

"It won't be necessary, Sergei, we'll turn back just before the CIA."

Sulitsky gave him a sharp look. "They'll send a chase plane up if we get too close, if that's what you have in mind."

"Not at all. In fact we're looking at a piece of property across the river in Maryland that we might want to buy. I just wanted to see it from the air first."

Minoru in the backseat behind the pilot watched out the window, getting his bearings until they approached a divided highway that crossed the river, Washington looming large in the near distance.

"Is that the Beltway below?" he asked.

"Yes," Lavrov said. "The small town just beyond is Cabin John."

The land here was heavily wooded rolling hills that rose up from the river. Minoru spotted the place almost immediately, the large house and several outbuildings at the center of a clearing. He took a dozen pictures with a digital camera. A long driveway looped up from the Parkway, but across the clearing behind the house the woods were very thick. As they passed over the property he could see no signs of any activity.

If McGarvey and the woman were down there they were probably alone, and vulnerable.

"Thank you," he said. "We may return to the airport now."

SEVENTY-TWO

The house was sprawling, a large stone fireplace in the great room, and wide windows looking out across the clearing, the horse barn and paddock off to the left. The previous owner, now in the federal penitentiary at Leavenworth, had bred Arabian horses as part of his old-money gentleman-farmer cover. The woods on the property were crisscrossed with bridle paths, the only road the one from the Parkway.

Kim was drinking a glass of white wine and she watched from one of the bay windows as the light plane turned and disappeared back to the northwest. "Are they looking for us already?"

"I think so, unless I've missed my guess," McGarvey said from behind her. Coming this soon meant that Turov had someone inside the CIA who was feeding him information. No one outside the Company knew where Huk Kim had gone to ground.

His daughter Elizabeth had called from her cell phone a couple of hours ago to make sure that they'd not run into any trouble yet, and to tell him that they were en route. Before he could object she'd broken the connection. He started to turn away from the window when her gunmetal-gray Hummer came up the driveway out of the woods, her husband Todd behind the wheel.

"Are these the people you were expecting?" Kim asked, stepping back. She'd been jumpy ever since Rencke had dropped them off. The house had been fully serviced recently, and Otto had picked up a couple of hundred dollars worth of groceries that he had brought out earlier. But the place seemed deserted, dry and dusty as a museum or mausoleum.

"Yes," McGarvey said, vexed. He went out to the stair hall and opened the door as they pulled up.

"Hi, Mac," Todd said, getting out of the Hummer, and going around back to get his and Elizabeth's things. He was a tall man, about McGarvey's height, and solidly built with a square pleasant face. He could have passed for McGarvey's son, which was one of the reasons Liz had fallen for him when they'd trained together at the Farm.

Elizabeth was tall and slender with a pretty oval face and short blond hair, the spitting image of her mother at twenty-eight. She and Todd were the youngest agents who'd ever directed the Company's training base, and they were very good at their jobs. Both of them were dressed in khaki slacks and CIA light blue T-shirts, pistols holstered high on their right hips.

"Hi, Daddy," she said coming up to him and kissing his cheek. She looked past him. "Who'd you bring with you this time?"

Kim stood in the middle of the stair hall watching them.

"You were sending me some help," McGarvey said crossly.

"We're not letting you face this alone," Elizabeth said. "And you sure as hell can't trust anyone else." She glanced at Kim. "Who is she?"

"Huk Kim. She and her husband were snipers for the South Korean Army until they decided to get out and turn freelance. They were the shooters in Pyongyang."

"Holy shit," Liz said. She turned back to her father. "You were there, you got her out?"

"It's a little more complicated than that, but yes I went up there," McGarvey said.

Todd had pulled a couple of nylon duffle bags out of the Hummer. "Went up where?" he asked, coming up on the porch.

"Pyongyang," Liz said. "And this is one of the shoot-ers."

"Holy shit," Todd said. He glanced over his shoulder toward the northwest. "We saw a light plane doing a one-eighty just a few minutes ago. Checking out the place?"

McGarvey nodded. "I expect we'll be having company, probably tonight."

"Maybe we should call for more backup."

"It's too late for that," McGarvey said heavily.

They all went inside where Todd dumped the bags in the hall.

"Why?" Liz asked Kim.

"For money," Kim replied evenly.

Elizabeth was instantly angry. "Do you have any com-prehension of what you started, you stupid little bitch?"

"Yes, I do," Kim said, meeting Elizabeth's harsh gaze. "We put into motion exactly what your country wants to happen; the end of North Korea under Kim Jong Il."

"But at what cost? If this goes nuclear millions of peo-ple will die, maybe tens of millions. Doesn't that mean anything to you?"

"Only my husband means anything to me."

"You're saying that it wasn't the North Koreans who made the hit?" Todd asked his father-in-law. "But then who hired her and how'd you get involved?"

McGarvey told them everything from the moment Col-onel Pak had showed up in Casey Key until his run with Kim to the Chinese Embassy in Pyongyang, including the business with Turov in Tokyo.

Kim hadn't known about the North Koreans coming to him for help. "But why you, if they suspected the CIA was behind it?" she asked.

"Because the Chinese respect my father, and North Korean intelligence obviously knows it," Liz said sharply.

"Do you think it's this Russian from Tokyo who's come here after you?" Todd asked.

"Either him or some of his people," McGarvey said, watching the realization of what that meant dawn on all of them.

"It means that I was right," Kim said. "It was the CIA who hired Alexandar."

"Dad?" Liz asked.

McGarvey shook his head. "We're talking a great deal of money, but Otto hasn't found a trace of it from inside."

"Black sources?" Todd suggested.

"That's the first direction he looked, and the money's just not there."

"But the small plane was no coincidence. No one else other than Otto and us knew that you would be here, except for housekeeping who've kept a watch out here."

"It's not the Company," Elizabeth said. "If that kind of an operation had been in the works we would have heard something. Even if the training had taken place offshore, someone would have let a word slip."

"We've got a mole," Todd said.

"A megalomaniac," Elizabeth said. "But you have to ask who is he working for and why? What's their agenda? Certainly not just a war between China and North Korea."

"That's why I brought her here. My first question has been answered, it is someone inside the Company."

"I told you," Kim blurted.

"Otto's looking for the money stream outside," McGarvey said. "And I'm going to find out just that, who hired him and why."

"If they're coming to kill us, I'll need a gun," Kim said, but Elizabeth just stared at the woman as if she'd crawled out from under a rock.

"We'll check around outside to see what we're up against," Todd said.

"Park your car in the garage, and keep out of sight as much as you can," McGarvey told them. "I'd like to keep you two as a surprise."

"There's still time to call for more help out here," Liz suggested.

"We'll do this on our own."

Something suddenly dawned on her. "You're expecting someone else to come out here. The one from the Building."

"It's a thought," he said. "You and Todd make your rounds and then get back here undercover."

SEVENTY-THREE

Minoru moved from the Hay-Adams downtown to a Holiday Inn Express just off the interstate outside of Rockville. It was about five miles from the CIA's safe house, and making it out to Dulles afterward would be simple. Lavrov showed up with a small duffle bag, and some equipment in a panel van just before seven in the evening.

"My operators will be here in a couple of hours," he said. "Have you spoken to the colonel about my request for more money?"

"He's agreed to pay whatever you want, provided you and your people do the job and get out clean."

"What guarantee do I have that you even called him?"

"None," Minoru replied. "Now come look at the images I took from the air, and tell me about your men so that we can devise a plan that will work."

The camera was a good one with a large LCD screen, and the ability to pan left or right and up or down and to zoom in for more detail.

The four men coming from New York worked for the Russian mafia out of Brighton Beach and Newark as enforcers. Whenever Lavrov needed some muscle to convince a business client to see things his way he called on one or more of them.

"They're reliable and damned good," he said.

"Do they trust you?"

"Completely."

"Too bad for them," Minoru said. He had spotted a narrow dirt track about two hundred meters from the driveway and had taken several pictures of it and the terrain above the house. He brought the images up on the screen one at a time. "We'll get off the highway here, and come by foot from the hills behind the house once it gets dark."

"Why not wait until just before dawn, they might be sleeping by then?"

"Because that's what they'll be expecting," Minoru told him patiently. "If we hit them in the early evening, chances are no one will suspect that anything has happened until the next morning.

"Fair enough," Lavrov said.

"What equipment did you bring?"

"AK-47s. It's old stuff, plus night vision oculars, and encrypted earpieces. My people will be carrying their own pistols."

"What did you bring for you and me?" Minuro asked.

Lavrov opened the duffle bag and pulled out a 9 mm Beretta 92F, two extra fifteen-round box magazines, and a Kevlar silencer. He laid all of it on the desk. "I have the same. For afterward. I figure that the house is far enough off the road that no one will hear the AKs. But when the job is done and we start the second phase it wouldn't do to make too much noise."

"You've thought of everything," Minoru said, handling the reliable Italian-made pistol.

"I always try to be thorough."

Minoru looked up and smiled. "Alexandar said as much." He picked up the camera and studied the image of the hillside above the house. "Your four operators will take the house from the rear once you and I have made our way around to the front. They'll go in first with a lot of noise—"

"While we wait in ambush to see what develops," Lavrov finished it. "But won't they call for help?"

"Not until it's too late. Alexandar thinks that they know someone's coming. It's why McGarvey's alone out there with the woman. He's hoping to spring his own trap. But like I said earlier, there's a possibility we'll have help from inside."

Lavrov was worried. "The bastard's got a hell of a reputation."

"Not against six of us," Minoru said. "And we'll have another advantage. He'll want to keep at least one of us alive, while we won't have the same consideration."

Lavrov grinned for the first time. "It's you who's thought of everything."

Minoru shook his head. "All but one."

"What's that?"

"Whatever it is that might go wrong and turn the advantage to McGarvey. If there's a way out of his predicament, he's probably thought of it."

"We'll have to be careful."

"Yes, and lucky."

SEVENTY-FOUR

At the safe house Todd came in the front door after making a quick look around the grounds. It was just after dark and he was dressed in black camos.

McGarvey came out of the study from where he'd been watching the road. "Any sign of the opposition?"

"Not yet," Todd said. "Maybe they'll wait until morning."

"If they're coming it'll be before midnight. It's when I'd make my move."

Todd saw the logic. "Nobody would miss us until tomorrow. Give them plenty of time to clear out of Dodge. But do you still think whoever it is in the Company will come out here?"

"I think so," McGarvey said. "He knows I have the woman with me, and he's got to be worried that sooner or later I'll figure out that it's someone inside who hired Turov. He'll want to find out if I'm suspicious."

"Liz and I are going to come as a nasty surprise. But won't he be running the risk of getting in the middle of an attack?"

"He won't think so," McGarvey said. "But that's exactly what's going to happen, because now that it's gone this far Turov will want him eliminated."

Elizabeth appeared at the head of the stairs and came down to them. "He'd be stupid to come out here."

"Only if he thinks I suspect something," McGarvey said. He glanced toward the head of the stairs. Kim had gone up to one of the bedrooms after dinner to get some rest. She was mentally and physically exhausted from the events of the past several days. "What about her?"

"Still asleep," Elizabeth said. She was angry again. "Why don't we take the bitch downtown and drop her in front of the Chinese Embassy? We could pin a note to her chest. Why risk our lives protecting her?"

"I don't care about her," McGarvey said, though in a way he actually did. From what he'd learned listening to her and seeing the material Otto had found in the laptop he'd come to the conclusion that everything she'd done was out of love for her husband. It didn't make her any the less guilty, it just made her situation tragic.

"We'll turn her over to the Chinese tomorrow and let them deal with her," McGarvey said.

"What about my husband?" Kim demanded from the head of the stairs, her voice shrill. She'd been listening.

"He'll be sent to Beijing," McGarvey told her. "What'd you expect?"

"I don't have to take this shit," she said, coming down the stairs.

"There's the door," McGarvey told her. "If you want to get out of here before your pals show up, be my guest."

"I made my way to Pyongyang without your help, and I can make my way back again."

"If Alexandar and his people don't kill you, and you actually do make it back to North Korea, which from what I've learned about you is possible, you'll still end up in Beijing," Elizabeth said. "You assassinated a Chinese general, what makes you think you and your husband shouldn't be turned over?"

"Someone in the CIA hired Alexandar to hire us, but you're not going to turn him over to the Chinese," she said defiantly.

She had a point. "What do you suggest?" McGarvey asked.

"You can stop the war, and for that Kim Jong Il will send Soon here to the States, where the two of us can go on trial with your CIA traitor and with Alexandar."

"Daddy?" Liz questioned.

"Let's get through tonight first," McGarvey said. "But the Chinese are going to want something."

"Alexandar," she said.

SEVENTY-FIVE

Turov's Nokia encrypted telephone rang and he answered it. The caller was Daniel. It was a little after eleven in the morning in Tokyo and 9 P.M. in Washington, fully dark, which meant that Minoru and the others would soon be on their way out to the Cabin John house.

"I have a solution to our mutual problem that's not nearly as blunt as yours, and certainly a whole hell of a lot neater and more elegant."

"Oh, yes?" Turov said, smiling. He was seated on the deck overlooking the garden, the sound of splashing water soothing.

"I'm going out to the Cabin John house and doing McGarvey myself. We know each other very well, and he won't expect something like this coming from me."

It was exactly what Turov had expected. "Where are you at this moment?"

"In my car. I'm on my way out there now."

"How far away are you, specifically?"

"Why does that matter?" Daniel asked, a sudden note of suspicion in his voice. "Were your people planning on attacking this early?"

"Not until just before dawn."

"Good thinking. They wouldn't have been at their sharpest then. At any rate I'll phone you when I've finished, and you can call off your people."

Turov looked up, the sound of splashing water in the pool soothing his nerves that had taken a spike. "What exactly is your plan? Tell me the details."

"Are you questioning my tradecraft again?" Daniel demanded angrily.

"Not at all. I'm merely trying to help."

"Remember it was I who contacted you, it's my money that's lining your pockets. Don't ever forget it, that is if you want to continue being my expediter."

"I won't forget it. But I want you to remember that we have had a long history together. One that has benefited you as well as me. You wouldn't be in your present position without the product I made sure got into your hands."

"It was never spectacular," Daniel said.

"No, but it was steady and most of all reliable. If you had brought back the sun and the moon both of us would have come under suspicion. As it is we have become rich men. I want to keep it that way."

"Very good," Daniel said, somewhat mollified. "I expect there'll be more work for you to do, but first I have to take care of this unfortunate turn of events."

"Yes, see to it," Turov said. "But will you tell me your plan?"

"He might be surprised to see me, but it won't worry him, nor will he suspect that when his back is turned I will put a bullet in his head. Afterward I'll kill the woman with his pistol, and putting my untraceable gun in her hands I'll fire another shot so that she'll have powder residue, and do the same with his body. She snuck up on him and fired a couple of shots, one of them mortally wounding the ex-director, and with his dying breath he managed to get off one shot which killed her."

"It's a brilliant plan. You'll be killing two birds with one stone, and no one will have any reason to suspect a thing."

"I knew that you'd see it my way," Daniel said. "Call off your people, they're no longer needed."

"I'll see to it immediately," Turov said. "Good luck."

Daniel chuckled. "Luck will play no part whatsoever."

After the connection was broken, Turov stood for a long minute, listening to the sounds of the water, the occasional splash of one of the golden carps, and a lark somewhere behind the house. His time with Daniel had been coming to a close; the relationship had become too dangerous. Time to end it once and for all. Perhaps even take the retirement he'd always planned on taking.

He speed dialed Minoru's number, which was answered on the first ring. "Yes."

"Where are you?"

"We're en route. About fifteen minutes out."

"There's been a slight change in plans," Turov said, and he told his chief of staff what Daniel had planned. "Hold up until he goes in. Once the shooting starts it'll provide the perfect distraction for you."

"He might be successful," Minoru said. "Crazier things have happened. How do you want me to handle it?"

"I want everyone in that house dead before the night is out."

"Including Daniel?"

"Especially Daniel," Turov said, and broke the connection. It was time for a bottle of Krug and within a few days he would be enjoying the opera season in Sydney.

SEVENTY-SIX

They took turns watching from the upstairs windows, scuttling back and forth between the front and the back. At nine it was Liz's turn. McGarvey was with Todd having coffee in the kitchen. The only light on in the house was from a small television Kim was watching in the breakfast nook.

"Somone's coming," Liz called from the upstairs hall.

"Shut off the TV," McGarvey told Kim. He grabbed

his pistol and hurried down the corridor to the front stair hall.

"It's a car from the highway," Liz said.

"Watch the back," McGarvey called up to her as headlights flashed from across the clearing. He unlocked the front door, opened it, and stepped back out of the line of fire.

Todd had gone into the living room where he was watching from one of the windows. "Shit," he said. "It's Otto."

Otto's battered gray Mercedes diesel came down the gravel driveway and pulled up in front, and the Company's Director of Special Projects, his frizzy red hair flying all over the place, jumped out and hurried up to the porch.

McGarvey would have bet his life that the traitor inside the Company wasn't Otto, but he hesitated for just a second before he holstered his pistol at the small of his back. A long time ago John Lyman Trotter, Jr., an old and trusted friend of his, had betrayed the Agency and had sold out to the Russians. It had nearly cost McGarvey his life. But not Otto, he could not believe it.

Rencke came up the two steps to the porch and stopped a few feet from the open door. "Mac?" he called softly, the frightened look on his face clear even in the dim starlight.

McGarvey hesitated just a moment longer. Todd was at the open French doors just across the stair hall, his pistol in hand.

"In here," McGarvey said, and he stepped around the corner to the doorway.

"You scared the hell out of me, I shit you not," Rencke said. "I thought I was too late and they'd already taken you down."

"We're expecting company at any moment, so get in here," McGarvey said. "And give your car keys to Todd. He'll put the car in the garage."

Rencke saw Todd holster his pistol, and realized at once what it meant. "You're expecting our resident bad guy to show up tonight, aren't you?" He watched Todd's eyes as he handed over his keys. "And you thought it was me. Cool."

Todd had to smile "You're not going to think it's so cool when we come under fire and you're in the middle of it." He went out to put Rencke's car under cover and McGarvey closed the door.

"Hi, Otto," Elizabeth called softly from the head of the stairs.

"Keeping watch for the bad guys?"

"Yup."

"What are you doing out here?" McGarvey asked.

"I know who our traitor is, and I'm a little surprised but not so unhappy, ya know," Rencke said. "I had to come out here in person to tell you, 'cause I didn't know how wired this place might be."

"Todd and Liz checked for bugs first thing. We're clean. But I'm sorry you're here, because now it'd be to risky for you to try to leave."

Rencke hopped from one foot to the other, something he did when he was excited or distracted. "I set one of my programs to look down Boyko's track while he was in the KGB and FSB, mostly his foreign embassy assignments, but also the periods he spent in Moscow. Then I started matching those dates and places with those of our own field people."

"And you found some matches," McGarvey said.

"Bingo, but just one. Moscow, Beijing, Kabul, Seoul, and Tokyo. He was at all those places the same time as Boyko."

"Don't tell me that it's Howard?"

"Correcto mundo," Rencke said. "Howard McCann, our own Deputy Director of Operations. How about them apples? But how did you know?"

"Just a guess, but I knew he'd been stationed in Kabul and Beijing, because he never stopped talking about it, and his product was always consistently good—not great, but good. But what abut the money? He doesn't have it, and you said it wasn't showing up in the black budgets."

"Unknown," Rencke admitted. "But if he comes out here tonight like you suspect he will we can ask him. Wherever it's coming from and however it's being transferred to Boyko's accounts, it's a slick operation because I haven't found even a tickle yet."

"Howard has to be working for somebody," McGarvey said. "He's not dealing on his own."

"Not unless he's a raving lunatic. I mean who the hell would try to start a nuclear war?"

Todd came back in a hurry. "I saw headlights coming from the highway," he said.

McGarvey switched on the hall light. "It'll be McCann," he said. "Turn on the light over the wing back chairs in the study and get into the dark corner by the desk. And you'd better open the French doors in case this thing goes down while he's here and we need to make some room for ourselves in a hurry. He'll be armed, he's come out here to kill me, but he probably doesn't know that Turov or his people will be coming our way too."

"Could get real interesting around here," Todd said.

"That it could," McGarvey agreed.

"Do you want to call for backup once he gets here?"

"I want him to open up first."

Todd went back to the study that faced the rear of the house and switched on the light. It would put them at the disadvantage if the attack were to start now, but McGarvey wanted to give McCann a false sense of security at first.

"Liz, we've got company coming from the highway," he called up to his daughter.

"I'll keep the back covered," she responded.

Kim stood in the shadows behind them. "Give me a weapon."

"Not yet," McGarvey told her.

"He's come here to kill me too."

"I want you upstairs with Otto for now."

"Goddamnit, I want a gun!"

"If something develops I'll think about it," McGarvey said, and he motioned for Rencke to take her upstairs. "Keep your head down, and try to keep her quiet."

"What if she doesn't cooperate?"

"Do you have a gun?"

"Yup."

"Shoot her."

SEVENTY-SEVEN

As soon as Rencke and Kim were upstairs, McGarvey went into the dark living room and watched from one of the windows as headlights flashed along the driveway in the woods beyond the clearing. If it was McCann he was driving slowly, probably nervous about what he'd come out here to do.

Unlike Otto he was surprised that the traitor was the DDO. He'd never particularly liked the man. McGarvey had always thought McCann was an officious little bureaucrat with a tight rein over the National Clandestine Service, which was the official name for Operations, but he'd never thought that the bastard had the imagination or the guts to play the role of a double.

There'd been others who'd seemed equally bland, unimaginative, and ordinary until after they'd been outed;

the FBI's John Hanssen a few years ago, a couple of years before that their own Aldrich Ames, and earlier John Trotter. And when the last day finally came everyone was surprised. Everyone had the same question: Why?

The CIA had an acronym for the reasons most intelligence officers turned against their own countries. It was MICE, which stood for money, ideology, conscience, and ego. Hanssen had played the game because his ego led him to believe that he was better than everyone else. Ames had done it for the money, nearly five million dollars from the KGB. And back in the fifties, the British spy Kim Philby had spied for the Russians because he truly believed that the Soviet system was better than Western democracies. He had been an ideologue. Others had become traitors, usually when their nations were at war, because some warped sense of conscience affected their understanding of what was morally right or wrong.

A dark Lexus SUV came into the clearing and made its way to the house, pulling up where Rencke had parked, and the headlights went out. McGarvey couldn't make out the driver until he opened the door and the dome light came on. It was McCann, and now there were almost no doubts left except where the DDO was getting his money, and what the long-range agenda was.

McCann got out of the car and as he came around front he absently patted his right coat pocket. He was wearing a lightweight pin-striped suit and despite the warm weather a vest, and his thinning light hair was mussed as if he had driven out from the city with the windows down.

He stopped and looked up at the mostly dark windows, then made his way up to the porch and hesitated a moment longer before he rang the doorbell.

McGarvey waited long enough for McCann to ring the bell again before he went out into the hall and opened the door.

"What the hell are you doing out here, Howard?" McGarvey demanded. He looked beyond McCann. "Are you alone?"

McCann was as indignant as he usually was. "I'm alone, and I'm here because I heard you'd brought one of the Pyongyang shooters with you. Is it true?"

"Yes, she's here, but you'd better come in and get out of sight."

"Are you expecting trouble?" McCann asked, coming into the stair hall.

"Yes," McGarvey said, closing and locking the door. "I'm using the girl as bait."

"Who do you expect is coming after her?"

"The man who hired her. Ex-KGB living in Tokyo under the name Alexandar Turov. Otto's working on finding out who he really is, might be a guy named Boyko but we're not sure yet."

McCann was obviously shook. "Well, for heaven's sake, you should have let me in on your secret, we could have sent some muscle out here to help out. Haven't you even told your daughter and her husband? I'm sure they would have dropped everything to come out. In fact we should call them right now." McCann reached for his right pocket, but McGarvey held him off.

"I don't want my family involved. Not until we get through this."

McCann looked up toward the head of the stairs. "She up there?"

McGarvey nodded. "Keeping watch. It was she who spotted your car coming up from the highway and I thought it might be starting already. But I don't think it'll happen until just before dawn."

"You're probably right," McCann agreed. "Which gives us time to get both of you out of here and to someplace safe." He stopped, an odd expression coming into his eyes as something else occurred to him. "What makes you believe this Russian knows you're out here?"

"I think there's a better than even chance he has a contact inside the Company. Someone with access to either the DO or housekeeping."

The same odd look came into McCann's eyes as if he were trying to figure the odds of pulling out his pistol and having a shoot-out here and now in the stair hall. "I think that's far-fetched. But do you have any idea who it might be?"

"A couple of possibilities," McGarvey said. "I have something back in the study I want to show you." He stepped aside to let McCann go first, which the DDO did reluctantly.

When they reached the study he went to the desk, his back to McCann.

"It's just here," he said.

"Take your hand out of your pocket, Mr. McCann," Todd said. "I don't want to shoot you, but I will if I have to."

McGarvey turned around. McCann had reached into his pocket for a pistol and he stood perfectly still, the color gone from his face.

"Is that why you came out here tonight, Howard?" McGarvey asked. "To kill me?" He walked over to McCann and took the Russian-made 5.45 mm PSM pistol out of the man's pocket. It was the sort of pistol that Kim would have used. "A woman's gun, but pretty effective at close range. Make it look as if the girl shot me. You'd probably use my gun to shoot her. Neat and tidy."

"I don't know what you're talking about," McCann blustered.

"Did Boyko have something on you from your days when you two were stationed in the same cities? Is that it, Howard?"

McCann held his silence.

"If it wasn't blackmail, what then?" McGarvey pressed, his tone reasonable. "Not money, you're not a rich man. So tell us why."

SEVENTY-EIGHT

At the edge of the woods, one hundred meters west of the house, Minoru held up a hand for Lavrov to stop. They were dressed in black slacks and pullovers. A couple of lights were on downstairs, one in the front and the other in the back. A dark SUV was parked in front.

"They've got company," Lavrov said.

"It's Daniel, the colonel's contact inside the CIA," Minoru told him.

He'd sent Lavrov's four operators up the dirt track to a point where they could come down the hill and approach the house from the rear. McGarvey would be expecting an attack sometime later tonight or early morning and might have set the woman to watch the back. He wanted to be in place before the shooting began.

"How do you want to play this?"

Minoru pointed to the lights from the French doors at the side of the house near the back. They could see shadows moving through the curtains. "I want to take a look. Maybe we'll get lucky and Daniel will do the job for us."

Lavrov grinned.

"Find out if your people are in place yet."

Lavrov spoke into his lapel mike. "Oleg, have you reached the clearing yet?"

"*Nyet,* but we're close."

Minoru heard the transmission in his own headset, but

he preferred that Lavrov give them the orders. They had worked with him before and they trusted his judgment. "As soon as they're in position tell them to hold up until you give them the word to go in."

Lavrov relayed the message.

"Will do."

Minoru waited for a moment, blackened his face with camouflage salve, then took his pistol out of his pocket. "No one leaves here alive tonight."

"Except us," Lavrov said, blackening his face and taking out his gun.

"That's right, so take care where you shoot."

"That goes for you as well. I want to live not only to spend my money, but to earn more from Alexandar. I'll do whatever it takes to become a multimillionaire."

"You'll be one after we're done here," Minoru promised, and they moved out of the woods and trotted toward the house.

The evening was very nearly silent, only the far-off screech of some night hunting bird, and their own soft footfalls on the grass to disturb the peace for the moment. But that would soon change, and Minoru found that he was looking forward to the coming action. He had always been a man of supreme patience. Like Turov he practiced Bushido, which taught endurance of mind and body. But when the time came to kill, the blood in his veins sang and he was truly alive.

Following the colonel's briefing he expected that Kirk McGarvey was a man of a similar stripe, and that fact would make tonight's work all the more enjoyable.

They made their way past the back of the empty horse barn, and had started the last forty meters to the house when Oleg's voice came over the headset.

"We're above the house just now."

"Hold up there," Lavrov ordered.

"Is something wrong?"

"*Nyet*. We're checking something out on the west side of the house. I'll tell you when you can come in."

"If they've posted a lookout in one of the upstairs rooms we'll be spotted the instant we move out into the open, unless you've started your diversion."

Lavrov glanced at Minoru who nodded.

"That's exactly what we're up to. Standby."

"Roger."

A few meters from the house, Minoru could see that the French doors were slightly ajar, the billowy curtains moving in the slight breeze, and he heard voices, one of them a man's raised in anger.

He motioned for Lavrov to go around to the front of the house to cover the SUV and the main entrance while he cautiously approached the French doors. Before he opened fire he wanted to know who was inside and what they were talking about.

SEVENTY-NINE

In the study, McGarvey was perched on the edge of the desk, McCann staring at him with extreme contempt, a thin line of spittle at the corner of his mouth.

"You and Rencke, that freak friend of yours, can't prove a thing. You won't ever come up with enough evidence to take this to a court of law, and I don't think Dick will even have the guts to fire me."

McGarvey shrugged. "You know what I did for a living, Howard. Maybe I don't care if you go to jail. Maybe I'll just shoot you right now and save us all a big headache."

"You wouldn't," McCann said, his bluster beginning to fade.

"Don't push me, Howard. I don't like sons of bitches who sell out their country no matter the consequences. If the Chinese try to take North Korea down a lot of people will die out there. Did you consider that bit of blowback, or didn't you give a shit?"

A range of emotions played across McCann's round face. Suddenly he stepped aside and reached into his left coat pocket and started to withdraw a second pistol, this one a much heavier weapon.

Todd fired one shot, catching the DDO in the shoulder shoving him backward against the bookshelves, momentarily stunning him.

Elizabeth appeared at the doorway. "We have company," she said softly, glancing at McCann's struggling to sit up. "It was him?"

"Yeah," McGarvey said. "How many?"

"Four of them coming down the hill from the rear. Otto's called for help."

"Cut the light in the living room," McGarvey told her, "and get back upstairs."

She disappeared down the corridor and Todd went over to the study light and switched it off.

EIGHTY

Minoru had heard everything, including the second man besides McGarvey, the woman, obviously an American, warning that four men were coming from the back, and that a man named Otto had already called for help. He hesitated for just a moment, angry that Lavrov's men had stupidly started their attack before the order had been given, and that more people were inside the house than just McGarvey, the Korean woman, and Daniel.

He'd taken out two of the spare magazines, and the moment the lights went out he reached around the corner and fired all fifteen rounds into the study.

Almost immediately Lavrov began firing into the house from the front, and the four Russian operators opened fire with their AKs from the rear.

Minoru ejected the spent magazine from his pistol, rammed one of the spares into the handle, charged the weapon, and unloaded another fifteen rounds as fast as he could pull them inside the study before he fell back out of the line of possible fire from inside, reloading for the second time.

Gunfire from the rear of the house was very nearly continuous, but Lavrov had stopped, realizing that shooting indiscriminately without clear targets was just wasting ammunition.

No one was returning fire from inside the house. At least three people were in the study, including Daniel and McGarvey, and Minoru was realist enough to understand that he might have taken down one or perhaps two, but not all of them. If it were McGarvey still alive inside it would explain why they were disciplined enough not to shoot at something they couldn't see. In that case tonight's assignment just got tougher.

"Cease fire," Minoru spoke softly into his mike.

If anything the AK gunfire at the rear of the house intensified, and a moment later Lavrov's voice came over Minoru's headset.

"Cease fire, immediately. Oleg, do you copy?"

The gunfire raggedly came to an end.

"We're going in," Minoru said, momentarily turning away from the open French doors in case someone was just inside listening. "Standby."

The night was silent again, and Minoru strained to

listen for a sound from inside the house. Any kind of a sound. But there was nothing.

"Mr. McGarvey," he called. "Can you hear me?"

No one answered.

"Send Huk Kim out to us, along with Daniel, the man who just arrived, and we will leave you and your friends in peace. We only came for them, no one else. You have my word."

"Do you want me to disable the SUV?" Lavrov's voice came into his earpiece.

"Standby."

"Roger."

"Your last chance, Mr. McGarvey. Send them, or their bodies, out and we will leave."

EIGHTY-ONE

McCann had taken two more hits, one in the center of his chest and the other in the bridge of his nose. Todd bent over him and felt for a pulse. He looked up and shook his head.

The shooting had stopped for now but McGarvey figured that the cease-fire wouldn't last much longer. They were outnumbered and outgunned. Liz had counted four at the rear of the house, armed with AKs, plus one just outside the study and at least one out front, armed with handguns. The last thing Turov's people would expect was a counterattack.

McGarvey motioned for Todd to go upstairs, and his son-in-law straightened up and cautiously checked out the corridor, before he gave the all clear.

"You needn't die this evening, Mr. McGarvey," the man from just outside the French doors called softly.

Todd slipped out into the hall and silently made his way to the stairs, McGarvey, keeping an eye on the front door, right behind him.

Elizabeth, a pistol in her left hand, was waiting for them at the door to one of the back bedrooms. Blood seeped from a wound in her right arm, which she held to her chest.

"Christ, you've been hurt," Todd whispered urgently and he went to her.

"I'll be okay, sweetheart," she said. She turned to her father. "What about McCann?"

"He's dead," McGarvey told her. "Where are Otto and Kim?"

"Watching the driveway from the master bedroom. He's got an old military .45, but he's all jazzed up and I'm afraid he's going to have an accident and shoot himself in the foot. What do you want to do?"

"We'll never be able to hold out long enough for help to get here, so I'm going out the bathroom window on the east side and see if I can even up the odds a little. We don't stand a chance against those guys with the AKs in the back," McGarvey told them.

"I'm going with you," Todd said.

"Stay here, because the other two will be coming up the stairs."

"We can handle them up here by ourselves if we don't have to watch our backs," Liz said. She was fiercely determined, and McGarvey was proud of her and frightened for her at the same time. But she was a highly trained Company field officer, and she knew what she was doing.

He pulled out McCann's PSM pistol. "Give this to Otto and let Kim have the .45, she's a better shot."

"Do you trust her?" Liz asked, taking the small gun.

"We don't have any choice—"

Just then the firing started again from the back of the house, the heavy Kalashnikov rounds smashing windows and easily penetrating the walls.

They all ducked down, plaster and wood chips flying all over the place.

"Watch yourself, sweetheart," McGarvey said, and he and Todd raced to the large bathroom at the end of the corridor, unlocked the broad window above the Jacuzzi tub, and shoved it open.

Pistol fire came from the front of the house and outside the study as McGarvey holstered his weapon then levered himself out the window where he hung for just a moment before dropping ten feet to the ground. He pulled out his gun and quickly moved to the back corner of the house as Todd dropped down from the bathroom and joined him.

McGarvey looked around the corner long enough to spot four figures dressed all in black, directing a continuous stream of $7.62\,\text{mm} \times 39$ rounds slam into the upstairs of the house.

"I'll take the farthest two," he told Todd. "But get ready to move smartly when they realize what's going on."

"Right," Todd replied tightly, the fifteen-round SIG-Sauer P226 that he preferred over the more accurate Wilson at the ready.

McGarvey, a spare magazine in his left hand, raised the pistol in his right and stepped around the corner, leaving enough elbow room for Todd to join him, and both of them calmly began firing, one shot after the other in rapid succession as if they were on a simulated live tactical situation at the Farm.

One of McGarvey's targets went down immediately as did one of Todd's, but the attackers were professionals who immediately understood that they were taking fire from their right, and they switched aim, diving for cover as they opened fire.

Todd took a grazing hit in his left side as he and McGarvey ducked back around the corner. "Shit," he grunted

"You okay?" McGarvey demanded, reloading his pistol.

"I'll live," Todd replied, pissed off at himself that he had brought only one of the attackers down and had taken a hit himself. "What now? They'll fan out and be coming around the corner any second."

"Expecting us to be hauling ass for the front of the house to get out of their way," McGarvey said. He hurried ten feet along the side of the house then dropped to a prone position.

Todd was grinning when he joined his father-in-law, dropping to the ground a few feet away and slamming a fresh magazine into the SIG's handle.

"We'll only have the first second or two before they figure out that they've been had," McGarvey warned.

"They're good," Todd said.

"Yup, but we're better, and they're in a hurry."

One of the black-clad shooters cautiously peered around the corner of the house for just an instant then ducked back out of sight. He said something in Russian to the other man, not bothering to keep his voice low. Evidently he'd not spotted the two figures lying on the ground no more than ten feet away.

He came around the corner, the second man right behind him, and before either of them knew what was happening McGarvey and Todd opened fire, dropping both of them.

"Four down, two to go," McGarvey said, getting to his feet. The firing at the front and opposite side of the house had stopped, the night deathly silent again.

"What now?" Todd asked.

"Go around back and force the kitchen door. Soon as you're clear I'll go around front to take care of whoever it was knocking at our door," McGarvey said. "But watch yourself, son."

"You too, Pop," Todd said, and McGarvey winced. He hated the word.

EIGHTY-TWO

Minoru stood over the body in the study. It wasn't McGarvey so he had to assume it was Daniel. The man was dead, at least that part of the assignment had gone as planned. But McGarvey had evidently retreated to the second floor.

The AK fire from the back had ceased, and he thought he'd heard the small pops of perhaps two handguns before there was silence.

He bent down and retrieved the SUV's keys from Daniel's coat pocket. "Valeri," he spoke softly into his lapel mike.

"Here."

"What's your position?"

"I'm in front."

"Standby, I'm coming out," Minoru said. He stepped over the body, left the study through the French doors, and hurried around front to where Lavrov was flattened against the wall beside the open door.

The man was jumpy and when Minoru came around the corner he spun around and raised his pistol.

"Get a hold of yourself," Minoru told him sternly. "Have you any contact with Oleg or the others?"

"No, and I say we get out of here right now," Lavrov blurted and it was obvious he was spooked.

"Daniel's down in the study and we have only two targets remaining. We can get this taken care of and be away in the next ten minutes if your keep your wits."

"How do you want to play this?"

"They're all upstairs. We'll go in, lay down a line of fire, and rush them."

Lavrov was skeptical, but he nodded. "You'll be right there with me, I'm not doing this alone."

"At your side," Minoru assured him.

Lavrov rolled left through the door, and moved fast across the stair hall, Minoru right behind him.

What sounded like breaking glass came from the rear of the house. "Clear in back," a man's voice called.

"Clear in front," another man called from just behind them on the porch. It was McGarvey. Minoru recognized the voice.

"Upstairs right now," he whispered urgently to Lavrov. "No matter what happens, keep firing, I'll take care of the two down here."

Lavrov hesitated only an instant before he opened fire and charged up the stairs.

Minoru turned and sprinted down the corridor back to the study, ducking through the door and hiding himself around the corner as the shooting upstairs intensified. Someone was firing back at Lavrov, and a woman cried out in Korean.

A tall, husky man, holding what appeared to be a boxy SIG-Sauer, hurried from the back, passing the study door with only a glance inside, and then was gone.

"Upstairs," McGarvey said urgently.

"Me first," the other man replied. "It's my wife up there."

"Watch yourself, for Christ's sake."

Minoru knew that the odds had changed against him, but this time it was because of faulty intel from Turov. Daniel was dead and Lavrov might be getting unlucky upstairs with the woman.

Time to go.

He crossed the study, slipped outside, and cautiously walked around front and got behind the wheel of the Lexus. The firing inside the house had stopped for the moment, but it was unlikely that anyone would be paying any attention to the front.

Starting the car, he slammed it into gear and headed back up to the highway. Help was on its way, and if the authorities were looking for any vehicle it would be this one. But no one knew about the van parked up in the woods.

EIGHTY—THREE

Rencke was down in the corridor but conscious, blood coming from a bad wound in his side, and Todd reached him as they heard the SUV start up and drive off. "Rats deserting the sinking ship," Otto quipped.

A few feet beyond him, Kim lay on her back, her eyes open, McCann's PSM pistol still gripped in her right hand. She had been shot in the forehead

"Where is he?" Todd asked, keeping his voice low.

"Somewhere back there," Rencke said. He looked up at McGarvey. "Sorry, Mac. I don't think I did such a hot job."

"Liz?" Todd said.

"Go, but be careful."

Todd jumped up and cautiously moved down the corridor toward the bedroom where Liz had been keeping a lookout, as McGarvey knelt down beside his old friend and looked at the wound. It was leaking a pale fluid as well as blood.

"Hurts like hell, kemo sabe."

"I bet it does," McGarvey said. "I think he got a piece of one of your kidneys."

"Not my liver?"

"Wrong place," McGarvey told him. He moved Otto's left hand to the wound. "Press down, and keep pressing. We'll get you an ambulance."

"I don't want to die, Mac. Honest injun."

A deep black rage threatened to block McGarvey's sanity, but he managed to keep himself under control and he smiled. "Not a chance. Louise would never forgive me. Neither would Katy."

Todd had disappeared around the corner, and McGarvey heard Liz's voice from the bedroom. "Sorry, sweetheart, I sorta got distracted when Otto got hit."

"Put your weapon on the floor or I'll kill her," a man with a Russian accent said.

"You'll shoot her no matter what," Todd replied.

"I don't give a shit about her or you. We came for McGarvey. Where is he?"

McGarvey came around the corner. "Here," he said. A large man dressed all in black stood next to Elizabeth, the muzzle of his pistol inches from her temple.

"Put your gun down."

"The four out back are all down, and your pal who was outside the study is gone. It's just you."

A little wildness came into the man's face. "I said put your gun down." His attention was on McGarvey.

Elizabeth moved sharply backward a half step. "Now!"

McGarvey fired one shot, catching the man in his left eye, his head snapping back. His pistol discharged, the bullet plowing into the wall across the room, and he fell back. McGarvey fired a second round, hitting the man in the neck and a third and fourth hitting him in the chest.

"Daddy!" Elizabeth cried.

He looked up out of a daze, on the verge of firing again at a man who had died after the first bullet entered his brain.

"It's okay," Todd was saying at his side. "They're all down or gone. We need to help our people now."

Somewhere in the far distance McGarvey thought he could hear the sounds of a lot of sirens coming down the driveway, but he couldn't take his eyes off his daughter. She was hurt, but she was alive and for now that's all that mattered to him.

WASHINGTON/TOKYO

EIGHTY-FOUR

Rencke was nearly unconscious by the time the cleanup crew arrived from Langley in four unmarked vans and got to work. With them was Lance Karp, a Company medical doctor who quickly checked his vital signs.

"Is he going to make it?" McGarvey asked. He still hadn't completely come down from the action, something that took longer and longer for him to do the older he got.

"He's serious but not critical for the moment," the doctor said. "A chopper is on its way. We'll take him to All Saints and I'll put him on the table right away. I'll know better then." All Saints in Georgetown was a private hospital used exclusively by the CIA and the other thirteen U.S. intelligence organizations. All the staff held secret clearances. Nothing was ever leaked about the patients who were brought there.

Two technicians strapped Otto on a gurney and brought him downstairs to the front hall. The doctor took a quick look at Elizabeth's arm and applied a temporary bandage to stop the bleeding.

"You're lucky, the bullet missed anything serious, but you're going to be out of action for a bit. You're going aboard the helicopter."

"I'm coming with them," McGarvey said.

"No room, and there's nothing you could do to help," Karp said briskly. "Let me do my job, Mr. Director. I'd say you have your hands full here for the moment."

He had Todd take off his jacket and lift his shirt. An angry red welt oozed a little blood, but it was nothing serious.

"Have one of the medics put a bandage on that," the doctor said. "You'll be sore for a couple of days, but you're even luckier than your wife."

One of the techs, wearing white coveralls with booties over his shoes and a hair net, appeared at the door. "Chopper is five minutes out, Doc."

"Anyone else here needs tending?"

"We're taking care of them."

"I see," the doctor said. "Downstairs in five minutes," he told Elizabeth and he left.

The technician came in. "Dick Johnson, Mr. Director," he said. "What do you want done out here?"

"I want the place sanitized within twenty-four hours," McGarvey said.

Johnson glanced around at the destruction that had been wrought by the AK-47s. But he nodded. "We can take care of this stuff, but we've got two bodies in back, two on the east side, plus the two up here, and it's Mr. McCann down in the study."

"Take McCann and the woman to All Saints and put them on ice. Get rid of the other five."

The four shooters outside, plus the Russian lying in a pool of his own blood, would be taken to a crematorium used by the Company's housekeeping section and the ashes and bones, which would be ground to a fine powder, would be flushed down a floor drain.

"What about fingerprints, dental, and DNA for IDs?"

McGarvey glanced at the Russian who'd shot Otto, killed Huk Kim, and would have killed Liz, and shook his head. "No need. I know why they were here tonight and who sent them. I want them gone without a trace."

"Yes, sir," Johnson said. "By this time tomorrow they'll have disappeared and we'll have this place right as rain."

"We're taking the Hummer, but there's a Mercedes in the garage," Todd said.

"Mr. Rencke's. We'll have it driven back to the campus tonight."

"One of the bad guys got out of here with McCann's Lexus," McGarvey said. "He'll have abandoned it by now, but find it and get it out to Langley."

"Any chance of us bagging him?"

"No. He'll be on his way back to Tokyo and I want him to get there."

Downstairs, McGarvey, Todd, and Elizabeth held up as McCann's body was being removed from the study. "Turov had him eliminated to keep him from telling us where the money was coming from."

"Which means that Turov knows?" Todd asked.

"I'm not sure," McGarvey said, his heart already hardening again for the job ahead. "But I'm going to ask him just that before I kill him."

The helicopter was landing in the clearing twenty yards from the house, and they hustled Liz out to it as Rencke was being loaded aboard.

"We'll see you at the hospital," Todd told her and gave her a kiss.

"What about Mother?" she asked her father.

"I'll call her in the morning. She can fly up to be with you."

Elizabeth managed a slight smile. "She's already here. She checked into the Hay-Adams three days ago. Couldn't stand to languish in Florida while you were out on the firing line. Call her tonight. She'll want to know about Otto too."

"I'm not going to have much time for her or you, sweetheart."

"I know. But if you're going back to Tokyo, take Todd along. You might need the backup."

* * *

McGarvey used his cell phone on the way in to call his wife at the Hay-Adams. She was just leaving to have dinner alone in the hotel's Lafayette Room, and she was over the moon to hear from him. "Where are you?"

"I'm with Todd, we're on the way to All Saints."

"My God, are you hurt?"

"It's not me. Elizabeth has been shot in the arm, nothing too serious, but Otto's in rough shape. They'll be operating on him within the hour."

"I'll leave for the hospital right now," Katy said.

"I'm not staying for long," McGarvey told her. "This thing isn't over yet."

"I figured as much. The president's address to the nation is being postponed until tomorrow night, because of some new developments. Kirk, everyone I've talked to thinks he hasn't a clue what to do next. It's frightening."

"They're right. But it's not his fault."

"Can you do something to help him?"

"I'm in the middle of it, Katy," McGarvey said. "I'll see you at the hospital in about thirty minutes." He broke the connection and pocketed the phone.

Todd glanced over at him. "If you're going back to Tokyo I want to come with you. Liz was right, you might need backup."

"Could get messy, especially with the Japanese. And Tokyo might not be such a healthy place to be."

Todd grinned. "I'll take that as a yes."

McGarvey returned the smile despite himself. "Just don't ever call me Pop again."

By the time they got to the hospital, Elizabeth had already been treated as an outpatient, and they found her, Katy, and Otto's wife Louise in the surgical waiting room on the fourth floor.

Katy jumped up when they walked in and before she

hugged her husband she looked into his eyes, something she did when she needed to gauge his mood. "Will it be all right?" she asked, holding him close.

"If it isn't I'll have done a lot of work for nothing," he told her, trying to keep it as light as he possibly could under the circumstances.

"That's good enough for me," she said. "When are you leaving?"

"In the morning."

She smiled faintly. "Would you like to bunk with me tonight?"

"I was wondering when you were going to ask," McGarvey said.

A surgical nurse, in a blood-splattered gown, a mask hanging from her neck, came in. "Mrs. Rencke?" she asked.

Louise jumped up and went over. She was very tall and slender with thick dark hair and a homely face, screwed up now in concern. Otto thought she was beautiful, and she thought he was the smartest, kindest man on the planet. "Me," she said.

"His left kidney was destroyed, and it'll have to come out. But Dr. Karp is about the best there is in the business. Your husband will be just fine, the doctor wanted me to tell you that. But it's going to take several hours."

"I'll wait," she said.

"So will all of us," Katy added.

When the nurse was gone, McGarvey went out to the corridor and used his cell to call the Watch, which was the operations center in the Company's Old Headquarters Building. The watch commander answered. "O'Day."

"Good evening, Darrell, this is McGarvey."

"Mr. Director, how are you? I heard there was something of a dustup at one of our safe houses tonight."

"Otto's been hurt, but he'll pull through. I need to

borrow one of our Lears and a crew without attracting any attention from down the hall. Can you do that for me?" The CIA maintained a small fleet of the twin-engine VIP jets that were capable of transoceanic flights.

"When do you need it?" O'Day asked without hesitation.

"Right away."

"I think I can arrange that, sir. Can you tell me where you're headed?"

"Okinawa. And I'm going to need an assist from the Navy out there."

"Yes, sir. Anything else?"

"Some information."

"Anything."

"Who's the current bureau chief for Chinese intelligence here in D.C.?"

"As a matter of fact I have the Chinese file open at the moment, we're working on the Watch Report for the President's A.M. briefing," O'Day said. "Ma Pang-yu. He's an army colonel at their embassy under the cover of military liaison."

"How do I get ahold of him? Do you have his private number?"

This time O'Day did hesitate. "I suppose I should ask you why you want the jet and that particular piece of information, and make a note of it somewhere."

"Yes."

"I'll try to get to it before my shift is over," the watch commander said, and he gave McGarvey Colonel Ma's Washington number. "Good hunting, Mr. Director."

"Thanks," McGarvey said. He hung up and called the number.

EIGHTY—FIVE

Minoru had called ahead and the Gulfstream had been ready for him by the time he had driven the Lexus up the dirt road, switched for the van, and got out to the private aviation terminal at Dulles. They were airborne a few minutes after one in the morning en route to Seattle, and now at three eastern daylight time, he had composed himself enough to think about telephoning Turov on the Nokia.

The crew aboard the luxuriously appointed jet was Japanese. The pilot and copilot had been lured away from JAL by a fabulous sum of money, and Keiko, the pretty flight attendant, had been the mistreated girlfriend of a Japanese *yakuza* boss who Turov had killed eighteen months ago.

"Would you like me to prepare the bed for you, Hirobumi-san?" she asked.

"Perhaps later. For now I would like more tea and then some privacy. I need to make a call."

"Of course." The woman bowed.

She was back a minute later with a pot of water and the tea things on a tray that she placed on the low table in front of Minoru. She smiled at him and then disappeared onto the flight deck.

He took his time measuring the tea powder into the pot of water, stirring with the bamboo implement six times in a clockwise motion then pouring two-handed into the small handleless porcelain cup. He drank with a slurping sound until the cup was empty, then refilled it, his mind returning to an ordered state for the first time this evening.

It was a little after five in the evening in Tokyo when

Turov picked up on the first ring. He'd been waiting for the call. "Where are you?"

"Aboard the jet," Minoru said. "We left Dulles about two hours ago."

"Was the mission a success?" Turov asked, and Minoru could hear tension in the colonel's voice.

"A partial success. The woman is dead, as are Daniel, Lavrov, and his four shooters. No one left alive saw my face."

"McGarvey?"

"We could not get to him. He knew we were coming, and just like you he laid a trap."

"He's less like me than you could possibly imagine, Hirobumi," Turov replied coldly. "Tell me everything."

Minoru did, succinctly and precisely, leaving nothing out, including his estimation of Lavrov and the four men who'd been brought down from New York without blaming them for the partial failure. "But you have fulfilled your contract, Colonel, and you are in the clear."

"Loose ends are never *in the clear.*"

"This time may be different."

"Very well, how do you see it?" Turov often used Minoru as a sounding board.

"Of the two assassins you hired, the woman is dead so can offer no testimony and the husband is in North Korean custody, and at this point the Chinese would not believe anything Pyongyang told them, even if Kim Jong Il were to declare that on a clear day the sky is blue."

"Continue."

"Daniel is dead so the link from you to the Central Intelligence Agency has been severed."

"For now."

"No one is left who can prove a thing against you."

"Except for Kirk McGarvey," Turov said softly. "He will come here again."

"If he does we will kill him, my colonel," Minoru said.

"You and I together. But if he remains in Washington, or returns to his home in Florida he will be ineffective without the woman's testimony."

"I'm not so sure, Minoru-san," Turov replied after a beat.

Minoru closed his eyes and felt a profound sense of gratitude for his own Bushido patience and understanding. "Believe me, Colonel, McGarvey is no longer a threat to us. If he persists we will destroy him."

"We'll talk more when you arrive."

"In the morning," Minoru said. "We will make plans for Australia."

EIGHTY-SIX

McGarvey and Katy got back to the hospital around 7:30 A.M. Housekeeping had brought his things from the safe house over to the hotel so he'd been able to change into some fresh clothes. He'd repacked this morning and brought his bag with him.

Todd had taken a pale, exhausted Elizabeth to their quarters at the Farm, and had promised to be back first thing this morning with the equipment they would need.

Louise had slept on the chair beside Otto's bed, and both of them were awake now, though it was obvious Otto was in a lot of pain. His breakfast tray of tea, juice, and Jell-O was untouched.

"What, no Twinkies?" Katy asked. Rencke's idea of a balanced diet was junk food, especially Twinkies, and heavy cream.

Otto's grin was lopsided and his long red hair was even frizzier than usual. "Oh, hi, Mrs. M," he said, his voice weak. "They've never even heard of them."

Katy and Louise embraced. "How's he doing?"

"He'll be just fine in a few days," Louise said. "But he wants me to bring him a laptop."

"How're you feeling?" McGarvey asked, laying a plastic 7-Eleven bag on Otto's breakfast tray.

"I've felt better," Rencke said. He eyed the bag. "Emergency rations?"

McGarvey and Katy had stopped to buy a couple of packages of Twinkies on the way over. "Something like that. For when you feel up to it."

"They took out one of my kidneys, Mac. Makes us brothers." A number of years ago McGarvey had lost one of his kidneys because of a gunshot wound, the same as Otto's.

"Practically twins," Katy said.

Otto stifled a laugh.

A hospital security officer in plain clothes came to the door and knocked on the frame. "Mr. Director, could I have a word, sir?" He was an older man who looked as if had played pro football a while back and hadn't let himself go soft.

McGarvey stepped out into the corridor with him. "Is my guest here?"

"Yes, sir. We've got him in reception downstairs."

"I'm taking him down to the morgue. We're going to turn the woman's body over to him."

"Yes, sir."

McGarvey went back into Otto's room. "I have to go now," he told them. He and Katy embraced.

"Watch your back, sweetheart," she said.

"I'm taking Todd with me."

"I'm glad."

"Kick some ass, kemo sabe," Rencke said, and Louise nodded.

Colonel Ma Pang-yu, dressed in an English-cut business suit, was a small, dapper man with a very light complexion and round non-Oriental eyes. He was seated across from the security reception desk. He got to his feet when McGarvey appeared at the door.

"Good morning, Mr. Director," the Chinese intelligence officer said, his English good.

They shook hands and McGarvey gave him a visitor's pass. "Let's make this quick."

He took the colonel down to the pathology labs and the morgue in the basement. One of the technicians opened the refrigerated compartment where Kim's body had been placed, slid it out, and then left them.

"Her name is Huk Kim," McGarvey said. "She and her husband Soon were South Korean snipers, but they quit the service several years ago and have been working freelance ever since. They were the shooters in Pyongyang."

Ma glanced at Kim's body. "Yes, we received word from Major Chen that you were given assistance in Pyongyang getting this woman here to Washington so that you could prove North Korea's innocence. It appears you failed."

"Only in keeping her alive, for that I'm sorry. But the fact that we were attacked proves she was involved."

Ma shrugged. "It proves nothing, Mr. Director, although the fact that you are working for the North Korean regime has come as something of a surprise. I'm here out of curiosity. Nothing more."

"She and her husband were hired by an expediter living in Japan. An ex-KGB killer. It was his people who came here last night."

Ma was unimpressed. "The Russians have no reason to see the region engaged in a nuclear exchange."

"He was an expediter only. He worked for someone else."

"Who?" the colonel asked.

McGarvey was walking on shaky ground now. "I don't know," he said, and Ma started to turn away. "But I'm going to ask the Russian. It's a question of money."

"And motivation."

"Yes. I'll ask him that too."

Ma chose his words with obvious care. "From where we sit, Mr. Director, only one country would benefit from creating trouble for us with North Korea—other than the insanity of Kim Jong Il."

"That would seem to be the case," McGarvey said. He opened the drawer next to Kim's and unzipped the top part of the bag to reveal McCann's face. "He hired the Russian, and he was one of the raiding party last night who tried to kill Kim to keep her from talking."

Ma was impressed, and then angry. "I know this man," he said. "And if what you are telling me is true my government will have to immediately reevaluate who its real enemy is."

"You may take the woman's body with you, but his stays here," McGavey said. He rezipped the bag and closed the drawer. "I only showed you because I want you to believe that I'm telling the truth. Like the Russian he was only a middleman. He was getting money from someone other than us."

"Convenient for you to say so—"

"Bullshit, Colonel. I wouldn't have brought you here to blow smoke up your ass. My government did not engineer the assassination. We may have done some stupid things, but this wasn't one of them."

Ma took his time replying. "It's only your reputation that compels me to listen to you, Mr. Director. What do you want?"

"Time."

"To do what?"

"Prove that neither Pyongyang nor my government was behind the assassination."

"How much time?" Ma asked.

"As much as you can give me."

Ma nodded after a beat. "Forty-eight hours," he said. "I think that I can convince my superiors of that much." He shook his head. "Beyond that I don't know."

"Do you want the woman's body?"

"No," Ma said, and he glanced at the other drawer. "But I would take that one."

McGarvey shook his head. "I'll call you direct when I have something."

"Yes, do that."

EIGHTY-SEVEN

Todd was waiting in the Hummer just outside the ambulance entrance when McGarvey emerged from the meeting with the Chinese intelligence chief of station, tossed his bag in the backseat, and got in.

"How's Liz?"

"Tired, but she's okay. How's Otto?"

"We brought him some Twinkies."

Todd laughed, but then he got serious. "I brought everything we'll need for Tokyo. What's the drill?"

"I've got one of our Lears and a crew, who'll fly us over to Okinawa and from there the Navy will get us to Yokosuka. But it's not going to be easy getting to Turov."

"Do you have a plan?"

McGarvey nodded. "You're going to provide a diversion and I'm going over the wall. Not very elegant, but we don't have much time for anything more sophisticated, and we certainly couldn't show up in Tokyo with a big crew. The Japanese authorities would be all over us before we took two steps."

"Well, first we've got another problem right here," Todd said. "Dick called and asked me to bring you in. He wants to talk."

McGarvey had been hoping to avoid Adkins until after Tokyo. But no doubt the housekeeping team leader from last night had filed his report to cover his own ass. He had stuck his neck out taking orders from a retired DCI.

"Did he mention anything about McCann?"

They were in traffic on Wisconsin Avenue heading toward the Key Bridge across the river. Todd glanced at him and shook his head. "And I didn't mention it."

"Thanks, Todd, but you're going to have to start watching your ass if you want to stay in the business."

Todd hesitated a moment. "Liz and I were going to talk to you about that," he said. "We're thinking about pulling the pin. Starting up our own security consulting firm. We'd make ten times the money, and maybe we'd get into a position where people stopped shooting at us."

"You might give it a second thought, son. They need people like you and Liz. Badly."

Todd smiled wanly. "She predicted you'd say something like that."

"Okay, let's go pay Dick a visit."

Adkins was waiting for them in his seventh-floor office in the Old Headquarters Building, along with the Deputy DCI David Whittaker and the Agency's general counsel Carlton Patterson. None of them looked particularly happy, especially not Adkins.

"I understand that Howard McCann was shot to death last night at the Cabin John safe house," Adkins said, getting right to it. His eyes were tired, his narrow face lined and sallow as if he hadn't slept in a week.

"That's right. Houseeeeping took his body to All Saints," McGarvey said.

"You were there too?" Adkins asked Todd.

"Yes, sir. Along with my wife, and Otto."

"Both of them wounded, Rencke seriously."

"Well, Jesus H. Christ, Mac, would you mind explaining what the fuck is going on?" Whittaker demanded. He was a tall, lean man, who had served under McGarvey as assistant deputy director of operations, and again under McGarvey in the same number two position he held now. McGarvey had never known him to have such a short temper.

"Howard was the traitor here who directed and paid the Russian in Tokyo to expedite the hit in Pyongyang and at least two others, probably more."

All the animation seemed to leave Adkins's face and he was struck dumb for the moment, as was Whittaker.

"Do you have proof of this?" Patterson asked.

"I suspected someone within the Company was calling the shots with this Russian. Otto discovered that Howard's duty stations corresponded—same cities, same dates—and when he found out that I had brought one of the South Korean shooters back with me from Pyongang I knew whoever it was would come out and try to eliminate her."

"The duty stations could have been coincidences," Patterson said. "And him coming out to the safe house could have been a gesture of goodwill. He came to offer his help."

"He confessed."

"Do you have that on tape, or in his own handwriting, maybe his signature?"

"Just my word, Carleton."

Patterson started to object, the lawyer in him wanting to argue the point, but Adkins held him off.

"What next, Mac?" he asked. "What do we tell his wife?"

"Killed in the line of duty. Give him his star downstairs, and his pension. Ballinger and his people can work up something that'll satisfy the press corps." Logan Ballinger was the Agency's chief press officer.

Whittaker was incredulous. "We're making him a hero?" he demanded.

"The country needs a hero right now, and so does the Company."

"What about us?" Adkins asked. "What next?"

"You'll need a new DDO," McGarvey said.

"I meant the situation."

"I have one more thing to take care of."

No one said a thing for a beat.

McGarvey got out of his chair across from Adkins and glanced out the window at the rolling hills and woods, pretty at this time of the year. "Hang onto your ass, Dick, because if I don't make it and the shit hits the fan, you're going to take a lot of the heat."

"Will you come in for a debriefing?" Patterson asked. "We can't just sweep what happened out at Cabin John under the rug."

McGarvey nodded. "But that might be what you'll have to do in the end."

EIGHTY-EIGHT

Turov's Gulfstream touched down at Tokyo's Narita Airport just before dawn and taxied over to the Russian's personal hanger beyond the VIP terminal. As the engines spooled down Minoru thanked the pretty attendant and the pilot and copilot.

Out front he got into a cab and ordered the driver to take him up to Ueno, and he sat back with his thoughts. He considered himself lucky to have walked away from the Cabin John operation in one piece. Rather than cower in the house after the attack had begun, McGarvey had counterattacked. It was the last thing any of them had expected to happen.

All but one of the mission's goals had been accomplished. The woman was dead as was Daniel, leaving the American authorities with no proof.

He hoped it was enough to satisfy the colonel, but he had his doubts.

Turov, dressed in a deep scarlet kimono, waited on the teak deck overlooking the garden, a samauri short sword lying at his side, his expression one of Bushido serenity. The morning was absolutely flawless, the sky cloudless, the sounds of the city very distant, muted by the compound's high walls and the parkland's woods on the low side of the road, the tinkling water in the fountain soothing, and the occasional splash of a golden carp in the pond gentling.

He didn't look up when Minoru came to the doorway, but his posture stiffened slightly. "Welcome home," he said softly.

Minoru remained where he stood, not moving a muscle. The colonel was in his transition state—a zen time between deep contemplation and total wakefulness—which was extremely dangerous. His actions could be unpredictably dangerous if he were disturbed. Minoru had personally witnessed the decapitation of a *yakuza* foot soldier who walked up behind the colonel at just a time as this.

Finally Turov turned and looked over his shoulder. "Come, sit with me and tell me everything."

Minoru went and sat down cross-legged and listened to the sounds of the flowing water for a few sconds before he began to speak, going over in detail everything that had happened from the moment he'd left the compound and flown to Washington aboard the Gulfstream.

"He will come here to finish this business," Turov said.

"But why? Your death will serve no purpose toward stopping China from making its attack."

"He is of a different opinion, and we must respect him for it. I've set someone to keep watch for him at Dulles and let us know the moment he departs, and someone at Narita to watch for his arrival."

"He could be eliminated in the crowds at the airport, or on the highway," Minoru suggested. "An accident."

"We don't have the time or manpower. It'll have to be done here."

"*Hai*, Colonel."

"When it's over we'll destroy his body in the usual manner and scatter his ashes in Tokyo Bay before we leave for Melbourne. It will be a just ending for a fitting adversary."

EIGHTY-NINE

The dawn was beginning to brighten the horizon behind them as the CIA's Learjet en route to Okinawa's Kadena Air Base began to lose altitude. McGarvey had awakened forty-five minutes ago after a reasonable night's sleep in one of the soft leather reclining seats. He was having coffee that their flight attendant had laid out when Todd woke up and looked out the windows.

"We're on the way down. How far out are we?"

"About an hour, I expect. From there the Navy is giving us a lift up to Yokosuka. The *George H.W. Bush* is in port so they're landing us aboard. Less questions that way." The *Bush* was the CVN-77, the latest Nimitz-class carrier, and it had been deployed to Yokosuka a couple of months ago.

Todd poured a cup of coffee. "Do you think they'll go along with us?"

"They won't have much choice."

"Anything else come in during the night?"

"The Chinese have apparently backed off their rhetoric for now," McGarvey said. "And CNN is reporting that the White House postponed recalling our ambassador."

"Dick must have said something at the briefing to make Haynes change his mind."

"I'm sure he did," McGarvey said. "He bought us some time."

"It's a start," Todd replied. "You said last night that we were going in with one slight advantage. What'd you mean?"

"He thinks that I'm coming to arrest him and turn him over to the Chinese."

"But we're not."

"No."

They were served a decent breakfast of steak, hash browns, and eggs from the aircraft's tiny galley by a taciturn ex-Air Force staff sergeant who was used to flying with anyone from an Agency VIP visiting a foreign station to field officers either going into or coming out of some dangerous assignment somewhere. No one appreciated questions.

They landed at Kadena in the southern part of the long, narrow island a few minutes past seven, and taxied across the field to where a Navy C-2A(R) Grumman Greyhound Carrier Onboard Delivery twin-engine turboprop aircraft was parked, its propellers turning.

Their pilot, John Tillotson, turned in his seat as the attendant opened the cabin door and lowered the stairs.

"Do you want us to wait here for you, Mr. Director? My instructions were to follow your orders unless we were recalled to Washington."

"If we're not back in twenty-four hours you can get out of here," McGarvey told him.

"Good luck, sir," the pilot said. "And we'll be expecting you back first thing in the morning. The champagne will be on ice."

"Good man," McGarvey said.

He and Todd hefted their heavy duffle bags and went down the stairs, the morning bright and breezy. They were met at the bottom by an Air Force chief master sergeant who was driving a Humvee. His name tag read Johnson.

"Good morning, gentlemen," he said. "Anything else of yours we need to transfer?"

"This is it," McGarvey said.

"Then if you'll climb aboard I'll turn you over to the Navy."

The inside of the Grumman was starkly bare and utilitarian after the Lear. Once their gear was stowed, and the aircraft taxied out to the runway a chief petty officer in a flight helmet helped them don inflatable life vests before he made sure that they were properly strapped in. He gave them helmets and showed them where to plug in so that they could communicate.

"The name's Decker, sir," the crewman said. "Have either of you landed aboard a carrier in one of these buckets?"

"A couple of times," McGarvey said.

"Yes, sir. Then you'll know to tighten down your harness when we go in. It gets a little bumpy right there at the end."

"That it does," McGarvey said.

"It's three hours to the Big G. If you need anything

give me a shout, I'll be forward," Decker said. He nodded toward a pocket on the seat backs. "Burp bags."

"How far out is she?"

"About twenty miles by the time we get up there. The old man's looking forward to having you aboard, sir."

McGarvey had to smile. "I'll bet he is."

The flight up was noisy, but much smoother than the last flight McGarvey had taken aboard one of these things. Tokyo Bay appeared on the horizon, framing the *George H.W. Bush* that had been turned into the wind. On deck the Nimitz-class carrier was huge, more than one thousand feet long, but coming in for a landing it seemed impossibly small.

The Greyhound pilot searched for the groove, right and left, the slewing motion sickening, but suddenly they were down, very hard, and moments later the arresting wires snagged and they came to a bone-jarring halt.

Decker came aft and opened the cargo hatch as McGarvey and Todd unstrapped and took off their helmets. "Not so bad, huh?" he shouted over the noise of the Greyhound's still-turning engines.

"Piece of cake, chief," McGarvey told him. "Thank the pilots for us, if you would."

"Will do."

Chief of Fleet Intelligence Commander Leonard Stiles met them on deck and introduced himself. "Good morning, Mr. Director. How was your flight up from Kadena?"

"Long," McGarvey said.

"The captain would like to have a word with you before we get squared away." The giant aircraft carrier was turning to starboard, her deck obviously canted. It was impressive.

McGarvey and Todd followed the officer across to the island then down a labyrinth of corridors to the captain's quarters.

"We'll be docking in a couple of hours so he's got only a few minutes to spare for you."

"Have you been briefed on what we're doing out here?" McGarvey asked.

"Only that we're to give you just about anything you need, and not to ask too many questions."

"This could be ground zero," Todd said. "I'm surprised that you guys aren't beating feet for the open ocean."

"It's supposedly a show of confidence for the Japanese that we don't think this situation will go nuclear," Stiles told them though it was obvious he had a different opinion. "The president ordered us to return to port."

They came to the captain's quarters, the Marine guard standing watch snapping to attention. He was wearing his battle dress uniform, and was armed with an M-16.

"The captain is Thom Turner. Black Shoe Navy, but a straight shooter."

"Has he been briefed?" McGarvey asked.

"Yes, and he's likely to tell you that he thinks that you're certifiable, and that he doesn't like CIA people aboard his ship."

"What do you think?" Todd asked.

"I think that the pot out here has been stirred enough. If the Japanese out you guys—doing whatever it is you've come out here to do—we're all going to be in a serious world of shit."

"We already are, Commander," McGarvey said.

Except for the uniform with the eagles on the collar, Thom Turner could have passed for the executive of a Fortune 500 company, not a career fighting man. He was seated on the arm of a couch talking to someone on a telephone when they walked in. "They're here, I'll be up in a few minutes," he said, and he put the phone down and stood up.

"Captain, these are the gentlemen from the CIA," Stiles said.

"Yes, I met Mr. McGarvey once, when he gave a briefing on bin Laden to the president in the situation room, right after 9/11."

"I'm sorry I don't remember you, Captain," McGarvey said. "Those were busy days."

"We're busy just now too," Turner said. "The sooner you tell me what you want, the sooner I'll see that it gets done and the sooner you'll be off my ship."

"Fair enough," McGarvey told him. "We're going to have to use some of your assets and personnel tonight and it will get a little hairy. Somebody could get hurt, and your people would be in the middle of a mess with the Japanese authorities."

"We've been in messes here before. Will my people have to shoot anybody?"

"No. And when it's over you can fly us back to Kadena."

The capain was not happy. "I see," he said tightly. "What exactly is it you want from us?"

"If you have a map of Tokyo, I'll tell you everything you need to know."

ΠΙΠΕΤΨ

Minoru had spent most of the day packing for their departure to Australia and sterilizing the house and grounds of anything that might be incriminating should the Japanese authorites, for whatever reason, decide to issue a search warrant. He'd paid off the staff and let them go, leaving only him and Hatoyama alone in an empty house.

Despite his troubles as a young man, he liked Japan and would miss the bustle of the cities and the orderliness and beauty of the countryside. But it seemed increasingly likely that the entire region would soon go up in flames, for reasons Turov had never explained. This went well beyond the insanity of Kim Jong Il, yet Minoru could think of no reason for the coming war. He only knew that it was time to get out.

Turov had walked down the hill shortly before ten to take the train into the city, and when he came back around five he called for his chief of staff to have a drink. He seemed to be in a good mood, happy about something.

"What time does McGarvey's flight arrive at Narita?" he asked.

Minoru was confused. "I'm sorry, Colonel, I thought you would have been in contact with your people there and at Dulles."

"They were supposed to telephone you direct."

"No one has called."

Turov went to his study for the Nokia and made the call to Dulles, but he didn't like what he was hearing. "Check all the connecting flights no matter how long it takes and then call me." He broke the connection. "He hasn't shown up at Dulles."

"Maybe he left from Baltimore," Minoru suggested. "Either way he'd have to land at Narita."

Turov called his Narita contact, and briefly spoke in fluid Japanese, his mood deepening, and he hung up.

"No sign of him, Colonel?"

"No," Turov said. He walked back out to the deck and stared at the fishpond for a long minute or so.

"Maybe he's not coming after all," Minoru suggested.

"I don't believe it."

"There were others with him at the safe house when we attacked. Perhaps they were his friends, and one or more of them were seriously injured. He may have remained in Washington to be with them."

Turov glanced at his chief of staff. "Do you think that Mr. McGarvey is a sentimental man?"

"It's possible."

"It's not possible for a man such as him. In that much at least he and I are alike." Turov shook his head. "He will show up here tonight."

"I'm sorry, Colonel, but how can you be sure?" Minoru asked. He was straying very close to the line, beyond which Turov was capable of reacting instantly and with deadly force.

"Did you see the news this morning? The Chinese have decided to keep their ambassador in Washington for another thirty-six hours to negotiate with the White House for a settlement of the North Korean issue."

"Pulling him out would have been nothing more than a symbolic gesture. Washington is in no danger of being attacked."

"I might agree with you except for two things," Turov said. His anger was just below the surface, and he was doing everything within his power to remain calm. Minoru could see it in the colonel's posture, and the set of his mouth.

"Yes, sir?"

"Beijing may believe, or at least suspect, that the U.S. was behind the assassination."

"But Daniel was nothing more than a middleman."

"Yes, but for whom?" Turov asked.

"Don't you know?"

Turov shook his head. "I have some ideas, but none of them really make much sense except that his money came from somewhere within the U.S."

"Then the Chinese might be right."

"I don't think so," Turov said. "But they must have been given or shown something to make them back off for now."

"McGarvey."

"Exactly. He planted a seed of doubt, and he promised to hand me over to them."

"Within thirty-six hours," Minoru said. But then he had another thought. "He's been here, he's seen the compound, and has to believe that we have men stationed outside the walls. If he means to take you alive he'll have to bring help, and a lot of it."

"The CIA doesn't have that sort of manpower here in Tokyo," Turov said. "In any event I'm sure that the PSIA has most of them spotted. They couldn't make a move, especially now, without picking up a tail."

"They may have flown in a team directly from Washington. Andrews Air Force Base."

"They'd have the same problem landing anywhere in Japan," Turov said.

"If he's coming for you, as you believe, he has to land somewhere," Minoru said. "Where could a man like that, bringing a team of shooters with him, land in Japan without the Japanese authorities knowing about it?"

Turov looked at the fountain softly lit now as the daylight began to fade.

"Have you talked to your police contact? Maybe he's heard something—"

"Pizdec," Turov suddenly swore in Russian. "Pack whatever you don't want to leave behind. I'll call the hanger and have the jet fueled and preflighted. We're getting out of here immediately."

"What about Hatoyama?"

"Get rid of him."

"I thought we were waiting for McGarvey."

"He's coming," Turov said. "Tonight, and he's bringing help because I know how he got to Japan."

Minoru was at a loss. "How?"

"The U.S. Navy. The new carrier put in at Yokosuka early this afternoon and he's aboard."

NINETY-ONE

In the small temporary quarters they'd been given in officer's territory, McGarvey and Todd had laid out the gear from the Farm on the two bunks. In addition to Russian night fighter camos, which they'd donned, they had a pair of Austrian Steyr AUG 9 mm Para-silenced submachine guns, a few British flash-bang grenades, and an Italian 12-bore Franchi SPAS-12 automatic shotgun.

Commander Stiles knocked at the door a few minutes before seven thirty and McGarvey let him in. He pulled up short, and whistled softly. "You guys aren't screwing around."

"No sense in it," McGarvey said.

Todd put a pair of Russian-made night vision glasses in one of his zippered pockets, and stuffed several magazines of 9 mm Parabellum ammunition for his Steyr and for his SIG-Sauer, also Austrian.

The only U.S.-made equipment they would carry in was McGarvey's Wilson. But he figured if he lost it the game would be up anyway. If the Japanese got on to them the political fallout would be harsh and endless. The weapon's extreme accuracy made it worth the risk.

"The captain's authorized a Knighthawk helicopter for your ride. It's been fitted out with a battlefield infrared detector the Marines use to detect warm bodies on the ground. We figured it might come in handy once we're over this guy's compound."

"Is it ready now?"

"It's on deck."

"What about weapons?" Todd asked.

"A pair of 50-caliber machine guns, but you're taking off dry. No ammunition."

"I wouldn't expect so," McGarvey agreed with the commander. "If the Navy opened fire over Tokyo the shit would truly hit the fan."

"I couldn't have said it better, Mr. Director," Stiles said.

"What about our extraction?"

That had been a sticking point that Stiles had promised to take care of. The helicopter would not be able to stay on station no matter how quickly the situation was resolved. Simply flying from the carrier into the city and back would cause a lot of questions. And standing by somewhere in Ueno with a Navy staff car to come in and pick them up wasn't possible either. Someone would spot the vehicle in the vicinity and it wouldn't take the Japanese cops long to link it to the mess they would undoubtedly find at the compound, and even tougher questions would be asked.

Stiles tossed him a small Bluetooth comms device. "When you want out, transmit: Yankee needs a ride. A pair of ONI plainclothes investigators volunteered to help out. They've rented a dark blue Toyota van under assumed names from Hertz out at Narita and they're on the way back to Ueno right now. They'll wait in the parking lot at the train station for your call."

"We'll need to come back here and get down to Okinawa."

"The Greyhound will be warmed up the minute we get word that you're on the way," Stiles said. "Will you be bringing anyone out with you? A prisoner?"

"No prisoners," McGarvey said.

Stiles nodded. "One last thing. The ONI officers will not be armed, so if something goes wrong they won't be able to help out. In fact, if the mission falls apart their orders are to get away as quickly as possible."

"If it comes to that we'll figure out a way to get back here on our own."

"We'll arrest you at the gate if the cops are on your tail when you show up."

"You're all heart, Commander," Todd said.

"You have your job to do, and I have mine," Stiles said. "I sincerely hope that you find what you've come for, but except for your ride in and out, that's all we can do."

"We appreciate it," McGarvey said.

"When do you want to leave?"

"How long will it take to get us up there?"

"You'll be over the site in twenty-five minutes," Stiles said. "I imagine you'll want to wait until later tonight or sometime in the morning."

McGarvey shook his head. "We'll do it right now. I want to be on the way out of here no later than midnight."

Stiles nodded. "Then if you'll follow me, gentlemen, I'll take you topside. The pilot's name is Allen Kilpatrick. He's a good man."

NINETY-TWO

The house was deathly silent as Turov finished removing the hard drive from his main computer and stuffed it in the same case with his laptop and Nokia 110. He brought it out to the deck and set it next to his single hanging bag, all that he was taking from the compound.

Nothing else here could possibly point to him being anything other than a Russian ex-pat businessman who traded on the Tokyo Stock Exchange, and who was heavily involved in commercial real estate in the heart of the business district. It's what his meeting in town this morning had been all about.

The security systems in place were normal for a man

of his wealth, and although the weapons left behind would be considered somewhat excessive, his contact with the police would make certain that became a nonissue if this part of the city wasn't incinerated.

He looked up at the night sky and shook his head. Tokyo had been fine, but for the past year he'd been having the feeling that the time to leave was approaching. No place would last forever. The majority of his money was safe in Jersey, the Caymans, and Switzerland, and he and Minoru would be able to set up in Australia, at least temporarily until he could gauge which way the winds were blowing in the aftermath.

Having a lot of money smoothed the way almost everywhere. It had worked for him ever since he'd gotten out of Russia, and it would continue that way even after the small nuclear war that he had expedited, because the only man alive who knew the truth would never get the proof.

One day soon, Turov promised himself, he would kill the man.

He couldn't help but smile. The coming days and weeks promised to be the most interesting period of his life so far.

Minoru came from the front where he'd been loading his things into the Lexus SUV for the ride out to the airport. He pulled up short at the end of the deck.

Turov ignored his chief of staff for a few seconds, a little show of power, even though he felt the almost overwhelming urge to run right this moment and get out of Tokyo as fast as humanly possible. One-on-one with McGarvey would be an interesting challenge, but he wasn't equipped to fight a U.S. Navy detail. At least not here and now with inadequate preparations, although the blowback that would develop if the U.S. military fired its weapons on Japanese soil would be interesting.

"Are we ready to leave?" he asked.

"Whenever you are, Colonel."

"What about Hatoyama?"

"He just left."

Turov nodded. "In a few hours we will be out over the Pacific, well out of the battle zone and untouchable, sipping champagne and eating caviar."

"Mr. McGarvey will follow us," Minoru said.

"Yes, I think he will. But not immediately. I would like a few days to get settled in at the Melbourne house. Reconnect with some old friends. Reestablish a few of my club memberships. Make my courtesy call to the police."

"He'll want to get to you before Beijing launches its missiles and Kim Jong Il responds."

"What are you trying to tell me?" Turov demanded.

"Perhaps it would be better to wait here for him and have it done with one way or the other."

"What about the Navy?"

"They might arrange for a civilian car to drop him off nearby, but I'm thinking that they won't fire their weapons on Japanese soil. Only McGarvey is foolish enough to do such a thing."

In the distance to the south they heard the distinctive sound of a helicopter approaching. For a moment both of them stood motionless, but Turov was the first to respond.

"We'll find out if you're right or wrong, Hirobumi-san," he said. "Cut all the lights and see if you can get Hatoyama back. Let's end it here, as you suggest, one way or the other."

NINETY-THREE

The Knighthawk's crewman, Chief Petty Officer Dick Upton, opened the side door as they flew over the Ueno train station when the compound's lights suddenly went out. "Looks as if they might have heard us coming," he said. "You guys ready?"

McGarvey and Todd had gotten into their rappelling gear on the way out and they gave him the thumbs-up as the helicopter flared and slowed its rate of approach. "Find out what's on infrared," McGarvey said.

"What are you painting?" Upton asked in his helmet mike.

"At least two live bodies inside the compound," the copilot Lieutenant Dan Herbert replied over the ship's intercom. "One on foot approaching the compound."

McGarvey took off his helmet and pulled his Steyr AUG into firing position and went to the open door in time to see one man in civilian clothes racing up the street toward the compound's open front gate. He looked up and raised what, even from this distance, was obviously a weapon and began firing.

"Holy shit, we've got incoming!" Upton shouted.

"Hold it steady," Todd radioed the flight deck.

McGarvey picked off the shooter with one round, sending him sprawling, but the man got to his hands and knees and started scrambling toward the gate.

"He's hurt, let him go," Todd said, pulling off his helmet.

McGarvey squeezed off two shots, the first sending the man reeling and the second knocking him down as he tried to get up. This time he didn't move. "I didn't want him coming up behind us."

The chopper moved toward the open gate.

"Standby," Upton shouted.

McGarvey pulled the pin on one of his H&W flash-bang grenades but held the lever.

"Go now!"

McGarvey tossed the stun grenade just over the compound's wall on the other side of the gate, waited until it went off with a tremendous noise and a blinding flash of light, then leaped out of the hovering chopper and quickly rappelled the sixty feet to the pavement.

Todd was beside him an instant later, and they unslung their Steyrs and raced to the compound wall where they took up positions on either side of the open gate as the helicopter banked sharply to the right and, nose down, headed back to the carrier.

McGarvey figured they only had six or seven minutes tops before the police showed up in force. They had no time for niceties.

He nodded to Todd, who poked his suppressed submachine gun around the corner and emptied his first 32-round box magazine left to right inside the front courtyard, the heavy 9 mm rounds easily penetrating the lightly built walls of the main house.

The moment Todd fell back to reload, McGarvey tossed another flash-bang grenade across the courtyard then looked away seconds later as it went off with an impressive boom and a blinding burst of intense light.

The two of them rolled through the open gate and darted across the courtyard in opposite directions. According to the helicopter's infrared equipment two people were inside, one of them near the rear of the main house. McGarvey figured the one in back might be Turov using the other one as a screen through which his attackers had to come before they reached him.

It was one of the scenarios he'd discussed with Todd on the way up from the Big G, and one of the easiest, because they would only be dealing with a few men and not the ten or more he'd thought possible. The others had either slipped away in the night, or never had been here in the first place.

McGarvey reached the Lexus SUV, its rear hatch open. A couple of duffle bags had been tossed inside along with a hanging suitcase. Turov had been getting ready to leave.

He looked over his shoulder as Todd got to the east side of the house and took a quick look around the corner. Someone at the rear of the main building opened fire with an AK, shredding the wall as Todd fell back out of the way, apparently not hit.

Someone else suddenly opened fire on McGarvey with another AK, the rounds passing through the SUV's side windows. Dropping the Styer where he stood, and keeping low, McGarvey pulled out his much more accurate Wilson and two spare magazines as he jackrabbited to the front of the big car.

The firing from both positions inside the house momentarily stopped, both shooters probably reloading. With a quick glance over his shoulder as Todd disappeared around the corner, McGarvey charged around the front of the Lexus directly toward where he figured the shooter was standing and opened fire, emptying his eight round magazine, ejecting it and pocketing it, slamming one of the spares into the handle and firing again.

An Oriental man was crouched on one knee just inside what appared to be a large living room, blood oozing from at least three places in his chest and gut. The Kalashnikov lay on the floor next to him. He looked up as McGarvey appeared in the doorway, and with a grimace of intense pain tried to reach for the AK, but McGarvey fired one shot, catching the man in the side of the head, and Minoru fell back dead.

The shooter in back opened fire with the AK, but fell

silent after only two rounds, and the house became deathly still.

McGarvey reloaded again, pocketing the nearly spent magazine. All that he would leave behind were the .45 caliber shell casings, which might suggest the weapon used was the Wilson, but without the actual pistol or shooter, nothing could be proven.

The living room opened to an inner garden and as he approached the teak deck he could hear the sounds of water splashing from what was probably a fountain somewhere across the pond.

Holding the pistol under his arm for a moment, he pulled out his night vision goggles and put them on. The pond was brightly lit up in a ghostly green. Diaphonous curtains moved in the open sliding doors to what looked from here like a bedroom. A hanging bag and a smaller leather duffle or computer case had been set on the deck in front of the bedroom. A U.S. Navy helicopter showing up had to have come as a big shock.

Three shots from an unsilenced SIG were fired from somewhere on the other side of the house, and McGarvey stepped out onto the deck, where the muzzle of a pistol was jammed into the side of his head.

"Mr. McGarvey, I'm so happy that you could drop in on me this evening," Turov said.

McGarvey was disappointed in his sloppiness. His lack of skill could very well get him and his son-in-law killed tonight.

"Pull off those silly goggles, then decock your pistol and drop it," Turov said. "We wouldn't want an accident.

McGarvey did as he was told. "Howard McCann is dead."

"Yes. But I was through with him."

"Can you tell me why?"

"Why Howard wanted to engineer a nuclear war out

here? I have my thoughts, but honestly I don't know. If you mean why I hired the South Korean assassins, that's simple. For money of course."

"You don't give a damn that millions of innocent people could die out here?"

"*Eb tvoiu mat,* give me a fucking break," Turov said. "Now I want you to call to your partner. Tell him you're all clear back here."

"No need for that," Todd called from behind them.

Turov switched aim and as he fired McGarvey shoved him aside, the shot going wild.

"Dad, get out of the way!" Todd shouted. "We can take the bastard alive!"

Turov was bringing his gun hand around when McGarvey landed a roundhouse to the man's face, knocking him back. He hit the Russian high on the right cheek with a doubled up fist, rocking the man again. Methodically McGarvey slammed his fist into the man's face, blow after blow, until the Russian dropped his pistol and fell back on the floor, blood flowing from his mouth and nose and from several deep cuts. He was dazed but still conscious.

McGarvey kicked Turov's pistol away, a black rage threatening to blot out his sanity.

"For fucking money?" he shouted. "That's it?"

"We have to get out of here," Todd said. "We can take him with us."

McGarvey keyed the comms unit. "Yankee needs a ride," he said softly.

"Roger. ETA five mikes."

"That's right," Turov said, his words slurred because of the damage to his mouth. "Your deputy director of operations was a megalomaniac, I was merely greedy. But that means you can't turn me over to Chinese. Not with what I know."

"You're right," McGarvey said.

"You'll have to take me back to Langley for a debriefing. Who knows what other little secrets I might have for you?"

McGarvey shook his head.

"You have my computers, but you won't be able to make any sense of what's on their hard drives. My encryption programs are the best."

Still McGarvey remained silent, his control returning.

"Come on, Dad, we have to get out of here now," Todd said urgently. They could hear sirens in the long distance.

"You and your son will take me back," Turov said.

"No," McGarvey said softly, a dozen other faces from his past swimming in his mind's eye.

"We can't leave him here," Todd argued.

"You're right."

Sudden understanding dawned in Turov's eyes and he started to rise. "You son of a bitch—"

McGarvey raised the pistol and fired one shot, catching the Russian expediter squarely in the middle of his forehead, and he fell back, dead before his head hit the floor.

WASHINGTON

NINETY-FOUR

McGarvey and the dozen others seated around the long table in the White House Situation Room rose when President Haynes walked in and took his place. In addition to Secretary of State Brishon, the National Security Adviser Dennis Berndt, and Dick Adkins from Langley, the others gathered this evening included the directors of National Intelligence and the National Security Agency and the chairman of the Joint Chiefs.

"Five minutes, Mr. President," a chief petty officer seated at a computer console announced.

"We'll make this as short and to the point as possible," the president said. "Mr. McGarvey will conduct the briefing, and although some of his material may be disturbing there will be no objections. You're here as a show of unity."

Everyone around the table nodded their assent. Except for Adkins most of them knew little or nothing about what had been going on behind the scenes over the past week.

"Are you ready, Kirk?"

"Yes, sir," McGarvey said. On the way back from Tokyo he'd given a lot of thought about how this should be played. It had depended on Otto's ability to decipher Turov's laptop computer and the desktop hard drive they'd found in the bag.

Even lying in pain in a hospital bed, it had taken

Rencke less than thirty minutes to break both encryption programs. "Boyko was an idiot if he thought this system would have stopped anyone but an amateur for long."

"We're coming up now, sir," the chief said.

A large flat-panel monitor on the far wall suddenly showed a split image. On the left side, Kim Jong Il sat in what appeared to be a plain conference room. Seated next to him was Colonel Pak Hae. On the right side, Chinese President Hu Jintao sat at a table in a similar conference room. With him were Premier Wen Jiabo and a third man who McGarvey figured was either a translator or some high-ranking intelligence officer, or both.

Simultaneous translations had been arranged for all sides of the conference video call.

"Good morning, gentlemen," President Haynes began. "I hope to provide a solution to our mutual problem."

"Good morning, President Haynes," Hu Jintao said. He did not include Kim Jong Il, nor did the North Korean leader respond.

"You know my former Director of Central Intelligence Kirk McGarvey. He will conduct the briefing."

"Yes," President Hu said. "We were able to be of some assistance to him recently in Pyongyang, and he is why we accepted this extraordinary call."

"North Korean police did not assassinate General Ho, and I have the proof," McGarvey said without preamble.

None of the Chinese showed any reaction, but a brief flicker of emotion crossed Kim Jong Il's features.

"The two shooters were former South Korean army snipers, who were hired to go to Pyongang and murder the general in an attempt to destabilize the relationship between your two countries. We have one of them here, unfortunately she is dead. Killed in a shoot-out."

"We had the other shooter in custody," Colonel Pak said. "He hung himself in his cell last night."

"Continue," President Hu prompted, his expression blank despite the tremendous stakes they were facing.

"The assassins were hired by a former KGB officer who was living in Tokyo from where he expedited a highly successful murder by contract business. I just returned from Tokyo with one of his computers and the hard drive from another, both of which were heavily encrypted. We've managed to decode both."

"What of this Russian?" Colonel Pak asked.

"He is dead."

President Hu nodded. "Our embassy in Tokyo was informed of a disturbance in Ueno that may have involved U.S. naval personnel. The incident, I'm told, is under vigorous investigation."

"Our navy was in no way involved with the disturbance," McGarvey said.

Adkins was troubled, as were some of the others around the table, but everyone remained silent.

"We would like to examine this computer equipment at the earliest possible moment," President Hu said.

"If we can come to a preliminary agreement this morning, the laptop and hard drive will be delivered to your embassy here, along with the body of the South Korean assassin," McGarvey said.

"We will deliver the body of the second assassin to your embassy here in Pyongyang," Colonel Pak promised.

"You said this Russian was an expediter," President Hu said. "Who was he working for? Who but a madman would want to foment this trouble?"

The Chinese leader had given them the opening McGarvey had been hoping for, and he glanced over at Haynes who he could see also recognized what had just happened.

"He *was* a madman, Mr. President," McGarvey said. "He was shot to death shortly after he murdered the South Korean assassin who was in our custody."

"You took her from here to use her as bait," Colonel Pak said in wonderment.

"Yes," McGarvey admitted.

"Who is this man?" the Chinese president demanded. "We want his body."

"We cannot turn him over, Mr. President."

"Why not?"

"Because he's an American."

McGarvey's statement hung in the outraged silence for several beats. Kim Jong Il had visibly reacted, as had the Chinese president and the others with him.

"CIA?" President Hu asked tightly. "A rogue?"

"A former academic." McGarvey sidestepped the accusation. "Of foreign heritage."

"What were his motives?"

"As you guessed, Mr. President, he was obviously insane. We're sifting through his background to find out what motivated him. But we know that he had a great deal of money at his disposal and that he may have lived and worked for a time in China and Japan and for some reason had developed an intense, pathological hatred for the Orient and her peoples."

"We will need more than your word," President Hu said sharply.

"I'm afraid that's all I can offer you at this time, Mr. President," McGarvey said. "Perhaps in the future, when we've finished our investigation, I'll be able to come back to you with the additional proof you want."

"So simple," President Hu said after a long pause.

"Yes, sir," McGarvey agreed. "Very often the most difficult situations arise from simple causes."

Again everyone fell silent, the enormity of what had very nearly happened between Beijing and Pyongyang and what had gone on at this conference call hitting home.

Kim Jong Il pursed his lips and sat forward for emphasis. "One thousand pardons, Mr. President, if my government in any way was the cause of such unfortunate sentiments," he said, his voice soft, almost feminine.

It was unclear which president he was addressing, but Haynes responded first. "I'm only happy that we have managed to avert a war—"

Kim Jong Il's image on the screen went blank, and a moment later the Chinese president, premier, and the third man were gone as well.

Dennis Berndt started to speak, but the president held him off.

"Nothing that was said in this room this evening will be leaked," Haynes said, "I give you my word that it would be the worst mistake of your lives."

No one moved a muscle.

"We've stopped World War III. Doesn't matter how, but as of this moment we've stepped back from the brink."

"My God," Jane Brishon said. "Who was the American who hired the expediter?"

"Thank you, people," Haynes said, dismissing them. "That will be all for this evening."

His secretary of state wanted to object, but she got up with the others and headed for the door.

"Mr. McGarvey, would you and Dick remain for a minute?"

When everyone else was gone, including the chief who had run the computer link, the president sat back in his big leather chair. "Okay, what's next?"

"We need to find the source of his money," Adkins said. "Otto Rencke is already working on it. That should give us the why."

"We had the most to lose," McGarvey said. "Whoever engineered this wanted to hurt us worse than 9/11 and worse than shipping a hundred pounds of polonium 210 across our border."

"If you're suggesting al-Quaeda, I don't think it'll turn out to be that simple," Haynes said.

"I don't think so either, Mr. President," McGarvey said. He was bone weary, and wanted to quit and go home, yet he knew that the U.S. wasn't out of the woods yet. Not by a long shot. "We might have had the most to lose, but India could have stepped up to the plate as our most important trade partner, taking China's place. Or Russian oil interests might have wanted to keep China out of Iran. Even the Taiwanese would have benefited because a crippled China wouldn't be as great a threat as she is now."

Haynes sat back. "If you're right, and I suspect that you are, it means that our hands are tied until there's another overt attack against us," he said.

"We need to find out where the money is coming from," McGarvey said.

"From the drug cartels?" Adkins suggested.

"The U.S. is their biggest customer, they wouldn't want to destroy us," McGarvey said. "The source is right here."

The president was startled. "What do you mean?"

"The money is coming from inside the U.S."

Haynes shook his head. "Who?"

"I don't know," McGarvey said.

NINETY-FIVE

It was well past midnight when the cab dropped McGarvey off in front of the Hay-Adams Hotel across Lafayette Square from the White House and one of the doormen met him. "Good evening, sir."

McGarvey hesitated. He was dead tired. It seemed like months since he'd slept last. Yet his mind was alive with a thousand separate possibilities and scenarios for where McCann had gotten his money and why. All he needed was a start, which Rencke had provided for him from Turov's computer, which had among other things listed the name of one man other than McCann here in the States. Both had been erased from the hard drive and had not been brought up at the White House meeting.

"I have to take a walk first," McGarvey told the doorman.

"It may not be safe at this time of the evening, sir."

"That's okay, he knows how to take care of himself," Katy said, coming out of the lobby. She linked her arm in her husband's and they headed down the driveway and crossed the street to the park, the White House lit up like a jewel.

"How long were you waiting in the lobby for me?" McGarvey asked.

"Actually I just got back from the hospital and I was debating whether I should have a nightcap in the bar. When I turned around you were getting out of the cab." She held his arm a little tighter. "Is it over, Kirk?"

"The dangerous parts."

"No war?"

"No war," McGarvey said.

They stopped under a light and she studied his face. "Honest injun?"

He smiled and nodded. "Honest injun," he said, hating the lie.

"But there's more, isn't there," she said as a statement, not a question.

"There's always more, sweetheart," McGarvey told her. "We're going home in the morning and getting the boat ready for the Keys."

She chuckled from the back of her throat, her contented sound. "Not Vladivostok?"

He laughed. "If you prefer."